A
NICE
PLACE
TO
DIE

A NICE PLACE TO DIE

A DS Ryan McBride Novel

J. Woollcott

LEVEL
BEST BOOKS

First published by Level Best Books 2022

Author Photo Credit: Dawn Withers

First edition

ISBN: 978-1-68512-166-2

Cover art by Tory Woollcott

This book was professionally typeset on Reedsy.
Find out more at reedsy.com

To Emma and Billy.

Praise for A NICE PLACE TO DIE

"A conflicted police officer who falls for the sister of a dead woman on his own case. He knew he shouldn't mix business and pleasure, but....

Life and death on the outskirts of Belfast, Northern Ireland that's already had its share of grief and tragedy. *A Nice Place to Die* has fast-paced dialogue and a deep mystery that the author keeps unraveling like the skin of an onion. Like the dark complexity of Detective Sergeant Ryan McBride. A brilliant debut by J. Woollcott. Certainly, one author to keep an eye on."—Mike Martin, Author of the award-winning Sgt. Windflower Mystery series

"A real sense of authenticity, with great details on settings."—Dr. Katherine Ramsland

"DS Ryan McBride is engaged in a coverup: he'd slept with the murder victim, and as his investigation proceeds, discovers he's falling in love with her twin. Woollcott's accomplished debut is a perfect blend of police procedural and domestic suspense, offering an unsentimental view of the tangled, complex relationships that exist between career and private life and the deadly consequences that can occur when the two worlds collide. The Belfast setting is rich in local color and as multi-faceted and nuanced as Woollcott's characters who seem so real they must exist somewhere beyond the page. The dialog sparkles throughout. J. Woollcott is a welcome addition to the mystery landscape, a writer we look forward to seeing again, and soon. The novel should delight fans of Tana French and Hilary Davidson."—Marcia Talley, Agatha and Anthony award-winning author of the Hannah Ives mystery series.

Chapter One

Sunday, October 23

They reminded him of mourners at a funeral.

Down where the body lay, officers searched the undergrowth, their hands clasped behind their backs and their heads bowed.

Detective Sergeant Ryan McBride pulled on his gloves. He should really grab a Tyvek suit, or booties at least, but he'd run out of patience, couldn't be arsed to hang around any longer. Now that he was here, he wanted to get to the scene. The CSIs were clustered near the river and had locked the vans. God forbid, in the middle of an area crawling with police, they should leave the doors open. In Portglenone Forest's windswept car park, that scent of an Irish autumn, damp leaves and woodsmoke, hung in the air, while crows, black and boisterous, flapped and cawed in the dark trees.

Ryan's partner stood by one of the cars interviewing the man who had found the body. Tall and thin, DS Billy Lamont shivered in the cool air, his boyish face blotched red and his shoulders tight. The witness, a stocky man with a thatch of ginger hair, slumped sideways inside the vehicle's open back door, his feet touching the wet grass. A little black terrier jumped and yapped incessantly at his heels, aware perhaps of its owner's distress.

Ryan headed over to the burly constable manning the entrance and signed the crime log.

"Here," the officer said and, reaching behind him, produced a pair of booties.

1

"Cheers," Ryan nodded his thanks as he passed around the tape. The crime-scene photographer, carrying a large bag and a couple of cameras, huffed up toward him. He was a strapping, florid-faced lad. "I already took shots of everything, boss, but if there's anything extra you want, let me know. I needed to shoot the video before the FMO sees her, he should be here any minute. I'm going to grab a coffee—freezing my tits off here."

Ryan flailed a little on the way down and cursed under his breath. Too much of a hurry—too keen. He glanced around, remembering. He'd walked along the banks of the River Bann years ago with a girl called Maggie. He'd told her that the river had its source on Slieve Muck in the Mournes, and they'd had a good laugh at that—trust the Irish to name a mountain after muck.

But there was nothing to laugh at now.

An early mist drifted in fragments around a young woman's body. With her face twisted to the right and hidden by a tumble of copper hair, she looked like a careless sunbather. She wore a thick, cream-coloured sweater over black trousers. One of her red shoes had toppled away and lay abandoned by a mossy rock. It caught his eye, shiny leather. A shock of crimson in the weeds.

He crouched on a protective metal grid the crime scene techs had set by the body. For the first time he hesitated. Caught something about her, what was it? The shade of her hair? He took out his pen and gently lifted a glossy, reddish-brown ringlet from her cheek. His heart skipped a beat.

No, no.

He stood quickly and inhaled cold morning air. The sudden blood rush made him lightheaded.

He knew her.

Oh, Christ, he'd slept with her....

He glanced at the river—a pretty enough place, if a little gloomy when the sun went in. On the far bank, a willow tree's bare branches skimmed the water's surface like long pale fingers.

Further along to his left, two constables ran blue and white tape between the trees while scenes-of-crime officers searched the undergrowth. The little dog's sharp barks echoed across the water as he exhaled, hunkered down again, and focused on her body.

He studied her, the skin as white and textured as eggshell. A few faint freckles dotted the side of her nose. Half open eyes. Thick brown eyelashes cast a soft shadow across her cheek. She had been pretty in life—beautiful. And more than that, he'd felt a connection to her, a vulnerability. The beginnings of a bruise crept around from the other side of her face. She hadn't died right away, and that small detail bothered him. Someone had hit her hard, a brutal blow. Blood, viscous and matted, threaded her hair and had seeped into the ground at her head.

What was her name? Cathy? Catherine? It had been about six months ago. He'd had too much to drink, and as far as he remembered, she hadn't told him much about herself. They had talked, connected right away. What should he do? Would they take him off the case? Because of a one-night stand? No way of knowing. They might. If they knew....

A tall, dense grove of trees, shuddering in a blustery wind, hid this section of the path. Alone there with her, in the damp early morning, with the smell of mud and stagnant water, the rustle of beaten grass above him and the cawing of the birds, he knew he couldn't have this investigation go to anyone else. Didn't even want to risk the possibility.

The river slid by, unmoved by tragedy, dark, smooth, and silent under its own rising fog. He paused for a moment and thought about the situation, the implication, felt his throat close with anger and coughed to clear it. Christ. That's all he needed, Billy to see him choking up. Never hear the end of it. But, my God, she'd been lovely, and he'd thought about her a lot after that night. Even though things had turned out badly in the end. He wondered if she'd known she was dying. If she'd suffered. He hoped not. He remembered her laughing in the bar. She had small white teeth.

The sun came and went, clouds racing across a pale sky. The forecast for once promised a cool, dry day, although Belfast weather being famously capricious, they had a tarp and a tent ready.

"Heads up," one of the constables shouted as the pathologist's silver SUV pulled in. "It's McAllister."

Ryan made his way back up. No point in courting trouble. He wasn't in the mood for a lecture now. That single, bitter coffee he'd drunk earlier churned in his gut.

At the top of the path, Ryan nodded to McAllister. Tall and silver-haired, he was the senior man and meticulous in everything he did. Some of the other detectives thought him fussy and he had earned a nickname, Alice, because of it. Ryan didn't care about that. He liked him, liked his thoroughness. Not every pathologist came to the scene, but McAllister did, when he could.

He finished suiting up, snapped his gloves, and reached for his case. "You senior on this one, McBride?" He noted Ryan's lack of Tyvek with a raised eyebrow.

"Yes, DS Lamont has the Crime Scene Log and DC Maura Dunn will accompany and take care of forms at the mortuary."

"Good. Excellent. I appreciate procedure. Behave yourself down there?"

"Absolutely." Ryan glanced back to the distant figure on the grass. Shook his head.

McAllister paused for a moment, catching Ryan's hesitation perhaps, and followed his gaze down toward the river. Beside the water's edge, eddies of yellow and red fallen leaves swirled. The morning sun chose this moment to reappear and a shaft of light slid theatrically over the body and surrounding scene.

The pathologist, normally a man of few words, cleared his throat. "Looks like a bad one."

"Yes," Ryan said. "It's a bad one."

Antrim Road Station had been through it all—fire bombings, sniper attacks, explosions. Now a barbed-wire necklace decorated the old brick building, while out front a long stretch of corrugated iron displayed a smattering of profane and badly-spelled graffiti, and was a real favourite with local dogs.

Upstairs, the squad room was a soulless rectangle of desks and groaning office chairs. Ryan shifted in his seat and pulled up the latest missing-persons report. Billy had wandered off in search of tea bags because he didn't like to pay for a cuppa in the cafeteria when he could boil a kettle and slap in a bit of milk for nothing.

He frowned. None of the stats here matched the victim. Had she been in art? A consultant or something? God, what had she said? Yes, they'd talked about paintings. She'd mocked him gently about his taste for traditional Irish landscapes. But what did he know about art? What he liked, that was all. He'd had too much to drink that evening and so had she. Both of them coming down from a bad break-up, or at least that's what he'd thought. Of course, he had also thought they had all night to talk, to get to know one another.

There was no point telling anyone about his rendezvous with her, come on, no point. One night, Christ's sake, that wouldn't affect his judgement. Yes he'd liked her, but he wasn't even sure of her name, she'd been a little cagey, burned from her last relationship. And he'd no idea where she lived—no, wait, she'd said up the Malone Road, hadn't she? So what? He'd investigated and solved enough murders to know that there was nothing to be gained by his admission.

Behind him, occasional wind gusts rattled the big south windows, finding cracks and whining through them. He could hear phones ringing and mumbled conversation. Somebody coughed, deep and wet. Ryan had just closed his eyes to concentrate when the squad room door banged open with a clatter and Billy hurried over. Strange. Billy never broke a sweat.

"What bit you?"

"Ed Wylie is back." Billy nodded towards the far corner.

Ryan pushed away from his desk. This morning had gone from bad to very bad.

"No, no, no."

Billy nodded again, his lips a thin line. "Yes, yes, yes."

Inspector Girvan appeared on the other side of the squad room. "Briefing. Be ready in five. I want a rundown on current investigations. Make it succinct, I have a meeting to get to."

Groans from the back.

"I know it's Sunday, but crime never sleeps, or goes to church." He marched back into his office.

"Knows how to make an entrance, our boss, eh, Ryan?" Billy riffled in his desk. "Where's my festering pen?"

Ryan stood and threw a pencil over to Billy. As he did so Ed Wylie slid onto the desk behind him.

Wylie was tall, around Ryan's height, maybe a scant inch shorter, with the same dark hair and light skin. But Wylie had a drawn look to him, a bitter edge of discontent, sharp lines pulling each side of his mouth. Ryan remembered Billy mentioning that he and Wylie could have been cousins. He'd just mentioned it the once though. Knew better after that.

"Well, well, McBride and Lamont. Star detectives, God's gift to the PSNI.," Wylie said with a smirk.

"What do you want, Wylie?" Billy asked.

"Saying hello. I can do that, can't I?" Wylie pulled a sheet of paper on Ryan's desk towards him with his index finger. Tried to read it.

Ryan pulled the paper back and pushed by him.

"Easy there, Detective Sergeant McBride." Wylie emphasized the title, drawing it out. Ryan knew his rank pissed Wylie off. They had joined the force at the same time and Wylie for all his connections, he was the Chief Inspector's nephew, remained a Detective Constable, thinking it everyone's fault but his own.

Girvan re-emerged from his office with a coat thrown over his shoulders. A big man, almost six three, he had wavy red hair and a ruddy complexion. But it was his eyes, a light, transparent blue that unnerved Ryan. Girvan marched over to the assembled group and straddled a chair. He glanced at the whiteboard behind him.

"Right, you lot, give me a quick summary of your ongoing investigations. McBride, you have this morning's body. What do we know?"

"At this stage, not too much. No identification, no missing-person's report yet. Why was she even there? She was too dressed up for walking over muddy ground." Those shoes came to mind. "Dr. McAllister will expedite

6

the results, promised a verbal soon. Forensics, too. Foot traffic sparse in the area, it was early. Church still in. Not your usual victim, though." Shit, shit. Why did he say that?

Girvan raised his eyebrows. "Not your usual victim? Do we have usual victims, McBride? A list somewhere we can refer to? Because that would be so handy."

"Just an observation, sir. Sorry." Shit.

"The witness?" Girvan carried on.

"Dog-walker. We have his statement and he'll come in again for a formal. He left his car in the car park and walked along by the river. He met no one. The dog ran down and started yapping. He noticed a red shoe in the weeds first and then the body."

"Right. Hand your full report to Janice, and I'll look at it when I get back." Girvan paused. "In the corner there, Detective Constable Edward Wylie has joined our team from Musgrave. A couple of other boys are coming tomorrow. Nice to have more bodies on board."

Wylie leapt up, cleared his throat. "Inspector, I want to say how great it is to be here at Antrim Road. I'm looking forward to working with and learning from this team."

"Good to see someone appreciates the place," Girvan said. "We'll get you sorted with a desk and computer. Talk to Janice. She'll take good care of you."

New arrivals were usually greeted with a token round of applause and a few catcalls. This announcement, Ryan noticed, elicited silence, although someone at the back made a soft retching sound. Wylie wasn't shy about rubbing in his connections, he'd alienated most of his fellow officers, especially since this Chief Inspector was a bit of a dick and all. Girvan indicated to the nearest DS to get on with his report.

After the meeting, as the detectives and constables drifted back to their desks or outside for a smoke, DC Derek McGrath sidled over to Ryan and Billy. Derek was about five-seven, a wiry bicycling enthusiast, hyperactive and intense. His light brown hair, lightly gelled and spiky, shone under the fluorescent lights. He rubbed at the back of his neck where a tattoo peeked above his collar. He was one of the best researchers Ryan had ever worked with.

"That wanker, Wylie, what's he doing here?"

"You heard the guv, Derek." Billy grinned. "He transferred over from Musgrave."

Billy, Ryan, and Derek all stared at Girvan's empty office. Wylie leaned against the boss's door, holding court, while Janice giggled like a schoolgirl and swatted at him with a sheet of paper.

Derek scowled. "Bugger's back to his old tricks."

Ryan shook his head. "You're right, but..."

"Never lets you forget he's connected," Billy said.

"Let's see how he copes with Girvan as a boss. There's a man who doesn't suffer fools," Ryan said. "Although he seemed to lap up the arse-kissing there."

"Okay. I'm away to get a couple of teabags this time." Lack of caffeine always made Billy a bit edgy.

"Here, don't you take them from our kitchen," Derek warned him. "I know how many we have up there."

From the far side of the squad room Wylie glanced over and saw them talking. He made a pistol with his hand and fired three shots, blowing the tip of his finger when he finished.

"Ahh." Derek shook his head and twitched. "Fucken bastard."

Back at his desk, Ryan pushed away from his computer. Dr. McAllister, in an unusual burst of verbosity, had told him the victim had likely not been dead long. She had made an effort with her appearance. Her hair freshly washed and shining, a nice sweater, and those fancy red shoes. She was meeting someone, surely. Or going somewhere special? Ryan thought back to their evening together and remembered with a jolt that he'd given her his card. Ah, Christ. He'd even written his mobile number on the back. She hadn't called, maybe she'd chucked it...it would be hard to explain if she still had it. Maybe he should have...no—it was too late now, too late to tell. And even if it wasn't.... The phone interrupted his musing. He grabbed it.

"McBride, can you come down here? Got a young woman wants to report a missing person." The front desk sergeant lowered his voice and spoke quietly into the phone. "Sounds like it might be related to the situation earlier today. Can you come down, quick-like?"

Reception was empty. A few metal chairs leaned against the far wall, and a coffee table, canting to one side, held a diverse selection of books and magazines ranging from *Reader's Digest* to an old *Dandy Christmas Annual*. The sergeant had the desk phone pressed to his ear. He held up his finger and mouthed *toilet*. Fair enough. Ryan nodded and walked back over to check out the Dandy while he waited. A particularly good year. His mobile buzzed. Billy.

"Do you want tea? I managed to scrounge a few bags and I don't want to waste one if you don't want any. Friggin' hen's teeth these things. And Derek? He's standing up there guarding the blooming third-floor kitchen like a dog protecting a bone. Where are you?"

"I'm downstairs at the desk. Someone's reported a missing person and Big John thinks it might be the…" Ryan stopped speaking and stared.

The young woman from this morning, very much alive, stood in front of him.

Chapter Two

Sunday, October 23

Ryan took a step back. What the hell? She spoke and he missed the first few words.

"…to report her missing. It hasn't even been a day yet, but…." The woman glanced from Ryan to the desk sergeant. "It's about my twin sister, Kathleen McGuire. I'm probably overreacting." She hesitated again and looked at Ryan. She'd seen his reaction. "What's wrong? Something's wrong." She put a hand on the wall then dropped into one of the chairs.

"Let's go somewhere we can talk. What's your name?" Ryan held out his hand to her. He was probably shaking more than she was.

"It's Rose McGuire. Will you tell me what's happened? She's been in an accident, hasn't she?"

The desk sergeant glanced over. "McBride, why don't you take her to the main interview room. It's empty. I'll contact DS Lamont and see if DC Dunn's back yet."

"Right, thanks, Sarge."

Ryan helped Rose McGuire to her feet and they started slowly down the hall. Her sister for God's sake. *Kathleen.* Right, Kathleen. He'd been close with the name. He felt himself tense up. The women were twins then, identical. Had she mentioned this? A twin? He didn't think so. Maybe she'd confided in her sister, told her about the detective she'd met? When they reached the interview room, he saw Maura hurrying towards them with

Billy right behind her.

Inside, Ryan introduced everyone. "I'm Detective Sergeant Ryan McBride, and these are my colleagues, Detective Sergeant Billy Lamont and Detective Constable Maura Dunn. Please have a seat." He watched her. Had she recognised his name? He felt sweat prickle on his forehead, what a fool he was, he should have said something.

Rose sat still while Ryan broke the news. He recognised in her the features he had seen a few hours ago. Her hair lively, if a little shorter than her sister's. A striking young woman, for all her distress. What crazy, impossible situation had he let himself in for? Kathleen kept coming back to him in bits and pieces now, snatches of memory from that evening.

"Could you give us a moment or two?" With a subtle nod, Maura indicated the door.

"Come on, Billy." Ryan headed out, and they left her alone to comfort Rose. Maybe Maura had picked up on Ryan's hesitation and was giving him a moment too. That wouldn't surprise him. She was sensitive like that.

While he waited in the corridor with Billy, Ryan took a call from the coroner's office, glad of the distraction. Newry Police had pulled back an unidentified body due for autopsy and McAllister had slotted Kathleen McGuire in its place. She was going under the knife Monday evening.

When the detectives returned, Rose was red-eyed but composed. She took them through her day, stopping only for an occasional catch of breath and a dab of tissue to her eyes. She had left early from Derry heading for Portstewart. "I just got home. I work abroad most of the time. We were to meet for lunch but Kathleen didn't show. I waited almost an hour and tried to reach her over and over then I decided to go to her place in Belfast." Rose pulled another tissue free, roughly wiping her eyes. "When we spoke on the phone, I could tell something was wrong. I mean she sounded...anxious?"

"How long had she been living in Belfast?" Ryan asked. He knew it had to have been at least six months.

"About eight months. She used to live in Brighton," Rose answered. "She worked at a small gallery there for a while. Hated it."

"What about family? Do you have other family here?" Billy asked.

"Dad died in a car accident when we were about ten and Mum got married again about five years later to our stepdad, Leonard. A year after that Mum got cancer and passed away, too. We'd just turned seventeen. Dad had brothers and sisters in Belfast, and we have cousins, but no one kept in touch. Dad was Protestant and Mum was Catholic. You know what that's like. I'll notify Leonard. He lives in Donegal now, has remarried. I have his number somewhere. He won't care much. We didn't get along."

"Close friends, a boyfriend we can talk to?" Ryan asked. He could see her struggling to maintain composure.

"No, I'm sorry. Not here, I don't think. But as I said, I've been working abroad and lately our correspondence has been erratic."

In the middle of this, and he acknowledged it had to be a nightmare, Ryan picked up on a definite restraint in Rose McGuire. He couldn't put his finger on it. Was she lying about something? They left the interview room with enough important information to get started, including the location of Kathleen's emergency door keys. Her full statement could wait.

Maura accompanied Rose, ostensibly to help her get a room at the Europa Hotel but mostly, Ryan suspected, to keep her company. Before they left, he arranged for Rose to formally ID her sister's body at ten the next morning.

Late-afternoon gloom hung over the squad room. After finishing his report and making a few calls, Ryan shivered and pulled on his jacket.

"I'm off to look at Kathleen's place," Ryan said to Billy.

"Do you need to? It's getting late, can't we go tomorrow? The CSIs will have sealed the door by now. No one will go in." He slid his crisps in Ryan's direction. "Want one?" He wiped his hands over a pile of papers littered with crumbs and salt sprinkles.

"No, I'm good." For once, Billy's penchant for getting home to his family worked in Ryan's favour. This meant he could have a look around the flat in peace. "We have a lot on tomorrow. I want to go, you know, check it out. What's that?" Ryan pointed to the pile of papers, lightly spotted with grease.

"They're copies of those reports Maura wanted to discuss, the date rapes?"

"Right." Ryan scratched his chin, the faint itch of stubble annoying him.

He felt a pull to Kathleen's flat, a thin wire of tension twisting in his gut. The chances of her keeping his card were small. Still, no harm in being careful. And something else, perhaps. He wanted to see where she had lived. How she had lived. Rose's appearance had shocked him. He needed to get away, to process this.

"Maybe we can chat with Maura about that tomorrow. I want to get over to Kathleen's flat before it gets dark. What did you think of the sister?"

"She's a cool one, eh? She was upset but not hysterical. You would think she'd be, I dunno, more of a mess?" Billy stopped speaking. Wylie had appeared.

"What do you want, Wylie?' Ryan didn't have time for it, whatever it was.

"Keeping you two up to date. Thought I'd let you know I got the word: I'm fast-tracking for promotion. Not before time. Off for a detective training session in London next month. After that, the detective exam. Can't be that hard, eh? You two passed it." He stopped, did his signature smirk again. "Might even end up as your boss one day, and don't think," he glanced at the busy squad room and smiled, "that I can't make that happen."

"Jesus," Ryan muttered. He checked his pockets for keys and phone.

Wylie placed himself between Ryan and the exit. "Oh, and that weeping goddess I saw you two talking to earlier? Wouldn't mind a little piece of that. She could cry on my shoulder anytime."

"Rose McGuire lost her twin sister," Ryan said. "This morning's body? Have some respect for once."

"Ah?" Wylie was still talking. "Always fancied twins. Haven't you ever thought about it, two lovely ladies for the price of one?"

Billy leapt up at the last remark to grab Ryan and hold him back. Wylie moved off, raising his hands in mock surrender.

Billy pulled Ryan away. "You can be really stupid, you know that? He does it on purpose to get to you, and every time you fall for it. He loves winding you up."

"One day he'll wind me too tight." Ryan shook Billy off, angered.

"Come on," Billy said. "You lay a hand on him and he'll have you up on charges."

13

"Hey, you two, can we talk?"

Maura, great timing as always, back from settling Rose at the hotel.

"Sure, but it'll have to be quick," Ryan said. "Is it the rapes? Billy told me, but I'm trying to get out the bloody door."

She perched on his desk and crossed her arms. She didn't pay much attention to what you said once she had her teeth into something. Ryan sat down again. No point in arguing.

"It'll only take a minute. The thing is, this rash of sexual-assault complaints that have come in? I sent the files to Billy." Maura nodded at his desk and the greasy pages. "The women end up not filing an official complaint, a combination of not enough evidence and the general trauma of it all. And no one seems to be able to remember details." She stopped. "To me, this is a pattern. He's clever, though, never the same place twice. Varies his look, not that any of the victims remember much. Always crowded bars, drops them off back where it started. I don't know how he does it, but I'm convinced it's the same guy."

"What? Drugs, you mean?" Billy asked.

"They don't know. They'd all been drinking and met a fella, had a few more drinks, and then left with him. They aren't sure if they were too drunk and agreed to have sex or if maybe he used a date-rape drug. And it's always too late to test when they finally come in."

"You can detect it in the hair up to three months, Maura. Ketamine, anyway," Ryan said.

"Why don't you send it up to sex crimes?" Billy added. "If you think there's a pattern."

"I might mention it to them again, Billy, but they have that child-exploitation ring at the moment. Listen, I need some help with Girvan. He's not convinced it's one guy, and I think it is. We need a couple of extra bodies. Maybe this is a pattern that goes back much further? He may have moved from county to county, town to town, and we need to check all that." She started to wipe away the crumbs littering Billy's desk. "Girvan likes you two."

What a joke. "You think so?" Ryan grinned at Billy, who shrugged.

14

"Maybe *like* is a bit strong, but he listens to both of you. Couldn't you bring this up with him, try to get him to devote more resources?"

"I'll go over the files when I have a chance." Ryan started to edge towards the door. "It's this new murder, you know? By the way, what did you think of the sister, Rose McGuire? She's sorted with a hotel room, right?"

Maura took a moment to consider. "She's distressed. I expected her to be in bits once everything had sunk in, crying and all, but no, she seemed fairly calm." She waggled her fingers at them, snagged the last of Billy's crisps, and left.

Malone Hill Park, tree-lined and sedate, seemed quiet after the bustle of the main street. Kathleen had lived on the second floor of a large, rambling house. At the front, a few ragged rose trees still bloomed in a small, tidy garden. Ryan picked up keys from the lockbox and let himself in. He lingered, looking, getting a feel for the place. Dark wooden wainscoting ran around the grand foyer and continued up the stairs. The banister gleamed with the same polished wood and turned at a ninety-degree angle to the second-floor landing. To his left, he saw a door with a note attached to it. This had to be where the landlady, Mrs. Mary Doyle, lived. She didn't seem to be in.

Mrs. Doyle,

My name is Rose McGuire, and I'm looking for my sister Kathleen. Would you call me on my mobile number below when you get back?

Thanks!

The place reminded him of the house where he'd grown up, with its fine wood details and the pervasive scent of polish and disinfectant. On the way upstairs, an old memory stopped him abruptly, a sudden flash of his father, a respected solicitor, crisp and smooth after a day in court, whiskey in his hand, checking homework. Ryan and Erin, both of them pale-faced and anxious in front of his desk in the upstairs study, waiting for the verdict. Even back then, he'd worried about his big sister. Erin took their father's caustic remarks more seriously than he did. He shook the memory away, annoyed that it still had the power to bother him.

This was a fine house, solid and imposing, and it had been converted into two apartments. Only one door faced him at the top of the landing, Kathleen's. The crime-scene guys had been at the flat briefly, mainly to seal the entrance. They would return in the morning to search. If anything in the flat identified him, now was the time to find it. He pulled on gloves and booties, stepped under the tape, and let himself in.

He paused in the living room and watched dust motes float in late-afternoon beams of sunlight. The air smelled musty, with the slightest hint of fragrance. Kathleen's perfume, perhaps, still lingering. Did it remind him of her? No. Not much chance of smelling anything but beer and sweaty bodies when they'd first met on that busy Friday night. She'd been sitting with a girlfriend at a small table in the Chimney Corner. Tired of standing by the bar, he'd noticed the other woman leaving and asked if he could have the chair. She had half a glass of wine in front of her. She'd smiled, noticed he was alone, and said, *'Of course, join me if you like.'* And he had, just like that.

He came back to the present, headed to the kitchen, and opened the fridge. Mostly empty, a few jars and bottles. Drawers and cupboards held all the usual things. Down the hallway towards the back, the first door on the left led to a small bathroom. He searched the mirrored cupboard above the sink. A few scattered bits of makeup and some hair clips with red hairs still clinging to them. What happened to you, Kathleen? He stared at himself in the mirror, faint shadows under his eyes, his dark hair unruly. He raked it back with his fingers.

In the bedroom wardrobe, a few clothes hung beside a number of empty hangers. The drawers in her dressing table were half full. Had she left for a holiday? He searched for a diary or journal of some kind. Although what would he do if he found something? If his name was there? That would be important evidence, and he would have to hand it in, wouldn't he? See, this was the problem. He had started down a dangerous path. Maybe he could say he hadn't recognised her at first, maybe....

He thought back to that night again. They had hit it off right away, and later he'd asked her to his farm for a drink. He lived nearby, and the bar was so packed they could barely hear each other. He'd told her she was safe with him. He was a policeman. She'd laughed until he'd given her his card. *Oh, my God, you're a detective.* He fancied she'd looked at him in an odd way then. Some people were like that when he told them. Did they think he was different? Perhaps he was. He had written his mobile number on it. It seemed to him that at the time they had both purposely avoided personal details. All she would say was that she had left England and come back home to get away from her boyfriend, Liam. Nice guy, terrible boyfriend, she had joked. She was glad to be done with him. But she had been hurt, he could tell. For his part, there was Bridget, his on-again-off-again girlfriend. She had dumped him, taken him by surprise all right, on her way out the door the morning after his birthday, fresh-faced, showered, and primped. Ryan, reeling from an ugly hangover and battling with the coffee maker, nearly missed her parting shot. *Sorry, it's not working.* She'd said the words almost carelessly as she left, throwing them over her shoulder like a scarf.

He headed back to the living room. Another note lay on a small table by the answerphone near the window.

Kathleen, I waited for almost an hour in Portstewart. I'm worried. Where are you? Answer your mobile or ring me on mine when you get this. Rose. xxx.

One corner of the note was tucked under a little wooden box fashioned like a miniature chest. He opened it with his finger. Empty. The side table had a drawer, and he pulled it open. Pens, a notepad, and a little pile of cards. Business cards.

And there it was, right at the bottom. She'd kept it after all. He touched it with his gloved index finger, then reached in and removed it.

The sadness he'd felt at the scene that morning remained with him. Branches outside the bay window painted early evening shadows across the floor. She had lived here, that lovely young woman, and now she was gone. The street was quiet. He remained there in the silence for a moment with the business card in his hand, thinking about her. She had come back to his farm that night, and they had more wine—a lot more—and made love. She had been…enthusiastic. Later he'd been out in the kitchen, naked, as

17

it happened, putting some leftover pizza slices on a plate when he heard it—the throaty rumble of Bridget's Harley. Even the memory made him wince. No, that evening did not end well. By removing the card, he had broken the rules. He knew that, and he wondered if he had found a diary would he have taken that too? Probably. He thought back to Kathleen lying there on the grass. The complete and utter waste of it. He looked at the card again. He could be fired for this.

He put it in his pocket and left.

Chapter Three

Friday, August 5

BEFORE

Yesterday had been busy at the gallery. Thursdays especially were, something to do with the cruise-line schedules. The big ships poured lots of tourists and money into the city. Sales were good, brisk even. Prints, and a couple of small oils. The visitors, mostly Americans, wanted a little bit of Northern Ireland to take home. You had to love them, throwing their money around like confetti. She was tired and her feet ached. Angus, the assistant manager, had managed to wrangle an extra-long weekend. Jackie and Gillian, her boss's nieces, were there to help but were clueless. And if that wasn't bad enough, when the tourists had left, the security alarm went off for no reason and wouldn't bloody stop. From outside the gallery, Kathleen contacted the security company and, almost deafened, she locked up, and they all went to get a coffee.

Sophie's nieces were nice, silly girls. She had never had time to talk to them properly or more likely, never bothered. Kathleen was reflecting on this and enjoying a cream bun when the call came to say the alarm had been reset remotely and they could return.

They sat for an extra ten minutes, exchanging gossip and having a laugh. How nice, Kathleen thought, to sit and talk. Not dwell on things all the time. That fresh coffee smell, the whooshing of hot steam, and the constant chatter were intoxicating. Sharp sunlight sliced through the misted windows, and in that moment, she realised how much she missed going out, the social scene, life's interactions. Most evenings, she spent time with Mrs. Doyle, her elderly landlady. Except for *that* Friday night. She shivered, felt a little thrill remembering. God, she was a wanton hussy.

The three of them returned through late afternoon streets busy with office and bank workers heading home, or perhaps going to the pub for a quick one. As she unlocked the gallery door, Kathleen paused. What if coming back, leaving Brighton and Liam, hadn't fixed her after all? She felt a pulse of despair deep inside. She'd fancied that detective. God, he was attractive, the perfect brooding Irishman, in fact, but he had too much baggage, and she was done with all that. Nobody needed a Harley-riding ex-girlfriend as a rival, thank you very much. A nice, simple relationship, was that too much to ask for once?

"What a busy day," Jackie called over as the sisters headed for the back to grab their jackets. "And remember Gillian and I don't work tomorrow, right? We're off Friday."

"Yes, I know. You two are away for a long weekend. Everyone's having a holiday, except me. Must be nice."

"At least you get to have a quiet, boring day by yourself in the gallery. What will you do?" Gillian asked.

"I'll think of something."

Kathleen came back to the present and sat for a moment longer. No cruises on Fridays, thank God. She would be alone this weekend and Monday, too, as Angus would be in Dublin. Lost in her thoughts, the door buzz surprised her. The sun backlit the man who came in. Broad shoulders, confident walk. Hello there.

She slipped into her heels, stood up, and smoothed her dress, glad she'd worn the pale blue, fitted one.

"Hello. Sophie around?" he asked, smiling at her.

He was very good-looking.

"Sorry, no, her mum's been in an accident and—"

"Oh, for God's sake, has the old bag been riding again?" He kept the smile up; he had lovely teeth.

"I think it's horse-related, yes."

"It doesn't matter. She doesn't need to be here." He held out his hand as if to shake, and Kathleen reached to take it, then hesitated when she saw the business card. Embarrassed, she snatched it and glanced down. Had he done that on purpose to unbalance her? The way he did it? But why would he?

Kevin Coulter. Security Consultant. S.S.I.

"My old man's company, Security Systems International." He smiled again. "What's your name?"

"Kathleen McGuire."

"Hello, Kathleen." This time he reached for her hand and took it, shaking it lightly.

He was taller than average with dark brown hair and navy-blue eyes. He wore a well-tailored suit, a white shirt, and a maroon tie. Very nice....

"I'll have a look at the system back there. Should only take a moment. You've had some trouble with the alarm?"

"It went off for no reason yesterday, and we couldn't override it. Terrible racket."

"Sophie phoned my dad and gave him an earful. It's a new unit we're installing now, has some little quirks, but it's the best bet for here. Let me see. I'll be back." He walked on past her towards the office, calling out, "I could murder a coffee right now. Any chance?"

"Oh, right. How do you take it?"

"Black."

Her hands shook a little as she made the coffees, and as she turned to take them to the office, he came out.

"All done. You shouldn't have any more issues, but let me know if you do." He smiled at her again, and her stomach gave a little lurch. She handed him one of the tiny cups Sophie had chosen for the kitchen. He held it up. "Seriously?"

"I know." Kathleen laughed too. The cup looked silly in his hand.

21

"Tell you what, it's almost noon." He took the other cup and poured both coffees into the sink. "Come on. I'll buy you a proper coffee and a lunch. We'll beat the rush."

"But..."

"No buts, come on, let's call it a working lunch. The gallery is dead." He moved behind her and helped her place her arms one by one into her jacket, like a small child getting ready to go out. "There you go."

Belfast, usually a bundled-up, dowdy old lady, sprang to life in the good weather. The town buzzed with a joy that came with summer and warmth. Girls passed in bright frocks, chatting and swinging handbags, wearing sunglasses. Men, freed from heavy coats and sweaters, wore light shirts and khakis. Even the birds seemed happy, fluttering around like mad things. The city normally had a solid look to it. Older buildings, most of them built of Portland limestone or sandstone, gave it an austere, Presbyterian feeling—but not today. Today the sun shone through laneways and between shadowed side streets, creating shards of light and dark as they walked by. Kevin led the way, chatting easily, asking all about her, what she liked.

During that short walk to the restaurant, that brief slice of time, with its smells and sounds and brightness, she realised how lovely it was, having someone show an interest in her. And strange how the city felt different depending on her moods. Today it fairly sang. Two outings in as many days. Look at me, a regular social butterfly. Yesterday's gloom seemed ridiculous now.

When they arrived at the restaurant, a converted newspaper building, people were laughing and sipping drinks under colourful umbrellas on the patio. Charming and theatrical, it could have been a film scene, and Kathleen said so, but Kevin ushered her in past all that as if he hadn't heard her or didn't care. The young lady at the front desk smiled at him while checking Kathleen out with a sideways glance.

"Somewhere quiet. Thanks." He dismissed the hostess and turned to Kathleen.

"Nice here, isn't it? Food's good too."

A beautiful curved wooden bar gleamed in the dim interior. Kevin led Kathleen to a table at the back, and the waitress arrived with menus. Kevin waved her away. "It's all right, we'll have the ribeye and the sirloin. Medium rare. Oh, and give us a bottle of the Cigar Box Malbec, will you?"

Kathleen leaned back, looking around. No one had ever ordered for her before, and she didn't know what to think. Did she like it? The place was filling with the lunchtime crowd, young men and women laughing and flirting at the bar while the staff shook martinis and poured wine. Look at them, she thought, drinking and swanning about at lunch. The hostess led parties to tables and hurried back to the door.

If she was honest, Kathleen felt a little disorientated. Plus, this whole damn thing of being out. God, she was a bloody hermit. That last time back in May at the Chimney Corner, she'd gone to meet with an up-and-coming female artist she wanted for the gallery. And afterwards, oh, dear, look where that ended up. All this life was going on without her, this sunlight and shadow and … everything. She must have appeared a little dazed because Kevin glanced over at her, an inquiring look on his face.

"You don't get out much, do you?"

"No. I mean, yes, it's just that…." Was he making fun of her? A mocking edge to that tone?

"Shit, you're not a frigging vegetarian, are you?"

She smiled. "No, I'm not."

"Right then."

All during lunch, she watched this gorgeous man and listened to his easy chatter. She liked his decisiveness, his authority. She had wanted someone to take care of her for a change, and she suspected Kevin Coulter would do that. If he asked her out, she would say yes. Why not? He seemed so focussed on her, interested. She imagined being an actress in her own film, the scene after the sunlit patio outside, lingering in this dark and interesting bar with her new leading man. Strange that yesterday she had longed for something like this to happen. A new life beginning. An old one ending.

Chapter Four

Monday morning, October 24

Ryan rolled down the window to a crisp morning. A wind gust blew in, bringing with it the smell of exhaust and traffic sounds. A new day and the Europa was awash with tourists. A far cry from the old hotel that had struggled through decades of violence. Why do they come in October? And did they know the hotel had been bombed twenty-seven times? Yes, probably they did. Part of the attraction, maybe. Sparrows fluttered about, pecking at the few remaining leaves on trees by the forecourt, rising up occasionally to twitter and fight. He'd arranged to meet Rose at nine-thirty. He checked his watch; she was late. While he waited, with the thin October sun slanting across his windscreen and the breeze lifting his hair, he listened to Chet Baker sing *Let's Get Lost.* In the middle of the piano and trumpet and Chet's smooth voice, he felt an unfamiliar flicker of uneasiness. He should have told them about Kathleen. Let Girvan know. Now it was too late.

A few minutes later, Rose appeared at the entrance and glanced around, frowning. She wore the same clothes as yesterday, tweed skirt, cream sweater, and a brown leather jacket.

He got out and walked over. "Hello. How're you doing this morning?"

She didn't respond to that and said, "Maura called and offered to meet us, but I told her not to. I would prefer to get this over with. I want to do it and ..." She jumped as a loud bang sounded behind them. The birds rose again in a feathery jumble of wings, and some people on the pavement turned, but it was only a cement lorry hitting a heavy metal plate on the road.

"Never a dull moment in this town," Ryan said.

"We are in Belfast," she replied. A bit on the sharp side.

He felt unaccountably annoyed. He'd been joking—sort of. Still defensive of Belfast, then. *Get over it, boyo.* His father's voice, laconic in his ear.

"Shall we head on?" He'd been with enough people going through loss, knew it affected them in different ways. Maybe this was her way of coping. He didn't know what he would do if he lost his sister. If Erin died, he would go mad, couldn't imagine living without her late-night calls, her emotional meltdowns—her constant drama. So different from him. He opened the door for Rose, and she slipped in, folding her skirt primly over her knees and crossing her arms. Protecting herself. Not from him, surely?

On the road, she remained quiet in the car for a long time, then asked, "How does this work?"

"It can be fairly quick. I'll bring you in, and you'll be shown a photograph. You identify the photo. Then we leave."

"What if I want to see my sister?"

The way she said it, it sounded almost like an accusation. Was she accusing him of something? Insensitivity?

"You can do that if you want," he replied. Still a bit on the defensive side. Jesus.

"I do want," she said.

They drove to the mortuary in silence. Had she felt it? The edge? He didn't think so. But in these first impressions, she seemed quite different from her sister, what he remembered of her anyway.

He pulled into the Royal Victoria Hospital complex and parked in a *Do Not Park Here!* spot outside the NI Regional Forensic Mortuary. Dead bodies, after all. Techies throwing their weight around. Always putting up signs, locking vans. He tossed his PSNI card on the dashboard. Two can play at that game. Rose gave him a look when they got out. He shrugged. What?

A white-clad technician led them down wide stairs to the lower level where marble turned to concrete and the hardwood floor to cracked porcelain tile.

The man had a limp, and his shoes made a clip-clop sound on the floor, like a clock ticking. It echoed as they followed him slowly along a corridor with walls the colour of old parchment. As they approached the mortuary, Ryan picked up traces of formaldehyde in the air and something else, distant fires smouldering perhaps. Or maybe the smell was in his head.

In the cramped viewing room, the technician drew back short maroon velvet curtains. Rose remained dry-eyed and silent for almost a minute, staring through the glass.

She took a step back and turned to Ryan. "Yes. That's my sister, Kathleen McGuire. Can we go?"

When she turned to him, her eyes were luminous. Tears?

Back in the car, he pulled on his seat belt. She had to be hurting, yet she said nothing. And there it was again, that edgy feeling. He was apprehensive. What was that? And why was it happening with this strange, aloof woman? He'd always been comfortable in female company, on the surface at least … but this one? Christ's sake, he was a detective. He'd dealt with all kinds of villains—hard men, killers. Why did she make him feel uneasy? The fact that he'd slept with her sister notwithstanding. And God knows he was uncomfortable with that situation. He suspected it wasn't Kathleen's death that made her…so unapproachable? Maybe it was her composure that intrigued him. She didn't go in for small talk or feel the need to fill in silences. He had never met anyone like her before.

"Back to the hotel? You don't need to be at the station until later for your full statement."

She shook her head. "I need to pick up some things, clothes, personal items. I have nothing with me."

"Want me to drop you downtown, then? Castle Court, Victoria Square?"

"It doesn't matter," she replied in an offhand tone.

He wasn't a taxi service, but he was intrigued. He'd drop her at Victoria Square. And as he maneuvered through morning traffic, she surprised him again.

"I haven't eaten anything since yesterday evening, and I only had half an egg-salad sandwich then."

"There are a couple of decent little cafés in the mall there." He glanced at her, unsure.

"I don't want to eat by myself." She said it as though he should have known, then she faltered for the first time, and when he looked again, he saw something cross her face—embarrassment? She turned away. "Not after everything that's happened. I won't bother."

"Ah." What the hell? She wanted his company for lunch? Christ, so confusing. She was so confusing. He felt the air around him expand and contract minutely. "We can go grab something together if you like."

"Yes," she said.

They drove through the city center. Sun and cloud, a day like any other October day. Pigeons flapping on ledges, housewives bustling about with shopping bags, schoolkids mitching. He continued on to the Cathedral Quarter and parked. They walked along in silence to Commercial Court and the Duke of York. As they turned down the charming old laneway he wondered if she'd noticed the white-fronted bar with its red benches and clumps of geraniums still blooming in window boxes. He was pretty sure she hadn't. He felt acutely aware of her beside him, her heels clacking on the cobblestones. A few hardy souls congregated outside with drinks in hand, smoking. They huddled in groups. One youth coughed and spat loosely. Stamped his feet.

"They'll inherit the earth, they will," he said. Didn't know why he said it. Wished he hadn't.

"Who?" she asked, distracted.

"The smokers, out in all weather. You'd think they'd all be dead of pneumonia by now."

She didn't answer.

Why did he bother? He should shut the hell up. Seriously.

He had to put this behind him, this mixing of emotions, this second-guessing. She was who she was. Rose, not Kathleen. This woman was working through grief in her own way. He didn't know her. He'd hardly known her sister.

The bar smelled of hearty food and spilled beer. A comforting combination, and he relaxed a little. A quick lunch with the victim's sister. Call it community service.

"Have you been here before?" he asked.

"No, I haven't been to Belfast much." A quick glance around the bar.

They grabbed a spot at one of the wooden tables, and a waiter came over with a couple of laminated menus.

"Everything's on today, and the special's not bad for a change. If youse want drinks, away on up to the bar, it'll be faster. I'll be back in a minute for your order." He gave their table a cursory wipe, leaving it smeared, and left.

Rose settled into the velvet seat.

"Do you want a drink?" he asked. "I know it's a bit early."

"Yes, I do. Could I have a white wine? Chardonnay if they have it, or anything." She reached for her handbag with shaking hands. When he saw it, that little tremor in her fingers, it hit him. Hard to imagine her sister had been brutally murdered the day before. If she was upset, he couldn't tell. She didn't give much away. God, it must be exhausting, tamping your feelings down like that all the time. He went up, got her a Chardonnay, and a Coke for himself, and watched her in the mirror behind the bar while he waited. She sat still at the table. Sad. Closed up.

Rose thanked him for the drink, took a sip, then set down the glass.

They were in a corner with advertising mirrors on the wall beside her and a stained-glass window behind him. Passing rays of weak autumn sunlight lit the window and briefly daubed her face with colour. Looking at her, he saw a flash of Kathleen's cheek in his mind's eye, long lashes and shadow. How could he not? Sitting here in the bar, his memories of that night with Kathleen were coming back. Maybe he shook his head—okay, he did. That image, inappropriate as it was, wouldn't go away.

She mistook the gesture. "I'd better slow down until I get some food, I suppose." She hesitated, took another sip. "Or not."

They had both ordered the special, steak and Guinness pie. It arrived quickly, steaming and fragrant, and they ate in silence. Later, after the waiter took the plates away, Ryan leaned back.

"What do you do for a living?" He'd been wondering.

"I work for World Relief. It's an international aid organization," she said. "I work with disaster-relief teams, managing logistics."

"That must be a hell of a thing. I don't think I could deal with that."

"It's a challenge, but then I don't know how you do your job either…" She let the sentence hang and finished her wine. She toyed with her paper napkin, tearing it. The floor beneath her was littered with shredded bits of paper.

"I would like another drink, would you mind? I'm fine now I've eaten, and I want to relax for a few moments." A hesitation. "I can't seem to breathe properly." She touched her chest lightly with those long fingers.

"No problem." He acknowledged this small crack in her shell with a nod of his head. Even that minor revelation had been difficult for her.

When he came back with the new glass, she picked it up immediately.

"I'm not usually like this. I don't drink a lot. It's…"

"Don't worry about it. I can't imagine what you're going through."

He couldn't. He didn't want to hit her with platitudes, figured she'd see through them.

They sat there while the lunchtime crowd moved noisily around them. The bustle of normal lives. In the midst of it, being with her, he had a feeling of loss—and yet not loss. Of something else entirely. Now their conversation, while casual, was easier. The wine had relaxed her.

They filled the time discussing books and music. Then, as they drank coffee, and as if he'd passed some test or another, she started to talk about her dead sister. She'd never once looked him in the eye.

"We'd grown apart a little, but lately, her emails stopped almost completely. I've been away working in Africa, and service wasn't always great, but something was wrong. When I got home, I barely had time to unpack, and she wanted to see me right away. But then it was always some drama with Kathleen." Her face crumpled. "She's dead, and I'm still judging her, picking at her. I can't take it in, can't believe it…."

This time, and for the first time, she looked right at him, distraught.

What could he do? He reached across the table and laid his hand lightly on hers. Half consoling…half what? What was he doing? Would she snatch it away?

She didn't. She kept it there, warm under his.

This was good.

This was not good.

Chapter Five

Monday night, October 24

The long white limbs, like a marble statue under lights, the flayed chest. The weighing of organs. Jesus. It was more than he could comfortably handle. Thank God it was over.

Back home at his farmhouse, Ryan headed for the kitchen. A stiff drink—maybe two, and something to eat might help. At the autopsy, he'd remained stoic, thought he had, anyway. The same crime-scene photographer huffing and puffing, his flashes bouncing off the white tile walls.

The metallic clatter of instruments tossed into a bloody surgical tray.

And that smell.

He'd been right there in the autopsy room, listened to Dr. McAllister documenting for the record, but wasn't present. The report would follow, everything would be covered. This was a forensic autopsy, and he'd asked for the works, stomach contents, nail scrapings, all the bloodwork. And as this was an early postmortem, he knew that evaluation of potassium levels in the vitreous humor would be useful in estimating the time since death. He didn't want to miss anything, and McAllister was the man for that. But in the end, he'd needed to get it over with. It had been more difficult than he'd imagined. And right before he left, it had only taken Alice's casual reassurance to finish him off.

'And of course, I'll include histopathological/microscopic examination of various organs as well as chemical/toxicological analysis of body viscera and fluids.' Christ, Ryan thought, I could murder a whiskey right now.

All he had to do was find out who did it and why. He tolerated autopsies as part of the job and didn't think of himself as squeamish. This one, though.... He thought back to that night with Kathleen months ago, then to lunch in the bar, of Rose's hand under his. It was doing his head in. Doing it in, honest to God.

Even Alice had noticed.

"Looking a bit peaky, McBride. You feeling okay?"

In reality, rather than going on about his feelings, he should be more worried about his deception, his lack of disclosure. Sometimes it hit him. What would happen if someone found out? If she had told someone? But then he always pushed the thought away, compartmentalizing—something he had always been able to do. A blessing or a curse, he didn't know. Maybe both.

After dinner, he poured himself that whiskey and stood by his Belfast sink, looking out over the back garden. This old farmhouse kitchen suited him. He had upgraded it, yes. Pale yellow cabinets, big old beams in the ceiling, and grey slate tiles on the floor, but the Aga cooker stayed. It reminded him of his granny. He could feel it at his back, belting out heat. He topped up his drink, moved to the wooden table in the middle, and sat down.

Rose's second interview in the station after lunch provided them with some names and numbers of Kathleen's colleagues and the like, but not many close friends. He'd speak to Kathleen's coworkers at the gallery tomorrow morning, see if he could get a better idea. So far, Kathleen's personality seemed undefined—and he couldn't add anything, could he? He hadn't had much time to talk to her because Bridget had stalked in that night, all righteous indignation. He was glad she hadn't ridden the Harley right through his front door.

"Didn't take *you* long. Whose fucking car, McBride?" She'd stared at his naked body, shook her head, smiled.

He'd flinched. Makes a guy vulnerable. "Bridget, Jesus."

He had to physically restrain her from storming his bedroom. She had left, finally, and a few minutes later, Kathleen emerged from the back, fully dressed, a little shaken up.

"Christ, I'm sorry. Please don't go. You don't have to." He'd moved towards her but she shook her head.

"No. I think I'd better, don't you?"

He hadn't wanted her to leave, but what could he have done? He wasn't going to plead. Not his style.

A mad scratching announced his dog, Finn, at the back door. The dog shot in, ran around the kitchen table in circles, then trotted over to his bowl. Patricia, his neighbour and Finn's surrogate owner, must have seen his house lights and sent the dog over.

"C'mon, boy, let's walk."

He should go to the gym, do a few rounds with his mate, Abbott, but he couldn't face it tonight. Boxing usually calmed him, allowed him to let off steam, but tonight he needed the steam.

A wind gust shook the front windows. He threw on an old raincoat, because you never knew, and set off down the Shaneoguestown Road towards Dunadry. This helped him think, walking with Finn, daylight fading and a soft rain beginning to fall. The trees, their leaves getting heavy, hung over the path, and all he could hear when he stopped for a moment was distant crows cawing and a muted, constant dripping as the rain increased. It suited his mood. Almost fully dark in that green, peaceful dusk, he inhaled the dense, damp smell of rotting leaves and thought of Kathleen. What could she have done for this to happen to her? Love, hate or money. Had to be one of those. Or some madman on the loose? All the same, he doubted that. Something personal clung to this. He could feel it.

Finn came crashing through the hedgerow.

"Come on, boy, it's starting to bucket." His warm kitchen beckoned. Perhaps another drink. He was restless tonight. The damn autopsy had rattled him. He headed back through the steadily falling rain. Finn, taking a last look behind, trotted after.

Back at the farm, he cleaned up and went through to the conservatory. A little jazz, Amy Winehouse low in the background.

Rose. She was an odd one. Attractive, of course, another Kathleen, but—no, don't even go there. He shook the thought away. He was lost in the music when his mobile buzzed. Finn regarded him from his spot by the heater, attuned to the sound. He seemed to echo Ryan's thought. Not work, not tonight. Ryan checked the screen. Bridget.

"Good. You're in." She sounded breathless on the line. "Can I come over?"

Long black hair, hazel eyes, smooth olive skin. And that temper….

Inside it was warm, the air redolent of Irish stew from dinner. Outside, rain poured down. A lone light at the back of his garden winked at him through slender tree branches swaying in the wind. Wet gusts slapped against the windows. Finn gave him his sorrowful face. Here he was giving his dog opinions and feelings. He did want to see Bridget, despite pretending to himself that he didn't care. It would be nice, even, to have her in his bed again, feel those breasts pressed against him, his hands down her back, her skin…but he couldn't deal with her right now. He needed to concentrate on Kathleen and Rose. Too many reasons to say no.

"Ryan, did you hear me? I want to come over."

And there it was. That pushy, entitled Bridget. A side of her he didn't like.

"Bridget, not tonight, I can't. I have a lot going on at…."

She clicked off in his ear.

It had been a few months since she had dumped him for good. After that night with Kathleen, she had come after him like a freight train, part jealousy, he supposed. She'd always been a fiercely jealous person, although there had never been any real long-term commitment between them. She'd never seemed to want that, and Ryan didn't, either. It felt fine the way it was. They had resumed their relationship only to have it collapse in on itself again. His sister Erin was the only woman he came close to understanding, and sometimes even she baffled him.

He locked up and turned off the lights. His other problem was Ed Wylie's reappearance. The two of them had worked together briefly during training at Musgrave, and back then, it had not gone well. To Ryan, there was something pathetic about him, something desperate, trying to live up to an uncle who was widely despised and feared. And recently, he'd noticed something else in Wylie, something he didn't like, a new smugness, a satisfaction. And it wasn't the fast-tracking. Wylie was up to something.

Chapter Six

Tuesday morning, October 25

Ryan's desk phone buzzed. Janice, Girvan's secretary, asked him to come over to the office. He hung up and signaled Billy. "Maura's got a couple of minutes with the big man before this morning's meeting. She's in there and wants to make her case for a few extra bodies to look into the rapes. Are you in or what?"

Billy nodded to a haphazard pile of paperwork on his desk. "Bit busy at the minute, let me know."

Ryan shook his head. "Right, Billy, keeping your head down as usual?"

"Bugger off, Ryan. I'm looking into the victim's background. We've got a blooming murder case here. I don't take on extra work because a pretty girl butters me up. Too much to do."

Unless, God forbid, Billy would have to miss one of the kid's birthday parties, or laundry night for that matter. Ryan bit back a reply, snatched up his jacket, and headed for Girvan. Billy, number-one frigging househusband. One year younger than Ryan, Billy had married his high-school sweetheart, and now they had three kids.

'He's happy as a clam,' Maura had pointed out to Ryan, one day on a lunch run.

"What does that even mean, Maura?"

She didn't know what it meant. *'But he loves being a dad. All those kiddies. I know that.'*

Inspector James Girvan sat behind his desk in a creaky leather chair. A wan morning sun struggled to brighten the room. On Girvan's credenza, a photo of his wife and two children took pride of place; beside that, his dog's photo. His wife and kids had red hair, his dog was a Red Setter, and the remaining photo, his parents Ryan supposed, revealed they, too, were redheads.

'Those weans had no chance,' Billy had whispered to Ryan the first time he noticed the family groups behind Girvan. 'Gingers, the whole pack of them.'

'It's not a death sentence,' Ryan had quickly pointed out, but Billy had shaken his head. 'That's a terrible colour they've got there, desperate bright.'

Girvan finished rustling papers, while Maura, who had dropped the report in question on Girvan's desk with a flourish, fidgeted beside Ryan.

"I have a busy schedule this morning, but DC Dunn, you're right, this is beginning to develop into a pattern." He shuffled a stack of sheets, and Ryan grinned. Maura had smothered Girvan in paperwork, as per.

"Thank you, sir."

"And DS McBride agrees to lend a hand? His busy schedule notwithstanding?" Girvan turned his head and narrowed his eyes at Ryan.

In Girvan's presence, Ryan felt guilty about something, wasn't sure what.

"Absolutely." What could he say in the face of the mountain of work Maura had done?

"I do take your point, DC Dunn," Girvan rattled on. "More needs to happen. Fortunately, those new constables from Musgrave have to be assigned to cases. Let me consider the logistics, can't have officers swanning about with nothing to do, right, McBride? Can't have them thinking too much on their own, getting into trouble."

"No, sir," Ryan said.

"Right then, see you all in a few minutes at the meeting. I'll let you know."

Maura said nothing as they left the office. Usually, he relied on her insight. But something was up.

"What's going on?" Ryan touched her arm lightly. "You're upset."

She seemed subdued. More than usual. No one could ever accuse Maura of unbridled exuberance.

"Nothing."

"Come on, give me some credit, Maura. Something's wrong."

"No, it's...."

She walked over to the door and pushed into the hall.

Ryan followed her. "Out with it."

"I had a young woman in earlier this morning. She thinks she was raped on Sunday night. She can't remember, and she's shattered. She told me she's a virgin, or was. Her mum forced her to come in. It had to be him, and I told her that, but she's still not sure, thinks she might have been off her face and let some random guy, you know, do it." She laughed sourly. "You know what? He even dropped her back outside the bar. Left her wandering around in a daze, knickers on backwards."

"Bastard." Ryan pushed his hands through his hair and leaned against the wall. He studied Maura as she stared down the corridor, hugging herself.

"You need to pull back a bit and not get emotionally involved, Maura. You're making yourself crazy. I know what happened to you at Christmas is—"

"What?" She wheeled around to him, furious. "You think because Wylie tried it on with me, I have some special rape agenda? What? Like, only now it's personal? Fuck off, fuck the hell off." She turned away, shaking.

When Maura had joined the squad, her straight black hair fell past her shoulders. Two weeks later, she arrived one morning with a short, no-nonsense cut. 'Makes me look older, more serious,' she'd confided to him the day after. He'd been disappointed that she thought she needed to do it, lose her lovely, long hair. When he told her that, she'd punched him lightly on the arm.

You don't know anything about it, DS McBride. What it's like being a female officer in the police. Not a bloody clue.

And he didn't. Not back then. He waited for a minute before he replied.

"Maura, no. I thought it made it more important, you have a connection. I didn't mean it in a bad way. Come on." He reached for her but she shook his hand off.

"What Wylie tried to do to me doesn't change things. I want this bastard

38

caught. I want to catch him and…." She turned around and slammed the wall with her open palm.

"Hey." Ryan grabbed her arm this time. He didn't want her to lose that empathy. Jesus, her sensitivity was one of the reasons he liked her, because most of the time, he didn't seem to have it. "I didn't mean you shouldn't care just…don't let it get to you."

"You think I don't know that? You think I want to feel this way every time I get a report? Jesus, Ryan." She turned away. "Maybe I'm not suited for this kind of job. It gets to me. Sometimes I want to…."

"What? Move to traffic?" The idea of it. "Maura, channel this anger into getting the guy. Keep doing what you're doing. You'll get him. We'll get him." Ryan opened the squad-room door. "Come on, we have to go, the meeting's starting soon, and Girvan will expect to see us there."

"I needed a moment, Ryan. Going over all the rape reports for Girvan brought it into focus."

"Yeah, well, I'm here and Billy's here, any time you need to talk. Hell, even Derek, for a fresh perspective. You know, on how your pain affects him."

That made her smile, and she punched his arm. He let her off with it. This time.

After the meeting, Ryan and Billy were about to head downtown to the gallery where Kathleen had worked when they were notified that her car had been located. Ryan made some calls. He needed the scene protected and forensics over there. He'd barely hung up when the phone rang again, and pathology informed him the victim's preliminary tox results were in. As they headed towards Ballymena and Kathleen's car, Ryan let Sophie Walton, who owned the gallery, know they would be late to the interviews, then he rang the coroner's office.

"Give me a quick verbal, Mervyn," he asked the assistant pathologist on speaker. "An overview for now and email me the rest, yeah?"

"Xanax. That's what she had in her system. A lot of it. That's a brand name for Alprazolam. It affects chemicals in the brain that tend to be unbalanced in people with anxiety. Oh, and some bruising down the arm, someone

39

knocked her about recently. You'll have seen that at the autopsy."

Ryan sighed. "Could she drive?" Mervyn was an old friend, but it was still hard to get preliminary numbers out of him. McAllister had trained him well.

"Unlikely." Mervyn rustled papers.

"Would it have killed her?" Billy piped up, trying for a two-pronged attack.

"Oh, no, Billy, nothing like that. And a heads up, looks like gunshot residue on her hands. Alice will confirm that shortly. Gotta go, see you girls later." Mervyn clicked off.

An unexpected development, the powder residue and Xanax. Ryan glanced at Billy. "What do you think? I don't get it. Gunshot residue?"

"Drugs? Guns?" Billy screwed up his face. "No, she doesn't fit the profile."

"Let's see what this scene says. If her car has information for us." Ryan accelerated. Billy grabbed the dash, and Ryan shook his head. Same old Billy, nervous Nelly.

They headed on up past Ballymena, and Billy lowered the window briefly. A brisk wind skittered around the car, bringing with it the scent of autumn and manure's fecund undertone. Muddy fields stretched away, stitched with white drystone walls and dotted with sheep and cattle. Billy quickly raised the window again.

"Such a sensitive flower," Ryan said, grinning.

Billy fanned himself. "That's stinking, that is."

They pulled in on a side road well back from the scene outside Portglenone. A passing cyclist had noticed the half-hidden red Fiesta and decided to call it in as abandoned. The area was roped off, and the team had already set up. Over at the edge of the lay-by, a few men searched the undergrowth. DC Derek McGrath was hunkered down, examining a small pile of debris.

"If it isn't Constable McGrath himself. A man of many talents. What brings you outside?" Billy said.

"I was in Doagh checking into another case, and I heard this on the radio. I called in, and dispatch told me to head over and wait until you two got here. Said you might need me. Buffeted by many winds, I am."

"Outstanding. I like the police tape and everything."

"Fuck off, Billy, why don't you?" Derek said conversationally, then pointed to a number of plastic evidence bags on the ground. "Ton of shit around here. People are pigs, you know? Very untidy. Look at all this stuff. I think there's some kind of Fixed Penalty Charge bylaw or something for chucking things out in a lay-by."

"Yeah, Derek, Jesus. I'll look into it right away." Ryan shook his head and zipped up his Belstaff jacket, getting chilly. "The car's been moved, right? It must have been parked in the lay-by first, then driven into the bushes to hide it. And we're close to where Kathleen's body was found."

"Yes," Billy said. "We are indeed, what, five, ten minutes away by car?"

"Yes." Ryan picked up a couple of bags and examined the contents: a biro, a matchbook with no markings on it, a plastic Pepsi cup, general debris. And a diabetic bracelet. That was interesting. He held it up.

"Was she a diabetic?" Billy asked.

"No, I don't think so. No mention of it anywhere. I could call her sister and double check, I suppose," Ryan said.

"Might as well." Billy inspected the other bags. "Hang on, is that a Rolex?"

"Looks like it." Ryan took the bag from Billy and poked at it through the plastic.

Billy grabbed it back. "A real one, do you think?"

Derek laughed. "Yeah right. Come on, Billy, nobody would leave a real Rolex behind, broken or not. I haven't had a chance to properly check it out. I'll let you know."

Ryan slapped him on the shoulder. "Stay and keep this lot at it, I want it all."

"What? You're joking, right? You want me to stay?" Derek gestured around at the scattered bits and pieces.

"They're almost done. Half an hour, tops. Better to have it. Don't be such a big girl's blouse."

"He's totally putting that on," Billy said as they headed over to the abandoned car. "Let's see what the techies have to say."

They heard a yell behind them and turned to see a squad car parking on the soft verge.

41

"Move that bloody car, you moron. This is a crime scene." A CSI ran over and berated the driver, who then reversed, fishtailed, and parked further back. Ed Wylie got out, pulled a jacket from the back, and sauntered over to them, unfazed.

"What the hell?" Billy murmured to Ryan as Wylie approached.

"I've been assigned to this investigation," Wylie said. "You're the go-to guys, apparently. According to Uncle George, the Chief Inspec…"

"We know who he is, Wylie." Ryan turned away and started walking. "Scram, we don't need you."

"Hey," Wylie called after him. "Detective Sergeant McBride, it's not your call."

Billy caught up. "He's been assigned. You can't blow him off."

"That asshole," Ryan said, without slowing down. "He's up to something."

"Ever think he might want to work on a decent case? And it's not our decision to make. You know that."

Billy turned back and called to Wylie, "Keep up."

The Fiesta was swarming with CSIs and surrounded by dense bushes. Beyond it, green and muddy pastures stretched into the distance, ending at a tree line. The same chill wind picked up, and Ryan shivered again. A tall, Tyvek-clad man broke away and came over to them.

"Holy moly it's the terrible twins. Hey, Ryan, Billy. And who's this?"

"DC Ed Wylie. Just assigned."

"What do you want first? The good news or the bad news?" Feely rubbed his hands together.

Ryan groaned. Jim Feely was a joker, an excellent CSI but, God, he dragged it out.

Billy said bad, Ryan said good, Wylie hung back. Feely smiled broadly.

"Bad first. Not great impressions to work with. It looks like another car was here, small, with a short wheelbase. Messes things up unless it's related, hard to tell. The best tyre tracks are over there on that muddy patch. We'll get casts and let you know. Beneath them, other tyre tracks from a bigger car. We'll do them, too, but concentrate on the top ones. This isn't a proper lay-by. I doubt it gets a lot of traffic."

"Anything in the car? A phone, maybe?" Ryan asked.

"No such luck. No bag, no phone, nothing. It's not locked."

"Shit. What about this wider surrounding area? Did you find anything?"

"Ask them over there. I'm focused on her car right now...."

"Right, thanks, Jim." Ryan started to back away, figuring, as always, it would be quicker to read the report later. They had to get to the gallery. "You'll keep at it, yeah?"

"Hold on, you haven't heard the good news."

Billy turned back. "Something else?"

"We didn't notice it at first because, as you can see, the damn car's been driven right into these thick bushes. We've been checking for footprints and anything outside the doors, close to the car—ground debris, fingerprints, too, you know the drill. We don't want to move it until we have everything documented in situ." He paused. "It's painstaking work, and with this team, nothing gets by us. Handpicked by me, every one. In fact...."

Just shoot me, Ryan thought—or better still, shoot him. "Jim," Ryan said, "fascinating as this all is, we have to get going. Interviews, you know? Will you get to the point? Anything unusual?"

"Excuse me, Detective." Feely bristled. "Depends what you think is unusual." He gave a little smirk. "She had a bullet through her back tyre and a tracking device way under the bumper. Is that unusual enough for you?"

Chapter Seven

Tuesday, October 25

They walked toward Sophie Walton's gallery, past the Duke of York, and Ryan thought back to his lunch with Rose. He wondered what she was doing at that moment, remembered the touch of her hand.

Sophie waited for them with a tall, big-boned man of about sixty whom she introduced as her husband, Anthony Walton. Walton carried a large portfolio in one hand and had some small oil paintings under his arm. He had a red, windblown face, a nose laced with a filigree of fine veins, and a casual indifference that irked Ryan.

"Are you sure you don't need me? I'll stay if you want." He inclined his head to Ryan and Billy. "This lot can overstep if you don't keep an eye on them."

Ryan glanced over, and Anthony Walton stared back at him. What, Ryan wondered briefly, was his problem? They were trying to solve a murder here, not hassling him for parking.

"Anthony, it'll be fine. They're only doing their job." Sophie Walton ushered him out and patted her hair self-consciously when he had gone. "Sorry about that. He's a little touchy with all this, protective. He was a lawyer before…he can't help himself. I assume you didn't need to speak with him?"

"Did he know Kathleen? Has he met her?" Ryan asked.

"Only in passing. He comes in occasionally to pick up old frames to restore and some paintings that require cleaning. He usually wouldn't be here."

"We can chat to him later on if necessary."

Sophie Walton normally lived in London, but was in Belfast because her mother had taken a fall, and she didn't have much information about Kathleen.

"Normally, mother is self-sufficient, but I've been here for almost six weeks now. Months ago, she hurt her leg badly with the horses. It got progressively worse, and now she can't get about. She has to go in for surgery. It's a bloody nightmare." She paused. "I'm sorry, this has me all rattled. I'm going on about nothing, and there's poor Kathleen."

She seemed charming but a little scattered. What had attracted her to the dour Anthony Walton, Ryan wondered.

"I can't help you too much. I didn't know her well at all. Just work-related. We didn't socialize. I'm not here all the time. She runs the place with Angus, the assistant manager. I oversee it from London. She reminded me a little of myself when I was younger. I suspect that's one of the reasons I hired her." She gave a little self-conscious laugh and touched her hair again, embarrassed. "She had been working in Brighton but wanted to come back to Belfast. I interviewed her in London. But Angus can perhaps tell you more. They were friendly. He'll be devastated, poor man. And my nieces, Gillian and Jackie. They're on their way in. They'll be upset too. They weren't that close but still, you know young girls, they can be emotional."

As Sophie gave her statement, Ryan glanced around. The gallery was high-end and modern, with a few traditional Irish landscapes among more contemporary pieces. He studied her again. She was a shapely woman, with dark blue eyes in a wide face, and full lips painted red to match her dress. Attractive, her long brown hair curling over her shoulders. She had a small bruise on the side of her face and a light scratch below her eye. He had a quick flash of that surly husband. He touched his eye and gestured to her. She seemed taken aback at first, then smiled.

"Oh, this? Gardening. Word to the wise, Detective: Avoid rakes in dark garden sheds. Now." She changed the subject. "Coffee? It'll only take a second."

"There is one more thing, Ms. Walton," Ryan said. "Where were you last Saturday night, Sunday morning?"

"You can't seriously think...."

Funny, Ryan thought, how some people took offense and others didn't. How they became defensive. "Routine. Have to ask."

"Oh well, I..." She paused and cleared her throat. "I'm sorry, this is...I was with my mother. We watched television Saturday evening and went to bed around eleven or so. I had some work to do. I woke her in the morning early with a cup of tea."

"What time would that have been then?"

"The tea? Oh, about six-thirty, then we had a little breakfast about seven-thirty, eight o'clock?"

"There you are, not so hard." Ryan smiled at her. "We'll send someone over to take her statement later."

The front door buzzed. A young man, somewhere in his late twenties, bustled in. Sophie jumped up and ran to him.

"Angus. My God." She turned towards Ryan and Billy. "These two gentlemen are policemen, here to take statements."

Angus placed a briefcase on the floor and unwrapped a bulky scarf. Distraught, no doubt about that. Short, dark-blond hair, styled and shaved at the sides, framed a long face with high cheekbones and watery, pale-blue eyes. He reminded Ryan of a goldfish staring out from an aquarium.

"You poor thing." Sophie lifted his briefcase and shooed him over. "Let me get you a coffee." She took his coat and pushed him into a seat.

Ryan looked around. "Is there a room we can use?"

"Of course, sorry. You'll want some privacy."

She walked them further back to a small office. White walls hung with bright, modern paintings and a sleek grey desk piled with papers.

"I'll leave you to it then." Sophie pulled the door closed.

Ryan began. "Angus, I'm going to ask you the obvious question: Is there anything you can tell us that might help us find who did this? Did she have enemies? Problems with people or anything like that?"

"No, no. I wish I could. I don't even know what happened to her. Did she suffer? I'm horribly upset. I don't get it. Why would anyone hurt her? She was such a nice person."

Angus seemed genuinely distressed, rambling and sniffling.

"How did she seem lately? Did you notice a change in her behavior?" Ryan asked.

"Yes and no. I thought, she's settling in, making friends. And lonely, you know? When she first got here. Sad too. I can tell, I've a good sense of people."

"Do you know if she had a boyfriend?"

"I don't think so, at least no one special. We talked a lot. She had an ex-boyfriend. A real Casanova. Nothing violent, but sometimes emotional pain can be worse."

"Any details we should know about this ex?" Billy asked.

"His name is Liam. They were a couple on and off for about two years. He wasted her time if you ask me."

Billy made a note. They knew about Liam. Rose had mentioned him, and Brighton had been contacted.

"Lately, though," Ryan insisted. "Anyone lately?" He waited, hoping she hadn't mentioned their night together.

Angus took a moment. "I'm pretty sure she would have told me if she'd met anyone, but she did seem, how do I put it? Brighter maybe? I don't see why she wouldn't have confided in me. And there's Mrs. Doyle, but she's old."

"That's the landlady?"

"Yes, they had become close. Sort of a mother-granny figure. You know Kathleen's family history? Her parents dying, all that?"

"Yes," Ryan said. "Her sister told us."

Everyone jumped at a sharp rap on the door. Sophie entered carrying a tray with three coffees. "Here you are. Need anything else?"

"No, that's grand. Thanks, Ms. Walton."

"Sophie, please. And my nieces are here." She closed the door.

Ryan took a sip of coffee. "Where were you, Angus, this Saturday night to Sunday morning?"

"Dublin, with my partner Calvin. We try to alternate weekends, one here in Belfast next one down there. I left Friday evening and got back late Sunday." He stopped and thought for a moment. "She suddenly decided to take this week off, though. She didn't come in to work last Thursday or Friday, called and asked me to cover for her early on Thursday morning. Did you know?"

"No," Ryan said, looking at Billy. "We didn't know that."

"She wouldn't tell me why." Angus hesitated. "Very secretive. Sometimes she could be like that." His face sagged, and he turned away.

Sophie herded her two nieces in like a couple of puppies and directed them to chairs as if they weren't capable of deciding for themselves. "Tell the police everything you know. The sooner this maniac is found, the easier I'll sleep. Gillian, is that gum?"

Gillian grimaced and spat a small piece of chewing gum into a tissue. She turned around and handed it to her aunt, then turned back with a shy smile.

"Right, I'll leave you to it." Sophie closed the door, and both girls blew out a great breath in unison.

"Sorry about Aunt Sophie," Gillian said, "She thinks we're like, twelve. She's worse than our mum, right Jackie?"

The girls, eighteen and nineteen years old, while not alike in physical appearance, behaved almost as one. They wore the same kind of clothes and styled their hair in the same way. Both girls had swollen eyes.

Billy fancied himself good with kids. He'd three of his own, after all. He took the lead. Bless you for that, Ryan thought.

"You first, Gillian. Did you know Kathleen well?"

"Well enough. She was nice. I mean, we didn't go out for coffee or drinks together or anything, but we chatted."

Jackie added, "We all went that time for coffee at Costa when the alarm went off for nothing, and we couldn't stop it. Remember?"

"Oh, yes, right. That once then," Gillian said.

The sisters were somewhat subdued and upset. While Ryan knew very little about Kathleen, he couldn't imagine her confiding in them. They seemed so young to him.

Jackie spoke again. "This is awful, you know. We can't believe it." She glanced at her sister. "We liked her."

Gillian nodded. "We were talking earlier, and we think it was her boyfriend."

"Liam?" Ryan asked. "Do you know anything about him, Jackie? Did he come over here, to Belfast, to the gallery?"

"Oh, no, not him." Jackie rolled her eyes a little. "Not the old boyfriend. She didn't fancy him anymore if you ask me."

Gillian broke in, "I think she still liked him a bit, Jackie."

"Yeah, maybe, but not him. The new guy."

Ryan's cottage sat on about five acres of land. A nearby farmer kept sheep on it, and as Ryan pulled in, an old ewe dandered across his driveway and started to munch on the grass verge. Ryan parked, shooed, and then had to push the bloody thing back to the field and resecure the gate.

After he washed his hands, which smelled like old socks, he made a beeline for the kitchen, phoned Patricia, and asked her to send the dog over. Finn came home by himself. Ryan looked out at the back garden, wind picking up. He'd stayed here as a kid many times, helping his grandfather in the fields during the summers when it was a working farm. All but the five acres had been sold. Now it was his.

Tonight, he had a few things to deal with. Kathleen's new boyfriend, who was he? And Liam seemed to be MIA. Ryan put a stew in the oven for his dinner—thank you, dear sister—and let Finn in the back door. The dog trotted over to his bowl and sat down.

"Live in hope there, old buddy. I know Patricia will have fed you already," Ryan said, then grabbed a bone-shaped dog biscuit and threw it at Finn, who caught it like a pro.

After dinner, he cleared up and took some notes into his conservatory. Should he call Rose McGuire? There it was again, that little spike of anticipation. Yes.

She answered after a few rings. "Hello?"

"Hi, it's DS McBride. Not too late to call, is it? This can easily wait until tomorrow."

"No, it's fine."

"A couple of things. We found your sister's car. I can't discuss all the details, but I wanted to let you know the investigation's moving forward. We have some new information to work with."

"Where did you find it?"

"Abandoned near the crime scene. As soon as I have anything else relevant, I'll tell you. Did she have diabetes, by the way? And did she own a Rolex?"

"No, she didn't have diabetes, and I don't know if she had a Rolex, although I doubt it. Why?"

"We found some items while sorting through debris at the scene. And another thing. We were at the gallery today, and the two assistants, Jackie and Gillian, said your sister had a new boyfriend. Dark hair, tall. Kathleen drove off with him in a nice car, dark grey or maybe black. This was one evening a while ago, down the street from the gallery. She kept him a secret, according to the girls; never mentioned him."

"Not Liam then. His hair's light brown and short. And he wouldn't be driving a fancy car, not unless he won the lottery. He rides a battered old motorbike. Have you spoken to him? They were together for a couple of years."

"We haven't, not yet. We're actively looking but can't seem to locate him. She never mentioned another man at all, not even a hint?"

"No, she didn't. The last words I had with her were sharp. I was tired and jet-lagged."

She said nothing for a moment, and Ryan thought he heard something, a muffled sob perhaps.

"I'm sorry," he said. "For your loss."

As they continued to talk, fat raindrops hit the conservatory roof, tentative splatters at first. She's loosened up, Ryan realised. Maybe because of our lunch together, or that we're not face to face? He heard a whine. Finn waited by the kitchen door.

"You want to go out?"

"Pardon?" Rose asked.

"My dog, Finn, he's standing by the door. I think he needs to go out. Hang on a minute, will you?" He opened the back door to a blast of wet wind. Finn hesitated. "Finn, make up your mind." He pushed the dog out, closed the door, and picked up the phone again, breathless. "I kicked him out. It's bucketing."

"What is he? What breed?" she asked.

"A wire-haired fox terrier."

"We had a fox terrier when we were kids. I loved that dog. Silver. We called him Silver."

"Hang on, he's back," Ryan said. Finn slunk in, bedraggled, trailing water. He shook himself dry spectacularly in the middle of the floor. Ryan picked up the phone, huffing. "Friggin' dog. I'm soaked. He does that every time."

"Maybe you should learn to stand back then."

"I do, but I think he waits and does it on purpose."

In the background a clock chimed.

"What time is it?" Rose said.

"Half-past ten. Sorry, I'd better let you go."

"You'll let me know as soon as you hear anything?"

"Of course."

"Goodnight then, DS McBride. Thanks for the call."

"Goodnight, Rose," he said, and thought of Kathleen.

Chapter Eight

Friday, September 16

BEFORE

"Can't you get around it?"

Kathleen sat in the back of the taxi and fretted. Outside, rain hammered down. Not one, but two accidents had twisted traffic into knots and caused her stomach to churn with anxiety. She checked her watch, a beautiful Rolex, gleaming on her wrist and mocking her. Kevin had given it to her on their first anniversary, a whole month. She'd been ecstatic, not just about the watch, even though it was a Rolex, for God's sake, but because of him.

He had his quirks, and his jealousy was a concern, but in some ways, she secretly liked it. Okay, maybe she had at the beginning. It was getting a bit old now, to be honest. She'd liked that he worried about other men coming into the gallery and flirting with her. As if anyone could compare to him. She told him this over and over again, and he seemed placated, then he would ask her if she thought the waiter handsome because she had chatted a bit too much to him. Did he not realise how gorgeous he was himself? Traffic had loosened up, and they were moving along the Malone Road now. She would be about fifteen, twenty minutes late at most. He would see the rain and understand. Nothing to worry about.

In the short sprint from the taxi to the restaurant door, she was soaked.

The hostess let her in with a sympathetic smile and handed her a couple of tissues.

"I see my friend," Kathleen said.

Kevin sat in a corner with his broad back hunched over the table.

"Here she is at last," the smiling girl said, walking her over. "I'll send the waitress now, shall I?"

"Give it a minute, will you?"

Kevin had a half-empty glass of red wine in front of him, and a full glass sat at her place.

He was white-faced with anger, his voice a low hiss. "What is it this time? You have a fucking Rolex and still you're late."

Here we go again...she should have known. Who was she kidding?

"Kevin, look at the rain. I left in plenty of time."

He broke in, "Kathleen, you're almost a half hour late, and I look like a fucking idiot sitting here waiting for my girlfriend to show up."

"I left forty-five minutes early. How could I have known about the traffic?"

She thought about her plan to stand in a doorway in the pouring rain and watch the restaurant until Kevin arrived, then walk in right after him. That's what he liked. But those damn car accidents. And it wasn't her. She wasn't the cause of his temper. It depended on how his day had gone. On his mood, not hers.

"I'll go to the toilet and fix myself up. I'm soaked." She forced a smile. "I'm sorry, I know you hate waiting." Did she ever.

"No. Don't go and leave me here again. Drink your wine."

He waved at the waitress.

"You can bring the salads now."

Kathleen had long since accepted Kevin would decide what they would have. It seemed natural now. She sat back and tried to smooth her hair. He seemed unsettled tonight, even more than usual. "Did you get that big contract? The one for the leisure centers?"

"What did I write on the note with the watch? *Now you have no excuse for being late.*"

Not willing to let it go yet. She thought back to the evening of the gift. He always said something, didn't he? Some little jab to make her lose a little more confidence. She had opened the fabulous box and had seen that watch. He had looked her in the eyes and said, 'No excuses now. You'll always be on time, right?'

She was rarely late. The only other time, she had been trapped at the gallery on a Friday evening, with Sophie pacing and worrying about her husband. He had decided to come over to Belfast unexpectedly.

She couldn't even mention Kevin to Sophie. He'd warned her about discussing their relationship at this point, especially at work. Some bad experience previously when a woman he dealt with had developed feelings for him. They had dated briefly, and when he wanted to end it, the woman had taken a long stress leave and started to threaten some kind of legal action.

"She said I was abusing her. Can you believe it? Said she was going to bring charges, sue for pain and suffering." He shook his head. "It always comes down to money, doesn't it?"

"Did it go to court?"

"No, because she was involved in a hit and run and killed. They never found the driver, and in case you're wondering, I was in England at the time. The police talked to me." He'd shaken his head again. "Bottom line, my father warned me against getting involved with clients. Best not to mention you're seeing me."

She told no one at the gallery they were dating, not even Angus, but she had already mentioned him to Mrs. Doyle and didn't see the harm. After all, Mrs. Doyle was a pensioner who had no contact with anyone Kathleen knew. And for goodness sake, she had to tell someone.

She drank her wine, feeling it relax her. Kevin ordered another glass for both of them, and they sat waiting for their entrees without speaking. As he checked his phone, she gazed over his shoulder. Couples chatting and smiling. The space felt intimate with rose-coloured walls and grey velvet chairs. A gorgeous smell in the air, garlic, lemon, some hint of spice. She heard muffled chatter, all pleasant in tone. Mirrors of various shapes and sizes hung around the room, and she caught a glimpse of herself. A woman she hardly recognised. Oh God.

Kevin looked up from his phone. "Go fix your hair; it looks ridiculous. And hurry back before the food comes."

She closed the door of the ladies with a sob. What was going on?

Her hair in the mirror was wild from the rain, her face drawn tight with anxiety. Why did this always happen? Should she end this relationship? Could she? She shrank from the idea of it, pulled a brush through her tangled curls and applied fresh lip gloss. She smiled tentatively. It's fine, she thought. He'll get over it. He always does.

As she came back to the table, the food arrived.

"Good timing," he said. "You look beautiful. A little touch-up works wonders."

"Thank you," she said. What else could she say?

His point made, she supposed, he was as charming as ever. They had cognac with dessert. How can he drink so much and not show it? She, for one, felt wobbly. He took her arm on the way to the car and when they reached it, he pushed her against it and kissed her roughly. Then he opened the door and guided her into the seat.

"I'm not sure I've completely forgiven you; we'll have to see what happens when we get to my place."

He lived in a spacious one-bedroom in the Titanic area. They drove into the deserted underground car park. He pulled her from the car and hurried her to the lift. When the doors closed, he pushed against her aggressively, kissing her hard. Hurting her.

Once in his apartment, he led her into the bedroom and undressed her without speaking. The sex was rough, and she didn't like it, but she said nothing because she didn't want to set him off again. Afterwards, she went to the bathroom and saw her blotchy face and swollen lips. Her chest had a red flush across it, and her breasts were sore, with the smallest hint of a bruise near her right nipple. But it's okay, it isn't always like this. He's angry. He would be fine now, wouldn't he?

She pulled on a linen dressing gown, the only item of clothing she had in the flat. He had never asked her to stay over, no matter how late it got. What about tonight? If he insisted, would she have to stay? When she came out, he was sitting up in bed with a bottle of bourbon on his night table and a glass half full in his hand.

"Come back to bed and bring a glass with you."

She didn't like bourbon, but she walked out to the bar and picked up a glass, tipped some whiskey in, then came back to stand at the large picture window in the bedroom. She stared past her own ghostly reflection, blurry with watery rivulets. "How can it rain so much?" The apartment was fairly spartan, nothing on the walls, just an unbroken stretch of white. It was cold—and something else, something she couldn't put her finger on. Unwelcoming perhaps?

"Come back to bed."

He had a smooth, hairless chest. Does he shave it? She didn't know. She didn't know much about him, not much personal stuff. Those conversations, intimate ones, he kept to himself, way inside, encased in a shell. She felt like a beach ball, bounced around by his moods. Why did he have to be this way?

On the chest of drawers, there was a picture of him with an older man, one of the only personal touches in the whole place. His father, she assumed. He had never suggested she meet him, spoke rarely about him, and hardly ever mentioned his mother.

"Kathleen."

He pulled the duvet back. "Come back to bed. Come on."

No, she couldn't.

"Is this your father? He's handsome."

He pulled the duvet back over himself.

"Yes."

"You don't talk much about your mother."

"No."

Something popped inside her, a bit of the old fire, a memory of times when she spoke her mind and still had an opinion. Those blazing rows with Liam. She almost wished for them again. Oh God. Anything was better than this, this tiptoeing around all the time. Not knowing whether Kevin was in a fair mood or foul. And the beginning of worry. Could she leave him if she wanted to? Could she crawl, inch by painful inch, out from under the dead weight of his neuroses?

She stared at him, bolder now. "Why don't you talk about her?"

Kevin took a gulp of bourbon. He must be so drunk.

"My mother doesn't give a shit about me, never did. It was always about my dad. Like she didn't want to share him or something. She was a jealous bitch."

Now she knew where Kevin got one of his major personality traits from. She said nothing. Watched him.

He took a quick gulp from his glass, splashing himself, and for the first time she could see how drunk he was. Did he do that when things got too much? Drink himself senseless? Was this the only way he could cope?

"Kevin, I'm sorry." He had never shown her this fragile side.

"Hey, that's the hand I got. You don't need to feel sorry for me. You didn't do so well either, did you now? In the parental sweepstakes."

"I should go." She needed to get out, didn't need him dragging up her past. That's not what this was about, was it? He was the fucked-up one in the relationship, not her.

Kevin didn't look at her when she left. Down in the lobby she peered out into the rain. The taxi she'd called idled there already. She rushed down the steps and tumbled into the back seat. A young woman turned around from the driver's seat and smiled at her.

Kathleen didn't expect this slip of a girl. Couldn't imagine driving around in the night, picking up strangers. "Aren't you a bit frightened working late like this?"

"Augh, no, the company screens the calls, and I get a lot of women like yourself, coming home late and all. Sometimes they even ask for me. And I can take care of myself, I box. It's brilliant exercise."

Kathleen sighed and studied the driver. She had razor-short, white-blond hair, a nose ring, and a thorn tattoo circling her neck. Thin and wiry, she didn't seem big enough to punch anyone out.

"Bad night?" the young woman asked, pulling away and glancing at

Kathleen in the mirror.

"Oh, you know, boyfriend stuff."

"Yeah, well. If he's a bastard, dump him. Life's too short and you're too good-looking. Get somebody else."

Kathleen was about to protest, but maybe the girl was right. "What's your name?"

"Annabelle. Ridiculous girly name, isn't it?" She laughed. "I'm gay too—oh, the irony."

"I'll be honest, Annabelle, I don't know where I am with him half the time."

Annabelle studied her in the mirror again. "You're out on your arse at two o'clock in the morning. That's where you are."

Kathleen stared out as the taxi splashed across the Albert Bridge, passing the Lagan river as it drifted by, black and cold. Belfast was deserted and dark now, except when they passed through the city center. Tall streetlights topped with misty white halos edged the pavements, and bright electric neon zigzags quivered in puddles. This was not her city, but tonight she felt a certain kinship with it. Its soaking, deserted streets and windswept alleyways. Slick sheets of rain thrown sideways across deserted intersections. Loneliness. God, she was lonely.

She crept in so as not to disturb Mrs. Doyle. Always a relief to get home these days. Grabbing a glass, she filled it with water and tiptoed into her bedroom. She undressed and decided against a shower even though she needed to feel the water washing everything away. Kevin. The last few months...everything.

She wiped at her face and gave her teeth a cursory brush. She'd had too much to drink and would pay for it tomorrow. The bruise on her breast had spread a little, and her lips were still puffy. She could also see marks on her hips where he had manhandled her. Right from the beginning, he had been demanding, even aggressive, during sex. At the start of this relationship, she had liked it. Deep down in some dark corner, she had found it exciting, but ultimately this was not what she wanted. She choked back a sob. Surely by now there should be some tenderness between them? He had changed. It was subtle, but she felt it. He had always been controlling and determined, but lately, she felt a shift to a more ominous, darker Kevin, more physical and aggressive. He had hurt her, hit her even, and threatened her. Why did she let him? What was wrong with her? What was wrong with him? She thought back to that night with the detective. The sex had been passionate and exciting, but he had not hurt her. He had been tender. Totally focussed on her. That's what she wanted, not this.

In bed, the night replayed over and over in her head. She had to do something. And when, somewhere around seven in the morning, the rain stopped and a watery sun began its tentative climb into a swollen sky, Kathleen made her decision.

Chapter Nine

"A harsh sea crashing over the pier, seagulls soaring high on clouds the colour of slate, and the wind, blustery and damp, pushing at your back.'"

"Shut up, Ryan. I'm not going, so you can forget whatever that crap was—you and your fancy school."

"Christ, Billy, head over there for a few days and ask around," Ryan said.

Still on Liam's trail, Ryan knew Billy didn't want to go to Brighton. He wanted to tie up loose ends by phone and email from Belfast. He was doing Ryan's head in, hence the poetic ramblings.

"Piss off, will you? Why in God's name would I want to trade one cold, grey, miserable, sea-swept town for another?" Billy lived happily in Carrickfergus but felt the need to complain about it regularly. "I talked to his best mate. Liam is some kind of artist." Billy made a sniffing sound. "He's not even in Brighton anymore, supposed to be on his way to Dublin to settle down with the love of his life." He pushed a couple of sheets around with his pencil. "Thing is, he left a couple of weeks ago, and nobody's heard from him since. Free spirit, apparently." Billy sniffed again.

"Got a cold, have you?" Ryan couldn't be bothered with Billy's disinterest in anything remotely artistic.

"Na, I'm dead on," Billy said, missing Ryan's snide comment altogether. Another thing Ryan hated.

"He's on a shitty old bike, and his friend said it's not reliable. It sounds to me like Liam's not too reliable, either, I managed to get a number for this new girlfriend. I've left her a message and might have to make a run to Dublin, but that'll be okay." Billy slapped his desk for emphasis, and a splash of tea slopped onto some papers. "Ah shite."

"Dublin, eh? All those Fenians. Will you be able to handle it?" Ryan said, only half-joking.

"You shut up about that, Ryan, nothing wrong with being an Orangeman. It's only a club now, a social thing, cheap drinks on a Friday night."

Billy started mopping up the spilled tea with some paper hankies.

Ryan said, "Speaking of, Bridget called me on Monday night."

Billy stopped wiping and turned to face Ryan again.

"What did *she* want?"

"She asked if she could come around, and I said no."

"Huh. You want to steer clear, Ryan. I've told you, that one's trouble."

"It's not that she's Catholic or anything, is it, Billy?"

"I'm not going to dignify that with a reply." Billy turned back to his tidying up, huffing.

"I know you never liked her, but why? You never told me why."

"I don't trust her or her bloody family. They're all bitter, Ryan, and you a policeman."

"Oh, it is because she's Catholic."

"No, it's not. She's too good-looking for a start and knows it, and it's hard to get past that family. Let's say she doesn't care that you're Protestant and what you do, but her brothers do. And they've been in trouble, you know they have. The dad too. Once they're in with that crowd, the Republicans…."

Billy let his words trail off and turned back once again to his desk.

Ryan could imagine Billy and Margaret discussing his love life. Any social gathering with the department, Bridget always appeared sleek and sexy. Wore tight little dresses and flirted with the guys, showing off for him, he supposed. And there was the whole motorcycle-chick vibe too. That had caught his attention, the Harley, the leather pants and jacket. Problem with Bridget, that wildness was part of her, not for show. That unpredictability was a turn-on for Ryan—up to a point.

Margaret usually sat demurely by Billy's side. Pretty too, but low-key, with her short brown hair combed neatly, plain little beige frock, and sensible shoes. Her face set in a disapproving smile. Often with a half pint of Guinness in front of her, one point in her favour at least.

"It couldn't have been that important to her. She hung up on me." And why did she? Ryan thought. They could have talked for a while. Much as he hated to admit it, he missed her sometimes.

"I would say give Bridget a wide berth. She's a sly one, and you're well out of it."

"Thanks, Billy, for the relationship advice."

"You asked me,"

"No, no," Ryan said, "I did not. I said she called."

"Why did you even tell me then? Huh?"

Capitulation was the only way. Billy had perfected the art of constant, relentless negotiation and argument. He'd had years of practice with Margaret and his three children. It was why he was so good at witness interviews and interrogations. Armed robbers, murder suspects, they all took one look at Billy, all freckles and silly hair, and thought, he'll be a pushover, harmless gobshite. Ah, so wrong. He had them begging to confess to get out of the interview room. He could drive a sane man mad, and some of the guys they interviewed were halfway there already.

But Billy, for all his smarts, was easily distracted, a little nugget Ryan had picked up over the years. "I still think it would have been a nice break for you, Brighton—get a bit of rock."

"Ha, ha. I think not. You go then if you're so keen. Margaret would kill me. We've wee Alison's birthday on Saturday. It's at the house, and the place is a tip."

"How's that your problem?"

"You're kidding me, right?" Billy turned to face Ryan. "Tell me you're joking."

"What? What did I say?"

"We share the housework, Ryan. She expects me to do half the tidying up."

"But you work, and Margaret doesn't. I don't get it. I'll never get it. Your lot are in school now, or pre-school or bloody kindergarten or wherever the hell parents dump kids now...."

"Oh. Here we go again. You're a right chauvinist, you are. She's a housewife. That's her job. We've three weans, Ryan. And you don't dump kids. It's a process, deciding where they go. Our children are all highly strung and emotional. It would do your head in."

Ryan said nothing. As far as he was concerned, Billy and Margaret's kids were spoiled rotten. He'd no desire for children, neither had Erin, and it was his father's fault, no question. Ryan and Erin had never gotten away with anything. Strict rules for homework and social behavior. It had soured him on family, he knew it. And Erin. It had damaged her in other, subtle ways. She never thought she was good enough.

"All I'm saying is this is a tough job; not sure I could go home to everyone's dishes and laundry. I've enough of my own," Ryan added.

"You get used to it. Hey, you know what?"

This time, Ryan noted, Billy distracted himself.

"You should find yourself a nice girlfriend and settle down, good-looking fella like you. Half the ladies in Musgrave fancied you." Billy grinned.

Ryan smiled back. "Why, thanks, Billy, that's flattering."

"And the other half fancied me." Billy snorted at his own joke.

A setup, then. "Humour, Billy. I don't think it suits you."

Billy's phone rang, and he grabbed it. And thank Christ, too, Ryan thought. "Detective Sergeant William Lamont."

Billy nodded to Ryan and turned back to his desk. After he hung up, he nodded over. Liam's girlfriend from Dublin had returned Billy's call, and she wasn't happy.

"Your woman's hysterical near enough. She's convinced something has happened, and wait until you hear this: She tried to report him missing to the Guards over a week ago."

"Why didn't we see that report?" Ryan said.

Billy sat back in his chair and blew out a big breath. "She tried to file one, but they didn't take her seriously. He's a grown man, and he'd only been missing a few days when she called. The Guards told her to come back later on. She did, and they sent out a missing-person report a few days ago. It hasn't been widely circulated yet. Not up here, at least."

"Damn. What do you think? Is he our man? Done a runner? I mean it sounds like he was in Ireland when she was killed. And by all reports, they had a fairly contentious relationship. Although…" Ryan thought for a moment. "You did a check on him, right? No criminal background there?"

"No, nothing like that. A few parking tickets, speeding on the bike, the usual stuff. I think I'll go talk to the girlfriend in person. You want to come with?"

"No thanks, away and enjoy yourself. I'm waiting for some CCTV footage to come in from outside the gallery and on that intersection where the girls saw Kathleen with the mysterious boyfriend. Might get lucky, see the car and that license plate. I don't want to hang around on this one."

"Why don't you take your own advice and get Wylie to do the CCTV? One less thing. I want to meet this girlfriend, make sure she's legit. See if I can get more information on Liam from her." Billy grabbed his jacket. "Make sure there's no chance he's hiding out in Dublin. I'll run it by the boss and see what cars they have downstairs."

He hustled back ten minutes later, car keys in hand.

"I'll call you if anything interesting turns up. Otherwise, I'll see you tomorrow morning at the briefing." He jangled the keys. "And you're sure you don't need me here?"

"Go ahead. I doubt anything major's going to happen in one day," Ryan said.

Billy shook his head. "You're asking for trouble saying that."

Erin phoned about ten minutes later. "Lunch, no excuses. I'm buying." She lowered her voice to a breathless whisper. "I need to talk to you." Always the drama with his sister.

"Why are you talking like that, Erin? Where are you?"

"At home. Where'd you think I am?"

Of course. "Okay, sure, but a short one, you'll have to come down here.

What's going on?"

They met at The Chester cocktail bar, not his local, but he'd been before and liked it. He got there first, headed to the back, and snagged his favourite corner banquette by an old fireplace, logs smouldering and crackling in the grate. The room was smoky and warm. He ordered a half pint and sat down to wait. Erin arrived ten minutes late, not bad timing for her. A few heads turned when she walked in. Still a stunner, Ryan thought, although it caused her more problems than not. That and the money she'd inherited from their grandparents, a dangerous combination in a headcase like her. He waved her over. "How's my girl?"

"Shut up and order me a large martini, will you?"

Ryan signalled the waiter. "A vodka martini for the lady, please."

"Paul telephoned." She challenged Ryan with a look.

"Ah, and what did your feckless ex-husband want?" Ryan knocked back the rest of his beer.

"Feckless? Really, Ryan, you should get over yourself."

The hint of a smile in her voice settled him a bit.

"And Paul, you know, he wanted to talk," she said.

"Erin." He let his tone speak. He couldn't bring himself to chide her. Everyone else had, and his sister was exhausted with it. The warnings, the remonstrations.

"I know. Please don't start."

"Okay." Not okay.

"He's not with her anymore, Ryan. They broke up. He wanted to be the one who told me."

"Nice guy. Considerate."

"Don't be sarcastic. That's not why I wanted to meet. If I needed sarcasm, I could call Dad. Take one of his classes in it."

He studied her. Black pixie hair and fair skin. She had his hazel eyes and long lashes, but her face was oval, her lips full.

"Then what do you want from me, Erin? You want me to sympathise with him losing his girlfriend? She was his main source of income, wasn't she?

After he left you."

Why couldn't she see that Paul Crawford was a dick? Pretty much everybody else could.

"He's not a bad person, he's an artist. He has integrity."

Paul Crawford. *Integrity?* Art photographer and ex-husband, he didn't know what hit him when their father had finished with him. Oliver McBride, *Lawyer Extraordinaire,* was not good for much as far as Ryan was concerned, but their father had stripped that bastard clean. Crawford may have married Erin with some good intentions, but her bank account wasn't one of them. She'd inherited a sizable amount of money from their grandparents. Ryan had, too, and bought Erin's half of the farm, a nice car, and banked the rest. Erin bought a husband.

"Does Paul want you two to get back together?"

"No, that's not why he called. You're so cynical. He wants to meet for a coffee. He doesn't want this bitterness between us, and neither do I. And what Dad did during the divorce, God, he's ruthless, relentless. I didn't want that."

Ryan knew what she meant, but Erin's wishes hadn't counted for much. Not with their father. No one got the better of the McBrides. "Don't meet him, Erin. Don't do it."

The waiter appeared with Erin's martini. She thanked him and took a sip.

"You never liked Paul, did you?" She took another, larger drink and turned her attention back to him. "Never gave him a chance."

"He had two affairs in three years. I didn't have time to give him a chance, did I?"

She ignored him, never listened when it came to Crawford. That was the problem. Another larger sip.

"And he didn't even have the courtesy to not get caught, every time." Ryan felt himself getting wound up.

Silence. Then...she exhaled.

"I'm lonely, Ryan. I don't want to do the singles thing again. What's wrong with having a drink or a quick get-together with your ex? And you're no good to me, always working. Don't you ever think about Bridget? Meeting for a drink, even getting back with her? I thought you two were so good together."

"Erin, Bridget broke off with me, remember?" He changed the subject. "Hey, when do Mum and Dad get back from Spain?"

She choked back a laugh. "Not helpful, Ryan. But my God, it's been great them being away. Not Mum, I miss her, but Dad. I could breathe there for a while. Didn't you feel it? The relief?"

Yes, he had felt it, sure he had. That subtle lifting of weight. No required Sunday-night dinners with his parents. His dad poking away at his life. Granted, he had been a major disappointment to the man. Graduating from Queen's University with an honours law degree, he had blindsided his father by joining the police, not the prestigious firm of McBride Law as expected. Now nothing he did would ever be good enough.

"Let's order. I don't have much time. What was it you wanted to tell me?"

"Oh, about Paul, you know...."

He left it. She'd already told him she was lonely. That was all right; he got lonely too sometimes.

She finished her drink. "Get me another, will you?"

"Erin, are you driving?" God, he sounded like their father.

"No. And you sound like Dad, you know that?" She swatted at him, smiled and grabbed the menu.

Back at the station, Ryan barely got his bum in the chair when a young constable approached him. Shiny, that was Ryan's first impression of him. His hair trimmed almost to his scalp, his skin, smooth as a baby's.

"DS McBride?"

"Yup."

"Sir, I'm PC Samuel Burns—Sam. I'm with the group over from Musgrave?"

Sam smiled down at him, fresh-faced, eager. Probably a probationary constable, Ryan thought. Hadn't had the enthusiasm beaten out of him. Still keen by the looks of him.

"Right, nice to meet you, Sam."

"Yes, well, I wanted to say hello, and if there's anything you want help with, any investigations you need an extra pair of hands for, let me know." He hesitated. "DS Anderson is keeping an eye on us and told us to make ourselves useful. He didn't want us hanging around with nothing to do, getting in the way. So—you know, I would love to help you, DS Lamont, and the group in any way."

"That's great, Sam, but—"

"The others, PC Wylie and his two friends, they said I should stick to old case files and the material Inspector Girvan has left for us to read over, but I want to help on real cases, not cold cases, you know? I want to help now. And like, computer work, going over files or anything like that? I've studied all kinds of techniques and forensics, on my own time. I want to be a detective. I've already told DC Maura Dunn, I graduated top of my class in computer science at Stranmillis."

Oops, best not let Derek hear that little nugget. "Let me think about it."

"Right, great. I'm off across the street to get proper coffee for the lads. Can I pick one up for you? Cappuccino, espresso?"

"They've sent you off on a coffee run?"

"Yes," he hesitated. "I don't mind. I pick up lunch for them sometimes, too, so if you fancy pizza or anything?"

"No, I'm good, thanks, Sam."

Jesus, typical of Wylie, got himself an errand boy already.

Ryan had finished a report and was eyeing the coffeemaker when his phone rang. Derek had big news.

"Mrs. Doyle, Kathleen's landlady? I've been checking up on her, and that's not all she is. She owns that house and a couple of other properties."

Ryan whistled. "Seriously?" That place alone was worth a fortune.

"All in that same neighbourhood," Derek said. "She owns three properties that I've been able to find, and not easy information either. Held in companies and trusts, etcetera. All told, she's worth a fortune. Oh, and Ryan, it might mean nothing, but she has some scary family connections too."

"Scary?"

"Patrick and Brendan Doyle. Patrick is dead, as you probably know—but yes, Brendan Doyle is her son."

"Piss off. You're pulling my leg." Although, to be fair, Derek didn't have a sense of humour, per se....

"No. Her sons."

"Bring me the paperwork. I need to see this."

"Right. Give me a minute to print it."

"And Derek, any chance of a coffee from your superior coffeemaker up there?"

Derek appeared ten minutes later carrying two coffees and a thick bunch of papers. He sighed dramatically and placed the coffees on Ryan's desk.

"Where's Billy?" he asked, glancing around.

"Gone to Dublin's fair city. Chasing Liam, Kathleen's ex."

Derek passed some of the paperwork over to Ryan.

"Names from the past, eh?" Ryan said, scanning the pages.

"Aye, her two sons were big shots back in the day, the Doyles. More the drugs and armed robberies, right? A large operation." Derek sat in Billy's chair, started to swing from side to side. "Brendan and Patrick would have paid off the Provos and the IRA, they would have had to," Derek added.

"Then Patrick got himself killed. That was a horrible murder, as I recall," Ryan said.

"Some talk the Russian Mafia were coming in back then. Patrick didn't want to pay protection to foreigners, and they don't like that, the Russians. They tortured him something shocking." Derek tried to swing the chair all the way around.

"Jesus, the Russian mob?" Ryan let that cheery thought settle in for a minute. "Derek, will you, for the love of God, sit still?"

"That's one theory." Derek grinned. But he stopped with the chair.

"Looks like Brendan got the message. No more bad guy. A gentleman farmer, you say? He got out of it all?"

"Yup." Derek finished his coffee. "He's making a packet from EU friggin' grants. Wind farms, tree farms, and farm farms, you name it. Who says crime doesn't pay? And they couldn't prove anything. This Brendan Doyle, he's no mug, I'll give him that. Smart bugger."

Ryan leaned back and put his feet up. Someone had opened a window at the back, and a cold draught ruffled the sheets on his desk. Sirens sounded outside in the distance. "Buying properties in the Malone Road, there's another nice little investment."

"It's not right, that's all I'm saying." Derek crumpled his cup and tossed it towards the bin, missing spectacularly.

"What about Mrs. Doyle then?"

"Her husband died years ago. A right bastard, apparently. Beat her senseless half the time when the boys were young. I have a couple of police reports here submitted by the local hospital. I'm reading between the lines, but it's pretty obvious she was a battered wife. They never bothered about that sort of thing back then. And here's the other thing, Ryan. Word was—Brendan murdered his father when he was old enough. Pulled him off his mother one last time and beat him to death with a hurley stick. Never proven. They claimed someone broke in, a revenge killing or some such nonsense. Oh, and she also had a wee girl named Ailish. Brendan and Patrick's little sister. Ailish died of pneumonia." Derek hesitated. "A shame, she lost her little daughter, her youngest son, and now only has her eldest son, Brendan, left."

"Right. Leave it with me. And can you gather CCTV footage from the streets around the gallery? I've decided to get Wylie to look for this elusive new boyfriend. Keep him busy. I have to use him, Girvan's orders, so don't give me that face."

Derek shook his head. "What? I do that, Ryan. I'm the expert with all that. He'll miss something. He's a tool."

Here we go, you never knew what would set Derek off. Might not be the best time to mention PC Burns then. "Look, Derek, this is rote work. I need you on other important stuff. We all do. You'll keep an eye on him."

"I don't want to keep an eye on that bastard. I don't even like talking to him. You're foisting him off on me. I do have other cases to work, you know.

You take advantage of my good nature."

"Oh, for God's sake, Derek, get a grip. Stop whingeing."

"See how much superior coffee you get from now on." Derek sauntered away.

"Great work on the Doyles, Derek, and don't forget to send the link to Wylie," Ryan shouted after him. "Today."

Ryan straightened the papers and began to reread them. Now, where the hell could Mrs. Doyle be? Probably with her son, Brendan. He glanced at the clock. Almost five now. He snatched up his desk phone, hoping Derek might have a number for Brendan Doyle. As he did so, his mobile buzzed.

"Detective McBride?"

Rose. Her voice in his ear caused a small thread of electricity to form in his stomach.

"Yes."

"There's a man in the downstairs flat."

Chapter Ten

Wednesday, October 26

R yan could hear the panic in Rose's voice.

"Look, it's likely Mrs. Doyle is home," he said. "But I'll come over in case. I'm at the station. I'll be there in about fifteen, twenty minutes. Is your front door locked?"

"Yes, and the chain is on."

"I'll see you shortly." He clicked off.

When Ryan arrived, he called her. "I'm downstairs. It's Mrs. Doyle. She's home. I'm coming up now."

She let him in. "I'm such an idiot, I'm sorry. I fell asleep, you see, and then I heard voices downstairs. It frightened me. And a man's voice, he was angry."

"Yes. Her son dropped her off. He didn't want her to come back here, but she insisted. She went to him because Kathleen decided to go away for a few days. Only yesterday she heard about Kathleen on the news and had a *turn*. Her son called the doctor, and they advised bed rest."

"Why didn't she stay with her son? She could have called the police from there and told them where she was."

"She intended to call tomorrow but insisted on coming home first against her son's wishes. That's why he sounded angry. He made her take something for anxiety. She's upset. They were close, Kathleen and her. Did you know that?"

"No, I didn't."

Ryan glanced around. "This flat, there's something about it, I felt it when I first came in. Peacefulness."

"Yes, I know what you mean," she said.

"You don't find it uncomfortable being here?"

"No. A bit lonely sometimes, but that's me."

She's more relaxed, he thought. "I'll head on then."

"You'll be right in the middle of rush hour," she said.

"I know it." He made for the door, heard a slight intake of breath behind him...waited for Rose to speak. Waited.

"You're welcome to stay a while. Maybe have a quick bite? You'll miss the worst of it then, and to tell you the truth I would appreciate the company. I did bring you out on a wild goose chase. You were probably heading home for dinner, right? And I'm making spaghetti, there's lots." She stopped speaking, seemed to realise she'd been babbling.

Was she nervous? That was a laugh, him making *her* nervous. "Spaghetti?"

He did love spaghetti.

"Spaghetti Bolognese. It's pretty good."

Two wine bottles sat on the counter. He thought idly about drinking some with her.

"I hope you weren't planning on drinking both of those tonight?"

"God no, one—part of one, I mean. A glass." She smiled briefly, her first smile. He liked it. A jolt of memory, Kathleen had smiled a lot.

"In that case, I better stay, if only to save you from yourself."

There. It was done.

"Great, that's great. Will you open the wine then? You can have a drink, right? You're off-duty?"

"Yup. Shift ended at five."

"You must think I'm stupid, worrying about some noise downstairs."

"No, it's fine. I usually stay a bit late at the station and, hey, looks like I might get a free dinner."

Rose moved to the kitchen, grabbed an apron, and placed a corkscrew on the counter.

"Wine detail then."

"Let me call my neighbour, she has the dog. She won't mind; she's used to it."

"I hope the wine is drinkable." She smiled.

He liked that she had relaxed at last. He poured a generous glass for each of them and went to the window armchair. "I do have to drive later."

"You'll have a full meal in you," Rose called over.

During dinner, she talked briefly about her work, that she felt she was making a difference. He saw her then in a new light, understood a little more about her. Her introspection. Why she spent months on end in dangerous countries, living in field hospitals and makeshift camps. They took their glasses into the living room, and Rose put on *Astral Weeks*. He finished his wine. "I saw Van once, in a bar in Belfast. He looked miserable."

"I don't think he drinks," Rose said. "Not anymore."

"He's brilliant. This is a fantastic album."

"Yes," she said.

"Have you ever heard Johnny McEvoy sing 'Carrickfergus'?" He almost added, *I'll play it for you next time,* before he stopped himself. What was he thinking? He wasn't thinking.

"No, I don't know him. I know the song." Rose saw his empty glass and stood up. "How much have you had? Can you have a top-up?"

She reached for his glass, and he caught her wrist.

"Better not." Better not pull her to him, better not kiss her. Her hair fell around her face, her skin gleamed. He saw Rose's face, not Kathleen's. He could smell that floral perfume he'd noticed the first time he'd been there. Tonight, it was fresh and light.

He pulled her to him. He knew he shouldn't, a vulnerable woman who was part of the investigation. No, don't do this.

A pause, she leaned closer and placed her other hand on his cheek. "I've lost Kathleen. What's wrong with me?"

"There's nothing wrong with you, but I can go if you want."

"No. Don't go," she whispered.

They made love on the living room floor, then he pulled her up, and they went to bed. They made love again.

Afterwards, she fell asleep. He held her and stared outside at shadows and the movement of treetops and dark clouds. What the hell was he doing? He stroked her hair and saw the curve of her neck in the half-light. He watched her breathe, watched the soft inhale and exhalation of air, her lip quivering. This evening had been her first time, he felt sure. Something about her, she seemed tentative, shy. Different from her sister. Kathleen had been an eager and energetic partner in bed. With Rose, he'd realised early that he had to be gentle.

"I have to go. I need to get home."

She stirred, drowsy. "Can't you stay?"

"I wish I could, but I have to be at the station early."

He kissed her, then got up and dressed. She saw him to the door naked, her hair tangled and her face soft with sleep.

"See you." He touched her cheek.

"Yes."

He took the stairs quietly and pulled the front door closed behind him, grimacing at the click. As he walked to his car, he glanced back at the dark bulk of the house and thought he saw a curtain twitch downstairs at the back.

Mrs. Doyle? Perhaps not asleep after all?

Chapter Eleven

Thursday, October 27

R yan made it home by half past three and was in bed asleep by a quarter to four. His alarm buzzed him at half seven, and he opened his eyes, squinting a little at the weak band of sunlight flickering across his ceiling. He lay there for a moment, watching it dance.

Something had been there, between him and Rose, almost from the beginning. At their pub lunch, or maybe before, sneaking up on him. It hadn't been entirely because of that evening with Kathleen either, although that played a part in all this. Rose had a completely different personality from her sister. Last night she had fallen into a deep sleep right after they made love, as if she hadn't slept for days—and perhaps she hadn't.

She'd been a virgin. She didn't mention it, and neither did he. How come? So beautiful and seemingly self-assured. Had she never been with a man? How could that be possible? He'd listened to her rhythmic breathing and occasional sigh, her hair messy on the pillow. It was strange, he thought, that he would be drawn to a woman whose emotional reserve mirrored his own. They hadn't spoken about Kathleen after they'd made love, and Ryan was well aware it had only been four days since her sister had been murdered. Was he a distraction? Was he being used? Somehow he didn't believe she would take their night together lightly. He hadn't.

After showering and dressing in jeans and a white tee shirt, he grabbed his leather jacket and jogged over the back fields to Patricia and Colin's home. Way in the distance, he could see a tractor as it moved across a fallow field. He could hear its engine on the breeze. The hedgerows edging the fields twitched and shook with birds and small animals, he heard something, the rustle of a rabbit perhaps as he approached Patricia's wooden gate. Originally a farmhouse like his own, they had renovated it and added another floor. Halfway up their back path, he heard Finn at the door, barking. He knocked, and Patricia yelled to come in.

"Hello, stranger," she said.

His neighbour's farmhouse kitchen smelled of bacon and coffee. Patricia fussed around wearing a pink quilted dressing gown and white slippers. She was a pleasantly plump woman in her late thirties with curly blond hair, a round, open face, and a wide smile. Finn jumped up and down like a mad thing until Ryan finally told him to stop.

"I'll take him down the road for a wee. To clear my head."

"That's brilliant, Ryan. The boys are still in bed, and Colin's running late."

He shook Finn's lead. "Let's give Patricia a minute." And a minute for him, too—he needed to let last night settle in before he went to work. He had so much to think about because here he was again, breaking rules. The tractor had finished. He walked in country silence with only wind sounds and the whisper of long grass for company.

What had he done?

Back in the warm kitchen, Patricia thrust a bacon bap into his hand.

"Away on and protect us, will you?"

Her husband Colin thumped down the stairs and popped his head in.

"Bloody hell, is that you, Ryan? When are we going to do our run? Patricia's tormenting me about my weight. Can't help it, I've a sedentary lifestyle. It's the job."

Ryan backed out. "Right, I'm away on." Ryan knew that Colin, ruddy-faced and jovial, owed his extra weight more to Guinness than the job.

"Here, is that a bacon bap?" Colin called after him.

Ryan finished the bap on the way to work and then brought a coffee up to the squad room. He walked over to the McGuire whiteboard and studied Kathleen's picture in the center. Now he saw Rose, her eyes closed and her lips parted as she lay beneath him. He knew it was wrong. But he couldn't push the image away.

"Hey." Billy arrived, lunch in one hand, his old leather briefcase under his arm, and a mug of tea in the other hand. "You were miles away."

"This case has me distracted. What did you get in Dublin?"

Billy dumped his stuff on the desk. "I did try to call you last night to fill you in."

"Oh, yes. Why?"

"An update. Not that much to tell."

"Sorry I didn't pick up. Mrs. Doyle is back."

"Anything?"

"She wasn't able to talk, so we're heading up there after the briefing. Rose McGuire called. She heard voices in the downstairs flat, a man's voice, angry, but it was the son bringing his mum home and not pleased about it."

"Brendan Doyle." Billy whistled. Ryan had emailed him the files Derek had uncovered on Mrs. Doyle. "And did you speak to the legend?"

"I did not. He'd left by the time I got there." Ryan changed the subject. "So, Dublin. What did you get from the trip?"

"The girlfriend's right. This is too long for Liam to be away without contacting her with a phone call or something. She had a studio set up for him. I didn't mention we suspected him, nothing like that. Just that we wanted to talk to him. She wasn't listening, more worried about where Liam was, that's all."

Ryan consulted his desk calendar. "Something's not right."

"Aye, if Liam took off for a holiday, even for a week, he should be in Dublin by now. Christ, Ireland's not big. She showed me emails they'd exchanged. Seemed legit, you know? I'll detail it in the report."

Ryan tapped his teeth with a pencil. "Thing is, we have nothing pointing to him. Nothing to suggest he came here to murder her. I mean, why would he want to? I can't see him placing a tracker on Kathleen's car, either. He has no history with firearms. Strange he turns up here now, though. Could it have been a catalyst for something else? And why hasn't he contacted us? If he was her boyfriend, you'd think he would want to know what happened to her."

"Unless he already knows," Billy added.

"Yes, but as easily this could be a separate thing altogether. With this tracker and the bullet hole, who springs to mind?"

"Brendan Doyle," Billy said. "With his background."

"Let's get this briefing over and go see Brendan's mum."

They had reached the squad-room door when Ed Wylie appeared.

"Where are you two heading?"

"Off to interview the victim's landlady," Billy said.

"Why don't I ride along? See how the pros do it." Wylie sauntered over.

"What about the footage on the victim and the mysterious new boyfriend?" Ryan wished he had left it with Derek. "You got those files from Derek, didn't you?"

"Yes, I did, but that's Derek's work. Let the nerd do it. I'm trying to get up to speed here, play a real part in the investigation."

"Listen." Ryan turned back to Wylie, got in his face. "I want you to look through the CCTV and try to spot Kathleen McGuire with a guy getting into a dark car anywhere near the gallery, around the timeline provided. You find that and we have a real lead. It is important, I'm not jerking you around here. How do you not get that?"

Wylie took a step back. "Lord it over me while you can. But the time will come...." He left the sentence unfinished and walked away.

As they clattered down the stairs, Billy looked over at Ryan.

"You know your problem, don't you?"

"Ah, Billy, why don't you tell me."

"You hold grudges. And there's your temper...I have to step in all the time. I'm not your mother, you know. You need to snap out of it, let it go. Lord knows Maura's over it."

"Jesus Christ, Billy, can we not? I don't lecture you, do I? And she's not bloody over it. Who are you to say she is? What about your wife? How'd you like it if he'd tried it on with Margaret in an alley, huh? Think she'd be over it by now? Maura hides it better. Wylie has serious issues."

"Look, I know he's an arse, a lazy shite, but Maura said he tried to apologize to her, said he was drunk, misread things. Can't *you* hide it better? We're all in the same boat, after all."

"Are we, Billy? Are we? It's not only the Maura thing, you don't see that? He's being fast-tracked for promotion? His uncle's doing, everyone knows it. He can barely be bothered to follow a simple order, doesn't want to do any work—doesn't think he needs to."

On the drive to Mrs. Doyle's, Billy sulked, and Ryan thought back to that night last Christmas, a few of the Antrim Road guys out for drinks to celebrate the season. Bridget, sexy, always flirting. He'd had a few too many drinks at the party, had the anticipation of heading back to his farm for quite a lot of sex that night, and again in the morning. Then Wylie turned up with some cronies. Hard to know why.

Billy had whispered to Ryan, "Don't they have their own bloody party to go to instead of crashing ours?"

Ryan had nodded, wondering himself.

Wylie chatted with Bridget at the bar and went in for a slow dance, hands sliding up and down her back, and maybe Ryan would have left it if Wylie hadn't glanced over Bridget's shoulder and given him a triumphant look. A smirk. He imagined Bridget had claimed some sort of personal victory when he interrupted them more aggressively than necessary, jostling Wylie and threatening him. He shouldn't have lost his temper. He should have left it. What he didn't know until later was that Wylie, drunk and frustrated, had gone outside for a smoke and bumped into Maura arriving late via the back alley.

The next morning, Maura called Ryan at home and told him in confidence that Wylie had tried to assault her. Ryan knew that for a young female PC to bring any kind of charge, especially against Wylie, it would have been a nightmare all round. Maura had decided not to pursue it.

"Accusations and recriminations, Ryan, I can't face it. It would hurt my career. I kneed him in the balls and left him there. And let's not forget his uncle."

"Who gives a damn about his connections? Maura, you have to report him."

"He'll say I encouraged him. You know what he's like. No, I've thought it over, and I'm going to leave it. I've made up my mind, and I feel better after talking to you. I'm going to call Billy too."

Afterwards as he lay in bed, he'd traced Bridget's shoulder with his finger and wondered if Maura was right. An investigation. He would be interviewed, and his altercation with Wylie would be questioned. And Maura would have a reputation, no matter the outcome. The small Christmas tree in the bedroom corner twinkled, its multi-coloured fairy lights glowing rosy on Bridget's naked skin. He could smell her body, its spicy perfume, and a lingering trace of sweat and sex in the air. The radiator ticked under the window.

Bridget stirred. "Who was it? You haven't been called in, have you?" She groaned and turned away from him. He felt her back, soft and warm on his side. If Maura wanted to forget it, who was he to argue? It was easier to let it go.

Mrs. Doyle seemed fine when they got to the house. A slight woman with tightly permed grey hair, she had bright blue eyes, currently red-rimmed. She wore a wraparound floral apron.

"A cup of tea? Bit early for a sherry or I'd have one meself."

"Oh, aye, thanks. I'll have a cuppa." Billy sunk down into the sofa.

Ryan followed Mrs. Doyle into the kitchen. "How are you feeling today? A bit better?"

"Yes, thanks, love. It's always nice to be back in your own bed. I'm that ready for a bit of peace and quiet. I'm glad I was with Brendan and the family when I heard, though. It hit me hard." She tapped her chest. "My heart, you know? I was exhausted last night."

Had she seen him leave? He wondered about that. Or even, God forbid, Kathleen had told Mrs. Doyle about him.

"Have you spoken to Rose?"

"She called me this morning, and we talked. It'll be difficult to see her. With her looking like Kathleen and all, very hard. Go on in and sit down. I'll bring the tea."

Ryan did as he was told and joined Billy on the oversized floral sofa. They'd called a tentative truce on Wylie.

"Nice flat," Billy said, impressed.

The room was similar to Kathleen's, with a bay window on the front wall and sunlight streaming in across a thick carpet, heavily patterned with whorls of colour. An old-lady smell, sort of dry, Parma violets and talcum powder. Doilies everywhere.

"Our place seems small compared to this. At least it's easier to keep clean."

"Again with the housework, Billy...."

"Here you go, boys, clear a space."

Mrs. Doyle came in with a tray loaded with mugs, a bottle of milk, a small bowl with sugar, and a big bar of Cadbury's chocolate.

"I've no biscuits, me being away and all, but this was in the cupboard."

"No worries there, Mrs. Doyle, I'll have a couple of squares," Billy said. "Oh, Fruit & Nut, my favourite."

After tea, they ran through the list of questions Ryan had prepared. She seemed happy to answer but surprisingly vague with her replies. She's running rings round me, Ryan realised. She should be in politics.

"Did she not discuss a new boyfriend with you at all then? I thought you were close?"

Mrs. Doyle's bright blue eyes flicked in Ryan's direction.

"We were close, but I never heard anything about a new boyfriend. What makes you think she had one?"

"She was seen with someone near the gallery, friendly like, you know?" Ryan sipped at the strong tea.

"Maybe she didn't like to discuss her love life with an old woman like me."

And maybe she did, Ryan thought.

Billy took more chocolate then added conversationally, "She was a beautiful young woman to be alone for that long, wouldn't you say? You would have thought she'd be more popular."

"Her choice. That bloody Liam put her off men, you know." Mrs. Doyle made a little tutting noise.

"You know about Liam then?" Ryan placed his mug on a doily.

"Oh aye, he was here a while ago. Wanted to see her before he got married. She told me he was coming."

"What?" Billy sat up. "Liam, here? When, exactly?"

"I told you, a while ago."

"Yes, but when, what date? Mrs. Doyle, the date is important." Billy looked at Ryan, raised his eyebrows.

"Oh, for goodness sake. I can't remember." She huffed a bit. "Maybe it's in my calendar." She hurried off to the kitchen. "The eighteenth," she shouted in. "Yes, a Tuesday night, they went out for a drink. That's right, I remember now." She came back and sat down.

"And? What time did he leave?" Ryan could feel his temper building. It's her nature. She didn't trust the police; that was obvious. But why did he have to drag every last thing out of her? If she was close to Kathleen, you'd think…

"He stayed over, didn't he?" she said.

"What? You mean he spent the night here? So, were they…you know?" This time, Billy raised his eyebrows at Mrs. Doyle, hoping no doubt to get the intent of the question to her without asking directly.

Billy didn't like to talk about sex, skirted the subject, except for Ryan's personal life, which was accepted as fair game by Billy, Derek, and Maura.

"No, no, they were not," Mrs. Doyle replied, affronted. "He had a bit of drink on him, she told me, and she didn't want him going off on that motorcycle of his. A right wreck. She let him sleep on the sofa. Good thing, too, that bike would have wakened the dead. We'd have had the police here if he had started it up at two o'clock in the morning. Last thing I want."

That's pretty obvious, Ryan thought. He waited, hoping for more. He did the eyebrow lift thing, seemed to work for Billy.

Mrs. Doyle sighed. "They went out in a taxi and came back in one. I heard them come in. It was late—and that racket…you could tell he'd been drinking. He's a loud sort of fella. Kathleen was trying to shush him."

"And he didn't leave until the next morning?" Ryan said.

"Isn't that what I told you? There's not much around here I miss."

She gave Ryan a sidelong glance, and he tensed. He hesitated, and Billy jumped in.

"You saw Liam leave in the morning?"

"I saw him and heard him, I'm telling you, I heard him turn on to the flippin' Malone Road! Are the two of ye not listening to me?"

So much for that, Ryan thought. Kathleen was alive when Liam left. Of course, he could have come back…but it did help them place Liam in Belfast on the eighteenth and nineteenth of October. He sighed and checked his notebook.

"Did you know Kathleen took a week off?" Ryan asked.

"Yes, I think she wanted a little break. She said it was quiet in the gallery. The cruises were mostly over, and Rose was coming home…" Mrs. Doyle paused. She's wondering, Ryan realised, how much she should tell us.

"What?" Ryan asked, leaning forward. "Please, Mrs. Doyle, if you know something that could help us…"

At this, Mrs. Doyle lost her composure and started to cry. Billy pulled a small packet of tissues from his pocket and passed one to her.

She blew her nose, sniffed, and smiled at him. "Thanks, pet."

Then she dropped the smile like a stone. "I may be an old woman, but I'll tell you this." She squeezed the tissue tight, transparent skin over white knuckles shining in her fist. "You better hope I never find out who killed her."

Chapter Twelve

Thursday, October 27

"Mrs. Doyle's lying, you know, holding something back," Ryan said.

"Oh aye, through her teeth," Billy agreed. "And wasn't she alarming for an old dear? A lot of menace in that threat. Scared the life out of me at the end. I liked her too. She reminds me of my granny. What do you think she plans to do to the killer? Slap him with a doily?"

They headed back through the city, boisterous with lunchtime crowds. Ryan thought he should come downtown more often, maybe take Rose out for dinner when this was all over. After they found the killer.

When they got to the station, he sent Billy ahead and trotted back to his car. Should he see Rose again? No, of course, he shouldn't. Last night had been a mistake—a mistake on top of a mistake. He would contact her and explain, she would understand. He made the call, and at the sound of her voice, he changed his mind. He wanted to see her. This was his problem. He had very little self-control when it came to women.

"Come over to me, Rose. Maybe bring an overnight bag?" For God's sake, what the hell was wrong with him? Some other little Ryan speaking for him.

There was a pause. He could hear her breathing, then… "Yes."

"Seven good? I'll text you the address."

"Yes."

Jesus, I'm a fool. He headed for the door, smiling.

A few minutes later, as Ryan stared gloomily into the snack machine, his mobile buzzed. Abbott, his mate from boxing.

"Missed you Monday night," Abbott said. "And Wednesday too. You giving it up? Slacking? Taking up ballet?"

"Hey yeah, sorry, I should have called. It's this new case—"

"Do you have time for lunch?" Abbott asked. Not a man for chat.

Ryan took one last look at the machine and its contents and said he'd see him in ten minutes. Abbott was nearby, grabbing supplies for the club.

They arranged to meet for a quick bite. The Chester again, nice and handy.

"Got you a Stella." Ryan had arrived first as usual and nabbed his favourite seat by the fire.

"Yeah, great."

Abbott was a good-looking man. Born in London, he'd joined the Army right from school. It had taken time, but Ryan had learned a bit about his friend's past. Some of it from Abbott himself and some from Bernie—short for Bernadette, the wife of the boxing club's original owner.

After serving with the SAS in Ulster, Abbott had returned to the province when he was honourably discharged. He'd lost his only daughter to a heroin overdose in London when she was sixteen, and his wife had left him a year later. *'Didn't blame her. I'd have left me too.'* It had been the job, the army, and the anger that came with it. He'd rarely been home when he had a family, he told Ryan, and now London reminded him of a past he'd lost and wanted to forget.

"So," Ryan asked him, a little puzzled. "What's this about? Not like you to show up out of the blue. And I know you've no shortage of sparring partners."

"Dorothy. It's about Dorothy."

"What about her?" Dorothy was the club's part-time accountant and general secretary. Somewhere in her early sixties, Ryan reckoned, a nice wee lady, quiet and unassuming. Always wore the same cheap and cheerful Primark blouses and trousers. "She okay?"

"See, that's the thing. She needed help reaching something from a high shelf yesterday, and I went over to help her. I touched her shoulder to get by, and she gave an almighty yelp. What's wrong? I ask her, but she said she'd slipped in her kitchen."

"So?" Ryan asked.

"Last week, she was limping a bit, and she said she'd tripped on her front steps. Ryan, I checked, and she'd a nasty bruise on her ankle. I don't like it. I'm thinking back. She always wears long sleeves and trousers. Remember about six months ago she had a broken finger? What d'ye reckon?"

"I don't know, Abbott. You work there. Have you talked to Bernie about this?"

"Bernie says Dorothy's always been quiet. Never any trouble. She's known her for years. Dorothy was in the hospital for a minor fall a while ago but came back right as rain. Now she's wondering about that, like me. I've seen the husband. He comes for her in the car. Big man, heavyset. Miserable looking git."

"Any other family?"

"There's a daughter, according to Bernie, but she works at a law office and lives at the top of the Newtownards Road." Abbott hesitated. "That's miles away."

"Still, you would think she would have noticed if anything was up."

"I don't know how often they see one another, and those visits could be managed. I think Dorothy is good at keeping it quiet." Abbott sipped his beer. "She told Bernie there's some bad blood between the father and daughter...and look how long it took me to notice."

"What do you want to do? Try talking to Dorothy again? Or we could go chat to the daughter. See if she could help," Ryan said.

"I'd rather talk to the husband. Wouldn't you?"

Back in the squad room after lunch, Ryan quickly checked out Dorothy's husband, George Kerr. But there was nothing, not even a parking ticket. He finished an overdue update for Girvan and did some preliminary digging on the Doyles. Derek could do a proper in-depth workup later. Then he re-read Kathleen's initial post-mortem results. Billy pulled his copy too.

"So, some faint older bruises, maybe not related? And blunt-force trauma to the side of the head, no rape or sexual interference, died where she lay, not moved, and no defensive wounds. Perhaps she knew her killer?" Ryan said. "And the murder weapon? Any sign?"

"No to the weapon, couldn't find it. Probably a rock, too many down in the river there. Might have rolled away or been thrown," Billy said.

"This mysterious new boyfriend, why hasn't he come forward?"

"Or Liam?" Billy said. "Still no sign of him."

"And don't forget the bullets and the tracker." Ryan leaned back in his chair. "I keep thinking about the Doyles. That family has the background to carry it off."

"Why would Mrs. Doyle lie, though?" Billy said. "Is she protecting someone? Protecting this secret boyfriend? Does she know who it is?"

"I don't know, but I'm going to get Derek to go deeper into the Doyles' background. Might be something there."

Forensics had swabbed Kathleen's hands and found gunshot residue. Where did the gun go? Where did a nice girl like Kathleen even get one? So many questions....

"We have to talk to Mrs. Doyle again, once we have some more information on her and her family."

"I'll sweet-talk her." Billy grinned.

"And who are you planning to sweet-talk, DS Lamont?" Maura appeared at Ryan's desk with a file, her coat, handbag, and a sandwich.

"Hey, how's it going? That's a fine-looking sandwich."

"You and your sandwiches, Billy." Maura smiled at him. "It's from that new machine outside the cafeteria. It's my dinner."

"What is it?"

"For goodness sake, I've no idea, some kind of meat. Listen, Girvan called me in. He said yes to a few bodies to assist with the rape cases."

Then she sat down heavily on a spare chair and sighed.

"I saw Wylie's uncle leaving for lunch with Girvan yesterday. Next thing I know, Ed Wylie's one of the newly assigned officers. Although, he also gave us PC Sam Burns. He at least seems like a hard worker. Introduced himself to me earlier. I gave him an armful of files to read."

Billy shook his head. "You'll get no sympathy here. Girvan's dumped Wylie on us too, to assist with the McGuire murder."

"We might be able to use Burns, but I'd keep him away from Derek. You know how touchy he gets," Ryan said. "This whole computer genius thing has gone to his head."

"Seriously." Maura started to unwrap her sandwich. "At least the Musgrave lot are way over there. They started setting up while you were out."

Ryan glanced towards the back. "Will you be able to work with Wylie?"

"Why not?" She pointed her sandwich at the far corner. "He's hardly spoken to me since our little romantic encounter and his *heartfelt* apology afterwards."

"I notice he walks with a bit of a limp now, you know, on damp days," Billy said, grinning.

Maura slapped his arm. "I kneed him in the balls, Billy. You'd have done the same."

"Oh, I dunno, he's a hunk...."

"I still think you should have reported him," Ryan said. "And it pisses me off that we're the only ones who know about it." Ryan didn't think it was something to joke about, although maybe Billy was right, and Maura was over it. How would he know? He normally took what she said at face value.

"I told you I'm going to leave it." Maura paused. "And there's his apology. He should have gotten an Oscar for that performance. I ended up hating myself for what he'd done to me."

"Did Girvan assign a DS to that lot?" Ryan asked.

"Yes, thank God," she said. "DS Anderson's wrangling them, and he'll oversee the rape cases. You two will still help, though, right? Jump in when you can?"

"Sure," Ryan said. "And any problems with Wylie, let me know."

Billy got up. "I'm heading home. It's our anniversary. We're going out for a nice curry."

Billy's tastes were fairly provincial, Indian food being his only weakness.

"Terrific. Have fun, yeah? Who's minding the kids?" Ryan asked.

"Oh, are you offering, Ryan?" Billy gave a hoot of laughter. "My mother-in-law, and we'll never hear the end of it, believe me. So I'm out the door here on time for a change. Don't want her charging overtime."

"For a change, Billy? That's a laugh," Ryan called to Billy's back.

"Shut up, Ryan. Not my fault you've only poor old Finn waiting for you to come home."

"Hang on, I'll walk down with you," Maura shouted to Billy. She took a bite of her sandwich and headed off.

"You staying?" she called back, her mouth full, very unladylike.

"No," Ryan said, standing up. He was not staying. Rose was on her way to his farm.

Chapter Thirteen

Saturday, September 24

BEFORE

K athleen had tossed and turned through another sleepless night, and coffee didn't seem to be helping. Nothing did, if she were honest. It felt like she was in withdrawal from drugs or alcohol. Was that what Kevin was to her? A drug? Luckily, Angus was at the gallery and it was a blessedly quiet day. He fussed and fretted, finally telling her to go home.

"I can manage. Go home and lie down. You look awful."

"I'm tired, Angus. I'm not going to die."

"Was it worth it? Did you have a fun night?" He nudged her with his elbow.

"I haven't been sleeping well, that's all. I think I'll pop over to Costa for a proper coffee. Do you want one?"

"Oh yes! Something sweet and foamy."

Angus, bless him. Kathleen smiled despite her headache. He's like a little boy sometimes. As she queued in the crowded coffee shop, she couldn't help but notice that most of the customers were couples, chatting and laughing. Why did Kevin have to be the way he was? Although she might not have to worry about that for much longer. He hadn't contacted her, and she didn't intend to call him. She had decided to hold firm.

Back in the gallery, Angus told her it was Calvin's turn to be in Belfast. "We have lots of straight friends. Nice guys. We'll match you up, I am determined. Come meet us at our local. You're such a dolly bird."

Dolly bird? She imagined being alone for another night, maybe a cup of tea with Mary, then off to bed with a book. For heaven's sake, why not?

She arrived at the Botanic and climbed the stairs, trying to remain calm. The bar was busy and she hit a wall of heat and beer as she searched for Angus and his friends.

"Hey you, get over here." Angus waved and raised his glass. "I'm skundered."

Later, laughing at somebody's stupid joke, she realised that her time with Kevin had taken away her self-confidence. Sitting with this raucous group and a second glass of wine in front of her she felt almost euphoric.

She had just lifted the wineglass to her lips when Angus materialised at the table. He fell down beside her and nodded towards the bar.

"Look over there. Our handsome security expert. Yum."

And there was Kevin, the broad shoulders and dark hair unmistakable to Kathleen.

"I must go over and say hi, invite him to join us."

Angus made to get up and Kathleen pulled him back down.

"Could you not?"

"Oh, come on, he's not that bad. I know he seems a bit standoffish, but there's no need to be rude. Plus, he's gorgeous, might make Calvin jealous. Give me a minute."

He jumped up and, before Kathleen could say any more, trotted over to the bar and tapped Kevin on the shoulder.

Kathleen lay in bed that night thinking back. She'd joined the main group and ordered a Coke; she'd had enough alcohol already—especially with Kevin on the scene. But he had been gracious to everyone, especially her. Later on, he asked her how she had been, and as they all headed out, he touched her arm and asked if he could ring her. He told her he'd been away on business. He'd had time to think, and he missed her.

That night she tossed and turned. Would it be worth a second try?

The next day Kevin called to apologise. He'd never done that before. "I'm sorry, Kathleen. I can't lose you. Give me another chance...."

When the call finished, she made coffee and sat in the seat by her window. She had something dark in her. She knew it. It had started to grow with her father's death and continued to haunt her when her mother died. She didn't know what it was or where it came from. But sometimes, like when she had seen Kevin at the bar, that flicker of anticipation she always felt with him, that recklessness, returned. What was wrong with her? Did she deserve to be punished? But for what? She'd known when she'd gone back to that detective's farm that it was foolish but she did it anyway and hell, she'd had a great time until his bitch of a girlfriend—crazy ex-girlfriend—had shown up like some character out of a Tarantino film. She finished her coffee and made up her mind. She would give Kevin another chance. Yes, he had taken some of her confidence away, but she had grabbed it back last night, hadn't she? If it didn't work out, she could always walk away.

Chapter Fourteen

Thursday, October 27

When he got home, Ryan showered and changed into a white shirt and jeans. He wandered into his conservatory, nursing a small whisky. Scotch tonight for a change. Finn sat in his dog bed, looking at him, sensing his mood. And what was his mood? He hardly knew. The idea of Rose arriving at his farm, to be here all evening with him, was intoxicating. What had happened? He'd never experienced anticipation like this before. He had no idea what to expect, and perhaps this was part of the attraction. Would she be cold and brittle? The way she'd been that first trip to the morgue? Or would she be vulnerable and enigmatic like last night in her flat? More than any other woman he had known, she remained a puzzle. A challenge—and he loved a challenge.

His phone rang—was she going to be late?

"How's my favourite brother?"

Erin. He couldn't tell her about Rose. She would keep him talking for hours. He heard tyres crunch on the gravel outside and felt a jolt of adrenaline. He jumped up. Finn did too. He hated lying to Erin, but.... "Listen, hon, I'm on my way out. Can I catch you tomorrow? Not sure how late I'll be."

"Oh," Erin said. "Don't forget dinner on Sunday. They're back from Spain. You have to let me know. I cannot face it alone."

"Okay. Bye, bye."

"Behave yourself, boy," he said to Finn. Honest to God, the dog looked puzzled. "No jumping, do you hear me?"

Rose had parked behind his car and was leaning into her back seat when he opened the front door. She turned around with her handbag over her shoulder, a paper bag in one hand and an overnight case in the other.

"Hey," she said.

He went to her. She passed him the paper bag with bottles clinking inside it, then the case. He placed everything on the ground, pulled her to him, and kissed her hard, pressing into her, feeling her breasts against his chest and her hair tangled in his hands. He drew back breathless, then kissed her cheek and down her neck, slowly. Inhaling her scent.

"Hello," he said into her hair.

She pulled away and took a breath. "Hello."

He picked up her bags and turned towards the door. She followed him, then stopped.

"Ah. This must be Finn."

Finn trotted over. A slow tail wag. Rose scratched his head right behind his ears. His tail picked up speed.

"You found the right spot. He won't leave you alone now."

Ryan carried the bags inside, and this time he went back and locked the front door, *just in case*. Rose followed with Finn right behind her.

"What a beautiful place. I love it. And not overly quaint."

"I avoid quaintness at all times. Drink?"

"Is that whisky I tasted?"

"It is."

"Then I'll have that, please."

She removed her camel coat and hung it in the hall. She wore a soft pink sweater over brown leather pants and boots. Beautiful.

"You look great."

She smiled. "Thank you. All new purchases."

So different then from the first time he had met her as a remote, grieving woman. And even last night, the tentative, unsure lover.

Whisky in hand, she strolled around the farm. Through the living room with its comfortable sofas and large stone fireplace. He'd lit the fire earlier, and a comforting, smoky scent hung in the air. And a flash of Kathleen now, chatting, a little drunk, sexy. Wandering through his rooms too, looking over her shoulder at him, teasing.

He watched Rose run her hands across the dining table's polished wood surface and lean over to smell a small bunch of wildflowers his cleaning lady had placed on the sideboard yesterday. He walked with her and showed her his kitchen. She loved it. The second bathroom and, finally, his bedroom.

"Very nice," she said.

He had left a lamp on by the bed, and it burnished her cheek. Stray beams edged her eyelashes and shone in strands of her copper hair.

"Are you always this tidy, make your bed?" she asked without looking at him.

"No."

"But you made it today?"

"Yes." He reached for her, but she turned away abruptly and walked back towards the living room. He followed her, unsure. "Rose?"

"I know I came here to be with you, but with Kathleen and everything that's happened between us. I'm confused. Ryan, I shouldn't be here."

No, she shouldn't. She was part of the investigation, and he was a fool to be getting into this with her. And that was apart from his connection to Kathleen, and how long since Kathleen's death? But, yet… "Let's go outside and get some air." He took her hand and led her into the rear garden. Darkness had fallen. A brisk wind pushed through the trees and all around them, from high branches, came that roaring sound he loved. Way back in the far field, occasional animal cries, forlorn and ragged.

"My God, when you listen, it's noisy out here. And cold." She slipped her hand free. "I wondered where you lived, that first time we talked on the phone. I tried to picture you."

"Did you? And is it what you expected?" Did she think he lived in a semi-detached? Or by the lough?

"I didn't know what to expect." She made a hand gesture as if presenting

him to someone. "You look like a tough guy. Jeans, black jacket, rough...."
She laughed. "I thought maybe a flat downtown? I didn't expect a quaint
old farm. That's the problem, isn't it? We don't know each other."

What to say? She was right.

The tall trees way at the back moaned again; occasional rain drops wet his
cheek. "If you just want to have dinner with me, that's okay. The last thing
I want is for you to feel pressured." He touched her arm. "Let's go back in.
I'm friggin' freezing. Are you hungry?" Normal things. They had to eat.

"I'm starving," she said and smiled.

"Good, because my sister Erin sent me a beef stew. She writes a food and
lifestyle blog when she can be bothered. It's popular."

He followed her back to the kitchen.

She had finished her whisky and nodded to the sideboard. "May I?"

"Absolutely, and top me up too." He moved close behind her, could smell
that perfume, light and floral. He remembered it from last night, or maybe
it was coming back to him from that evening back in May. Kathleen here
with him, no hesitancy that night, no reservations. Not like Rose. He felt
Rose's hair stroke his cheek. He reached around and lifted down a bottle of
The Balvenie, brushed her shoulder.

"Oh, Scotch—not Irish?" She turned, her face an inch from his.

"I am an equal-opportunity whisky drinker."

She laughed and nodded at the stew. "Nice of your sister to feed you. Are
you close?"

"A bit too much sometimes. She's had some issues lately. A divorce. Her
ex-husband's an ass."

"Sorry, I didn't mean to pry."

"No, it's okay. Right, this stew has to go in the oven, I should have put it
in earlier. You distracted me."

"Did I?" Rose wandered back to the living room. Soft jazz in the
background. Etta James singing, "At Last."

He joined her moments later and pulled her into his arms. She seemed
calmer now, more mellow. Got to love whisky, the great relaxer. Or his
irresistible personality finally kicking in.

"Want to dance?" He nodded outside. "Or, what about a walk?"

"A walk? Are you mad?" She kissed his neck. "How long will the stew take?"

"As long as you want." He pulled back, smiled at her. "You think I look rough?"

She smiled back.

In his bedroom, she undressed, pulling the pink sweater over her head and starting to unhook her bra. Ryan went to the open door where Finn sat, resolute, watching them. He closed it in the dog's face.

She paused with her hands behind her back. "Poor Finn."

"He's fine. Here, let me help you with that."

A little before nine o'clock, they made it back to the kitchen, and Ryan rescued the stew. Rose opened a bottle of red wine and brought it through to his dining room with two Waterford Crystal glasses she found in a small hall cabinet. She set the table, adding some old linen napkins from the same place.

"Nice," Ryan said as he brought the plates in.

"You have some wonderful old pieces, lovely linens, and crystal."

"That was my granny. She collected all that."

"It's a beautiful place."

"Yeah, I love coming home here."

They ate while Finn lay under the window gazing balefully at Ryan, who normally gave him a little something from his plate. When they had finished and moved into the conservatory, Rose grew quiet again.

The investigation was the last thing he wanted to talk about, but did he have the right to deny her the few details he could discuss?

"What do you want to know?" It was on her mind. How could it not be?

"I know you're doing everything you can, but the murderer is still out there. I wonder sometimes if I'm in danger. I mean it's possible, isn't it?"

"It depends on the why of it. Why did it happen?" he said.

She paused. "You have to find this killer. You have to—for me and

Kathleen."

He took another sip of wine, refilled her glass, and hesitated.

"Will you stay here tonight?"

"Yes. I brought my little case."

"Is there enough in that little case for tomorrow night too?"

"Are you sure?" she said.

"I would like you to be here when I get home tomorrow night. You'll be safer here." Did he believe that? Or was he saying it to make her stay? He saw something in her expression, conflict, a furrow in her brow. He studied her face. She was difficult to read. He wanted her to stay. And oh yes, this was at best a lapse in judgement, and at worst? He didn't know the answer to that and didn't care. This little problem of his, rearing its head.

"Yes," she replied and lifted her glass. "I'll stay."

Friday morning, back at his desk. He'd left Rose in bed, and he thought about her as he turned on his work computer, sipped his coffee.

Billy called over. He'd come in early too, and had just put down the phone.

"Here Ryan, yer man Angus from the gallery? That was him."

"Yeah?"

"He doesn't know if it's important, but he forgot to tell us Kathleen had a locker in the gallery's lower level. He thinks maybe she stored a few things in hers? Wants to know if he should open it? Have a quick look."

"Christ, no, tell him not to touch it. We'll be over as soon as we can."

Then his phone rang. "Good morning, Ryan, it's Janice. Chief wants to see you."

"I don't care, McBride. Unless you have something more meaningful for him to do, he can ride along and observe." Girvan tapped away at his computer while he spoke, frowning.

"But sir..."

"Have I not made myself clear? Take him along. I've the Chief Inspector asking how he's doing. How much he's learning. He's being fast-tracked, God help us, so have him ride with you once in a while. What is the problem?

Be a bloody mentor or some damn thing. Now get out." Girvan squinted over Ryan's shoulder and shouted, "Janice, get in here. This bloody computer has frozen again or some damn thing…."

A mentor? Do I not have enough to worry about at the moment? Back at his desk, Ryan glared at Billy and called Wylie.

"Car park, now."

The ride was icy. Billy exchanged a few words with Wylie, who seemed oblivious to the atmosphere and sat in the back checking his phone, clicking away, annoying the hell out of Ryan.

At the gallery, Angus led them down narrow stairs and into a cellar that had been tarted up. He chattered on. "I think this cellar used to belong to the Duke of York, the pub? For the beer kegs and that. Sophie and Anthony own the whole place and did a nice renovation. They have a studio flat on the third floor for sleepovers after openings etc. Lots of money spent. God, I sound like a real estate agent, but this property is worth a packet now." He pointed to a door right at the end. "Staff can park out there if Sophie is away." He walked on. A side room to the right contained a few metal filing cabinets and a row of rusty old lockers. Angus stopped and tutted. "Spiders and earwigs. Bit musty." He swatted the air. "This room's for us."

He jangled a keychain and approached the last locker.

"Hang on, Angus, let me do it." Ryan snapped on his gloves.

Angus raised an eyebrow at Billy and Wylie and stepped back. "God," he said with a nervous laugh. "And to think I would have opened it, you know, like a normal person."

"A precaution, Angus, can't be too careful." Ryan opened the locker.

An old sweater hung on a hook. Ryan shone his torch around. A pair of flat shoes lay discarded on the bottom, the heels worn on the outsides. In a corner at the back, he noticed a dark green leather box.

"What's that?" Billy peered over Ryan's shoulder.

"A Rolex box," Ryan said.

"Is it real, not a knockoff?" Billy said.

"No way she could afford a real Rolex working here," Wylie said casually.

"Right, and here's me forgetting how well-paid police officers are," Angus said tartly in response.

Ryan grinned. He brought the box out into the light and opened it. No watch, but a small nest of booklets tucked neatly inside.

Angus came over. "She started wearing a Rolex a while back, but when I asked her about it, she laughed and said it was a fake. You're saying it's real? Why would she fib?"

Billy slipped on his gloves and placed all the papers from the box on top of the file cabinet. "Now, where would she get the money for something like this? Or maybe she didn't buy it."

"The box looks real enough. Hey, Billy, you don't think that one at the car site is …?"

"Ton of paper here. I didn't get this much certification when I bought my car."

Ryan grunted. "It's a Renault Twizy, Billy. No offense, but…."

"Hey, that's a great little runaround, and it's earth-friendly. Excuse me for not having a BMW."

"Hang on, what's this?" Ryan said.

A small card was wedged between the top shelf and the side of the locker. Ryan eased it out. White, heavy vellum. Rolex embossed on it. Someone had scrawled a note. Billy and Angus crowded in to look.

Now you have no excuse for being late. xxx K.

"K. Who the hell is K?" Ryan said. "Would Kathleen have bought it for someone?"

"Why keep the box then? And again, where would she get that kind of money?" Billy asked.

"Angus, any idea?"

"What? Don't look at me. I told you she was private about that sort of thing. First name? I know tons of people with names starting with K. None of them have anything to do with Kathleen as far as I know. And that doesn't look like her writing either."

Ryan went through the papers in the box again. "We might be able to find out where this was bought and who bought it. Not a fake with all this paperwork, surely." He nodded to Wylie, who took the booklets, walked away, and called Derek. Over in the corner, Ryan could hear him arguing. "Christ's sake, Derek, give over. Just do it."

Ryan turned away, smiling. He would talk to Derek later, get him moving on it. Derek was naturally a pain in the arse, but when he actually worked at it.…

Rose's car was gone when he got home. For the first time that day, he tried her mobile. It went straight to message. No answer on the phone at Kathleen's flat either.

"What's going on, boy?" He patted Finn's head. "Where is she?"

He checked for a note. The place felt empty and cold. He walked out to the back garden smelling woodsmoke in the air. The darkening sky held strands of white haze. Puzzled, he went back inside. Her case wasn't on the floor in the bedroom, and her things were gone from the bathroom. She'd left. Phone in hand, he walked into the kitchen and saw the blinking red light. He clicked it on.

"Ryan, listen, I'm sorry about the other night, I shouldn't have gotten angry, but you know how I am, right? Call me back?"

He listened to Bridget's message. Rose must have heard that. Shit.

"Come on," he called to Finn, who, after a hurried pee, jumped into the back seat of the BMW and settled down.

When he got to Kathleen's, it was in darkness, and Rose's car wasn't there. A single dim light shone somewhere in the rear of Mrs. Doyle's, but he was reluctant to involve her. Could Rose have gone back to Derry? He tried to reach her continually for almost two hours. Dispirited, he finally gave up and headed home. Back at the farm, he stared at the phone. Thought about the message. What should he do?

He made the call.

"What is it, Bridget?"

If his tone surprised her, she didn't let on. He could hear a TV in the background with some sitcom laugh track erupting every few seconds.

"Hang on, let me turn this off."

The phone rattled in his ear, and the noise stopped. She came back on, breathless.

"How've you been?"

"Bridget, get to the point." Did she think this was a social call?

"Come on, Ryan."

He waited her out. What does she want? Because she always wanted something. He pushed Billy's words away. She was trouble. But then, wasn't that part of her attraction?

"Can we meet for a drink?" she said.

Something in her voice, a catch. This didn't sound like the Bridget he knew.

"What's the point, Bridget?" He could guess, though. This was her usual pattern. She had decided it was time to resume the relationship.

"I want to see you. Can't we meet and talk?"

"Look…" He took a breath. "I'm seeing someone."

He didn't mean to tell her. He didn't want anyone to know because it was still too delicate a situation. But it had come out. And, of course, he didn't know where that someone was at the moment. He wanted to yell at Bridget, tell her she might have screwed things up, lash out, but something in her tone stopped him.

Silence. He was about to ask if she was still there when he heard her inhale.

"Since when?"

"Not long, but I like her. You can understand if I don't want to mess it up. You and me, we've tried, again and again."

"I want to talk, that's all. We were together over two years. You know I still care about you. You have to know that."

"Has something happened? Tell me."

"I need a shoulder, you know. Come on and meet me for a drink. For old times."

He imagined the fuss if he refused. She could never take no for an answer. When he spoke to Rose again and straightened this out, he didn't want Bridget calling back. And she would if he didn't deal with this.

"Tomorrow night then?" she asked.

He hesitated, then replied, "Okay."

Chapter Fifteen

Sunday, October 16

BEFORE

K athleen didn't regret her decision to start seeing Kevin again, but the time apart had subtly shifted her perception of their relationship. He travelled a lot these days, and that was a big relief—although she didn't like to look at it like that. She had more independence when he spent time away. Sometimes she picked up on the old edge, that control he liked to have, mostly when he'd had too much to drink. Even so, Kevin seemed more subdued now they were together again. And she'd decided to look for another job. She knew that getting to a new place would give her a bit more independence from Kevin. Not that he spent much time at the gallery, but he had that connection to Anthony and Sophie, and if she decided to break up with him—not that she was thinking of that, but in case it ever came up, better she was elsewhere. A clean break. Something had opened up at the Ulster Museum, and it could be the perfect position for her. She'd finished Sunday dinner and turned the news on when her phone rang.

"Hello."

"Hello, doll."

The voice, with its soft brogue, brought back memories. Some good, some bad.

"Liam?"

"The one and only."

"My God, where are you?"

"I could be in Belfast on Tuesday." He laughed. "And listen, I'm a changed man. Swear to God. I'm engaged."

"Come on...."

"Mad, isn't it? She's great, though. You'd like her. I want to see you on my way down to Dublin. That's where I'm heading. I'm moving in with her, God help me. But before all that I want to have a last holiday by myself on the bike, visit a few mates, take my time. And I have to see you and sort of apologise."

"Sort of apologise?" That was a good one, verging on hysterical.

But it would be nice to catch up. She saw him in her mind's eye, the bad boy, the clown. Handsome, though, and he had the old Irish charm in buckets. Too much of it for his own good. How many times had he talked his way out of a messy situation with her? Ah, but he had been fun. She smiled at the memories. So different from her relationship with Kevin.

Night and day.

Of course, Kevin and his mad jealousy remained an issue. What should she do? She tensed up thinking about it. Could she not have a drink with an old boyfriend without worrying about how Kevin would take it? Wasn't she past all that with him? They had a dinner date planned Monday night. Possibly, maybe, she might tell him. Play it by ear.

"Right, what's the plan?"

"Text me your address, and I'll come to see you, maybe this Tuesday night? I could be there around sevenish. We'll go out for a few drinks...my treat, the whole night."

Kevin was pensive over dinner Monday evening, but after a drink or two, he loosened up and seemed to relax. She went for it. "You'll never guess who rang me last night."

"You know I hate games."

"Liam." She held her breath.

He put his wine down and scowled at her. A crease formed between his brows. "Liam. The Liam who messed you about over in Brighton?"

"Yes, that one. But Kevin, he's engaged. He's going to Dublin to be with his fiancée. He wants to drop in for a drink on the way, to say hello." In for a penny, she thought. "Why don't you come and meet him? We'll all go out. He's a nice bloke, good fun. It's over between us. Please don't even worry about that. Let's all go out. Tomorrow night, the Bot?"

"Yes, you'd like that, wouldn't you?" Kevin's mood turned dark.

She should have kept her mouth shut. Would she ever bloody learn?

"Nice and cosy for you, right? Two of us hanging on your every word, Miss Popular, Kathleen McGuire, look at me. One guy's not enough. I have to keep them all hanging on, buzzing about like flies on old meat."

His voice had risen, and some people nearby glanced over.

As he wound himself up for another scene, she sat there, a huge battle raging inside her. The old Kathleen would take it, wait for the humiliation, the ridicule, and worse to come later if she went back to his place. It was as if a switch had been flipped in his head. It all rushed back, crowding her thoughts. That night in the rain outside his place. Annabelle, the taxi driver, and the marks on her skin. She remembered her life before Kevin, when she made her own decisions, chose her own wine, and decided what she wanted to wear. Why, even now, when he had seemed changed, she still dressed to please him, wore the perfume he liked, and did her hair the way he preferred.

He tossed money on the table.

"Get your coat."

Kathleen lifted her drink. She had more than half a glass of wine left.

"I'm not finished."

He regarded her with that old contempt. "Drink it or leave it, I don't give a fuck, but get your arse out of that chair."

She dropped her eyes to the table and began to scratch a design with her fingernail in a spill of salt. Inside her, a dense knot of fury formed like a living thing. Something had changed. The time apart had readjusted her settings. Like turning something off and turning it back on again. She wanted to slap his face. She wanted to wipe that look right off it.

"No." She continued to push the salt around. Conflicting emotions. Fear. Anger. She was afraid of him, damn right she was. She could feel his furious physical presence looming over the table.

"What did you say?" He spat the words out.

Suddenly ignited, her frustration and rage flared. She had struggled to ram it down deep, this fury and resentment. Rose choosing to work as far away from her as she could. And she knew Rose's defense well—oh yes. That cool exterior and fragile interior. Her sister chose to run away, physically and emotionally, to let nothing affect her. Was it Kathleen's fault their father had died and their mother too? *Was it?* No. And yet she had given up. Letting Liam lie and cheat and forgiving him, always. Losing touch with Rose and allowing her sister to retreat into herself while pretending everything was fine between them. And Kevin? A different deception. A darker one. Worse, and by Christ, she'd had enough pretending.

"I said no, Kevin. No."

"You little...."

She flipped her hand up in a defiant *stop* gesture, her palm right in front of his face, salt crystals cascading onto his jacket and down his tie. She could taste the anger in her mouth, sour and metallic. Taste it.

"Listen to me." She lowered her voice and hissed at him. "Don't you shout at me in front of these people. I'll have you arrested. That's all you need with your history, right? I'll sue you for abuse. I'll sue you for everything you have, and don't think I won't." Oh my God—her chest swelled with it, the power of release, of not caring, not being afraid. "I have photos of bruises you gave me, and Mrs. Doyle will back me up. She helped me many a night. I kept those messages you left on my answer phone, those drunken rants and threats. Don't you fucking touch me."

She didn't have photos, no saved messages. She had erased them all, shaking and overwhelmed, sometimes not listening to them. And Mrs. Doyle didn't know most of the bad times she had been through.

That calmed him. Calmed the bastard right down.

"Let's go to my place and talk this out."

"No chance. I'll get a cab. You go. And leave that money for the bill."

She lifted her wine again, surprised at how calm she felt. He had risen from his seat and stood there looking down at her. For once, he seemed unable to make a decision. The restaurant around them held its collective breath, the air thick with expectation.

"Kevin," Kathleen looked up at him. "Fuck off."

She waited until he had snatched his coat from the hostess and stormed off before she made a call. Then she poured the rest of the wine into her glass and sipped it, her right hand trembling. She steadied it with her left, then sat for a moment, adrenaline draining out of her, the aftermath settling in. What had she done?

After fixing her face and hair in the ladies, she took her coat and sat on a stool in the small bar by the door. Here she could see out through the restaurant's front window. In a little while, a taxi appeared, Annabelle in the driver's seat with her short, spiky platinum hair.

He was still there. Kathleen knew it. Could she make it from the restaurant to the taxi? She eased outside and hesitated by the door. Had he gone? Humiliated and shocked, had he fled? That didn't seem like Kevin, although she had never defied him before. She moved quickly towards the taxi, head down, purposeful strides.

Annabelle had her hand on the back door. "Hiya. I thought I recognized the name and home address. Boyfriend acting up again?" Her grin dropped when she saw Kathleen's expression. "What's—"

"Look out!" Kathleen yelled.

Kevin hurtled towards them, his footsteps pounding the pavement, his arms pumping.

Annabelle whipped the door open and unceremoniously dumped Kathleen into the back seat. She slammed it shut and leaned against it, crossing her arms.

Kevin crashed into the car and shoved Annabelle aside, almost knocking her to the pavement. He pulled frantically at the door handle, yelling, "Kathleen, open it!" then pounded on the window.

Annabelle stood and grabbed his arm. "Hey! Don't touch my car. Back off! I'm fucking warning ya!"

He turned, considered her, then shook his head and laughed as if it was absurd, this tiny girl threatening him. He pushed her off and started beating on the car window again.

"Open the door, Kathleen, open it!" he yelled.

"Hey, ya big bastard!" Annabelle pulled her fist back in one swift motion and punched him on the side of his face so hard he staggered and would have fallen if he hadn't banged against the taxi. He slid down, shaking his head, trying to clear it.

Annabelle was winding up for a kick when Kathleen lowered her window and yelled, "Get us out of here! Bloody hell."

Grabbing Kevin's arm, Annabelle roughly dragged him away from the back wheel, jumped into the car, and roared off with a screech of tyres. They raced through side streets, Annabelle clipping red lights and screaming around corners.

"God knows what he would have done if you hadn't shown up." Kathleen sat, shaking yet exhilarated in the back seat. Must be the shock....

"Call me any time you need a lift until two weeks Monday when I'm off to fucking Spain. And don't forget to lock your doors and threaten to call the police if he does show his face. I'll say one thing for him, he's dead good-looking."

"He won't be too good-looking tomorrow, I daresay," Kathleen said.

Chapter Sixteen

Saturday, October 29

A burst of laughter hit Ryan when he entered the Chimney Corner lobby. Wide stairs flanked by an impressive wood banister led to the second floor. A group of early drinkers jostled at the door to the lounge, waving pints around. Ryan maneuvered his way through, paused, and scanned the place. Bridget was already there, sitting by the window. She had someone with her, a young man, straddling a chair. She waved and smiled when she saw Ryan, and her companion leaned in, kissed her on the cheek, and left. She looked great, short black dress, glossy hair. Not riding the Harley tonight, then. She hugged him, and as he pulled away, he became aware of her heady, spicy perfume, the smell instantaneously triggering memories.

"Who was that?" Ryan lifted his chin at the stranger, now at the bar with a few others.

"Victor? A friend. Jealous, are you?"

"What would you like to drink?" He didn't want to get into it with her.

"I've the early shift at the hospital tomorrow, so a tomato juice with lime; don't forget the Worcestershire sauce. But you know that, right?"

He did. He knew a lot about her, but didn't think she knew much about him, how he felt about things. He brought his double whiskey and her drink back and sat down. He took a quick gulp and felt it warm him. She always did this to him, put him on edge. He used to like it.

"What's going on?"

"I told you, Ryan, I've missed you. Can't we talk for a while?" She tossed her hair over her shoulder in a gesture he remembered well. He felt a little visceral jolt.

"I wanted to see you. You listened to my message, didn't you?" She placed her drink on the table. Moved her hand towards him, her fingers touching his. "This woman, you say you like her, but…" She stopped. "C'mon, Ryan, you know me, how I get. I needed some time to think. Lots of couples split up and get back together."

Oh, that was it.

"What is the point of starting again, Bridget? How would it be different?" This constant cycle of breaking up and getting back together. Was that what she wanted? More of the same, over and over.

"I thought I needed a change." She studied him, a high flush on her cheeks. "Ryan, I know you hated me flirting with other men. That's all over with, I swear. Honestly, there were times I never knew where I was with you. I suppose it was a cry for attention. You can be a cold bastard sometimes." She smiled to soften her words. "Look, I'm not blaming you. Please, let's give it another chance." She reached across the table and took his hand. "I love you. I didn't realise it then. I've been thinking about you a lot. You could have called, you know."

He held her hand and squeezed it gently. Bridget was so sure, so confident. And why not? She was gorgeous, they had been happy enough together, great sex, and probably he would have said yes. Before Rose. And he didn't know if it was Rose or the realisation that he could have such intense feelings for someone. It had surprised him.

"No, Bridget. No. I'm sorry." He didn't want to hurt her.

He slipped his hand from hers and tossed back the last of his drink. He shifted his chair back a little—it wouldn't stay empty for long he knew, and stood.

Then he saw her face.

"Bridget? You okay?"

She dropped her head, long, shiny hair falling forward. When she looked up again, he saw it, the quiver in her lip, the tremor in her hands.

"I'm pregnant."

He sat back down, stunned. He couldn't take it in. He jumped up, went to the bar got another drink, brought it back.

"How far along?"

"About two months; that last time we were together. You were pissed, remember?"

His birthday, for God's sake. Indeed, he'd been a little too drunk to take precautions, even though she had warned him. *I'll be careful, don't worry,* he'd said. *What are the chances?* High, as it turned out.

His fault, then.

"Ryan, I'm giving you a choice here. I'm going to keep the baby. Do you want to be involved? I know you've never been interested in being a father, but you need to know to make a decision. Do you want to be in the child's life or not? I won't force you."

"Bridget, Jesus. I don't know what to say."

"This is a shock. Take time to decide. I know this isn't what you want or need right now, I understand—but would it be so bad? We could get back together and raise the baby." Bridget reached for his hand again. "Together."

"I need some time…to think things through. I know it's about us. We have to sort it out between us, one way or the other."

"Don't tell anyone, and for God's sake, don't tell Erin. I need to talk to my parents face to face. They'll be home shortly. My mum, she'll be happy, a grandchild. But Dad, well, you know."

"Your dad hates me."

"No, Ryan, not you, just that you're in the PSNI."

"And a protestant."

"Yes, that too. But he'll get over it. It's my brothers. I need him to deal with Malachy and Marcus. He needs to speak to them. They'll listen to him."

Her mother had been ill for a while, and her parents had gone on a cruise to celebrate her recovery. Bridget wanted to tell them when they got back.

She didn't pressure him, but he knew the social situation it put her in.

And he had put her in it. Northern Ireland was a fine place to live, but on moral and societal issues, it was in the dark ages. He had never planned on children. But now, if he even contemplated walking away from this, Bridget and the baby, it would be a nightmare when his family found out—and they would. Oh Christ. Erin, his mum. Not to mention Bridget's family. Throw me in Magilligan and chuck the key away.

Ryan thought of Billy's words. Her brothers were hardened IRA republicans, and this would not sit well with those lads. He didn't give a damn about them and what they might do; he could take care of himself. It was his family, his father especially. God, he could imagine that conversation, and he'd deal with it when the time came, but Rose, Rose must be told. He thought Bridget would object, but she didn't.

"Of course, you must tell her. If it were me, I'd want to know, no matter what we decide."

After he left Bridget, he drove to Kathleen's flat, although it was Rose's now. Her car still wasn't in the driveway. He scanned the side streets in case she had parked farther away, but with no luck. Out of options, he called the mobile number Mrs. Doyle had given him, not expecting her to answer, but she did. When he asked about Rose, Mrs. Doyle had been a little evasive, but relented when she realised he was worried.

"She did come back, I heard her in the flat, and her car was outside. Then I saw her on the driveway with a suitcase, and off she went. Not a word to me, mind. I called my son, and I'm down here with him now. I don't like being alone, not after what happened to Kathleen."

She sounded a little put out, Ryan thought, at Rose's abrupt departure. That made two of them. Where the hell had she gone? Not back to Derry so soon, surely?

The next day was Sunday, and his parents had arrived home from Spain. He had to have dinner with them. It was the last thing he needed. He went to the gym before heading over there, trying to sweat out his frustration with the case and with Rose, and pretty much everything. He was about to leave when Abbott arrived. Ryan grabbed some bottled water and pulled his mate into a far corner. He told him about Bridget. Yeah, yeah, but he had to tell someone. It was too big for him. And Abbott never repeated anything to anyone. The original quiet man. Abbott's introspection was what made him interesting. Ryan wished he had more of it himself.

"What are you gonna do?"

"Abbott, I don't know."

"It's a gift, man. A baby."

"But I have my job, my own life—everything. I can't take it in."

"Ryan, listen to me. I fucked up. Don't do the same thing, don't let work take over. It'll be a family. Think about that."

"I know, I know, but I never expected it. I...I have to let it settle. I have some time to decide if I want to be part of it, you know?" Ryan paused and drank some water. He didn't want to think about it anymore. "What about Dorothy? Did you talk to her or the husband?"

"No, she hasn't been in. Bernie called her, said she sounds okay, has a cold, that's all. I'll let you know if and when action is required."

"Oh, great," Ryan said. That's all he needed, more action.

He went straight to his parents from the gym, and his mother insisted on washing his workout clothes. He wouldn't have been surprised if she'd offered to give him a bath and wash his hair.

"Go on in and see your father. He's in good form for a change." He left her shaking clothes by the washing machine.

In the sitting room, Erin was subdued, thinking about bloody Paul Crawford, no doubt. His father, on the other hand, was in uncharacteristically good spirits.

"Golf, Ryan. We have to get you started on golf. Lots of contacts there. The chief constable, everyone's at Royal Portrush. More help to your so-called career than boxing. Where's that going to get you? And your friend from the gym, Abbott. Special Forces, right? You'd do well to steer clear."

"Special forces?" Erin perked up. "How exciting."

"You liked him enough before, Dad, when he did that bit of dirty work for the firm." Ryan had recommended Abbott for a small surveillance job.

"I never said I liked him, Ryan. He was useful, that's all. And that's my point, isn't it? He does the dirty work." Oliver McBride took a sip of sherry

115

and studied his son. "I might have known you'd start hanging around with people like that. It's the job you're in."

"You defend murderers, Dad. Don't come on all self-righteous on me."

"Of course, I defend the accused, but I don't make friends with them, don't socialize with them, and take them to the club for dinner. Do you not see the difference? You hang around with these lowlifes, these...."

"Oliver." Ryan's mother came in and put her hand on her husband's shoulder. "Darling, we're all tired." And to Ryan and Erin, "After dinner, let's go through to the drawing room for some brandies. And holiday photos. We have lots."

"Oh yes, let's." Erin rolled her eyes and took Ryan's arm. "By the way, dear brother, why have you never introduced me to your dodgy friend Abbott? He sounds interesting. Is he married?"

Chapter Seventeen

Monday, October 31

Halloween.

Ryan stared at his computer. Some eejit had carved up a turnip, put a little candle in it, and stuck the bloody thing in the squad-room kitchen. The place reeked of that burny-turnipy smell. With Bridget's news, his life had done an abrupt turnaround. And he was worried about Rose, she could be anywhere, and Kathleen's killer was still out there. The investigation into Kathleen's death had stalled....

He called over to Billy, who had a mini glow-in-the-dark skeleton hanging on the back of his computer. "Hasn't Derek traced that bloody watch yet? Where the hell is Liam? And sweet, suffering baby Jesus, that's a sickening smell that is, burning turnip. Who in their right mind would do that?"

Billy's head popped up. "Steady on, Ryan. What's your problem? Our wee Allison made that turnip lantern last night for the squad room. Spent hours on it, too, ye grumpy auld fart."

Billy's phone rang, and his head disappeared again.

Saved by the bell, Ryan thought. He turned back to his computer.

Billy put the receiver down and popped up, shaking his head.

"We have another body."

"Is it Rose McGuire?" Ryan said. She was on his mind. She was missing.

"Rose McGuire?" Billy hesitated, confused. He'd picked up the receiver again, and he held it midair, poised like an auctioneer's gavel. "No, no. Sounds like they've found Liam. Man's body near Enniskillen."

The relief was overwhelming. Ryan felt almost lightheaded with it. "Who's in charge over there?"

"DS Malloy. He's responding to my request about a motorcyclist. We should head over," Billy said.

"Yup, and Billy, I'll drive. It's about two hours to Enniskillen, and we'll want to get there before we lose the light."

"Ha, ha, very funny. I'm driving. It's not bloody Le Mans, you know. I have a family waiting for me at day's end."

"Oh Christ, not that again."

"Deaf ears, Ryan, deaf ears...."

Wylie tagged along. Always appearing when they tried to leave. Is he sitting like a little garden gnome in the corner watching us, Ryan wondered? He didn't care, though—not now, not today. Things were moving forward again, and Rose was not dead in a ditch. Billy did drive, and Wylie sat in back, glued to his phone, silently clicking away. What the hell was he writing? Or studying for his sergeant's exam? Unlikely. Traffic lightened up once they got to the M1 and then the A4. They managed a fair clip until they hit the smaller towns.

Billy had slowed down to his usual, unhurried pace and was looking around, taking it all in. "It's pleasant here, eh? Nice wee towns, Augher and Clogher? Quiet though. I don't think I could take the quiet."

"Yes, Billy, after the bright lights of Carrick."

Billy lived in a new estate of tidy bungalows in Carrickfergus. Last time Ryan had picked Billy up, it was about nine o'clock in the evening, and you could have heard a pin drop, as his granny used to say. They passed Fivemiletown and started winding their way toward Enniskillen. Finally, Ryan saw Belview, a small road to their left.

"On past here to the right, Billy."

They pulled over and headed for the activity. They had arrived at a small, heavily-wooded section of the local area. The further they walked in, the denser the trees grew. Where the side road ended, they spotted DS Martin

Malloy speaking to the techs. Ryan called, and Malloy waved them over.

"Hello, lads. And this is?"

"DC Wylie." Wylie nodded up ahead. "How's it looking here?"

Malloy hesitated, possibly at Wylie's tone, and indicated activity further in the trees. "It could be an accident. Weather here's been awful over the last week, but...." He shook his head. "The pathologist has been here awhile. I've had a look at the bike, and if you ask me, he was hit from behind. The damage could have been from before, but I doubt it."

"Why would he come up here?" Ryan said. "Would someone have been following him?"

"I don't know." Malloy shook his head again. "We'll have more when they get the bike back to the shop and have a proper look at it. Let's go see the body."

"It's him for sure?"

"Yes, identification on him. We'll get a proper from dental if we need to, but it's him, the guy you were looking for. What's he done?"

"Nothing we know of. We wanted to speak to him regarding a murder. Any idea how long?"

Malloy shook his head. "You know what the doctors are like about time of death, but he thinks, and don't quote me, about two weeks, give or take. And you can forget tyre-track evidence and all that, the way the weather's been here."

"How come it took so long to find him?" Wylie waved his hand around. "Doesn't anyone walk around here?"

"They do." Malloy gestured at the path. "But not right here so much. It goes nowhere, and like I say, the weather's been bloody miserable. A dogwalker found him. A poodle, to be exact. A white poodle."

They trudged through the damp undergrowth, raindrops spotting their trousers and dark, loamy soil sticking to their shoes. Ahead the bike lay on its side, mangled at the front end where it had hit an oak almost head-on. Two old trees growing close together had given him nowhere to maneuver, and he had plowed into the biggest one. The bike was hard to see. It lay almost hidden by a stand of bushes.

"Where is he?" Billy asked.

"Over there." Malloy pointed into dense foliage where several crime-scene techs were crouching.

"You mean he flew all that way?"

"He hit hard." Malloy gestured around him at the damp bushes.

Malloy addressed the tech closest to him. "Give us five minutes, will you? Away and have a cup of tea."

"We're not done with the surrounding area yet. Please be careful what you touch—hey, you." He motioned to Wylie, who was wandering into the bushes. "Back on the path. Jesus Christ."

"Calm down." Wylie stepped back, casually dismissing the guy. He looked over at Ryan and Billy. "What? Those guys always miss things."

The men in white suits walked away, pulling off gloves, talking quietly, and shaking their heads.

"Not wearing a helmet?" Ryan asked.

"They've taken it away for analysis. Here, I'll read you what we have so far." Malloy consulted his phone. "Hit the ground head-first, broke his neck. That's as far as the doctor will go at the moment. It does look like he died instantly. We've taken scrapings of dark paint on the rear of the bike. Looks fresh. Multiple lacerations and some broken ribs, but," he paused, "the neck did it."

Liam wore leathers and lay sprawled on his stomach in the middle of the bush, barely recognizable from the picture Ryan had seen. Decomposition, small animals, and the elements had taken a toll. The suit covered most of the body, but it seemed about to burst. His face, turned to the side, was dark and bloated, almost black, with reddish trails staining the nose and mouth. Small white patches bloomed on his cheek. Malloy saw Ryan looking at them, was about to speak when Ryan said, "Fungus. It'll be all over him."

Malloy nodded. "The post-mortem's going to be a nightmare."

Ryan took a moment to consider that. This was one P.M. he did not intend to watch. "When do you think?"

"Later in the week, I expect. I'll get you what I can when I can, but you'll want the info on the paint samples ASAP, I suppose?" Martin said.

"Yes, please, Martin. See if we can get a model and colour."

"Right you are..." Malloy lifted his hand in farewell and hurried off.

As they walked away, Ryan turned to Billy and Wylie.

"There goes our first viable suspect. Was he murdered, or was this an unfortunate accident?"

"I'm thinking deliberate," Billy said. "You saw how bashed up the back of the bike was."

"Who is this new boyfriend? Why haven't we heard from him? I'm thinking the new guy became our next prime suspect." Ryan turned to Wylie. "Will you please get back to that frigging CCTV and find me something?"

"Christ." Wylie kicked at something on the path. "Not that again. I'm going cross-eyed looking at the bloody screen." He took out his mobile and started to scroll through his messages.

Erin called Ryan on his way home. "I'm coming over with sparklers and champagne for Halloween so don't say no." She had a forced gaiety to her voice that tugged at him.

"Sure, why not?" He didn't want to sit on the farm and worry about Rose, and he reckoned that's what he would do by himself. He knew she had to be out there somewhere—just needed to know she was safe, wanted the call. Why did she not call? It was frustrating. He could do nothing. He'd be laughed out of the station if he tried to get an official search underway. Lover's tiff? He could almost see Girvan's face. He shuddered.

Erin barged through his front door as the kettle started to boil. "I'm here," she shouted. Finn had a fit as usual, and she crouched down to pet him. She was burdened with stuff. Two shopping bags and a handbag slung over her shoulder.

"What the hell did you bring?"

"Food for you. Frozen dinners, couple of stews, bits and pieces. Did you eat the last lot?"

"Course I did."

"Well then. Help me unload."

"You don't have to feed me, you know. I can fend for myself." But he'd rather not....

"I have to cook for my blog, can't eat it all myself, or I shouldn't, so you're lucky. Hi, Finnie, good boy." She tossed her coat on the nearest chair. "I should have brought some fireworks. We could have let them off in the back. Some firecrackers. Some kids down the street from me were throwing some bangers around."

"They're illegal, you know, since 1997."

"Oh, do get a grip, Ryan. You can still order them online."

She grabbed the bottles and headed for the kitchen. "Never mind the tea, you daft bugger. Let's get the booze open, celebrate Halloween like the two old losers we are. Sad, right, spending tonight with me? How'd I know you'd be available? We're a pair."

She chattered on, forced gaiety, breaking his heart.

Ryan took the champagne off her, went to the back door, and eased the cork out. "Put a stew on, would you, Erin?"

Ryan stacked the dishes when they finished eating and swallowed the last of his champagne with a gulp.

"That's dead common, you know, stacking dishes at the table. The waiter's supposed to do that." Erin smiled at him, bleary from the booze.

"Call him in then, will you?" Ryan said, and they grinned at each other.

By the time Ryan had made it to the kitchen, Erin was already there and had opened a bottle of red.

He shook his head. "No, no. I have work tomorrow, and you're driving. A cup of coffee?"

"I can stay here tonight, can't I?" Erin poured herself a glass and joined him in the living room. "How's your love life, baby brother?"

God, if she only knew.

"More to the point, big sister, how's yours?"

"I have a confession to make." She got comfortable on the sofa and sipped her wine. "I met Paul for a drink."

"Jesus, Erin. Really?"

"I knew you'd say that. She turned to him, her eyes shining. "A drink, I promise."

"You could get any man you want. You know that, right? Why him?"

"You wouldn't understand. You've never loved anyone. Have you?"

Had he loved Bridget? Could he love her? He'd pushed those feelings down. They'd never seemed important in the scheme of things. Some of that blame had to lie with her, though. She'd never been the needy type, and he had responded to that. Now with the baby, everything was different. And what about Rose? He couldn't let himself think about her. God, had he ever loved anyone? Had he? He got up and poured himself a glass of red. All this soul searching, very stressful.

"Top me up, will you?" Erin held her glass for him to fill.

"You'll be seeing Crawford again then?"

"Maybe. Oh, I don't know."

What could he do?

Erin talked and drank steadily until, at about eleven, she fell asleep. Ryan carried her into his spare room and put her to bed. He could still hear fireworks cracking outside. She had asked him who he loved. He loved her; he knew that. A fierce protective emotion that scared him. He touched her cheek. She sighed and turned away from him. He covered her up, heard her little snuffling snores, and smiled as he pulled the door to. "Finn, let's head out."

Chapter Eighteen

Tuesday, November 1

Derek appeared out of nowhere as Ryan waited in the cafeteria line. "Who's that knob hanging around Maura?"

"I haven't even had my morning coffee yet. Give me a minute." Ryan picked up his mug and headed back upstairs to his desk, Derek trailing behind. "And never mind that, what about the bloody watch?"

"It's a real Rolex. I had to contact the main office in London." Derek paused. "Snotty bunch. Did you get my email? Did you read it?" Derek was bursting. He had cycled in to work, obviously. Too much oxygen.

"Took you long enough to find out. Can't you tell me now?"

"Yes, I suppose so. Had to beat bloody Wylie off with a stick. He's useless, that one. Saunters in late, sits around looking over my shoulder. Won't do any work, wants all the credit."

"Right, Derek, got it. What about the watch?"

Billy wandered in and sat at his desk with a grunt, setting his sandwich bag and thermos in front of him with a brief smile to Derek and Ryan. "Alright, you two?"

"Billy, I got the results on the watch from Rolex London. And who's that guy hanging around Maura?"

"How should I know? He'll be one of the new lads from Musgrave. Why?" Billy poked at his sandwiches. Frowned.

Please let the sandwiches be ham and tomato, Ryan thought.

"And never mind that, what about the watch?" Billy said, wrapping his sandwiches up again and smiling.

"Derek? Derek?" Ryan couldn't take it any longer.

"Lunn's Jewellers."

"Lunn's? In Queen's Arcade?"

"Yes."

"Right, this is good news." Billy unlocked his drawer, placed his sandwiches inside, and relocked it. "Come on, Ryan, let's head there."

Ryan gulped his coffee, made a face, and grabbed his jacket.

"I'm driving, Billy, no arguments."

"Where's our enthusiastic sidekick Wylie?" Billy made a show of looking around when they got to the car.

"He drew a blank on the CCTV. Malcolm's got a couple of PCs off sick with colds, so I kicked him over there. I've asked Derek to have a quick look again."

Billy shook his head as he clicked on his seatbelt. "You're a hard man to please. Poor Wylie."

"Poor Wylie? Honest to God, why don't you ask him to move in with you?" Ryan drove on in silence.

"Park in Castle Court, will you? We can walk up Royal Avenue, look at the shops. There, turn there. That's the entrance to the car park." Billy pointed ahead.

"Oh? That's it there, the big sign saying Castle Court Parking?"

"Yes, there," Billy said again, exasperated.

What was the point? Ryan pulled in and found a spot. They walked briskly up Royal Avenue and Donegall Place, enjoying the weak sunshine and the crowds.

"It's great to see people out and about again." Billy held his fair, freckled face up to the sky. "Not worried all the time and skittering about like nervous wrecks, you know? Years there you couldn't enjoy a pint without worrying you'd lose a leg."

Ryan turned his face to the sun, too, enjoying the warmth. "It's a beautiful city, even after the bombings and all that shite. The people brought it back."

"Aye, they did," Billy agreed. "We're a rare breed, the Norn Irish."

They both smiled at that. Up ahead, the City Hall gleamed white in the sunshine.

"I've never been inside that building," Billy said.

"I did not know that, Billy, but I do know that it was built by architect Alfred Brumwell Thomas in the Baroque Revival style and constructed in Portland stone. And, interestingly, much of the interior was done by skilled workers from Harland and Wolff, the same men who built the Titanic. It has a similar look to the lounges and suites on the ship."

"I love that Titanic Exhibit. Have you been?" Billy said, missing the point again.

Billy wasn't much of a history buff. Didn't give a toss about architecture either.

Queen's Arcade was quiet as they strolled toward the jewellers.

"Lovely wee place here, isn't it?" Billy glanced around him. "I've always liked it. Feels like you're away on your holidays, to Paris or Rome or somewhere like that."

"And here's me thinking you didn't appreciate structural design."

"Eh?" Billy said.

Indeed, the arcade had a European feel to it, with a high, arched glass ceiling and an echoing tile floor with inlaid coloured stones. At Lunn's, Ryan pulled out his warrant card and waved it at a big man in uniform standing inside the door. The security guard nodded and buzzed them in.

Lunn's was a high-end shop of pale polished wood and gleaming cabinets full of expensive watches and jewellry. A young woman at the back rubbed furiously at a counter. She had a bottle of glass cleaner in her hand. She blew a curl of dark brown hair out of her eye.

"Oh, hello. Police, are you?"

Ryan smiled back. "Yes, we are. Is it that obvious?" He didn't think they looked like police. Maybe Billy, with his wrinkled suit and daft tie. He, on the other hand, wore jeans and his dark grey Barbour jacket. Rather dashing....

"Oh, aye. Either that or the Mormons," she said.

Not so dashing then. "Do you have a moment? We're interested in a Rolex watch we believe was purchased here."

She led them past a number of counters and stopped at the one branded Rolex.

"Please take a seat. I'm Connie, by the way. I'll call my uncle. He's at the back somewhere. He has all the records."

Her uncle, a tall stooped gentleman, hurried from the back at Connie's yell. He was apologetic but unable to provide more information. "The buyer paid cash. He had researched the price. We don't usually handle that much cash, but a sale is a sale. I took the money right to the bank. Sorry I can't be more help."

"What did he look like? Can you describe him?"

"Been a while, old memory's not what it was. A youngish man, dark hair, I think? Tall. That's about all I remember. We get a lot of traffic in here. The cruises, you know."

"What about cameras? CCTV?"

"Eh, yes." He nodded to the corner in the ceiling. "But only held for a week. Don't need them after that."

Ryan handed him a card. "Call me if you or Connie remember anything."

"I will. Connie wasn't in that day. She's the one with the good memory."

Back out in the arcade, Ryan paused for a moment, disappointed. This could have been the break they needed. He felt it again, that spike of anxiety. It had been more than a week since Kathleen's murder, and they were nowhere. Liam dead now too. What the hell was going on? Brendan Doyle, Mrs. Doyle, Sophie Walton, and her brooding husband, Anthony. And Rose.

"So, what next, Ryan? That had to be the new boyfriend, right?"

"Had to be. Damn it. The bastard covered his tracks. He didn't want anyone to know about him and Kathleen."

"Doesn't mean he's the murderer, though."

"No, but what's going on? Why go to so much trouble? Unless he likes paying in cash. Surely he wasn't planning something that far in advance. And if he was, why buy your victim an expensive watch, then kill them? It makes no sense. Let's grab a coffee and something to eat. I'm starving. Plan our next step. Maybe we could get CCTV from the arcade? Worth a try."

They wandered into the Queen's Café Bar. Ryan ordered a sandwich. Billy sat down with a cup of tea and checked his Timex.

"Here, Ryan, worth a few bob, the stuff in there, eh? Did you see those watches? Fantastic—how's your sister, by the way?" Billy said, changing the subject. He had a minor but persistent crush on Erin.

"Not great. She still has issues to deal with, the divorce and all. I don't know what to do. Not good at that stuff. And Mum and Dad are no help. Sometimes they make things worse. She writes for that online business she has and cooks, but I don't know. She never seems to get out and meet new people."

"She still drinking?"

"Yes, a bit."

"She's lonely then. Maybe you should...."

"Billy, leave it. I can't...." Ryan pushed his sandwich away. "What's it like, coming home every night to Margaret and the kids? Don't you sometimes wish you were alone, had a bit of space?"

"What, me?" Billy looked affronted. "No, course not. What's gotten into you? That's a funny thing to ask."

Ryan's mobile buzzed. "DS McBride." He didn't recognise the number.

"Hello? This is Connie...from Lunn's? You two gentlemen wanted a name for the bloke who bought the watch?"

"Yes, Connie, we really do."

"I have it."

Chapter Nineteen

Wednesday, October 19

BEFORE

I
t had been two days since Monday night's debacle with Kevin and the punch Annabelle had landed on him. Kathleen still half-expected him to appear at the gallery, although that didn't seem like Kevin, to show weakness in front of others or to cause a scene for that matter. He liked to intimidate her in private. She thought briefly about last night, her fateful date with Liam, as she thought of it. Drinks and a bit of harmless fun at the Botanic Inn.

But how could she have spent those years with him? He was an eejit, a wild man—and good luck to his fiancée. She would need it. Last night's date had turned into an all-nighter. Not that kind of all-nighter, but Liam, drunk as a skunk, had slept on her couch. Please, God, let him be gone by the time I get home. As the bus edged along, she was struck again at how simple life could be—should be. Her fellow passengers chatting on mobiles or to each other, laughing and gossiping. The city alive outside the bus window. A weak October sun, pearly behind thin clouds.

Kevin would laugh if he could see her now, jumping at shadows and not at all like that scary bitch she had been on Monday night. Where did that all come from? A different Kathleen, a new and improved version. In the past, he had hit her, yes, and she had let that happen. He had couched it in different ways. Sometimes as a kind of sexual play, and sometimes an argument gone a little too far. Always lighthearted afterwards, always playing it down. And she had taken him back. What had she been thinking? That she deserved the abuse? Maybe that was it. She'd been lost for a while there.

She had some holidays, and she intended to take them next week. She would email Sophie and let her know, unless she got up the courage to phone her. Sophie wouldn't be well pleased, but the gallery wasn't busy. This new job search would take priority over everything. If she had reservations about leaving before, that had all changed. No more interactions, business or otherwise, with Mr. Kevin Coulter. She never wanted to see him again. Sophie would not be in until Saturday. She stared out at the trees flashing by and noticed for the first time the darkening sky, big ominous clouds building in the west.

Kevin came to the flat about seven-thirty.

Mrs. Doyle had invited her downstairs for dinner. *I've a nice piece of halibut, dear, too big for me.*

Kathleen had a bottle of white languishing in her fridge and brought it down with her. She'd unscrewed the top when the outside bell went. She jumped, and Mrs. Doyle touched her hand.

"It's all right, pet. It'll be her next door returning my big bowl. Don't worry about yer man. He won't come here after what you did." Mary winked. She took off her apron and fluffed her tight perm in the little mirror beside the door. "And good riddance to him too."

Kathleen turned back to the wine. Mary's right. She had to stop worrying. He hadn't shown up or even tried to contact her at work. His ego had been badly bruised. If she could get a new job, she never needed to see him again.

The door crashed open first, then shouting and the sound of something breaking.

"Kathleen!"

Kevin. His voice high and frantic. She'd never heard it like that before, and she'd heard him angry many times.

130

"No, no."

She rushed for the hall as the wine tumbled to the floor. Kevin stood inside the door. Mrs. Doyle lay crumpled at the foot of the stairs.

"What have you done?" Kathleen ran at him, but Kevin grabbed her wrist and twisted it.

"We're leaving. Come on." He pulled her.

She swung at him, and he grabbed her other arm.

"Think you can throw a punch like your little friend the other night?"

She tried to twist her arm free. "Are you off your pills or something? Who are you?"

That struck a nerve. He squeezed her arm harder and pulled her to him. "Don't worry about my fucking mental health. I've never felt better. I can see what's going on now. And your ex-boyfriend stayed the night, didn't he? And guess what? Now he really is your ex-boyfriend."

What has he done? Has he hurt Liam? A thought, unbidden, roared into her head, surprising her. If she had a gun, she would shoot him. Oh yes, she would.

"Kevin, let me call for help. Mary's hurt."

He ignored her and started to drag her towards the front door. In the distance, sirens whooped.

Mary Doyle stirred. "That'll be the police. I hit my panic button as soon as I saw you at the door." These days, with her bad heart, Mary wore a small plastic alert unit around her neck.

"Don't think this is over." Kevin shoved Kathleen hard, and she stumbled away. Then he turned to Mrs. Doyle, who had pulled herself halfway up onto the first stair. He pushed her again, and she fell back down. He walked to the door, pausing before he slammed it shut. "I'll see you again soon," he said.

Kathleen rushed to Mrs. Doyle. "Mary?"

"I'm fine, pet."

The sirens had almost reached them when Mrs. Doyle grabbed Kathleen's wrist.

"No police. Let the ambulance people in, but tell them to send the police away. Say I fell on the stairs." She grabbed Kathleen's arm harder. "Do you hear me, love? No police."

"Mary, I think he's done something to Liam. We have to stop him."

"No, we don't. My son Brendan will sort it. I'm sorry about your friend, but we have to leave it for now."

"But Kevin's dangerous, Mary. You saw him. I think he's mentally ill."

The door banged open and two hefty EMS guys, and an equally hefty woman, burst into the hall.

"Okay, love, we have you."

Mrs. Doyle gave Kathleen a sideways glance.

"You can cancel the police if they're on their way. It's just a fall, and she doesn't want a fuss. Can you do that?" Kathleen said. "Cancel everyone else?" What was she doing? Was she risking Mary's life?

The burlier of the two men turned to Mrs. Doyle. "You want us looking to you then, love, no need for the whole circus?"

"Yes, boys, a couple of sticking plasters, and I'll be right as rain."

"Let's have a look at you."

The woman pulled a radio off her belt and cancelled the police and fire response.

"Thanks, it's a busy night."

Kathleen went into the flat and put the kettle on because she didn't know what else to do. Soon they had bundled Mrs. Doyle onto a gurney and brought her through to her bedroom.

On the way out, the EMS woman turned to Kathleen. "She'll be all right, but she'll need to rest. Maybe a bruised rib or two, but she flatly won't go to the hospital. She insisted on making a phone call to her son. I think he'll be heading here by the sound of it. We gave her a little something, but you can talk to her for a while. Tough old bird, eh? If she sleeps, she wants you to wake her when he arrives."

Brendan Doyle arrived red-faced and breathless, looking like he'd run the whole way from his farm. A tall man, solid and imposing, he held himself like a brawler, his chin pushed forward. He had a fleshy, sunburned face under a thatch of short, dark-brown hair threaded with grey. His broad nose canted to the side, broken a few times by the look of it. Kathleen put him in his late fifties. She knew almost nothing about Mary's family.

He shrugged off his overcoat. "Mammy's in her room?"

"Yes, I finally got her to settle, and Brendan, she's okay. I'll make us all a nice cup of tea and bring it in. She said to wake her if she's sleeping."

When she brought the tray in, Brendan jumped up from his mother's bed and took it from her. What would he think of her, a stupid girl, duped by a manipulative man and ultimately putting Mary in harm's way? She sat down in the small chair in the corner.

"Brendan, I'm sorry I brought your mother into this."

She rubbed her wrist and noticed for the first time a bruise forming from her hand to her elbow. Her neck and upper shoulders ached where Kevin had wrenched her toward him. Mrs. Doyle, on the other hand, looked the picture of health, with a cup of tea in hand, several pillows fluffed at her back, and a pink eiderdown tucked around her.

"Mary, how do you feel?"

"I'm grand, pet. I've had worse in my time," she said.

Brendan took his mother's hand and squeezed it.

"Here's what we're going to do," she said. "We're all heading to Brendan's place, let things settle...."

"But," Kathleen interrupted, "I've work tomorrow and Friday and...."

"Didn't you say you were only going in to sort out a few things? Your wee friend will cover for you, won't he? If you take some extra days. And pet, you've already let your boss know you'll be away next week, right?"

"But—"

Brendan came over and knelt in front of her. "Look, Kathleen, I'm not leaving you or my mammy here for that bastard to come back and terrorize. Sorry, Mammy," he added.

"Brendan's right," Mrs. Doyle said. "We have to go. I don't want to be here when he comes back, and neither do you. Brendan will talk some sense into him, won't you, son?"

Kathleen paled at the thought, the idea. "No. Oh, my God, Brendan,

Kevin's dangerous. He works in security, and he might even have guns. In fact, I'm sure he has them. That's his business. He as much as told me he killed my friend, Liam—although he may have been trying to scare me." She hesitated, unsure, unwilling to believe.

Brendan touched her arm. "Kathleen, don't worry about me. I'll talk to him. I've dealt with worse. Come on, girl, away upstairs and pack some things. Clear the fridge, too. Turn off your phone before we go. Try to get some sleep, and we'll leave in the morning."

He turned to his mother, and Kathleen saw Mary nod to him.

"And one more thing," he said. "I'll need Kevin's full name and address."

Chapter Twenty

Tuesday, November 1

"The customer didn't want a warranty at first, then changed his mind and came back the next day to register. We're not supposed to keep a copy, I did, you know, in case I had to contact him for anything." Connie blushed. "I didn't know that was the watch you were after. Uncle Trevor was out at lunch, and I forgot to tell him." The blush deepened. "Name is Kevin Coulter. Here you go, Arc at Titanic. I love that building."

They called it in as they headed toward the Arc Apartments. Billy pointed over at Titanic Belfast. The exhibition on their left soared like a huge ship's silver bow. Towering steel ripples formed the sides and reflected the early afternoon sun.

"Funny, we were just talking about that earlier. I'm thinking of taking the kids again. It's brilliant," Billy said. "I like that wee hanging car that takes you up through the ship, and when you pass the engine room, you can feel the blast of heat. Oh, and even the café is great, smashing lunches and everything. Fantastic." He craned his neck around to catch a final glimpse.

Ryan nodded his agreement, swung the wheel, and parked. Curved, and in three sections, Arc's modern high-rise apartments perched right on the Lagan's edge. A young couple held the door open as Ryan and Billy got there, and they entered a large, wood-panelled foyer with marbled floors. Ryan thought it a bit too impersonal, but beside him, Billy whistled quietly.

They headed up.

"This Kevin guy might have nothing to do with it," Billy said.

"Why hasn't he come forward then? She's been in the news."

The apartment was on a high floor facing the city. They knocked and waited.

"Derek will get his phone number and details." Ryan had taken out his phone when a door down the hallway opened, and a young woman stepped out. She struggled to lock up while holding a heavy coat, a handbag, and a small white dog. The dog saw Ryan and Billy and began to yap.

"Sugar! Stop that!"

But the little dog continued to yap. She finally locked her door and slipped her coat on, put the dog down, and came toward them, smiling uncertainly. She was a wide-eyed blond with high, arched eyebrows and a startled expression.

"Sorry about Sugar. She's harmless."

Sugar was about the size of a teacup. "No problem." Ryan showed her his card, then leaned down and tickled the little dog. Sugar rolled over, exposing a pink belly which Ryan obligingly scratched. He imagined Finn and Sugar together. What a picture. He could sell postcards on the beach at Bangor with that shot. Sugar's back leg jiggled.

"Police. We're looking for the gentleman here." Ryan nodded at the door.

"Oh. Mr. Coulter?"

"Yes. D'you know him?"

"No. I think he travels a lot. Almost every time I've seen him, he has one of those wheelie cases, you know? Keeps to himself. I don't think he likes dogs." Her pretty forehead furrowed. "Something wrong?"

"A traffic thing, that's all. Where's parking for these floors?" Ryan asked.

"He'll be on P1 like me. Apartment number on the spot."

She smiled and left, trailing the dog behind her.

Ryan slipped his business card under Kevin's door. "Do you want to go and check for his car? It's a dark-coloured Mercedes, according to Derek."

"Sure." Billy headed for the lift. "That might be why we haven't heard from him. He may not know yet."

Kevin's spot was empty.

"Not much going on here." Billy squinted. looking around. "C'mon, let's head back. I've missed my lunch. You had that sandwich."

They headed for the car, and Ryan's phone buzzed. It was Malcolm calling, Maura's DS on the rapes case.

"Maura said you'd like to know; another girl's come in. She was out the night before Halloween, had a few drinks at a costume party with a guy in a Dracula costume, and doesn't remember much after about ten o'clock. The place was packed, she said. They left, and he took her somewhere. She's positive she was drugged and raped."

"Does sound like another one, Malcolm." He passed the word to Billy.

"Malcolm, we're on our way back to the car, be there shortly. Thanks for the heads-up." He had just clicked off when it rang again. This time the number was withheld. He debated and decided to answer.

"DS McBride."

"Ryan, it's Rose."

He motioned to Billy he'd see him at the car.

"Rose. Are you okay?"

"Yes, I'm fine."

"I'll have to call you back in a little while, I can't talk right now."

"Yes."

When Ryan climbed back into the car, Billy glanced over at him.

"Who was that?"

"Nobody."

"You seem a bit tense."

"I'm fine."

Billy had the common sense to keep quiet on the drive back. Ryan leaned over and switched the car radio on low until they entered the station car park. When they got upstairs, Malcolm and Maura were leaving the interview room. A female PC escorted a young woman off in the other direction.

"Is that her?" Ryan asked Maura.

"Yes," Maura replied and nodded to a plastic evidence bag in Malcolm's hand. "And we may have caught a break. She brought a lighter with her.

She thinks the guy may have used it."

"See you all later then." Malcolm turned to leave. "I'll have someone send the lighter out. We'll have it swabbed for DNA and fingerprints."

As the three of them headed back to their desks, Maura called out to a constable at the far end of the corridor. "PC Burns, do you have a minute?"

Maura introduced them to PC Sam Burns. She was extremely enthusiastic. "Sam here has been helpful. He's great on the computer, could give Derek a run for his money."

"Hello, again, Sam. Maura got you working hard?" Ryan asked.

"Oh yes, great, it's great. I'm hoping to get some proper experience, help out if I can. DC Dunn has been terrific."

"Good to hear. Yes, Maura will take good care of you, I'm sure." Ryan turned to leave, then had a thought. "Hey, Maura, you said this guy always changes locations, right?"

"Yes, Belfast and a little cluster out of town—Hollywood, Bangor, and Newtownards."

"But he never uses the same place twice, right?"

"Not the same bar, the same towns."

"He seems to spend a lot of time in County Down."

"Yes. Why?"

"Could we do call ins to various bars in the areas he likes? Put a word in the ear of a few bartenders. Ask them to keep an eye out for suspicious behaviour."

"I hear what you're saying, Ryan, but we don't know what he looks like, and it's a zoo most nights at the bars. He always picks crowded ones. And there's a question of manpower."

"Yes, manpower is always a problem." Ryan gave a tiny nod in Burns' direction.

"No, it's a thought. Let's talk later." She left with PC Burns trailing behind her.

"Oh, oh. Derek won't like this." Ryan watched them leave.

"What? Burns's computer skills or Maura's little crush?" Billy said.

"Both I think, wouldn't you say? I'm going to call the gallery, see if anyone there knows Kevin Coulter. Will you see if you can find out who he is? See if Derek has found anything?"

Billy jumped up. "I'll pop up to the third floor then, shall I? Check in with Derek."

Angus answered the phone at the gallery.

"Kevin Coulter? He's our security guy. Sophie's husband has always used them. They aren't based here, though. They're in London. Kevin's father is the president and owner. Why do you want to know?"

"Pursuing a line of inquiry, Angus. Trying to talk to anyone who may have known Kathleen."

"Yes, but Kevin's only been here a few...."

Angus stopped abruptly.

"Oh my God! Is he the mysterious boyfriend? The *K* from the note?"

"We would prefer it if you kept that kind of speculation to yourself at the moment. Will you do that?"

"Of course I will." Angus sounded hurt. "But can I tell Calvin?"

With the name and number of Kevin's father and Angus's solemn promise to keep the conversation private, Ryan hung up and called the security offices in London. Adam Coulter was not in, but his secretary assured him her boss would call back as soon as he got the message.

He hung up and called Rose back.

"Look, Rose, I'm sorry I couldn't talk earlier. Can we meet tonight? I need to speak to you. Not on the phone either. I need to see you." He could feel himself tightening up. He had to see her face to face, had to explain. "Will you meet me? Where are you?"

"I'm outside Bangor. I'm staying with my cousin and her family."

"Cousin?"

"It's complicated." She paused, then, "I'll meet you if you want me to. Can you come over this way, to Bangor?"

"Of course. About seven?"

"Do you know the bar Jenny Watts?" she said.

"Yes," Ryan said. "I'll see you tonight."

Ryan liked Jenny Watts, a traditional bar on Bangor's main street. Rose was there when he arrived, and he went straight to the bar and grabbed some drinks. He, for one, needed something to fortify himself. She'd found a nice quiet spot at the back. Her face seemed almost chalk-white in the glow of the pub's wall lamps.

He put the drinks on the table and sat down. He hesitated, then took a large swallow of whiskey.

"Bridget's pregnant."

There, he'd said it. No mucking about, no excuses. He drank the rest of his whiskey in one go.

Rose lifted her wine and took a sip. She didn't reply.

"I had no idea until now. No idea at all, Rose."

"You haven't seen her since we've been...." She hesitated. "...going out?"

"If you mean have I been seeing you both at the same time, no. I saw her last Saturday for the first time in ages after I heard her message. That's when she told me. She's asked me to decide if I want to be part of it. It's up to me."

Rose lifted her glass again and sipped, looking thoughtful. "You've decided then, Ryan. I think you have."

He realised that he had. He could not ignore a child of his. He couldn't. And his family, Erin, his parents, even if he wanted to, that would not work.

"I'm sorry, Rose. I never meant for..."

"I know. I'm pleased for you. A baby." She smiled, but only for a moment. "As long as you care for Bridget, and I think you do."

"It happened before we broke up. I'm an idiot."

They sat there in silence for a few moments. Rose finally spoke. "It's funny, but I'm relieved in a way. I thought you had been stringing me along, lying to me, and I was devastated. This was my first real relationship, you probably figured that out, and I felt like a fool."

"No, no. Don't think that. It was never that. Look, I don't want to lose touch. Can I call you to talk sometime? Where are you staying?"

"With my cousin, Anne Magee. I got a message from her when I returned to Kathleen's flat from your farm. We've been estranged from that side of the family for years. Anne heard about the murder on the news. She found my stepfather, Leonard, in Donegal, and he gave her my number at Kathleen's. We hit it off right away. She has two kids and they're great. I'm staying with her and her husband here in Bangor until I can plan the funeral."

"Rose, you understand that might be a while. I can't release the body, and the coroner won't either until we're completely satisfied we have everything we need."

She nodded. Said nothing.

In the warm, intimate bar, he reached for her hand and thought briefly of their first lunch. She let him hold it for a moment, then slipped it away.

He drove straight home and, with Finn eyeing him disconsolately, drank whiskey in the conservatory. He couldn't believe he'd said goodbye for good.

He couldn't let that be, could he?

Chapter Twenty-One

Wednesday, November 2

Ryan picked up the phone at the first ring. It was the desk sergeant. "Lady down here with her wean needs to talk to someone about that murder. Something about the car we found."

"Right, Big John, I'm on my way."

Five minutes later, Mrs. Cathy O'Hara sat across from Ryan, stiff-backed and fuming. She had gathered her blue-black, badly dyed hair in a tight ponytail. It tugged at her face and slanted her protruding eyes upwards. She had small black commas for eyebrows. Her son, Stevie, squirmed and fidgeted beside her. They looked nothing alike. Stevie's mass of fine, fizzy, ginger hair floated around his face like candy floss.

"He's a flippin' wee hallion, so he is. I blame his father—my side were never like this. Stevie, tell the policeman what you did."

Stevie sat there looking all around him, slack-jawed.

Mrs. O'Hara, nerves on a knife-edge, or so it seemed, leaned over and smacked him.

"Tell him, ya wee shite."

"It was open."

Mrs. O'Hara smacked him again, and Ryan mouthed an unconvincing protest.

"He's a policeman. Call him sir or something."

"It was open, mister. I had a look, didn't do any harm. Just a stupid phone,

142

no games or nuthin'."

"And a packet of Polo mints." His mother added.

"So," Ryan said. "You mean the little red car in the news? Found in the lay-by and connected to the murder investigation?"

"Yes," Mrs. O'Hara said. "I found the phone in his tip of a bedroom. Finally got it out of him, where he got it. When he said a red car and where it was, well, we've been talking about it, me and Cam, that's my husband, about that poor lass that was murdered. Too close for comfort, you know? We come all the way down here from Portglenone in the car to tell you. You was in the paper. Lead detective and all, thought we'd come right to the top man. No reward is there?"

"I'm afraid not, Mrs. O'Hara." Ryan turned to the lad.

"This is a murder investigation, Stevie. Did you know that?"

"No. Me mam told me after."

"You are an important person now." He leaned in to the boy. "I need you to tell me what you took and when you took it."

Ryan stared at the mobile, now in an evidence bag.

Billy grinned. "At least we got it back. Many a mum would have chucked it, right? Afraid she'd get her wean in trouble."

"I think she's counting on it, Billy. Maybe get rid of him for a while to Child Services. Where the hell is Derek? Thing is, this is a burner. I'm thinking the killer didn't know about it."

"What did the kid say?"

"He was off with his mates on their bikes about ten Sunday morning. He said they stopped for a break. He went over into the lay-by for a pee and noticed the car. He said his friends dared him to look inside; the door was open."

"And what all did he take?"

"Not much. He took the phone. It had fallen between the seats and some Polo mints. He got chatty after I told him he'd been a major help. I gave him a packet of your crisps."

Before Billy could protest, Derek appeared. "You want this off to those clever guys upstairs?" He grabbed the mobile in its evidence bag.

"Yes," said Billy. "So don't you touch it."

"Ha, ha. You're a laugh a minute, you are." Derek turned to Ryan. "I wonder where her handbag went."

"I'm thinking the murderer must have taken it."

Billy scribbled in his pad. "Kathleen's car must have been there and empty at ten o'clock."

"Her body was found shortly after eleven," Ryan added. "And Alice says she died around ten or thereabouts."

"She stops at the lay-by earlier. There's an altercation. She's forced into another car and driven to the river park area? But who drugged her, and when did they?" Billy said.

Ryan shook his head. "I can't see it. How could the murderer force her down to the river and get her walking? She died where we found her; Alice is sure of that. Plus, remember, she had gunshot residue on her hand, she fired a gun. Where did she get it, and where is it?"

"Maybe wee Stevie has it after all."

"My God, I hope not. His mam better watch out…."

Ryan's phone rang. Adam Coulter returning his call. He hit speaker.

"DS McBride? I got your message. You needed to speak with me?"

"Yes, sir, it's about your son, Kevin. We want to talk to him in connection with an investigation we have here. Do you have any idea where he might be? I have been calling him. I left my card at his flat."

"What kind of investigation?"

"A murder investigation. We believe he knew the victim. We need to talk to him."

"He never mentioned this to me, a friend being murdered. When did this happen?"

Ryan ignored the question. "When did you last speak to your son? He may not have heard, perhaps?"

"I'm sure he hasn't. I saw him this morning. I'm here at the office in London, and he's on his way back to Belfast. Should be there later today sometime. He comes back and forth all the time."

"How long has he been over there with you?"

Adam Coulter hesitated, and Ryan said, "Mr. Coulter?"

"Ask him yourself. I'm not comfortable being interrogated like this about my son's movements."

Ryan absorbed the tone in Adam Coulter's voice. Here was a man used to getting his own way.

"No problem, we'll do that."

Ryan hung up. "Did you hear that, Billy?"

"Yes. His dad seemed a bit touchy. Kevin will be back later today then. Maybe that's why he hasn't contacted us. He's been away and didn't know?"

"I think I'll go back over to his flat in a while," Ryan said. "You want to come?"

Billy shook his head. "What about first thing tomorrow?"

"No, I'll run by there myself. Derek can check with the airlines and ferries. I'll hurry him up on that background check too."

Billy unlocked a drawer and took out his lunch.

"What do we have today?" Maura had arrived at Ryan's desk and nodded at Billy's bag.

"Hey, Maura, I dunno. Let me check."

Here we go, Ryan thought.

Billy took his sandwiches out and inspected the filling. "You know, I'm not sure."

"Let me see." Ryan, intrigued, had a look. "Bocconcini. Little bites."

Billy was dubious. "I don't like the sound of that."

Maura lifted one up and sniffed it.

"Oi, do you mind?" Billy took it off her and sniffed it himself. "It doesn't smell of anything."

"It doesn't taste of anything either," Ryan added.

"What's the point of it then?" Billy, scandalised, waved the sandwich around like a hanky. "This'll be her sister's fault. Always trying fancy new stuff out. I'm not eating them."

"That'll teach her. Can I have them then?" Ryan held his hand out.

"Give me one too." Maura grabbed a sandwich and bit into it.

"You know, it's not bad," she said.

Billy huffed and headed for the door. "That's it. I'm away to the cafe. Enjoy yourselves now. Don't mind me."

Ryan waved with his mouth full.

"Aye, not bad. What's up?"

"One of the girls from before remembers something else. The rapes?"

"The same girl who brought in the lighter?'

"No, this girl was assaulted a month ago, but I asked her to come in again, could be nothing, but she desperately wants to help. She doesn't seem as upset as the others, but she's angry, you know?"

"What time?"

"About three. Do you want to sit in?"

"Sure, then I have to fly, heading over to see if Kevin Coulter is home yet."

Evelyn McCracken was an attractive brunette. Well turned out and self-assured.

"The stupid thing is, as far as I recall, he wasn't bad-looking. Why would a guy like that have to drug a girl? It makes no sense. Why did he have to do that?"

"You started out in Bangor?" Ryan checked his notes. "Tell us what you remember again."

"Not too much about the whole incident. I only know it started in Wolsey's. I had a glass of wine with my mates. Later they saw me talking to a bloke further along the bar." She paused and fidgeted a little. "Sorry, the bastard got me smoking again, but I'm trying to give it up. I ended up sitting with him, way at the rear. That's the last they saw of me. Wherever we went, and it can't have been too far, it felt dreamlike. Almost like I was in a fairy tale. And I don't know why I think that. Thing is, I didn't drink all the drinks. I dumped part of the second one when he went to the gents because I had a slight hangover from the previous night. I did see something, I think, in his car. Don't ask me the make and model because I don't know, but for some reason, I saw this golf shirt, and it had a badge embroidered on it. I'm a graphic artist, and I tend to remember logos and things."

"Can you describe it?"

"A star or a cross with maybe an outer ring? Here, I'll draw it. Don't expect much. It's vague in my mind. Maybe he's a golfer? My dad plays and has a shirt like that. He's a member at Royal Portrush," she added.

When she had finished, Maura, Billy, and Ryan exchanged glances.

"And you had a vague description?" Ryan asked.

"I think he had, like, longish dark hair and stubble. Oh, and glasses too. Tall, and like I said, not bad-looking. That's the half-arsed consensus of my mates. They remembered more than me, but they'd all had a few by then. Although, it might have been anybody I met that night. Sorry."

"Are you game for an e-fit, Evelyn? See if we can get a likeness?"

"That's like a drawing of the guy? I'll give it a go."

When Evelyn McCracken had left with Maura, Ryan turned to Billy. "Are you thinking what I'm thinking?"

"Tall, and what looks like the Police Service of Northern Ireland logo on the golf shirt?" Billy said, a bit on the sarcastic side.

"Don't mention this to Maura. Let's wait and see if she arrives at the same conclusion. I don't want to influence her. We'll wait for the e-fit, but she has to recognize the logo."

"No way it's Wylie," Billy said. "What are the chances? This isn't you getting hung up again, is it?"

Billy was entitled to his own opinion. Ryan said nothing.

Chapter Twenty-Two

Ryan got to Kevin Coulter's building before five o'clock. He didn't intend to stay long and pulled in next to the Public Records Office at the back, across from the exit ramp. He waved off a security guard by flashing his warrant card.

A damp, skittery wind had sprung up, pushing dead leaves, bits of sweetie wrappers, and scraps of debris about in front of it. Rain on the way, too, as usual, and he'd left his overcoat in the car. Chilled, he slipped in a side door, putting him on the other side of the lobby. As he turned the corner towards the front, he saw a crowd of young people in the lobby. He could hear them talking and laughing. He didn't want to share a lift with a noisy group, couldn't be bothered with it. He would head to the garage and check if Kevin's car was back. Derek had found a black Mercedes registered in Kevin's name. After a bit of wandering around, Ryan spotted a door to parking and headed downstairs. On the first landing, an electrical panel stood open. A bunch of wires lay in a tangle outside an open door marked maintenance. A dim light glowed inside.

"Hello?" Ryan called into the room beyond. Be good if someone was around in case he couldn't get into P1. He stepped in a little.

"Hello?" he called again. No response.

"Hey." A voice from the back. "This here's private." A small, overweight man appeared.

"I'm police. I need to get into P1. Is it open from the stairs?"

"Yup, it's open." The man stepped over to the wall. A high-pitched buzzing sounded, and the room flared with light. Short and red-faced, the man's bald head gleamed in the fluorescents. He pointed behind Ryan. "All them doors, some damn mess-up with the wires. I'm not a bloody electrician, I've a call in. Can't blame me; not my problem."

"Right," Ryan said and headed down another flight of stairs. The door to P1was ajar. The cold, metallic tang of old exhaust hit him like a slap. Ryan caught it as soon as he barged through to the garage. He heard raised voices, too, an outcry from the other side. He squinted, straining to see. Up ahead, at Kevin's parking space, he saw movement. Figures trying to force someone into the back of a dark van, its doors yawning open. More commotion. Parked in the spot, a dark Mercedes with a suitcase toppled on the ground beside it.

He took off running and yelling, "Stop, police, stop." The garage stretched out in front of him. He pounded forward, tugging at his gun, dragging the stale air into his lungs. Closer now, one of the men turned a sallow, surprised face to him, then rammed a struggling figure inside the van and jumped in with him. Ryan had only a second to see, but it was enough. They had taken Kevin Coulter. Another man followed, slamming the door shut after him.

A cloud of white spewed from the back as the driver started the engine. A large man burst from the passenger door, his arm raised, pointing a gun directly at Ryan. Dark overcoat flapping like wings behind him, he strode through the billowing exhaust like some avenging angel.

Ryan didn't expect it, the shot—even though—Jesus, he should have—but while attempting to dodge the inevitable, and before he could even raise his weapon, he felt something hit him like a splash of acid. His body burst with pain all over. He spun and crashed into a support pillar headfirst. Acid, then a brick to the head. He'd been shot—was he dying? Is this what it was like? No time to think. Tires shrieked. The engine roared as the van backed up, spun around, and hurtled toward him. The blazing headlights almost blinded him. As it skidded past, he rolled away and felt another bullet kick up the concrete beside him.

His head pounding and his arm throbbing like hell, pain coming and going with every heartbeat. He pulled himself up and leaned against the pillar. Blood soaked his jacket sleeve. He had been hit in the arm then. It galvanized him, the sight of his blood slowly seeping through like that, a heavy dark stain creeping down his left arm. He staggered towards the ramp, half shuffling, half running out to the street, his breath coming in shallow gasps.

He emerged into a dark, wet evening. Up ahead, brake lights flared at the corner. He hobbled across to his car, rain hitting him in the face. He slid in, grimacing with every movement, and took off fast along Queens Road, gritting his teeth and wiping his blood-soaked palm across his thigh. Adrenaline coursed through him, and he powered the big engine forward, emergency lights flashing blue into the darkness. Have to catch those guys, probably shouldn't be driving, but what the hell…up ahead, the same van, had to be. The wind had brought the rain slashing across the windows. He could barely see. One minute the van was there, then it was gone. The wipers on the old patrol car smeared the streetlights ahead into starbursts.

He grabbed the radio. "Dispatch–dispatch, come–in–come–in…."

A crackle in response, then, "Dispatch here."

"This is DS McBride," he yelled into the radio. "Shots fired, a dark-coloured van heading east on Queens Road from the Arc car park. At least four men inside, probably all armed, they have grabbed a witness, Kevin Coulter. I'm hit but am in pursuit. I…."

Something rocked the car. Hard. He felt the vehicle lurch sideways.

He lost control on the rain-slick road, and the vehicle drifted sideways in slow motion. *I'm on a merry-go-round,* he thought as the car pulled a graceful ninety-degree turn, then slammed into a concrete post with a sickening crunch. He hit the steering wheel, then felt himself tossed to the side against the passenger door. *Always fasten your seatbelt.* A little voice in his head lecturing him…*Erin?*

Everything went black.

He woke up in the Royal Victoria Hospital with Erin and Billy beside the bed. His arm was bandaged, and he felt pretty good.

"Finally." Erin leaned in and kissed his cheek. "Billy called me, said you have a mild concussion, but you were always such a big baby I thought I had better come and hold your hand.

Erin was paler than he was. He turned to Billy, who sat snacking on a packet of crisps.

"Listen Billy, they grabbed Kevin from his parking space. He'd arrived home, suitcase by his car. I've the van's description but no license plate or anything. How long have I been out?"

"About an hour and a half. It's only nine o'clock, but I think they gave you something in the ambulance. Our boys are all over the car park, and we're looking for the van. A couple of witnesses gave a description, but I'm not hopeful. They could have gone any which way and the cameras are next to useless, especially on a night like this. I doubt they would have risked the city center. Back streets probably, then onto the motorway." Billy shifted in his seat. "The bloody K&E lot are on it. They have an SIO there already. He's taken over. Asking lots of questions, answering nothing."

"Christ, kidnap and extortion already on it? That was fast."

"See, that's his flippin' father again, isn't it?" Billy tutted. "Adam Coulter, pulling strings."

"Bastards shot at me. I wonder what the doctor gave me? I feel pretty good."

"You only got hit by a ricochet, then you slammed your head, no actual bullet wound as such. You'll be fine."

"Jesus, it feels like they shot me." Ryan looked at Erin for support. She patted his hand.

"Yes, they missed," Billy said, finishing his crisps and tossing them towards the corner. "And the doctor said you have a nasty bump on your head. They did shoot at your car from their van with heavy-caliber bullets and took out the tyre, the first one did. An ambush likely. That's why you lost control. Not your rubbish driving this time."

"Oh, cheers for that, Billy. Who's the K&E senior officer by the way? Do we know him?"

"No. Some twat from Knock Road. They've taken over one of the larger interview areas as a Green Room. Oh, and they brought in their own computer whiz." Billy grinned. He picked up his coat. "I'm away then. Got some work to do on this. We have background on Coulter now. He's had some trouble with the ladies before. One girl even sued him."

Ryan threw off the sheets and sat on the side of the bed. He felt a bit light-headed.

"What came of that? Anything?"

"No." Billy put his overcoat on. "She ended up dead, killed in a hit and run."

"Seriously? That's got to be suspicious."

"Not so much at the time," Billy said. "They assumed it to be what it was; plus, according to the report, Kevin Coulter wasn't even in the country. Away on business with his dad."

"Not the best alibi, though."

"No, but it checks out. They did a thorough search at the time, immigration, everything. His alibi is solid." Billy headed for the door.

"Hang on, I'm coming too." Ryan started to get up.

Erin touched his arm. "You can't leave the hospital. Sit back down."

"No, I'm fine."

"Ryan, you've been shot. Oh, my God, don't you dare."

Billy held up his hand. "It's a flesh wound, Erin. Like I said, the bullet nicked him. A ricochet and not a direct hit. He bled a fair bit, but the doctor said he'd be okay. Are you okay, Ryan?"

"Look, I'm fine, and I'm heading out. Erin, love, thanks for coming. I don't want to stay here overnight. I want to get up to speed with Billy, then I'll go home, get Finn, and go to bed."

"I could come back with you if you like. Look after you."

"No, no, Erin, I'm fine. No need."

She nodded, forlorn. "All right."

They sat in the hospital car park for a few minutes, but there was nothing else they could do for the moment. It was late, and Ryan felt weary, frustration and sedatives churning inside him. "To tell you the truth, Billy, K&E can take this and run with it. I want to concentrate on the murder. They have the resources; I'll get Girvan to keep us up to date on their progress. Let's head to the station, and I'll pick up my car." He wanted to be home at his farm, by the fire with his dog.

"Are you sure you're good to drive? I can take you," Billy said. "I can send someone to pick you up tomorrow morning."

"No fear, I'm not leaving my own car in the compound overnight and me not there."

"But, don't you when you're on night shift?"

Ryan rolled his eyes, wished he hadn't. "Yes, but I'm there."

"What about when you're on a callout?" Billy persisted.

Ryan considered his options. It was irrational, and he knew it, but.... "That's different."

"Then I will take you back to your car, assuming it's still there, of course." Billy drove off at his usual stately pace, shaking his head.

Chapter Twenty-Three

Thursday, November 3

B illy had a bit of pink-tinged Kleenex stuck to his chin when Ryan rolled into the station the next morning.

"They're planning to kill him, or already have." Ryan sat down. Gingerly. "It has something to do with Kathleen's murder. Has to be that." He was in good shape, he knew that, but even with the running and boxing, he felt shaken up, a bit like he'd been dropped from a great height onto something soft. Or not soft.

"Yup." Billy nodded. "Someone knows more about Kathleen's death than we do. Oh, and Kevin's father is on his way over from London. Let's see how he behaves himself now."

Derek appeared and leaned on a chair. "Hey Billy, that's a nasty cut you've got there on your chin." He pointed to Billy's chin as though Billy perhaps didn't know where it was. "And Ryan, you got shot? I hear it's not too bad."

"Grazed by a ricochet and mild concussion," Billy added. Unsympathetically.

"Ahh, you're lucky. I'm a bit off myself, you know. I think I'm getting a cold. There's one doing the rounds." Derek gave a sad little cough, sniffed, and sat down. He started waving a sheaf of papers about.

Ryan bristled. Apart from fairly intense body pain, his head ached, and a dull pain gnawed at his arm. "I don't feel lucky, Derek, I don't. My head hurts like a bastard, and what, you need to lose an arm to get some sympathy around here? Or cut yourself shaving?" He should have let Erin come over and look after him after all. At least he would have had breakfast made for him and a bit of consideration. Christ's sake. Maybe if Billy hadn't been at the hospital, he would have let her, but....

"Can we get back to the cases? We're not shooting *Casualty,* you know." Billy was getting bored but had removed the bit of tissue from his chin.

"Oh, right then, lots to tell." Derek produced a sheet. "Calls from the phone handed in on the Kathleen McGuire thing, only three, nothing else on it. And from the rape case, no hits from fingerprint found on the lighter, and no DNA except the victim's. And..." He produced another sheet with a flourish. "The e-fit."

Both Billy and Ryan leaned in to see.

"Ah ha." Billy nodded.

"What?" Derek took another look. "What does that mean, ah ha?'"

Ryan flattened the e-fit out a little and pointed to it. "Recognize anyone?"

Derek picked it up and squinted. "You know, now you say that, it does look a bit like the barman at the Bellevue Arms."

"What? Give me that." Ryan snatched it from him.

Billy poked it with his finger. "Could it be anyone else, Derek?"

"It's a bit vague, isn't it? A guy with dark hair, glasses, and moustache. What's gotten into the pair of you? Do you know who it is?"

Ryan lowered his voice and said, "Might be Ed Wylie."

Derek laughed. "Wise up." He hesitated. "You're not serious? I hate the bastard too, but..." He stopped and picked up the sheet again. "I mean, it could be him, I suppose, without the glasses. Or anybody, even you, Ryan, come to that."

"Take another look." Ryan flattened the paper again.

"The girl is positive. That fingerprint belongs to our rapist. It's not Wylie's. We're all on file. You know that. You don't like him."

Derek was right, and Ryan did know it. Still, he couldn't shake the suspicion that Wylie was up to something. He had this look about him and a whole lot of attitude. Ryan couldn't put his finger on it.

"Has Maura seen this?" Ryan asked.

"Not yet."

He sighed. He would leave it for now. "Let me see the phone log then, and Derek, keep this Wylie thing to yourself."

"No worries. Wouldn't touch it with a barge pole unless you have proof."

Derek took off, and Ryan studied the phone log.

"Jesus, Billy, have a look at this."

He handed it over. "Two short calls to Rose and one to Sophie Walton."

"Sophie Walton." Billy paused. "She never mentioned a call on the morning of the murder."

"No, she didn't." Ryan took the paper back.

He called the gallery, and Angus told them Sophie was working from home. "I'm supposed to be in Dublin, but Sophie can't face the gallery right now. We're closed, but I'm doing paperwork. I know she's upset, but what about me? She's at home if you want to talk to her."

"She's at home," Ryan said to Billy. "Let's just show up."

They headed for the car, and Billy said he'd be a minute.

"You know where we're going?" Billy said when he got to the car, placing a briefcase on the floor behind him and pulling on his seatbelt.

"Yup, I put it in the Sat Nav while you were dicking about."

"I grabbed my lunch, Ryan. I don't know about you, but I get hungry at noon."

"Yeah, yeah."

Great. No arguing about who got to drive for once, and he could probably cadge a sandwich from Billy. He'd a feeling he was going to need it. Kathleen's call to Sophie had surprised him. He hadn't expected involvement there. The woman had appeared open and somewhat vulnerable to him. He wondered if he had missed the mark completely with her, if he was losing his touch. Something else struck him as they got closer to Sophie's house. He figured Billy was thinking the same thing. "We're not that far from the murder site."

"No, not at all."

"She has to live somewhere. Maybe it's a coincidence?" Ryan said.

"I hate them, coincidences," Billy answered.

The Sat Nav directed them to open gates leading up a gravel driveway bordered by mature trees and shrubs. At the end of the approach, an impressive home with a soft yellow brick exterior and arched windows came into view. Ryan liked it. The yellow colour gave the place a cheery feel even though the day had grown grey and chilly. Topiary trees in urns flanked the front door while an old vine twisted up the right side. Behind the main dwelling, they could see outbuildings with black slate roofs. The front of a bright red Jaguar peeked out behind the wall, and a white Range Rover sat further back in its shadow. An intermittent wind scattered leaves around their feet. Silent crows wheeled high above them. The smell of livestock hung faintly in the air.

"Nice piece of real estate, eh?" Billy whistled.

"Think of the cleaning, though," Ryan said, smiling as they approached the door.

Anthony Walton answered their knock and regarded them with a blank stare. What did it mean to open your door to the police and show no reaction? You'd think there'd be something. He ushered them into a grand hall painted deep blue. Glossy white woodwork set off dark oak floors. Walton called upstairs.

"Sophie, those detectives from the gallery are here to see you." He turned to them. "We have a lunch engagement, if you can keep it brief?" He left them standing there.

Sophie came down to meet them. She managed a tentative smile and gestured to a room on the left. "Through here." She wore a beige woolen dress that accentuated her figure and matching heels. She hugged herself as she walked.

They followed her to a conservatory off the hall. Light streamed through a high glass ceiling, arched floor-length windows, and French doors. It was chilly, though, and Ryan rubbed his hands together; his arm ached, the cold made it worse.

"Would you like some coffee or tea? I'll put the heat on. I'm sorry, it's not too warm in here." She smiled. "Anthony's had it with the cost of heating, so we freeze most of the time. What's this about? Any new developments?"

"A few questions, Ms. Walton. Don't worry about tea. Shall we sit down?" Ryan said.

When they were settled, Ryan took out his notebook, and Billy withdrew a sheet of paper from his briefcase and held it up. "Why did Kathleen phone you on the morning of her murder?"

"I'm sorry?" Sophie said.

"Kathleen's phone call. Why didn't you mention it?" Billy handed her the page. "Three calls. The one highlighted in yellow. That's your number, isn't it?" he said.

She studied it. Ryan watched her. The paper trembled. Was she thinking, or trying to fabricate a lie? He saw her face soften.

"I'm glad this has come up, I am. Yes, I did talk to Kathleen that morning. I'm sorry—I'm sorry. I didn't want to get involved in it more than I had to. Anthony hates fuss, publicity, that sort of thing." She held her hands up in a helpless gesture. "Don't think I haven't regretted not telling you, but the longer it went on, the harder it became. And really, it had nothing to do with her murder."

Ryan thought suddenly of his fleeting relationship with Kathleen. Had he not told himself exactly the same thing to justify his actions at the murder scene? His own lack of full disclosure.

"What did she want, Mrs. Walton?" Billy asked.

"I don't know. It was early Sunday morning. I had given Mummy her breakfast, I wasn't dressed, and my mother..." She stopped. "My mother can be difficult at times. I don't like to leave her alone for long. The carer doesn't work on Sundays, you see. Kathleen called and told me she had a flat tyre and could I come fetch her. Said she was driving through to see her sister." Sophie paused again. "I know I should have told you. I didn't want to get involved. Anthony is...he can be...anyway, I told her I couldn't. I had no way of getting to her, my own car had a flat tyre, a horseshoe nail, and I had a call into the Car Club. I told her to call them too. I mean, they could get there and fix the bloody tyre, simple. But she said she wasn't a member."

At this, Sophie got up and crossed to the fireplace. She paused for a moment with her back to them, looking into the empty grate. While he waited for her to continue, Ryan thought he caught a noise, a soft scuffle from the hall. Could that be Anthony, the overprotective husband, listening in? The big man unsettled him, to be honest, something about him. the way he had said 'those detectives'. Of course, Walton was also a lawyer by training. Ryan allowed himself a brief smile. Maybe that was it.

Finally, Sophie turned back to them. "I said okay, but she would have to wait until the Car Club arrived here. Then whatever time the mechanic took to fix the tyre. I also needed to dress and sort mum. I told her it would take about—what? About fifteen minutes for me to get there from here. That meant it would be at least an hour and a half before I could get to her. She says to me after all that, 'too long.' Too long? What else could I do? I had no option, you understand? I thought I heard something over the line, a car, maybe? I'm not sure. And she said, 'Don't worry about it,' and hung up. Just like that." Sophie paused, searching for words. "I've tortured myself thinking about that morning. But what could I have done? She said it was sorted."

Ryan snapped his notebook closed. "And you didn't think that was important? Someone may have come along and picked her up? It could have been the killer."

"No, I didn't. I told you I wasn't even sure I heard anything. And how could I have known this would happen?" Sophie turned away. "I'm so sorry."

"Did you know she was seeing Kevin Coulter?"

"Kevin? No." She paused. "Adam Coulter's son? They install our security."

"You'll have to come to the station to give a new statement. And this time, don't leave anything out. We'll decide what's relevant," Ryan said. God, what a hypocrite he was.

She paced. "Kathleen didn't come here, and I didn't leave—couldn't leave, I told you that."

"You had no other car?"

"My husband has a Range Rover, but he was down in Dublin with it. And my mother's car is at my brother's house for Jackie and Gillian to share until she recovers."

"So, no other transportation then?"

"No. I don't even have a bicycle. This happens from time to time, nails in the tyres. It's a farm."

"You'll have to come in and make your statement first thing tomorrow," Ryan said. "We need all this in writing." He was glad to get out of the freezing conservatory and Anthony Walton's persistent, lurking presence.

"She's got an answer for everything, that one." Billy gazed out of the passenger window. He had been quiet for the first bit of the journey, eating a sandwich.

"Do you think she's lying?" Ryan said, "because I think she's telling bits of the truth." Sophie was hard to pin down, like Mrs. Doyle. Too much ambiguity in all the answers. If both women were so upset at Kathleen's death, why weren't they more forthcoming? They were both guarding secrets, but still, what secrets could Sophie be holding? He thought back to Anthony Walton. Something about the man didn't sit right. And Sophie's face, that bruise. "Should we haul her husband in for an interview? Sophie said Anthony barely knew Kathleen, and she didn't know about Kevin and Kathleen."

"Can we believe her?" Billy said. "Hey, Ryan, maybe she liked her handsome security consultant a bit too much? Jealousy's a powerful motivator. Did you think of that? She wanted Kevin for herself."

Ryan remembered her in the gallery that first day. He'd thought her attractive, charming. She'd been different today.

"And we didn't tell her about Kevin's abduction," Billy added.

"We'll tell her when she makes her new statement," Ryan said. "There's an outside chance Kevin might show up by then. Although I doubt it. I'd like to see how she behaves without her husband loitering nearby. Funny though, she knows Kevin's family, and the father doesn't even tell her his son's been kidnapped."

"Yes, and quite the coincidence, her car being out of commission on that morning," Billy said, rummaging around in his briefcase.

"I'll get Maura to follow up on that, check with the Car Club, and what were you saying about coincidences, Billy?"

CHAPTER TWENTY-THREE

"I hate them," Billy said and bit down on sandwich number two.

Some partner, Ryan thought. Gives me no sympathy and no sandwiches.

Chapter Twenty-Four

Thursday, November 3

At home that evening, Ryan put the kettle on, grabbed the phone, and dialed the gym.

"Hey, Abbott, what are you up to tonight? Let's go have a beer. I'm in no fit state to work out."

They settled on the Bellevue Arms. Abbott had not been there before.

"Does it have good beer?"

"Yes," Ryan replied patiently.

"Curry?"

"Yes, Abbott—probably."

"Not too fancy?"

"Eh, no."

Satisfied, Abbott said he'd meet Ryan at seven.

"Get over yourself. It's not that bad." Ryan signalled a waitress over Abbott's shoulder and ordered their drinks. He might have fibbed about the décor. It had been renovated, was a bit posh, but he liked it, liked the food and the crowd. They sat in a mustard-coloured banquette by the bar, exposed brick on the walls and mood lighting. Nothing wrong with going a bit up-market once in a while.

He told Abbott about his injury, why he couldn't box. Most people would have been impressed at his heroics, Ryan thought, but Abbott took it in stride.

"Sounds like that Kevin fella's not coming home, eh?" he said. "He'll be dead already. You were lucky."

"Yes, everyone tells me how lucky I am." Ryan took a swig of beer. "It's got something to do with Kathleen." He rotated his shoulder and winced. "Let's order. I'm starving."

"I don't see any curry," Abbott said, flipping through the menu.

"Oh Christ, shut it." Ryan signalled the waitress again.

Ryan's mobile rang as the food arrived. Erin calling.

"I'm about to eat, love. Can I call you later?"

"I had a drink with Paul, and you were right, he wants money, and we had a terrible argument outside the bar, and when I said no, he grabbed me and threatened me." She took a rasping breath. "It was terrible, Ryan, I ran to my car, and he followed me home. He's outside. He keeps phoning the house." He heard a muffled sob. "He's drunk. I never told you that sometimes he could be like this when we argued." She paused for a moment. "I know what you're like." Another pause. "Can you come over? Maybe if he sees your car. I know you frighten him."

Ryan explained to Abbott in the car park, and they made a plan with the sounds of the motorway heading into Belfast echoing loud from under the bridge as they spoke, the car headlights streaming away below them. Ryan, enraged, could barely get the words out.

"No, no, not you," Abbott said. "Let me. You're in no condition. You can barely move your arm. I'll talk to him, reason with him. He doesn't know me, no blowback, right?"

"A warning then," Ryan said.

Abbott did not like men hurting women.

"Right, you go in the back when we get there, don't let him see you. Leave it to me. Go on, I have the address now." Abbott turned and hurried to his car.

On his way to Erin's, Ryan called her, finally got through. "I'll be there in

163

ten, less. Are you okay?"

"Yes, but he's still outside."

"I'll come in the back. Keep the doors locked. I have my key. It'll be fine."

But would it? He'd seen what Abbott could do when he was riled up. He hoped Crawford kept his mouth shut and left quietly.

Paul Crawford's Porsche idled opposite Erin's place. Ryan had left his car a few streets away and walked up a neighbour's driveway. He slipped gingerly over a fence and jogged up to Erin's back door.

He let himself in. She sat in the kitchen, crying softly.

"C'mon, love." He pulled another chair over and hugged her with his good arm.

"Don't say I told you so, don't frigging say it." She sniffed. He got up and tore some kitchen roll for her. She blew her nose, then held up her arm for him to see. A slight yellowing circled her wrist. "That bastard. Oh, Ryan, what am I going to do?"

A sharp rap on the front door made her jump. "Oh, God!"

"No, that'll be my buddy. He had a word with Paul for you. Hang on."

Ryan met Abbott at the front door and motioned him to the kitchen. "Is it sorted?"

"Yes," Abbott said.

"Erin, this is Abbott."

"Hello." She reached for his hand and took it. Shaking it lightly. "You're Ryan's Special Forces friend?"

Only Ryan noticed Abbott's slight wince at the handshake. Crawford didn't just get a warning, then.

"I am, and I'm pleased to meet you," Abbott replied.

Erin wiped at her face and smiled. "I'm a mess. Give me a minute. There's beer in the fridge, or Ryan, make Abbott some coffee, for goodness sake. I'll be right back."

Abbott grinned at Ryan.

"What?" Ryan knew, of course.

"She's quite lovely. Isn't she?"

164

"Abbott..." Ryan turned to the coffee maker.

"Just a casual observation," Abbott said as he checked out the fridge.

"Here I am." Erin bustled back to the kitchen, energized, makeup reapplied. "Now, I know you two didn't have time to eat your dinner. Why don't I heat up a nice curry?"

Chapter Twenty-Five

Thursday, October 20

BEFORE

"Oh my God, Brendan, it's beautiful here." Kathleen had followed Brendan's Range Rover in her car. She'd parked and now stood in front of a stunning home set in manicured grounds.

"Aye, it's nice, isn't it?" Brendan said, smiling.

Kathleen had expected a farm. But Brendan and his wife Kelly lived in a lovely old place set away from the road. Stone-fronted and ivied, it had a Georgian feel to it, more like an exclusive country hotel or a stately home. She headed inside behind Brendan, who supported his mother up the front step. A smiling woman of about fifty or so came from the back of the hall to greet them. Sturdy, with a fair-skinned, country face and pink cheeks, she wiped her hands on a frilly apron. Grey hair, with some blond strands still in it, fell straight down below her ears in a heavy blunt cut.

"Mary, how are you feeling?"

"Kelly, I'm fine, dear, don't fuss."

"I'll have Donny get your bags sorted. And this must be Kathleen?"

"Yes." Kathleen extended her hand.

"Nice to finally meet you," Kelly said. "Mary's told us all about you. Right, Brendan?"

"Right, love, she has. I'm going to take Mammy up and get her settled."

"I'll put the kettle on. Mary, I've a barmbrack in, nice and fresh."

"Lovely. Well buttered, mind."

As Brendan helped his mother up the stairs, Kathleen hesitated in the impressive wood-paneled foyer, not sure what to do.

"Come on into the kitchen with me." Kelly headed down the hall.

"But my bags?"

"Oh, don't worry. Our wee Donny will sort all that. Come on. You can tell me all about this carry-on."

Kelly bustled about in her kitchen, all stainless steel, marble countertops, and sleek wooden cabinets. It smelled good and reminded Kathleen of something, maybe sitting with Rose in the kitchen in Derry when they were young, their mum making fairy cakes. The girls were allowed to ice a few each week and sprinkle them with hundreds and thousands—that was the best part. Although, being with her mum and Rose, it had all been the best part, if only she'd realised it then.

"Let me get this ready for Mary. She's a fusspot that one, but the boys dote on her." Kelly paused. "She's been through a lot, you know. Did she tell you?"

"A little bit, but she's a private person. Got my life story the first day, though."

"Aye, she told me. Sorry about your mam and dad. That's a desperate blow for young girls. But at least you have your sister. Isn't that a blessing?"

"It's just that Rose works abroad a lot, so we haven't been as close as we should be. I'm going to change that, though. She'll be back shortly, and we're going to have a real talk." She pulled out a chair and sat down. This whole experience with Kevin had been a nightmare.

"Kelly, everything is mixed up. I've been stupid, you know? I let myself be manipulated. I ignored my sister and put Mary in danger."

Kelly sat down across from her and reached for her hand.

"Brendan told me a bit about what happened to you. That bastard Coulter. Brendan's dad was abusive too. Back then, nobody took any notice if a husband beat the hell out of his wife and kids. It was family business. Their father was a brute." She put a pot of tea on a tray and the slices of loaf beside it. "You don't need to worry about Kevin Coulter anymore. It doesn't matter what he does or who he knows. Nobody touches Mary and gets away with it." She looked directly at Kathleen. "Brendan will keep you safe. No matter what he has to do. That's why the police won't be involved. Brendan and his mam will have nothing to do with them. They never helped Mary when she was being beaten half to death by old Mr. Doyle, and then they come to Brendan with accusations after the bastard was killed. No, we'll have nothing to do with the police in this house. Fair enough?"

Kathleen hesitated. "Yes. If you think so."

"I do." She lifted the tray. "I'll be right back. Then I'll bring you upstairs and show you your room."

Sitting in the conservatory the next morning, Kathleen sipped her tea and crunched through her toast. She had just reached for another slice when Brendan bustled in. He had a mug of coffee in his hand, and he sat across from her.

"Right, love, a couple of things. Yer man is a hard case. I've checked him out."

Kathleen stiffened. "I told you."

"Now, don't worry. It's good to know who you're up against, right?"

"Yes, but…"

"So, I'm going to give you a few pointers on how to defend yourself, should it ever come to that."

"Oh, Brendan, thanks and all, but it won't. I'm going to leave the gallery and never see him again." She thought back to Annabelle, how confident the young woman had been, and that punch. "Although, maybe boxing? Anywhere I could go in Comber? A YMCA?" She fancied boxing now, wished she'd been the one to punch that bastard in the face.

Brendan shook his head and reached behind him. He pulled a gun out from under his sweater.

"Oh, fuck, Brendan! What?" She closed her eyes. How had it come to this?

"Don't worry, the safety is on." Brendan didn't seem to care about her disquiet. He scowled at her. "And you've a terrible mouth on you, you know that? Talk like that in front of Mammy, and you'll get a thick ear."

"Look, I don't normally swear. I'm sorry. But I don't care if the safety is on. It's a bloody gun. No way am I carrying a gun. I wouldn't even know how to hold it." She thought back briefly to the night of Kevin's attack, her feelings then. That slam of hatred.

"I'll teach you."

"No." Was the man crazy?

"It's a precaution, till I sort this out. Mammy insists."

"What, Mary told you to give me a gun? Come on." The idea of Mary Doyle, that wee lady, telling Brendan to give her…a gun. What was that old saying? *If you didn't laugh, you'd cry?* It was all so ridiculous.

"Mammy told me to give you this Browning 9mm and teach you to use it."

"Oh, right, Brendan. Now I know you're joking."

But he wasn't.

It was a real gun. The thing had a recoil, but she started to get the hang of it. They practiced behind the garage, aiming at a few tree stumps with paper targets stuck to them.

"That's right, look down there. It's a three-dot sight, you can't miss."

She missed, a lot, but it wasn't as bad as she thought.

"Keep it with you for a while. After you get the feel of it, we'll keep it cocked and locked, and I'll show you how to turn the safety off quickly if you need to, either side, right or left."

"Yes, but Brendan…"

"No buts, it's simple. It won't fire unless you release the safety, and even if you do, the chances of you hitting anything are fairly slim to none. Think of it as a deterrent only. Kathleen, I promised Mammy."

Kathleen smiled at the big man. "You are so full of shit, Brendan."

"Aye, well, there's that mouth again. Lunch, I think. You hungry?"

Mary had taken her lunch upstairs, and Kathleen popped in to see her after she'd finished helping Kelly with the dishes. Sunlight streamed into the room; a stiff breeze moved the curtains.

"Do you want this closed?" She crossed to the window and looked out at the garden. October had taken its toll on the flower beds, decay setting in, but the brown and ochre landscape was beautiful. Kathleen wondered why Mary didn't stay here all the time. Personally, she would have jumped at the chance. Why remain alone in her flat in Belfast?

"It's lovely here. You didn't tell me Brendan's rich." Kathleen had to ask. "How come you're living in that house in Belfast and still working as a manager?"

"Oh, I like it there. And it's my house. I own it."

"You own that house?"

"Aye, and a couple more."

The Doyles were full of surprises.

"You're a crafty one, aren't you? Why do you even bother renting it out?"

"I like the company, and I wouldn't have met you, would I? Did I hear you shooting earlier?"

"Oh yes, at targets. It's fun, even though I can't believe I said that. I'm a terrible shot. And Mary," Kathleen laughed, "Brendan said you told him to give me the gun." She suddenly saw Mary Doyle, perm in place, swaggering over to the seafood counter at the local Asda with her gun. *This fish is off!* She was officially going mad.

"I told Brendan to give you the Browning, and I'm telling you to keep it with you."

"Come on, Mary, you told him that? How do you even know what a Browning is?"

"Never you mind, I'm asking you to carry it until we sort yer man out. I won't have him coming after you again."

"But I can't ask Brendan to put himself in danger for me. I should go to the police. I understand you don't want to involve them, but sometimes you have to."

"No, no police. And Kathleen, don't you worry about Brendan, you hear me? I'd worry more about Kevin Coulter if I were you."

The steel in Mary's voice surprised Kathleen. She dropped the subject.

After dinner, when they were sitting around the fire, Brendan handed Kathleen a phone.

"Use this from now on if you need to call anyone but don't, for the love of God, call your boyfriend."

"No worries on that, Brendan, but my sister is coming home on Saturday, and I want to go see her. She lives in Derry."

"Does Kevin Coulter know where she lives?"

"Probably, I did mention she lives there. He knows her name."

"If I can't talk you out of seeing her, then meet her somewhere else."

"I'll call her when she gets in on Saturday."

"You do that. And Kathleen? Tell her to be watchful. I meant what I said earlier about this man and the company his father owns. He has resources. I want to have a wee talk to him first. Resolve this."

"Promise me you'll be careful."

Brendan smiled at her, and despite the warm room, Kathleen felt a chill. Brendan Doyle, at his mother's request, had rescued her, taken her under his wing, and taught her to shoot for God's sake. And Kevin, Kevin had not frightened him, had not even ruffled this big man's feathers. Brendan knew what he was up against, yes, he did. Knew about the violence, the guns—and yet here he sat, calm as anything, stoking the fire and trying to persuade his wife to make him a cup of tea. What was with this family? She loved Mary Doyle. And Brendan and Kelly had taken her under their wing and vowed to protect her, and somehow she knew they could and would. She thought back to Mary's warning.

'I'd worry more about Kevin Coulter than Brendan if I were you.'

Chapter Twenty-Six

Friday, November 4

Sophie Walton appeared at the station early and sat quietly while Ryan and Billy went through Kathleen's last phone call in detail. When they were done, and she'd retrieved her coat, Ryan said casually. "Did you know Kevin Coulter is missing?"

"What?" She glanced at Ryan and Billy, shook her head sharply. "He travels for the business all the time."

"No, Ms. Walton. He was grabbed Wednesday night, and I suspect someone thinks he might be involved in Kathleen McGuire's death."

She fell back into her seat. "Could I get some water?"

Billy took off, and Ryan sat across from her. She was ashen.

"Is Kevin Coulter more than a friend to you?"

She looked up, shocked.

But was it, Ryan wondered, because she found the suggestion outrageous? Or because he had uncovered the truth?

"I'm upset for the family. Kevin missing. Can't I be upset if a friend's in danger? And I don't believe he's involved in Kathleen's murder. That's insane. Anthony and I have known the family for years."

God, she was difficult to read. She's used to this, Ryan thought. Used to keeping her emotions hidden.

"We're investigating his relationship with Kathleen, and suddenly he's violently abducted. Whether we believe he's involved or not is irrelevant if we can't find him. Especially if the people who have him believe he killed her."

Billy came back with the water, and she sipped it. Her hands were shaking.

"Look, I have to go. I'm sorry. My husband's downstairs. We must call Adam."

"You'll be contacted by the Kidnap and Extortion team. They have the lead on this," Ryan said.

"Yes, yes, anything I can do. Anything." She handed her glass to Billy, lifted her handbag, and left.

Ryan watched her go. "She took that hard. Any word from our illustrious kidnap team yet? They're putting out an appeal on the lunchtime news, right?"

Billy nodded. "According to Girvan, nothing on the van yet. No trace at the snatch site, no demand from the kidnappers. His mobile left in the Mercedes, charging, so no joy there. It's a business phone, seems like, he may have another, but we've no idea of the number. But that's not what this is about, is it? Searched his flat, nothing incriminating there. Clean as a whistle. Serviced once a week."

"No cameras in the whole damn car park?"

"Nope, some sort of malfunction." Billy consulted a thin file on the desk.

Ryan thought back to that electrical panel and the wire in the stairwell. That problem the janitor complained about. He'd already sent a team down to the Arc, to hell with the kidnap guys, had them ask around. Cameras had been affected by the outage, and nobody saw anything.

"Do you think there's a chance at all Kevin's abduction is unrelated to Kathleen's murder?"

"No, I do not," Billy said. "Although there's an outside chance it's something to do with their security business, right?

"I can't see it, Billy. Let's assume it has nothing to do with Kevin's business; who else could pull this off?"

They spoke at the same time.

"The Doyles."

"Mrs. Doyle had to know about Kevin. She was close to Kathleen, closer than she's letting on. I don't know why she's lying. You'd think she would want to find the killer. She's got to be hiding something, and if we're right about the Doyles grabbing Kevin, we're in a difficult situation. We have no proof."

"You should get that to the K&E team then, save some time," Billy said. "Fill them in on Doyle. I know you're pissed at them taking over, but it's procedure. Nothing we can do about it."

Ryan, even though he had professed otherwise, was pissed, and Billy knew it. A bunch of guys from downtown strutting around, insinuating themselves into the inquiry—his inquiry. "Yeah, I'll get this to them. I haven't had a minute."

One of the other detectives stuck his head in. "You two finished in here? I need the room. Bloody K&E jerks took the main interview suite." He left, muttering.

A little later, Ryan rattled the main interview room's door. It was locked. He was about to knock when a swarthy detective wrenched it open.

"Help ya?" Shaved head and heavy black glasses, his eyes red-rimmed and moist behind them. Belligerence in the tone. Trimmed beard, neat, about five seven.

"Ah, yes, can I speak to the SIO?"

"And you are?" The man said this carelessly, glancing over Ryan's shoulder, as if he really didn't want to know.

"DS Ryan McBride. I'm SIO on the Kathleen McGuire murder."

"DCI Tiller." The man rubbed a meaty hand over his scalp. Ryan could hear the bristles. "So, yeah?" Tiller asked again.

Ryan glanced behind the DCI, saw the room had been set up. A young woman sat in front of a couple of large computer screens. A whiteboard hung at the end of the space. Nothing on it yet. A few detectives huddled around a desk near the back.

Tiller moved forward, blocking Ryan's view. "We're busy. What is it you want?"

What the hell? "I want to brief you on the McGuire case. It's connected with yours. Kevin and Kathleen were an item."

Tiller moved forward again, crowding Ryan. "Look, McBride. Thanks and all, but we've got this. We've been briefed by Girvan, had a long call with Adam Coulter, and will be interviewing him in depth later today. We like to take a wider view, know what I mean? Adam Coulter has serious security connections making him a target. We can't discount that. We're looking at all the angles. It's what we do."

Did he say that? We're looking at all the angles? "Look, DCI Tiller," Ryan said, trying to be patient. "I don't believe this has anything to do with Adam Coulter or his background. Have you been briefed on Brendan Doyle?"

"Girvan sent over your past notes. I have the gist. Shoot me the rest. I'll read them. We'll take it from here. I have your statement; you witnessed the lift. We'll need to talk to you—but later. I have your report. We work with digital information and technology. May there," he nodded behind him, "she'll sort everything." Tiller stepped back smartly and closed the door. Ryan was left in the corridor with a waft of stale sweat and aftershave.

He legged it back to the squad room, royally pissed off. Billy sympathized but in the end, had he expected anything else? No.

Maura arrived shortly after. "I got the rapist's e-fit. Now we'll see if there's a response at the bars. That was a good idea, Ryan. I've asked Sam to drop them off."

It was a long shot, but sometimes these things paid off. Maura made no reference to Wylie and the e-fit. Could he be that blinded by dislike? Yup, certainly he could.

"How's it going with you guys on the murder?" she asked.

"Not well," Ryan said.

She pulled up a chair, and they filled her in.

"People are lying to us. Little lies, you know? But it's muddying the water."

"I think it's odd she had so few friends," Maura said. "You would think a nice girl like that would be popular."

"And," Billy said, "nobody knew about Kevin. Nobody."

"So they claim."

"And why keep him a secret?" Maura said.

"A business thing, perhaps? He had that issue in the past when he dated a woman he met through work." Ryan finished his coffee and threw the cup away. "When's his dad due in for the interview?"

"Eleven," Billy said. "We get him before the K&E boys. Maybe we'll find out more then."

The eleven o'clock meeting did not go well. Billy and Ryan learned before they entered the interview room that Coulter had insisted Inspector Girvan be present. For the first few minutes, they sat there as their inspector, red-faced with anger at the unexpected summons, quickly brought Coulter up to date on the investigation. When he had finished his basic overview, he stood, adjusted his cap and jacket, and pointed to Ryan and Billy.

"My detectives will fill you in on the remaining details, Mr. Coulter. They are running a parallel case, and McBride here was present at the kidnapping. I have to get back to work. Anything else regarding the progress of your son's disappearance, the Kidnap and Extortion team will connect with you. Now, if you will excuse me?" Girvan delivered all this in such a tone that Ryan and Billy winced and Coulter's mouth formed a thin line.

With Girvan gone Coulter got right back to it with the attitude. "My son's been snatched from a car park right under your noses. Tell me again, where are we in this investigation?"

A physically formidable man, Coulter was over six feet tall and solidly built. He dominated the small interview room. Kevin's father was a handsome, imposing man and really getting on Ryan's nerves. K&E had sent over up-to-date files, and Ryan opened the folder.

"Your son was taken Wednesday night. The car park has been searched, his car, and his apartment. Constables from the kidnap team have spent hours on CCTV trying to find the van. They have spoken to the building manager and as many residents as possible to see if anyone knew Kevin or saw or heard anything. A public appeal for help has been launched." He paused. "We need a list of his friends and colleagues from you, sir. There may be other motives we're not aware of."

Coulter snapped back, "You think he had something to do with that girl's

176

murder? That's why I'm here talking to you? This is ridiculous."

"Her name is Kathleen McGuire," Ryan said. "And it's not ridiculous. What we want to know from you is what other reason could there be for him to be snatched like this? We're finding it hard to build a picture of him. He doesn't appear to have friends. You're our only source, unless his mother can help?"

"Olivia and I are separated. We haven't been in touch for years. She won't care, believe me."

Billy took over. "Gambling debts? Drugs? Anything like that?"

Coulter leapt up, almost knocking his chair over. "Oh, for God's sake. No. This is all mad. It must be a random thing, for money. It has to be. Or me, someone targeting me." He remained there agitated, bristling.

"Kevin's had problems in the past, hasn't he? Anger issues. He was being sued at one point." Billy pressed.

"That's nonsense too. Money, again."

"But that went away, didn't it?" Billy said. "Pretty convenient for Kevin."

"The woman died in a hit and run. My son was with me, and we weren't even in the country at the time. Believe what you want—you will anyway."

After Coulter left, threatening to take the investigation private and trailing an atmosphere of outrage and indignation behind him, Billy and Ryan went back to their desks.

Billy nodded towards Girvan's office. "How did Coulter get him in the meeting?"

"Contacts Billy. Golf buddies or something like that. I don't know."

"Hiya." Derek appeared and sat sideways between the desks. He took out his own packet of sandwiches and started to examine them.

"How did the meeting with old man Coulter go?"

"Not good. Girvan came in for a couple of minutes," Billy said.

"What? How come?"

"We were speculating on Coulter's contacts. Maybe some golfing buddies at the top?"

"Oh no," Derek said. "Nothing to do with golf. I was going to tell you after I got my tea. It's part of that background check you asked for. Coulter has friends in high places because he used to work for the old Royal Ulster Constabulary in a civilian capacity. He was in the British army, too, when he was young, Special Forces. He's got quite the background. Lived all over." Derek paused for effect. "Some of it's redacted."

Billy whistled. "I, for one, am glad I didn't piss him off. Think you did, though." He grinned at Ryan.

"There's an outside possibility here that Adam Coulter's background, something lurking in the past perhaps, might be at the root of this," Ryan said. "What if one of the contractors Adam Coulter employed, or someone he's pissed off in the past, has decided to take revenge for something?"

"What? Might have grabbed his son, something like that?" Billy said. "It's not impossible, but Kathleen? Liam? No, it has to have something to do with Kathleen." He pointed at Derek. "Can you dig a little deeper?"

"Yes, I'll go even further into Kevin's background. See if other girlfriends have ended up dead. It'll take time, though. I'll have to check across the water and in the EU database. See if there's an accident or suicide, something like that. I'll do my best."

"Right." Ryan sat back in his chair, shook his head. "What we're looking for are mysterious disappearances, missing women connected to him." Ryan paused, frowned, then added, "Or his father."

Chapter Twenty-Seven

Friday, November 4

"It will have to be on his terms, if he agrees to see you at all."

Girvan had nixed Ryan's request to officially interview Brendan Doyle. The chief worried about consequences. Doyle, regardless of his background, had never been convicted of anything and appeared to carry a lot of clout. Ryan and Billy sat in Girvan's corner office, the afternoon sun fugitive behind grey clouds and grime-smeared windows. He had called them in for an update and beckoned Maura too.

"It's frustrating, sir," Ryan explained. "Kevin has to be the top pick for Kathleen's murder. I also think Mrs. Doyle is holding something back. We know Brendan Doyle has the resources, but no reason to hurt Kathleen. The Doyles may have suspected Kevin of Kathleen's murder and picked him up to question him. We need to talk to Brendan Doyle, if only to clear him. And then there's Sophie Walton. She didn't tell us about her phone call from Kathleen that last morning. And Adam Coulter. He has the background, but no reason we can think of to kill Kathleen McGuire, unless she threatened Kevin in some way." He checked his notebook. "Adam Coulter wasn't in the country at that time as far as we know, but he could have had it done."

"It seems to me, then, you have more questions than answers on this one." Girvan swung around in his chair. He stopped with his back to them. Outside his window, treetops thrashed back and forth against a gunmetal sky. A brisk wind picked up again, and the sun had finally given up and left for the day. Girvan turned back.

"What's the plan?"

Billy flipped his notebook open. "We're looking at Ms. Walton's background in more depth, same with Kevin, his father, and the Doyles. We're waiting for results from forensics on the paint from Kevin Coulter's Mercedes to confirm he made contact with Liam's bike. That's due shortly."

"Kevin Coulter caused the ex-boyfriend's death?"

"Yes, sir," Ryan answered. "It's likely. His car showed evidence of a recent altercation at the front. We have it at the police garage."

"Make sure you get that to DCI Tiller. And, on another topic, because we need to solve some crimes here, what about these rapes, Maura? I suppose we're no closer to a result?"

"We have moved forward a little. We have an e-fit, a possible fingerprint, and a shirt which bore a distinctive logo."

"Oh yes?" Girvan sat up.

Maura glanced at Ryan and Billy. "We're working on identifying it, sir, some possibilities. We'll let you know as soon as we come up with a solid lead."

"This e-fit, is it out there yet?"

"Yes, sir, we are circulating it widely to restaurants and bars in the area the suspect is known to frequent."

Back at their desks, Billy caught up on some phone calls and asked Derek to come down.

Ryan had a message from Abbott. He called him back. "What's up?"

"Ryan, can you come to the club tonight? We could discuss Dorothy's situation, and Bernie wants to have a listen in."

"Dorothy's situation? Why, has something happened?"

"No," Abbott said.

"Oh. I see." Ryan hesitated. "You want something to happen."

"Yes," Abbott said.

Ryan sighed. "Eight o'clock?"

"Yes," Abbott said and hung up.

Maura arrived then with a coffee, and Derek trailing right behind.

"Anything usable on Kevin Coulter yet, Derek?" Billy asked.

"No. I've questions in to different police departments in London and Interpol. We should have something back by Monday. They take the weekend seriously over there."

"That computer person, with K&E, I expect she'll be checking Kevin's background too?" Ryan asked, dreading Derek's response. But no, all was good.

"Oh yes, May. It's fine now I know who they're using. I trained her. She'll pass anything relevant to me. No worries there." Derek picked at something on his sweater. "All sorted."

Ryan turned to Maura. "Look, about that logo. On the golf shirt."

"Oh, the Police Service of Northern Ireland logo?"

"You know," Billy said.

"Yes, of course, I know, but I didn't want to be the one to suggest to Girvan a police officer is the rapist. That would make his day." She snorted. Unbecoming.

"And the e-fit?"

"Don't even say it. We need some concrete proof. Can you imagine?"

Ryan glanced at Billy for support. "So, Maura, you think...what?"

Maura shook her head at them. "For God's sake. I can guess what you think, Ryan, it could be Wylie. But then most of the officers we know fit that damn description. This guy could be wearing a wig and glasses. It could be anyone, but then there's that thing with me, right?"

Ryan slapped the desk. It wasn't him being an ass. It could be Wylie. It could be.

"And there's another thing. It's important, something from Janice." Maura added, checking over her shoulder.

"What?" Ryan asked. Derek sat on Billy's desk.

"Don't repeat it because she told me in confidence, but apparently, some of the officers who were transferred from Musgrave may have been involved in the disappearance of evidence from the lockup down there. No names, but still...now, nothing's been proved. Official line is an intake error, but guys, it was Rohypnol, among other things."

"Maura," Ryan said. "You have the dates of all the rapes. Let's start by comparing Wylie's days off to that schedule. I mean, if he was working, that pretty much clears him, right?"

"But the fingerprints, the DNA?" Derek added. "What about that?"

"Who would Malcolm have asked to send it out for analysis. I'm thinking...."

"My goodness, yes. Wylie?" Maura gasped and punched Ryan's arm. "Why don't you ask Malcolm who sent it out?"

"He'd think I was checking up on him. It's not my case. Why don't you?"

"Same reason, I suppose. Why would I want to know who sent it?"

They all looked down towards the back corner in time to see Sam weaving through desks laden with a cardboard tray of coffees and store-bought sandwiches. He saw them watching as he manoeuvred around a couple of obstacles, smiled, and lifted his hand in greeting to Maura.

"Who is that guy?" Derek asked. "I think he's a spy from the Musgrave group. He was up on our floor with a software analyst. I don't like the look of him. D'you know what? He offered to refile all the computer software manuals upstairs. Now, I will admit I have them filed to my own system, but all anyone has to do is ask me, and I'll find what they need. He'll mess it all up." Then he added, "Tool."

"You mean anyone who needs to find anything in those manuals has to ask you?" Maura shook her head at Derek and turned to Ryan. "No, I can't ask Sam to."

"Come on. Tell him to be casual about it. If Wylie did send it, and he's involved, it's a dead end. He'll have done something to it. What's the harm? He can inquire. He's part of their team."

Maura sighed. "Wylie's guys are odd. They mostly keep to themselves you know? If they think he's spying on them...."

"I don't want to cause him trouble. Use your best judgement then." Maura was always worrying about something.

"Now, there's one thing that bothers me about Kevin's abduction," Ryan continued. "How did they know when he got home?"

182

CHAPTER TWENTY-SEVEN

"Perhaps they were watching the Arc car park," Billy said.

"From inside?" Maura asked.

"But that would mean the van sat there for days, and no one noticed it."

"What about somewhere outside?" Derek stood. "I could have one of the guys take another look at the CCTV during the days before."

"Or," Ryan motioned for Derek to sit again, and continued, "maybe they already knew when he was arriving."

"But." Maura shook her head. "How could they? We weren't even sure until his dad told us."

"What if the kidnappers had inside knowledge? He came into an airport. George Best is closest to the Arc. Let's say he left his car there, long-term parking. Easy to drive to, fly out and pick it up when he came home. Had to book the spot and tell them how long. Or let them know roughly when he would pick it up. Apparently, he travels a lot. Might have been a regular, have a contract?"

"Someone in parking then? Or maybe at the airline?" Billy said.

Maura jotted something in her notebook. "I'll see if I can get an employee list from them, long-term at George Best Airport. It's somewhere to start. We can check Belfast International Airport afterwards. And I'll see if I can have a look at their pre-booked contracts, if they give out monthly passes etc." She stopped. "Are we sharing this, Ryan? With K&E?"

"Of course, if anything important comes of it. Not until. We don't want to waste their time."

"Right." Billy winked at Ryan.

Ryan left as twilight fell over the car park. Frustrated at the lack of progress, he could do nothing until the rest of the information came in, probably on Monday. He wanted a rest, he still ached, and his arm hurt. He decided to go in Saturday morning, get some paperwork done. Bridget was coming over after her late shift tomorrow night. They were going to make plans, talk about the future. She would move in with him when the news was out. Strange that he thought of the baby now with a mixture of fear and excitement. His child was growing inside Bridget's belly. He unlocked the car, threw his jacket in the back, and got in. He laid his head back, closed his eyes, and thought of Rose.

The car was cold. Almost half seven, and already getting dark. Floodlights illuminated the barrack's car park in a searing, sodium glare and caught raindrops as they fell on his windscreen, hundreds of diamonds. He started the engine, and a scattering of tiny dead leaves blew across in front of his headlights like confetti. He turned on Van Morrison and headed to meet Abbott.

Bernie, short for Bernadette, owned the Boxer Boxing Club. She was a short, stout woman with a square face, an iron-grey bob, and a permanently pissed-off expression. Bernie and her husband Andy had bought the rundown social-club building with Andy's winnings on the Bantamweight circuit, where Bernie had been a cigarette girl. Ryan had occasionally, and unsuccessfully, tried to picture a young Bernie in high heels, fishnet stockings, and lipstick, selling cigarettes to punters while wobbling up and down the aisles at the boxing venues. She must have made an impression, though, because Andy and Bernie were married within a year of meeting and quickly produced a couple of daughters, Shannon and Tara. They had a happy marriage, both of them involved in the club, Bernie even training with Andy sometimes, and their daughters getting involved. A real family business, until lung cancer took Andy at sixty. Their daughters, who had become gym teachers, had recently started a women-only Boxercise class in the back room—much to Abbott's dismay, although in the end, it was proving successful.

"It's a good thing, I suppose," was all Abbott would say about the gaggle of teenage girls and young women who arrived on Tuesday and Thursday nights to train.

"Do you boys want anything to drink?" Bernie had arrived with a big mug of coffee.

"Eh, no thanks, Bernie, I'm good." Ryan had tasted Bernie's coffee.

She stared at them. Scowling. "I phoned Dorothy's daughter this morning and had a quick word. I said her mum's been a bit depressed lately, and had she noticed? No, she hadn't, she said, because she'd not been over to the house for ages, doesn't get on with her da apparently. Left home in her teens...she sounded upset."

"You didn't mention the bruises, did you? We can't go around accusing people if we've no proof. That's not right," Abbott said.

Bernie gave him a look. "I told you, I said Dorothy's a bit under the weather, down in the dumps, you know? I'm not an eejit. Then I had a quick word with Dorothy—casual-like? How's everything going with you? She said she was fine. I don't know what to think, boys. I don't know."

"Do you believe her, Bernie?" Ryan didn't know Dorothy that well.

Bernie took another slurp of coffee. "No clue. I'll have to leave it in your hands. Keep an eye on her for me. She's great with the accounts." She headed out and turned. "Abbott, a couple of rowdies at the back need sorting. I'll call you if I need you."

"She won't need me. So, what do you think, Ryan? Should we investigate?"

"Where does Dorothy live?"

"Bernie said the bottom end of Rathcoole. I have the address here." Abbott waved a bit of paper at Ryan.

Ryan read the address and checked his watch. "We can go and do a quick flyby, check it out. It's on my way home. But that's all. This is getting to be a nightly occasion. My arm is killing me, and oh, yes, I'm investigating a murder."

"We should open up our own private detective agency, Ryan. *The Boyos' Detective Agency*. I like it, do you? I'll be the brains; you be the brawn."

Ryan sighed. "I'll follow you." Didn't think he could handle Abbott with a sense of humour. A relatively new and disturbing development.

After parking down the street, Ryan jogged over and jumped into Abbott's car. "Looks like they've gone to bed." He settled himself. Derrycoole Pass was a sad collection of plain, white-stuccoed, terraced houses. Not too much beautification here. Most front gardens held wheelie bins abandoned in weed-choked desolation.

Dorothy's house was an end unit much tidier than the others. It sat in darkness except for a bright pink smudge in an upstairs window. A hedge ran down the edge of a modest side garden.

Abbott turned. "Have you had any more thoughts about the baby, all that?"

"Bridget's coming over tomorrow night. I'm thinking she'll move in with me, and then, who knows?" He thought briefly of his parents and Erin and added, "Probably get married." His mum would want a big wedding, maybe in St. Anne's Cathedral, and Bridget's family would want it to be a Catholic service and the child to be Catholic, and he had no idea what to think, or if he even gave a toss about all that. He groaned.

Abbott chuckled in the darkness. "It'll be grand, just grand. Any ideas for names yet?"

"Give over."

"How about Abbott if it's a boy?"

"Will you...hang on—we have a visitor," Ryan said.

A small white car came out of nowhere, roared up, and parked outside number twenty-four. A bundled figure got out. None of the streetlights worked, and it was hard to make out details as the person barrelled up the pathway. Abbott lowered the windows a little, and they heard a loud bang-bang on the front door.

"Bit late for a social call." Abbott stretched around to get a better view.

A curtain twitched upstairs, and a moment later, the hall light came on. The visitor rapped hard again, and the porch lit up. The front door opened, and they heard shouting.

"Come on, boyo, let's have a look." Abbott slipped out of the car, and Ryan followed.

They approached the house, keeping low. The front door slammed shut. They crept to the living-room window, but the blinds were closed. Not even a chink to spy through. Ryan could hear yelling from the room.

"What the hell is going on?" Abbott whispered.

"Let's try the back. See if we can get a look inside," Ryan said.

They crept down the side of the house. What would happen, Ryan wondered, if someone saw us and called the police. He didn't want to think about it. What a cluster that would be....

They passed a kitchen window first, a square of darkness, but as they edged further along the wall, avoiding a back door, a larger window revealed the dining room with the living room bright beyond it. Ryan motioned Abbott to keep down, and they peered in from opposite sides. Ryan could see two figures, one he assumed was Dorothy's husband, George. A big, bald, heavyset man who carried most of his weight in the belly. The other person was a bulky woman with short, frizzy blond hair. She stood in the middle of the room with her arms raised and was shouting.

"What do you think?" Ryan whispered. "Could it be the daughter, come to check on her mum?"

"She's a big girl, takes after the dad then. He better watch out." Abbott grinned, his face pale in the darkness, his teeth a white crescent. "This'll be because of Bernie's call. She doesn't show it, but she's fond of Dorothy, known her since her daughters were small. Helped her a lot when Andy died, apparently. Shannon, the eldest daughter, told me that."

"We can probably leave them to it." Ryan had a full day tomorrow. "Looks like the daughter will sort it...oh, what now?"

Dorothy had appeared. She'd been out of sight. She approached the visitor with her arms raised in a placating gesture. Without warning, the blond pulled her arm back in a sweeping movement and slapped Dorothy hard across the jaw. Dorothy staggered and fell. George rushed forward, and the woman leaned into him and shoved him with both hands. He tumbled backwards. She started yelling again. Ryan and Abbott, stunned for a moment, looked at each other.

"What the fuck...?" Abbott slammed his hand on the window as the blond lifted her fist. She turned a pink, bloated face to them, her mouth a perfect O.

Ryan rushed to the back door. Tried it, put his shoulder to it, but it didn't shift.

"She's taken off," Abbott yelled, and they both charged round to the front, a comedy of errors in their haste, barging into bins and tripping over shrubs Ryan swore weren't there when they first arrived.

The woman had made it to her car, surprisingly agile for such a big woman. *Fight or flight*, Abbott offered later. She took off, tyres screeching, as they made it to the gate.

"Leave her," Ryan called out as Abbott sprinted for his car. "They'll know who she is. We'll get her. We'll get her later."

Back in the house, George lay slumped in a chair while Dorothy hovered over him, sobbing quietly. Blood trickled from her nose and a cut above her eye. Abbott went to her and guided her to the sofa while Ryan tended to George. The big man was panting and had gone a bad shade of grey.

"I'll call for an ambulance." Ryan took his mobile out.

"Give me a minute. I have my pills." George took a breath. "Dorothy." He looked over at his wife and shook his head. For the first time, he seemed to notice them. "Who are youse?"

"Dorothy's friends from work," Abbott said.

Ryan came back from the kitchen with water for George and a wet cloth for Dorothy's face. "Here you go, hold it to your nose and cheek. You'll have a nasty bruise there in the morning." He sat down in the other chair. Abbott remained standing.

"Who was that?" Ryan asked.

"My daughter, Hillary," George answered. "Dorothy's stepdaughter."

"George and I both lost our partners about twenty-five years ago," Dorothy said. "To cancer. We met at a bereavement group. We were both shattered. It was the grief that brought us together like, the shared grief. But Hillary never got over her mam's death. She's always been a belligerent girl, would never accept help. We never got along." Dorothy wiped her face and sat on the arm of the sofa. She sniffed.

"You tried." George's colour was coming back now. "Hillary left home years ago and went to England. She's been back about a year now. Still aggressive, and now she has this gambling problem. That online gambling. She owes money everywhere and comes to us when we get our pensions. Says she needs it, and we owe her. Has started to get—you know, nasty."

Dorothy shook her head. "We don't know what to do. She's George's girl, but she's going too far. George has a heart condition, and she's going to kill him." She choked a little. "We can't fight her off."

"I'll have a word with her," Abbott said. "I'll see she doesn't bother you again."

"You have to be careful. She works in a law office, an assistant. But she's got in the habit of saying you do anything to her, she'll sue you. She threatened George with child-abuse charges. She said even though she made them up it would ruin him." Dorothy patted George's hand. "He wouldn't hurt a fly."

George shook his head. "I never laid a hand on her. That's probably the problem right there. Her mum didn't believe in discipline. She was a right softy. See where that got us."

"What law office?" Ryan said, checking. Although, to be honest, she wasn't his father's type...

"Mitchell & Cobb," George said.

Ryan blew out a breath. Not his dad's office then, thank God. "Right, good. Look, we'll deal with this, don't worry."

"I don't think she'll come back now," Dorothy said. She had a thin, worried face, and her grey hair was pulled back in a loose ponytail. She wiped at the smeared blood again with the cloth.

Dorothy saw them to the door. She touched Abbott's arm. "Hilary said Bernie had called her. She didn't like that. You tell Bernie from me that something will have to be done. I don't want to lose another husband. That girl's never been right in the head, always been a bad seed. Sorry, but it's the truth."

Outside at Ryan's car, Abbott paused. "I'll talk to Bernie," he said. "She has the junior boxing lads under her thumb. I'll have them take turns sitting outside Dorothy's house, keep an eye out for a while."

"I have too much on my plate right now, I can't commit more time," Ryan said.

"I have it covered." Abbott smiled.

"Yes, that's what worries me," Ryan said.

Chapter Twenty-Eight

Saturday, November 5

When Ryan arrived early at the station, he could see Maura already hunched over her computer. She jumped when he walked up behind her.

"Two things about Wylie," she said. "Guess who sent the lighter out for processing? I ended up phoning the lab myself and pretending that I'd mislaid the form. They faxed me a copy, and there it was, Wylie's name."

"Yes!" Ryan said and slapped Maura's chair.

"And, before you ask," she continued, "Sam did try, but couldn't get Wylie's group to answer, not without being too obvious. About the rape nights, though, I told Janice to pass me schedules for the last three months. Said I was working on a new metric for scheduling." She paused at Ryan's blank stare. "You know I help her with all that paperwork sometimes? She forwarded them last night."

At this, Ryan grabbed a chair from the next desk, pulled it over, and sat down. Maura had indicated a tidy, two-inch paper stack to him. Did she want him to go through all that?

"Don't panic, Ryan. I've already isolated the pages we need." She waved some sheets in his face. "We do have a problem. Two of the rape nights, he was working a late shift. I asked Sam, and he said it's a community-outreach initiative. He's done it himself and said your time is your own. He enjoyed it, said you drive around certain neighbourhoods and talk to kids playing football. Hang about being friendly. I can't see Wylie getting into that, can you? Although, if your time is your own, who's to say he didn't sign off early...and let's not forget too that people sometimes swap shifts without logging it in."

"We can't prove he messed with the lighter." Ryan shook his head. "And yes, he might have swapped shifts or, as you say, or taken off early. No way to find out without raising suspicion. Damn it."

Sam had visited bars and hotels the night before and dropped off the e-fit. "He'll do a few more this evening, maybe Donaghadee and Hollywood. That should cover it, right?"

"Yup, worth a try."

"What are you doing here so early?" Maura asked.

"I wanted to get in before it gets busy. It's this case. It's like Kevin disappeared." He straightened up and stretched his back out. He badly needed a run. "Kevin killed Liam McKenna. On purpose, though? No way to know. I'd have to say probably. And that would naturally suggest crazy jealousy, right?"

"So," Maura speculated, "It's likely he killed Liam and possibly killed Kathleen, but I get the feeling you aren't completely convinced."

It was true, the way Maura put it. He was Kathleen's boyfriend. He tried to hide the fact from everyone. He had past issues, and he most likely ran Liam off the road.

What was it, Ryan wondered, that nagged at him? Because something did. Maybe it was the abduction. Someone else was involved. Doyle? "I'm not saying he didn't kill her. Just keeping an open mind." He shrugged. "I know it's crazy but I hate it when things are too obvious."

The door banged open, and Derek appeared, wearing an anorak over a cycling outfit and a rucksack slung over his shoulder. He was also carrying his bike and breathing heavily after carrying it up the stairs.

"Bloody lift's not working again."

"Why drag it up here?" Maura asked. "Can't you leave it in the car park?"

"Catch yourself on. Do you know how much this cost me? Don't want it nicked."

Maura snorted. "It's the bloody police car park Derek. Get a grip."

"Yes, so what?" Derek leaned the bike against the wall. He wandered over to the kitchen and switched on the kettle.

Maura looked at Ryan for support.

"To be honest, I wouldn't leave an old toaster in that car park if I could help it," Ryan said. "Especially weekends and overnight. The bike's safer here. I'd bring my car up here if I could."

Derek, when he had his tea and settled himself, had some information to share. "After high school, Sophie left Belfast to finish her arts education in Europe. Travelled a lot—lucky for some. She ended up in London. That's where she met her husband, Anthony Walton, a wealthy gallery owner."

"That's it? No dark clouds?" Ryan said.

"Not that I can see. Walton was a wild man before Sophie met him and straightened him out. He trained as a lawyer, ended up in the art business. Their galleries are successful. Her mother is a retired horse vet, and her dad was a businessman who died a few years ago. One married older brother and two nieces."

"I met the nieces," Ryan added. "Nice girls."

Derek continued, "There's money in the family."

"What about Kevin? Anything new there?" Ryan said.

"Nothing. Clean as a whistle, as far as I can see. Other than the previous transgressions we already know about."

"Excellent work, my man, now..." Ryan slapped Derek's back. "Can you see if any CCTV cameras have picked up Kevin going down the Malone Road after Liam?"

After some moaning, Derek headed upstairs to his computer. Maura and Ryan headed for the little kitchen on their floor.

"That's a long shot, isn't it?" Maura said, dunking her tea bag.

"Maybe," Ryan said. "But I think he may have followed Liam from Kathleen's, might have been clocked by CCTV on or around the Malone Road that morning. That's the logical place if he was stalking Kathleen and saw Liam leaving her flat, assumed they slept together, and decided to do something about it. Worth a look. We have the date and rough time that

Liam left. Worth a try. Where else could he have picked Liam up?"

"Even though Mrs. Doyle said they didn't sleep together?" Maura said.

"Kevin wasn't to know that," Ryan said.

"And we assume Kevin put the tracker on Kathleen's car?" Maura asked.

"Yes, that's the most likely explanation. He is in the security business after all," Ryan said, splashed some milk in his tea, and headed for his desk.

Derek bounced back into the room before lunchtime. He had found the footage.

"I saw the bike first, then a couple of cars back...bingo. The Mercedes. That's pretty damning. If and when Kevin Coulter shows up, if he does, he's in for a lot of grief. I sent the files to you."

"Now we have proof he found Liam; he was watching Kathleen's place," Ryan said.

Maura gave a little shudder. "That is seriously creepy. A stalker." She punched Ryan on the arm. "What made you think that?"

"His history, and his dad's defensiveness. And...I hate to admit it, but the abduction. Somebody knows something we don't. And that may be the least of it," Ryan said. "Derek, you might as well send that over to DCI Tiller and the gang. Now, I'm starving. Anyone for Chinese?"

After lunch, Ryan was re-reading Anthony Walton's file when Maura came over and sat down.

"Shit."

"What? What's wrong?"

"It's Sam. You know he has that lovely old Morris Minor? The lavender one?"

"Oh, is that his?" It was a ridiculous car. *'Wee girl's car,'* Derek had casually suggested when it had appeared in the lot.

"Don't tell me he's had an accident?"

"Somebody keyed it last night, did a number on it. He's devastated. He was so proud of it. It's a collector's car. His dad passed away a few years ago, left it to him."

"Do you think Wylie and his friends realise he's been asking questions for us? Would they have done this?"

"They know he's been distributing the flyers, Ryan. He's been making copies, and he had a pile on his desk. And he's been seen with me." Maura shook her head.

"Where is he now?"

"Up on Derek's floor. Filing. Said it takes his mind off his poor wee car and gets him away from Wylie."

"I'm sorry, Maura. I suppose there's no way we can tie this to Wylie?"

"No, I don't think so. The car was parked on a side street when he was having a drink with friends. Anyone could have done it. No cameras either. He checked."

"There are some guys in the motor pool garage can help with that sort of thing."

"I'll tell him." And, on the bright side, guess what?"

"There's a bright side?"

"This girl has a date Monday night. Mind you, I had to ask *him* out."

"Finally." Ryan smiled. "Every cloud and all that, eh, Maura?"

She punched his arm, and he flinched. "Maura, that's my injured arm."

"I know," she said and sashayed off.

At about four o'clock, Ryan glanced at his watch and started to finish up. He sent a few emails and phoned Bridget.

"Bridge, I'm stopping at Nesbitt's Butchers to pick up steaks to barbecue. I fancy a Caesar salad with, any chance?"

He heard her chuckle. "Every chance. I'm making the dressing right now."

It struck him as funny, as he waited in the small shop for the butcher to wrap the meat, how quickly you could get back into a rhythm. He missed it in a way. He wasn't much of a cook, and with Erin dropping off countless dishes for him, he didn't have to do it often. But there was something enjoyable about picking up a couple of good steaks, then standing in the garden with that smoky barbecue smell billowing up around you, and maybe a beer in hand in case you got thirsty. He pulled into the driveway and saw

Bridget's motorcycle. How fast that old sense of familiarity came back, like slipping on a well-worn jacket.

"Hey," Bridget called from the kitchen. He heard bowls clattering and chopping and smelled garlic. Man, she had always been a noisy, messy, wonderful cook. Must be her Italian ancestry.

"Hey yourself. I have the steaks. Finn here?"

"Out back having a pee and a dander about. Wine?"

"Well, if you're not drinking…."

"Don't be daft. We both don't have to be miserable. Here." She handed him a glass of red after sniffing it luxuriously. "Ahhh. Honestly, I don't know how some women have eight children or more. I mean, that's what—nine times eight, which is fifty-six months, which is? Nearly five years without wine. My good God. And you have eight bloody children to deal with as well…."

Ryan went over and kissed her on the cheek. "Don't worry. We won't have eight children. Let's see how the one goes."

She stopped chopping and turned to him. She laid her hand on his cheek, reminding him for a dizzying second of Rose's first touch when they kissed in Kathleen's flat.

"It's going to be great, Ryan, it is."

She wore her bike leathers and a white tee shirt. My God, she did look good.

"Those leathers look great on you."

"I thought I'd wear them, might be the last time for a while." She patted her belly and smiled.

And he wondered then how it was possible to care deeply for two women at the same time. It felt a little like being on a seesaw. Up, down, up, down.

"Go on, get that bloomin' barbecue started. I'm eating for two here." She slapped him lightly and turned back to the salad.

Later, at about half past ten, they were on the sofa in the living room watching a thriller on Sky when his mobile rang. Ryan had his feet up and was sipping a second glass of wine. Bridget was half-asleep beside him with Finn's head on her lap. Like old times. He snatched it up, expecting Dispatch.

It was Abbott.

"That bitch came back to Dorothy and George's house tonight. Big Glenn was in his car outside. He caught her storming up the front path. She threw a punch at him, can you fucking believe the cheek of her, a punch at Big Glenn? Bernie's fit to be tied. I'm here at the club with her. She's vibrating. It's something to see."

Ryan heard Abbott draw a harsh breath.

"Abbott, don't…."

"No, I'm thinking this has to be the end of it. Big Glenn grabbed her and shoved her back into her car. Said there'd be someone there every night. And next time, she wouldn't get away so easy." Abbott paused again. "Something's wrong with her. That daughter's a mental case."

"What do you want to do?"

"Nothing we can do—for now. Just reporting in," Abbott said and hung up.

Ryan woke Sunday morning to a cool, dark bedroom. And silence. He'd given Bridget the guest room.

She had remained firm about keeping the pregnancy secret. And he was fine with that, for now; couldn't imagine what Erin would say. She'd always been fond of Bridget and had lectured him after the breakup. "Not my fault, Erin. She broke up with me," he'd said. "You have it backwards."

"No, but you caused it, bloody fool. Did you ever tell Bridget that you loved her? Did you?"

He hadn't, of course.

He had reluctantly lifted his house phone receiver off last night. Erin had a habit of calling early on Sundays to remind him about dinner with their parents, and he knew Bridget needed to sleep in. Beams of light slid through a thin chink in the curtains, coming and going as the sun disappeared behind clouds. So many things were spiralling away from him as he lay there without moving, watching small dust threads hanging in the air. Where was Kevin? Was he dead? Surely it had to do with Kathleen? Or Liam? Was it his father's background? Adam Coulter's reticence puzzled him. Had he been contacted privately—was he negotiating Kevin's release on his own? And why did Olivia Coulter not factor in? Most mothers would be frantic.

Finn's whining finally got him up at about eight o'clock, and he padded along to the kitchen to make both their breakfasts. He checked his mobile, low. He quickly plugged it in, should have done it in last night. He grimaced; Abbott's call had distracted him. Hopefully, Dorothy and George had slept through the night. Another problem to nag at him. Christ, family issues were the worst. He remembered back to when he was on patrol. They were always the most dreaded callouts. You never knew what to expect in a domestic situation.

Bridget still slept. He started coffee and left a loaf on the counter in case she woke and fancied toast. After he dressed, he sat in the kitchen looking out into the back garden. He finished his coffee, had a small bowl of cereal, then left his phone to finish charging and dragged the reluctant dog out for a quick walk. Ryan figured Finn liked to hang around Bridget because she gave him too many bone-shaped dog treats.

Clouds broke to sporadic sunlight, and a fresh breeze skittered through the leaves at his feet. He could feel rain in the air, and he could smell it too. He saw large cumulonimbus thunderheads forming. Agitated, the crows that met him most mornings cawed and flew from treetop to treetop. He fancied they followed him as he walked along the road and cut into the fields behind his farm. He'd been heading back home when the sun briefly burst through the cloud cover again and illuminated the countryside. For a few moments, Ryan saw splashes of bright green and ochre, a vivid combination of light and intensity of colour produced by the moisture-drenched air. His own forty shades of green. He loved this country. And he wondered if he would be walking here in a couple of years with a little girl or boy by his side. He couldn't picture it. Not yet.

What about Rose? Should he call her? He felt the need to talk to her, to see her even—but that wouldn't be right. Would she meet him for a drink if he asked her? She hadn't been in touch since that conversation in Bangor. Not a word.

As soon as he got back to the farm, he heard the low trill of his mobile from the kitchen. "DS McBride here." He didn't recognize the number right away.

It was Girvan. "McBride, get yourself over to Kathleen McGuire's crime scene, now. We have another body."

Chapter Twenty-Nine

Sunday, November 6

The threatening rain materialized. It lashed down as Ryan left his farm, and it continued throughout the drive. When he arrived at the side road, he pulled his old raincoat from the boot, stepped into a pair of wellies, and hurried to the scene through the torrential downpour. An early morning jogger had discovered the body, and Ryan watched as the witness compulsively shifted from foot to foot while giving his statement. The man had a silver blanket over his head and shoulders while the constable with him hunched under a large black umbrella held by another officer.

Girvan stood apart beside Dr. McAllister's Range Rover at the top of the embankment. DCI Tiller was there, too, talking on his phone. He looked wet and dour. Nearby, Billy held a wide roll of blue and white crime-scene tape for a drenched WPC as she pulled a black cape over her shoulders.

"Shit," Ryan said to Billy when he sloped over. "What a cluster."

"Yeah, I know," Billy said. "It's not like we didn't expect it. But here? At Kathleen's murder site?"

Billy had already sorted things, and the scene was hopping. McAllister had been and processed the body and had joined Girvan and Tiller. A tent had been erected down at the river bank, but the area ran with water.

"Looks like we can go and have a look." Nodding to Girvan, who gestured towards the river, Ryan approached a tech and grabbed some gloves. They pulled on their protection and made their way down the path.

"Waste of time," Billy lamented. "I swear, Ryan, this has got to be the wettest autumn in history. Has it stopped raining since October?"

Sodden clouds hung over everything, low and brooding.

They stepped under the canvas and scrutinised the body.

Kevin's arms were flung wide. He lay on his back with his head twisted around to one side, facing the fast-moving river Bann.

"Did you expect this?" Billy asked.

Ryan shook his head. "The way Kevin was taken, it was only a matter of time, but at Kathleen's scene? No, I didn't see this coming. Any info?"

"Couple of things so far. Not killed here, dumped. Oh, and get this, Alice says he's been worked over, but he thinks the killing blow came later. He'll know more when he—"

Ryan knelt down. "Worked over?"

"Yes, knocked about, fairly severe beating. You can see on his chin and cheek there, and his hands."

"Jesus, are those fingers broken?"

"Looks like it to me," Billy replied, joining Ryan by the body.

Ryan frowned. He had expected Kevin to be dead, but not here, not like this. The side of the tent facing the Bann had not been rolled down, and he could see rivulets of mud and rain surging from the banks into the fast-moving torrent as it raced past, brown and swollen. "God, it's miserable here," he said to Billy, icy rainwater trickling from his wet hair and slithering down his neck. "Let's head up."

Girvan called them over. Tiller had disappeared. "Dr. McAllister will be sending over a preliminary report right away. You might as well head back to the station. Not unexpected this."

"Has Adam Coulter been notified, sir?" Ryan asked.

"Yes, McBride. DCI Tiller has spoken with him. He'll fully cooperate now. We all want the murderer found."

They trudged up the slight incline. When Billy got to his car, he stopped. "Maybe now we'll get the truth from his dad."

It was full steam ahead at the station. Ryan hurried in, wet and cold, only stopping downstairs to grab another coffee. He could see Girvan in his corner office with Adam Coulter, DCI Tiller, and another man Ryan didn't recognize. Coulter was distraught. The other man, sharply dressed and animated, spoke earnestly to Girvan, who nodded along. Tiller leapt up, gesticulating aggressively at the others, turned, and stormed out.

Billy arrived next, taking off his anorak and shaking it out briskly, sending water everywhere.

"Hey, come on, Billy. You're worse than Finn."

Unconcerned, Billy draped it on the back of his chair and sat down. "Who's the suit in with Girvan and Coulter, then?"

"I don't know. Government?" Ryan said. "And I think we've seen the last of Tiller."

"Oh yes? Billy perked up.

"Girvan. I don't think he wanted the bloody K&E team in here any more than we did. Steals his thunder. Plus, Tiller was a bully. If he tried to push Girvan around, it was bound to end in tears."

Maura arrived next with a few others, wet and bedraggled. The floor started to fill up.

"Bad about Coulter then, eh?" she said, stopping by their desks.

"Yes, his father's with Girvan now." Billy nodded to the corner office.

The door banged open, and another motley group of detectives and constables hurried in, bringing with them a wave of damp, cold air redolent of cigarettes and wet sheep. At the back, Ryan noticed a group of Musgrave DCs. Maura saw them too and raised her eyebrows.

About ten minutes later, Girvan shook hands with his visitors. He led them out and came over to Ryan.

"They're taking a break now, but you can talk to Coulter around lunchtime. The desk sergeant will let you know when he comes back."

"Who was in there with him, sir?" Ryan asked.

"Someone from the Policing Board. Keeping an eye on things." He flashed a tight smile. "DCI Tiller's team are packing up. Bit of a cock-up, only focussing on Adam Coulter's business and not coordinating the search with us quickly enough. Where he was found obviously ties it with our case. A question of not reaching out. They'll review from Knock. The interview suite is free again." Girvan said this as he walked away. Ryan heard the smile in his voice.

Coulter entered interview room three, a changed man, just holding it together. He got right to the point. "I have some things to tell you. They may not be relevant to this investigation, or the wider issue of Kathleen McGuire's murder, but in the interest of clarity, I'm going to share them with you."

"Go ahead," Ryan said. About bloody time.

"Kevin had issues. Depression and possibly mild schizophrenia. Inherited. He had help when he was younger; that seemed to make a difference." He shook his head. "All this emotional mumbo jumbo. I don't believe in that nonsense. It was Olivia. She thought there was something wrong with the boy. To me, he was a typical lad. In life, you need to get on with it." He paused again, seemed unsure. "Girvan told me you appear to have some evidence he killed that motorcyclist?"

Ryan slipped a sheet from the folder in front of him.

"You can read it for yourself, Mr. Coulter. You know what it means."

Coulter scanned the page. "This still could have been an accident."

"Accident or not, he didn't call for an ambulance. He left Liam McKenna in a forest. And he'd been following him. We have the CCTV. He has a long history of tormenting ex-girlfriends, right? Liam McKenna was Kathleen's ex-boyfriend."

"I see now Kevin's problems were overtaking him," Coulter said. "It's difficult to explain, but in the past, things always seemed to get resolved. I thought he was taking care and managing his issues. He never asked me for help, didn't seem to need it."

"Look," Ryan said. "At this point, true or not, it's possible someone blamed your son for Kathleen McGuire's death. We have no direct evidence pointing to him. No proof. Someone either did have proof or firmly believed he murdered her. Everything comes back to that." Ryan paused, "Unless you can think of another reason someone would want to kill your son?"

"Where is his mother, by the way?" Billy cut in. "No matter whether she got on with her son or not, you'd think she would want to be here."

"No. Don't bother contacting Olivia. She won't speak to you."

"Still," Billy said.

Coulter shook his head. "Olivia's not his mother."

Ryan and Billy exchanged glances.

"He's adopted?"

"Yes. I hired a surrogate. Olivia couldn't have children, and I wanted an heir. Kevin didn't know. Few people did. Olivia wasn't happy about it but knew how much having a child meant to me. She never cared for Kevin, and of course, he never understood why. I was away working most of the time, and he was an unhappy child. In hindsight, I should have made more of an attempt to deal with the situation, but back then, it was all about the business. I'm still not sure this is relevant, but now you know everything." Coulter hesitated. He seemed unsure what to do next. This was the first time Ryan had seen that rigid façade slip, then he said, "I need to go."

"Weird, eh, Ryan? This whole thing, don't you think?" Billy said after Coulter had left.

Ryan pulled on his jacket and headed for the door.

"Come on."

"Hey, wait up!" Billy grabbed his lunch and hurried after him.

When they got out to the car park, Coulter had already left the building. Ryan threw his keys to Billy.

"Bring the car around, will you? I'll have a look and see where he goes."

Ryan sprinted to the front gate and eased around the guardhouse. He could see Coulter walking fast along the Antrim Road toward a line of cars. Parking outside the station, or even close to it, was not an option. Hurry up, Billy, hurry up, or we'll lose him. His car finally arrived, with Billy easing towards him.

Coulter stopped at a white Lexus RX. Ryan turned back and motioned Billy out of the driver's seat, then jumped into his BMW.

"White Lexus down the street," he said to Billy. "We'll take it easy." As he said that, the Lexus sped by. "We're on." Ryan pulled out of the car park.

"Where are we going? We can't legally follow him. You know that, right? We need surveillance authority."

"We're going for a drive. That's all. This case, don't you see? We've been looking for one killer, lurching from one prime suspect to another, but I think it's always been about love. Different kinds of love. Maybe Kevin killed Liam, but did he kill Kathleen? Did he? Somebody else out there killed him. That makes at least two murderers, right? But we have three murders—do we have three murderers?"

Chapter Thirty

Sunday, November 6

They followed Coulter up the Antrim Road, getting on to the M2 outside Glengormley. Past Antrim they turned off, and Ryan thumped the wheel. "There it is. Sophie and Coulter go way back, right? And she was fond of Kevin."

"I thought she fancied Kevin," Billy said.

"Yes, I did too, at first. But when you think about it, with his admission Olivia Coulter wasn't the mother..." Ryan paused. "It was Sophie's behaviour when I asked her if she was in love with Kevin. She was appalled, an immediate reaction—yet she was so upset by the news of his abduction. It struck me as odd. Did she care about him or not?"

As the Lexus slid into Sophie's place, Ryan slowed and pulled over.

"Let's hang back, eh Billy? Let them have a few minutes."

Billy whistled softly. "They do look a bit alike, don't they? Sophie and Kevin?"

"He looked like his dad, but, yes, there was a resemblance."

"He won't have phoned her. He'll want to break it to her in person," Billy said.

They sat there for a moment; Ryan lost in thought. He hadn't suspected this, not until that final piece of information about Olivia. Sophie, out of the picture for a few years in Europe, Adam Coulter's business mainly over there. The Coulters were old friends of Anthony Walton, yes, but who introduced them? Sophie. A way to keep an eye on her son and also her ex-lover. He was convinced there was a link between Sophie and Adam somewhere in Europe, before Anthony came on the scene. She'd been no surrogate.

"Let's get this over with," Ryan said. He reversed and turned into Sophie's driveway.

"Hey, Ryan, do you think Sophie's husband knew about Kevin?"

"I doubt it. She seems to like keeping secrets."

"It'll be a terrible shock to him, and it's bound to come out."

Ryan thought about Rose. "There's always collateral damage with murder."

"Yes," Billy agreed as the door swung open.

"You followed me."

Adam Coulter stood in the doorway.

"Can we come in?" Ryan moved forward.

"This is not a good time."

"No," Ryan said, "I expect it's not, but we still have to talk to her."

"You're wasting your time. She's a close family friend, that's all, and extremely upset about Kevin. You had no right to follow me. I'm not a fool. This is illegal."

"You're denying she's Kevin's mother, then?"

"I've already given my statement. And Mrs. Walton is not able to see you at the moment."

"Thanks, Mr. Coulter. Sorry to bother you. We'll set something up for her at the station."

Billy turned and headed for the car, and Coulter made to close the door, but Ryan put his hand on it, stopping him. He stared into Coulter's eyes, held his gaze. They could both hear it. A low, desperate keening from the conservatory. A terrible sound.

When Ryan got to the car, Billy sat in the driver's seat.

"Let me drive for a change."

Sophie Walton's anguish had unsettled Ryan. He nodded to Billy and got in, strangely disturbed. "I heard her crying. God, I feel sorry for her, I do."

206

Billy took off slowly and turned onto the side road.

"Do you think Kevin knew she was his mum?"

"I doubt it. You heard Adam Coulter. Olivia Coulter had things wrapped up pretty tight. She must have wanted to punish Sophie, denying her the right to claim Kevin. Or Adam Coulter didn't ever want Kevin to know Sophie was his mother. Make things too complicated for him. Who knows? He strikes me as a man who likes to get his own way, doesn't give a damn about the people around him."

Ryan found himself getting angry, and he took a moment. He lowered the window and looked out at the green fields and hedges slipping by. The rain from this morning had washed the landscape clean. A watery sun hid behind thin clouds.

"Adam Coulter wanted a child. As soon as he got one, he tossed Sophie away and lost interest. He married Olivia, and according to Derek's notes, got the money he needed to start his business, then ignored her too."

Billy drove at a regal pace, and Ryan felt himself settle. Sophie was Kevin's mother, Ryan was positive, could she be Kathleen's murderer? She had hidden her son's identity, and then there was the phone call from Kathleen on the day of the murder. But what motive did she have? Why would she? Maternal jealousy? She didn't seem the type. She also had an alibi and a lack of mobility on that day. No car, no way to get to the murder scene. He took out his mobile and pulled up Sophie's place on maps. Studied the house and grounds from above. Picked out the road they were travelling on. He noticed a nearby outbuilding at the end of a side lane that cut across in a diagonal to the main road.

"Billy, hang on, take that wee road there—there." Ryan pointed across Billy's nose.

Billy swerved to the right, dramatically and unnecessarily, in Ryan's opinion. They bounced along.

"What did you do with those sandwiches?" Ryan asked Billy. All this thinking was making him hungry.

"Never you mind about them, Ryan. I'm losing weight running around with you. I've a delicate stomach. Why are we going down this track.?"

Right. Billy and his stomach. Distracted, Ryan looked at the screen and out the window again, at the patchwork of fields rolling away in the distance. A bit like this case, rolling away from him. He seemed always to be running after it instead of getting in front and stopping it.

The sky was that cool, grey-blue that presaged the change of seasons. It would be winter soon. Where had summer gone? He knew, of course. Bridget had left and taken summer with her. Warm evenings at the farm, making dinner together and sex afterwards. Not lovemaking, he realised. It hadn't been that, had it? Bridget had known the difference. He hadn't.

So now, with a baby to raise, would love come? It would have to, wouldn't it? Last night together hadn't been too bad. It might work out for them all. Lost in his thoughts, he almost missed it, the structure half hidden by a small copse of trees. What was that? He checked the map again. Right on the edge of Sophie's property. Not far at all in a straight line.

Billy turned onto the main road.

"Billy, is that a garage?"

"Where?"

"There. Stop the car."

Billy pulled over, and they both stepped out onto muddy ground.

"My good shoes are getting ruined, Ryan. Why are we stopping?"

"I don't know. We're still close to Sophie's, and there are no other houses nearby. Let's have a peek. What's the harm?" He held up his phone and showed Billy how close they were to Sophie's house.

They both stared at a solid stone building with red bricks patched in. Big enough for two cars. Mossy green paint clung to sagging wooden double doors held tight to the front wall with large black hinges. Water had seeped upwards and the planks at the bottom were rotting and black with mould. Faint indents rutted the ground where the doors had been opened, although how recently it was hard to tell.

"We've no warrant, no right to go poking about." Billy glanced around him. Somebody had a wood fire going nearby. The smell of it softening the crisp air. Something else, too, on the wind.

"Is that turps, Billy?" Ryan sniffed, then lost it. It was probably from inside

208

the garage. He walked over to the closest window along the side, murky with grime and dirt.

"Give us a leg-up, will you?"

Billy muttered, but gave Ryan a boost. He grabbed hold of a wide stone sill to steady himself and looked in. He could see an old, bashed-up green Mini. He wrestled his phone out and took a picture through the glass.

"Okay," he yelled and jumped down.

"Short wheelbase, right Billy? The tyre tracks at the lay-by?"

"Yes, I think so." Billy wiped his muddy hands on his hanky.

"There's a Mini in there." Ryan stepped aside and walked over into the field, thick with dandelion leaves and patchy grass. "It's a bit of a wreck." He could clearly see the back of Sophie's house. He caught the smell of solvent again. Someone had been using the garage lately. He was sure of it.

"What do you think, Billy? Couple of minutes to Sophie's back door?"

Billy shook his head. "What's the motive? And she has a bucketful of alibis. It's all conjecture, no real proof. How do you even know if the thing runs. Look at this place. It's abandoned."

"Yes, I'm aware of that." Ryan shook his head in frustration. He knew more than anyone how pig-headed he could be. He was convinced it was someone close to Kathleen. Not a random attack. "If it's not Sophie's, we'll have to find out who owns this building. Let's head on, but turn the other way on the main road."

His mobile buzzed.

"McBride." Girvan sounded tense. "Where are you?"

"Up near Sophie Walton's place, sir, we've…."

"Harassing her?"

"No, sir. We found out that Kevin Coulter is her son and…."

"Do you have proof?"

"I…not yet, but…."

"Adam Coulter is close to bringing harassment charges. Did you follow him without authorization? I don't want this department involved in anything remotely like this, especially from him. Do I make myself clear?"

"But…."

Click.

Billy shifted beside him. "Don't tell me. That was Girvan telling us Coulter is pissed at us for harassing and following him."

"Billy, is there no end to your bloody talents?"

"No need to get nasty there."

Around a curve, they saw a small bungalow with a white stucco front and a well-tended garden.

"In here, let's see if anyone's home."

They pulled onto the tarmac driveway and got out. Billy rapped on the bubble glass of the front door and a shadowy figure approached. A woman opened the door, regarded them with interest. Balanced on her hip, she clasped a red-faced, hairless baby. The child sucked furiously on a dummy and stared wide-eyed at Ryan and Billy.

"Hello, there," Ryan said to the mother, who shifted the baby to her other hip. The child's eyes never left them. "Police. We've a quick question about those buildings back there. On that side road?" Ryan nodded towards the fields while holding out his warrant card.

"Thank goodness," she said, her expression softening, "I thought you might be here about my Frank or me dad. You do, don't you? When the police come to the door. No harm to youse, but you can tell a mile away."

"Does that garage belong to you? The one up the lane there?" Ryan asked.

"No, it belongs to me dad. Why, what about it?"

"We're in the middle of an investigation, and we wondered if we could get inside? To check it out. I see there's a Mini parked in there." Ryan nodded towards the garage.

"That's my dad's auld Mini. It's a wreck. Why do you care about that?"

The baby continued to suck heartily while resolutely staring at them. And suddenly, from inside, a loud crash and a shriek. A child began to wail. The woman turned around and shouted, "Wesley! Shut your bake."

She returned her attention to them, shaking her head, a menacing look on her face. Billy nodded in sympathy, a fellow parent.

"Right then, Mrs.?" Ryan smiled at her.

"Mrs. Moore. Lily."

"Could we have a word with your father, Lily?"

"No, sorry. He went to church this morning. When that's over, he goes fishing on the Bann with his mates, then they all go for a drink. I've no idea where, but he'll be back later on."

"Could we have a quick look in the garage then?"

"Oh, no."

Ryan waited for her to continue. She said nothing.

Billy waggled his fingers at the baby. "Do you know the Waltons at all, Lily?"

"Oh, aye. My dad works over there sometimes. Odd jobs and gardening, things like that. Why? Is this all the same inquiry, like?"

"Do you know if Ms. Walton has access to the garage?"

"She might have some stuff stored there. Her mam's horses are over in the other field in a small stable building." She gestured vaguely behind her. "Not much storage in them stables. But our old garage there, the keys are left in the Mini, and everybody round here knows that, so if you two are investigating break-ins or anything you best tell me now."

"Ma'am, may I ask why we can't check the garage out?"

"It's me dad's, that's why."

"Oh." Ryan produced a business card. "Would you give that to your dad and ask him to call me? I want to get in there and look at the Mini, and I need to ask him a couple of questions, need his help, that's all. He'll be done in no time. And don't worry about break-ins. This is a general inquiry."

When they got to the car and started off, Billy turned to Ryan.

"That wean was odd, eh Ryan? Staring at us like that? Sucking that dummy for Ireland he was."

"Yes, he was a grim wee thing."

They remained silent for a few miles.

"We need to get permission to check out that Mini. If Sophie has access to it and she flatly told us she had no other transportation—what did she say? Not even a bicycle? Plus, the phone call she omitted."

Billy glanced over at Ryan, frowning. "But why? That's what I don't understand."

"It had something to do with Kevin, had to have."

"But she didn't kill Kevin," Billy said.

"I'm thinking maybe the Doyles had something to do with that. Can't prove it. It's a hunch, but who else was close to Kathleen?"

"And Sophie? We have to be careful; we need proof, Ryan. Girvan's .…"

"Yeah, yeah, we'll get proof, Christ, Billy. Kathleen posed a threat to Kevin. Must have. It's like his father said, his problems seemed to disappear. Maybe they didn't resolve themselves. Kevin dealt with them, and Kathleen found out? It might be worth looking again into that original hit-and-run. And I wonder if Maura's found anything on how the kidnappers knew Kevin was coming home."

When they got back to the station, Billy closed his computer and got ready to leave.

"We've Margaret's parents coming for Sunday dinner, and I have to get home."

"No worries, I'll update Maura and see if Derek's still here. Girvan's gone, but I'll email him a report on today's findings. Keep you out of it. Away on then."

"Aye, grand Ryan. See you."

Billy disappeared, and Ryan wandered over to Maura's desk. She blew her nose and took a sip from a large mug of lemon-scented cold remedy.

"You all right?"

"I've a cold coming on, and there's me with my big date tomorrow night. I might have to cancel. I think Derek gave it to me on purpose."

He filled her in about the afternoon's discoveries. She had nothing back yet on the inquiries into the airport car park. He went back to his desk and sent a short update to Girvan, downplaying his interaction with Adam Coulter. He started putting his stuff away when a shadow fell across his desk. Ed Wylie. He was dressed to leave, overcoat over his shoulders.

"What? Don't tell me you're deserting your post, DS McBride." Wylie made a show of looking around. "I thought maybe you kept a little cot here, slept over, looking good for Girvan, always in early, always leaving late."

"Being here early is part of the job, Wylie. Not that you'd know. What do

212

you want?"

"Oh, nothing, being friendly, catching up. Say, how is the delectable Bridget? You are one lucky man...."

Ryan badly wanted to call him out on the rapes, beat the shit out of him, but one wrong word or move and Wylie would report him. He couldn't mention Sam and the attack on his car either. Wylie would know Ryan worried about the young constable, and that could make things worse.

"I gotta go, Wylie. Why don't you piss off home?"

Wylie snorted. "Why, thanks for your permission, DS McBride. But I've got better things to do with my time than sit at home looking at my dog." Wylie swaggered away.

A few minutes later, Abbott called with an update on 'the Dorothy situation,' as he called it. No sign of the daughter, no communication. Dorothy didn't want them to pursue it, hoping it was over with. Both Ryan and Abbott knew it wasn't.

When Ryan finally headed out, the evening had turned colder, but the rain had gone, and he walked through a scattering of leaves towards his car. He was tired but still hoping for a call from the old guy who owned the garage. He needed forensics to look at that green Mini. Needed Adam Coulter off his back and a way to understand how Sophie fit into all this.

Back home, he'd finished his dinner and washed up when Finn came into the kitchen and head-butted him.

"Fancy a walk, do you?"

The night wind felt raw and blustery on his back. It brought with it the rich odour of burning peat mixed with the sharper, more chemical tang of coal. Finn ran ahead into the darkness. It was exhilarating walking there with the wind roaring in the trees. His mobile went when he was heading back. It was nearly seven o'clock, and he didn't recognize the number.

"DS Ryan McBride."

"Jimmy here."

"Yes, hello." He took a leap of faith. "Is this Lily Moore's dad?"

"Aye."

213

"Sir, hello. I don't know if your daughter explained to you, but we want to have a look inside the garage, mainly at your Mini if possible? We think it may have been used without your knowledge. Possibly in the commission of a crime. May we enter your property, search it, and examine the Mini?"

"Aye."

"So, we can take a team up there, and you'll put your signature on that?"

"Aye."

He wrote up another report for Girvan, sent a quick email to Maura, Billy, and Derek about the permission given. Maura didn't respond right away, so he asked Billy to sort the team. Tomorrow morning they would get everyone up there.

He was watching the news when his mobile rang. Erin.

"Erin, I told you I wasn't up for the family dinner tonight. I'm still under the weather with this injury, and I had to work today."

"Oh, for God's sake, don't give me that. You couldn't be bothered. Admit it."

He ignored that. "You never call my mobile. What's up?"

"I tried the home phone, and you didn't pick up. I assumed you were avoiding me."

He settled in for a long conversation.

But only five minutes later, with Erin still chattering in his ear, his other phone rang.

"Erin, my other line's ringing, and it might be work. Can I call you back?"

He rang off and grabbed the phone. It was dispatch downtown.

"DS McBride?"

"Yes?"

"I've an Ivan Cameron on the line asking for you or DC Dunn. Can't raise her at all, and I've been trying to get you on your mobile."

"Patch him through." Who the hell was Ivan Cameron?

"This is DS McBride."

"My name's Ivan. I work as a barman at Jenny Watts in Bangor. Do you know it?"

"I do." Ryan felt a flicker of unease. He'd last been there with Rose.

"A constable was distributing flyers around Bangor a few days ago. Apparently, there's a suspicious character targeting young women. I drink up the street sometimes, and they had leaflets lying around. This fella at the back, I dunno. The woman he's with seemed fine when she came in around seven with a couple of others. Then he shows up, starts to chat her up. Mind you, it's packed here tonight, so I can't watch everybody, but she's slouching in her seat now, no sign of her mates. People sometimes go up the street to the other pubs for different music. The man doesn't look like the e-fit exactly. Maybe a wee bit, you know?"

"Describe him to me." Ryan felt his pulse rise. They could use a break in this case. Maura did, especially. It was wearing on her, but they all needed some damn thing to happen. Could it be their guy? If they got him, great. If not, some young woman would be traumatized. And they needed to catch him in the act too. There was nothing wrong with having a drink in a bar with a woman. How to get him? Follow them? Hope he attempted to assault her?

"I can't see them at the moment. I'm at the phone out here behind the bar. But he's tall, longish straight hair under a baseball hat and those aviator-type tinted glasses. I didn't serve him myself, but I could ask Sean if he remembers better. It's slammed in here tonight, though, with the band and all. It doesn't seem right."

"Listen to me, Ivan." The phone felt slippery in his hand now. "Do not let them leave. If that's our guy—he's going to assault her. We can't know for sure at this point if it's him, but just in case, you can't let them leave. Make an excuse, get the other barman to help if you need to, but stop them leaving. I'll be there in about twenty minutes or less. The Bangor police will be there sooner. Will you go make sure they're still there?"

The phone rattled in his ear as the barman put it down. He came back on, breathless.

"Yes, I can see his back. Looks like they're settled there for a while. She's a pretty young lady, hard to miss."

"Keep an eye on him. It's important you don't let him know you're watching and don't approach them unless he tries to leave. Improvise, can you do that? He hasn't done anything wrong at the moment, but I suspect he intends to. Any other doors?"

"No. They won't get past me. I can see the front door from here and the emergency side exit too. At the back our service door is locked."

As soon as Ryan hung up, he called dispatch, gave them the basic details, and told them to contact the local Bangor station and have them send cars to Jenny Watts to talk to Ivan, ASAP. They were also to contact Billy, fill him in. He tried Maura's mobile a couple of times as he drove, and it went to voicemail. Why wasn't she answering her phone? He redialed and accelerated hard onto the M2 while his heart hammered on.

Chapter Thirty-One

Sunday, November 6

Where the hell was Maura? She would want to be part of this. He hit redial again and again.

Someone answered. A flat, angry voice came on the line before he had a chance to speak.

"Who's this? Who is this ringing and ringing? If a person doesn't answer, it means they're not available."

"Let me speak to Maura." Ryan raced along the Sydenham bypass, pulling around slow-moving cars. He had his lights flashing.

"She's sick. She's a bad cold, and she's asleep in her bed."

"Is this Mrs. Dunn?"

A slight hesitation. "Yes."

"Wake her up. Get her on the phone. Right. Now."

He heard a sigh as Maura's mother presumably thought the better of further argument.

A few moments later, Maura came on, her voice rasping and thick with sleep. "Hello?"

Ryan gave her the rundown as best as he could.

"Shit. Where are you now?"

"I'm about ten minutes out."

"Shit. Shit." He heard more rustling and creaking.

"I'll meet you there. Sorry, my mum took the phone away while I slept.

She'd have turned it off but couldn't figure out how. I'll be there shortly."

He disconnected. The sign for Bangor flashed by. The phone rang again.

"DS McBride? It's Ivan. I'm dead sorry, but they've gone. I watched the door the whole friggin' time and checked on them every wee while. The Bangor police arrived a few minutes ago."

Ryan slammed the phone onto the seat, powered into the Bangor roundabout and onto Main Street. He double-parked in front of Jenny's with a screech of brakes, causing a constable standing inside the door to turn around, alarmed. He registered the flashing light and relaxed a little. Ryan jumped out.

He showed his warrant card to the young constable. "Anything?"

"No, Sergeant. My partner's in there, and I walked up and down Main Street on both sides but saw nothing unusual. We don't know what we're looking for. The couple you wanted us to watch had already left."

"How come it took you all so long to fucking get here? The station's just up the road."

The constable recoiled as if he had been struck, Ryan's anger coming off him like a physical thing.

"We're shorthanded with the flu going around. Gang fights at the seafront, and somebody tried to break into the Co-op. And we were only told of a suspicious sighting."

Ryan slammed his hand on the doorframe and rushed in. He saw the other constable at the bar, writing in his notebook and nodding at a long-faced barman.

He pushed through. "Ivan?"

"Yes. Look, I'm sorry. I kept checking, but I have to work, and I never let those doors out of my sight."

There was a slight disturbance at the front as Maura arrived.

Ryan turned to the barman. "Can you describe him again?"

"Tania's on the other bar. I'll get her. Sean, come here, will you?"

The waiter came over. He was ginger-haired and affable, but no help.

"I served him and all, but he kept his head down the whole time. Like, not obvious or nothing, but I never got a decent look at him, and to tell you the truth, all I remember is longish dark hair and a baseball hat, I think. But nearly everybody has dark hair, you know? He checked his mobile a lot. I'm dead sorry."

Tania was a bit more help. "I saw a man with a dark-coloured baseball hat and glasses. Maybe a black jacket? I took his order."

"Would you recognize him again?"

"I only saw him for a minute, and it was a big crowd at the bar. So probably not."

Ryan turned back to Maura.

"How come no one saw them leave?" He walked back to the table and looked around, then moved towards the back. Then he saw it. A hallway by a dark corner, hardly noticeable. He went over. The exit sign glowed dimly above the back door. Cardboard boxes, some big metal beer kegs, and a wheelie bin crowded the corridor. It was a tight squeeze. This was the service door and...it was open a crack.

Maura had come up behind him, and they both ran outside. "There's a big car park over there. What do you bet?"

"What kind of car does Wylie drive?" Ryan asked.

"He used to drive a red Ford. But Ryan, how do we know it's him? Listen to me, it might not be. We have to be careful. We can't broadcast an alert for Wylie, not on a hunch. And even if he rapes her, we have no proof unless we find them. The witnesses can't identify him."

They reached the pub's back door, and Billy rushed out.

"Any luck? The barman told me they must have left this way. It's supposed to be locked. The main fire exit and side door is over there." He pointed to a side corridor. "He would have seen them if they'd used it. He said this back door is only used to store kegs, bins, and recycle, and they take them out at shift's end. One of the staff must have opened it for quick smoke. It's the only way to duck outside without the manager seeing."

"Listen, would you get the two Bangor constables to check this car park and maybe keep an eye out for red Fords? I want to talk to the barman again." They headed inside.

Ryan scanned the crowded room. What could they do? Drive around aimlessly, searching? The noise, the heat, it was driving him crazy. He had to get out, to do something…and it wasn't just Wylie, it was the case. Kathleen, Rose, and now Bridget and the baby. How had he let his life spin out like this? "The last victim we spoke to, Evelyn, he lifted her from Bangor, didn't he?"

"Yes," Maura said. "But not from here, from Wolsey's. It's up the street."

"What did she say, though?" Ryan said.

"Something about a dream, but that sounds a bit, you know, far-fetched? Let's ask, what do we have to lose?"

"A dream? What do you mean, a dream?" Ivan said, puzzled.

"A fairy tale?" Maura added. "Something like that?"

"No, I don't know anything about fairy tales. Here, I'll get Sean and Tania."

The barman walked away, and they waited, seconds passing. He came back with Tania.

"Something about a dream, Tania, a fairy tale." Maura smiled at the waitress, encouraging her.

"I'm thinking, maybe stupid," Tania said. "Bangor Castle Walled Garden? I took my family there this summer when they came from Poland for a holiday. It's lovely in the good weather. Castle, fairy tale? Closed now."

"Can you drive through the castle at night?" Ryan asked.

"Yes, I'm sure. You park there for the offices as well, you know? Castle Park. And nice trees all around."

"How far?"

"Up the street and left at the roundabout."

Ryan glanced around for Billy but couldn't see him. He nodded to Maura. "Come on, it's worth a try. Call Billy for me Maura, and tell him where we're heading. He'll sort it."

They shot out of the roundabout with Maura holding onto the dash the way Billy did, sliding onto a straight road with trees either side. Ahead, they saw the park, and as they neared it, a sign for Bangor Castle Walled Garden.

"Funny how the mind works," Maura said. "Maybe Evelyn saw this and made it into a fairy tale."

"Who knows? We could easily be heading in the wrong direction. Probably lots of dark alleys off the main street. And there's Pickie Fun Park too. Those big bloody swan boats. All the fairy lights on the front there."

Ryan roared into the castle grounds and up a smaller road flanked by overhanging trees. The road emptied into a circular car park with a grassed section in the middle. The asphalt gleamed, the parking lines glowed white and precise in his headlights. It stretched before them, empty. The castle loomed black and impenetrable against the sky.

He drove slowly around the grassy island and, noticed a break near the top, headed through. They coasted along, their headlights only picking up shrubbery and trees. Ryan swore softly under his breath. No sign of them.

"Wait, what's that?" Maura grabbed his arm and pointed into the shrubbery.

Ryan could see nothing, then…a faint flash. He pulled towards it. Slowly.

A vehicle, tucked under a tree. Something flashed again. Ryan turned their car around and his lights swept a dark blue car, hardly noticeable among the bushes.

"Oh shit." Ryan cursed himself for not turning off his lights because as soon as he said that, a head popped up. "Christ, he's seen us."

The driver's door swung open. A dark figure bolted for the trees.

Ryan slammed on the brakes, jumped from the car, and took after him with Maura yelling, "I'll see to her. Get him, get him!"

The guy had taken off at speed and crashed ahead, barrelling through the undergrowth and the stand of trees behind it with his arms flailing wildly. Ryan could run. Normally, he was a sprinter, but the last few days and nights had depleted him. His wound still hurt as he swung his arms, pumping after the bastard.

He followed the fleeing figure down the long driveway as the guy shot by the tall bushes at the edge, dodging in and out, trying to find an escape before he came to the front gates. As they approached the main road, Ryan could see better—he was closing in, he could hear the runner's laboured breaths. He could see his outline, a black fleece, and dark trousers, white trainers.

Then, as they got to the end, instead of running out through the gates, the guy took an abrupt right turn and headed back into the dense hedges at the side of the driveway.

This move was so unexpected that Ryan, fuelled by rage and momentum was unable to stop. He slammed right into the stone wall by the gates. The body blow was shocking and sudden. He collapsed on the grass, his injured arm and side erupting with pain so intense it took his breath away.

As he lay there, gathering his reserves, he saw the guy's baseball hat lying nearby and reached for it. He caught his fingers in something soft—hair? It was full of hair. And where the hell was the guy going?

My God. He was heading back. He was doubling back to his car. He intended to get away. He was running back to the victim...and to Maura.

Ryan was up in a flash, pounding along the road. He didn't need to go through the trees. He knew where he was going. Halfway along, he found his stride, forgot the pain, increased his speed, and propelled himself forward towards the smaller car park.

He was almost at the car when he saw her, a bundle lying half on the tarmac half on the grass. It was Maura. He was about to stop when she yelled, "Get him. He's in the car."

Ryan flew by her, tossing her the baseball hat as he passed, and hit the car as the engine caught and the headlights splashed the bushes ahead with sharp white light, temporarily blinding him. He heard a frantic shifting of gears as he wrenched the driver's door open. The car started to move backwards. He reached in, grabbed the guy by the collar of his fleece, and violently yanked him out.

At this point, he should have pushed him onto the side of the car, cuffed him, and held him there while he read him his rights.

He should have done a lot of things.

Instead, he hauled the guy fully out onto the ground, dropped on top of him, knees on his stomach, and felt his breath whoosh out like a punctured tyre.

It was Sam Burns.

Ryan hit him, one side of his face then the other, frustration fueling his anger. It wasn't easy. His body protested with every blow. But it didn't matter. The pain felt good. He needed it to keep focused. The bastard had raped those women, and...he had hurt Maura.

Burns stared up at Ryan, his eyes wild. He seemed disoriented. He'd taken something, Ryan thought. He recognised the glassy look, the dilated pupils. Maybe that's why he'd been able to run away so fast.

Maura had, by this time, managed to stand up. She ran to Ryan, pulled him away, and looked at the cowering man. Her face twisted in shock and disgust.

"It's Sam! No, no." Maura reared back. "How can this possibly be?"

Sam Burns pushed himself up on one elbow. "She wanted to come with me. She liked me." He lay back down, brought his hands up, and covered his eyes, then whispered, almost to himself, "Everybody likes me." He pointed a quivering finger at Ryan and wiped his sleeve across his face. "I ran because you surprised me." He turned to Maura, "He hit me. You saw it."

She walked over to him, drew back, and kicked him hard in the ribs.

"I saw you violently resisting arrest, that's what I saw."

Ryan got his breath back. "How is the woman, Maura? Did he assault her?"

"I think we got here in time. He'd started to take photos with his phone, though."

"Watch him," Ryan said and walked around to the passenger side of the car. A young woman lay sound asleep, her blouse undone. Ryan covered her up a little and closed the door. It was a chilly night.

They had Burns restrained by the time Billy arrived with the Bangor police.

"Jesus, *Sam Burns*? Looks like he put up a bit of a fight."

"Something terrible," Maura said, "He came at Ryan like a wild animal. He's on something."

"You should have shot him," Billy said. "Save taxpayers' money. But don't ever tell Margaret I said that."

Ryan wiped his nose with the back of his hand. His face was slick with sweat. His arm was screaming. He'd have to take something when he got home.

"How's she doing?" Billy nodded at the ambulance with its lights flashing.

"She's still unconscious," Maura said.

"Do you think he...you know?"

"We don't know. He was warming up. We're hoping we got here in time."

The young constable from the front of Jenny's came over, shaking his head.

"Jesus, yer man's knocked about a bit, eh? He's a police officer, you say? You would think he would know resisting arrest is a mug's game."

"Yes," Ryan said, "you'd think."

Chapter Thirty-Two

Monday, November 7

L ast night had been a nightmare, what with the booking and the statements. Ryan dried his face. He needed to get over to Jimmy Blackwood's this morning, get the bloody garage processed. He'd been wrong about Wylie. Was he wrong about Sophie? Everything was circumstantial, wasn't it?

The old man signed the papers to allow the team to check the garage and haul the Mini away. He dandered around the field in Wellington boots and old dungarees, smoking a pipe. He seemed to be enjoying all the fuss. Good news for Ryan since the flatbed truck was on its way from the yard for that purpose. Lily remained at the bungalow, watching the vans and activity with placid interest. When Ryan approached her, she nodded and smiled. No wee bald baby boy on her hip.

"What are youse doing?" she asked.

"Having a quick look around the garage area and checking the car out. It may have been used without your dad's knowledge in the commission of a crime. Does he use it much? If he does, we'll fix something up for him."

"No, you're all right. He uses his bike mostly, and one of his mates can always come and pick him up. He's plenty of mates, my dad."

Walking back to the garage, Ryan tried to picture old Jimmy in the midst of a lively bunch of friends, chatting away. Couldn't see it. Nope.

Sunday night had exhausted him, physically and emotionally. Burns, protesting his innocence, had been remanded. The team had a warrant request for his flat and were, at this time, downloading the digital images from his camera and phone. They would forensically examine his personal computer. He had kept all that stuff; it was astounding. Something about the lad, Ryan had felt it, too eager. But Maura had liked him, and he hadn't wanted to burst that bubble. And the clever bastard had used Wylie as a foil, the enemy of my enemy and all that. Of course, Derek had been suspicious—but who ever took Derek seriously?

Ryan reached the garage and pulled on a suit and booties, then wandered over to the CSIs.

The high-pitched whine of a hand vacuum filled the space. Eddie, the senior tech, backed out when he'd finished and greeted Ryan with a smack on the arm. His bad arm.

"You owe me for this. Not everybody gets the team up on such short notice, although this is interesting. Just finished doing the carpet and upholstery." He brandished the vacuum for emphasis.

"Why interesting?" Ryan asked.

"Someone has wiped this car. On first blush, it's clean. Your average person usually leaves some traces. Nevertheless, we'll get old motor-mouth Jimmy down the road there to give us his fingerprints for elimination. We'll do the daughter, too, although she said she never uses the Mini. We'll know better when we get it downtown. That's if we find fingerprints or anything."

"The outside of this bloody car's a mess, dirt, and crap all over. Strange it's spotless inside."

"Ryan, my friend, that's your department, but I think someone's trying to pull the wool over our eyes. The thing won't start. Normally if it had not been wiped, I would have said you're wasting your time. Thing's an old wreck, doesn't even go."

"Hey, boss, come have a look." A CSI waved to them.

They walked around behind the garage to the far corner. Clusters of yellow dandelions bloomed. The man indicated an old metal oil drum. A photographer hung over it, shooting inside. He finished up and nodded to them.

"That's a solvent." Ryan caught a faint whiff in the air as he approached the drum. That's what he had noticed before. Turps.

"What is it?" Eddie asked the CSI.

"Looks like someone's tried to burn something in there. Did a great job, but I think there may have been some water in the bottom? How could there not be, the weather we're having lately? Smells like they used an accelerant. We'll test it."

Eddie peered inside. "Anything recoverable?"

"Like I said, it's been raining on and off recently. We might get lucky."

They moved away, and Ryan started to peel off the suit. "Thanks, Eddie, for getting here so fast and all. I know you're busy."

"The Justice Branch never sleeps."

Ryan yawned. "The Serious Crime Branch never sleeps either."

Back at the station, he saw Maura in Girvan's office with Malcolm Anderson, the DS assigned to the rape cases. He sneaked towards his desk until Girvan spotted him and waved him in. Girvan smiled thinly when Ryan sat down.

"Good work. Although this damn Burns situation, it's a PR nightmare."

"I hear we're coming at it head-first, sir," Malcolm said.

"Yes, the service is not whitewashing this. He's having the book thrown at him. I'll have to head the press conference on that." Girvan shifted in his seat, uncomfortable with this development. "Thank Christ he's a probationer." Then he brightened up. "McBride, we may have a breakthrough in the McGuire murder?" Then Girvan's smile vanished. "And what about Coulter?"

"Yes, we're cautiously optimistic about the Kathleen McGuire inquiry, and as I mentioned before, I believe Brendan Doyle to be the main suspect in Coulter's murder. I don't have concrete proof at the moment. He is experienced at covering his tracks. Kevin Coulter killed Liam McKenna. We have the paint analysis from his car back finally, and the CCTV to back that up. We can't say for definite that it was deliberate, but...while Kevin Coulter remains a suspect in the Kathleen McGuire case, there are a lot of signposts pointing to Sophie Walton."

"Yes, yes, I read the preliminary report. We're assuming you're correct, and she's his mother, eh? A matter of time, DNA will seal it. An end in sight, possibly." Girvan beamed. "So, we'll treat this like any other case. Anything else?"

"No, sir," They all said together.

Ryan wandered over to Maura's desk and found her typing furiously. She stopped and studied him for a moment before she spoke.

"A stash of roofies at Burns's flat, hats, wigs, and fake glasses—and it looks like that car's a cesspool of DNA and hair and all kinds of trace evidence. According to the boys in forensics." She frowned, looking at her screen. "It's not registered at all. If he had been able to get away, we'd have been back to square one. No way to trace him. Must have picked it up at a junkyard or somewhere. Although there was that baseball hat and the fake hair. We might have pulled some DNA from it...oh, I don't know. What a nightmare." She shook her head. "He had tons of police manuals and computer searches on surveillance and disguises. If he hadn't been such a fuck-up, he would have made a good undercover officer one day. I feel like such a fool. We had a date planned. I was looking forward to it. He seemed nice." She paused again. "His bloody Lavender Morris Minor is in his garage, not a mark on it. He made it up for sympathy and to throw suspicion on Wylie. Bastard."

"Maura, I liked him too. So enthusiastic. Almost too much so, but I thought that was me being my old jaded self." Ryan smiled. "Of course, he didn't fool Derek. Never hear the end of this...."

"Ah yes, Derek. He's been down already. I felt like slapping him. Right," she said. "I do have some information for you regarding those car parks. Let me finish here, and I'll send it over. Sorry, it just came through." She turned back to her screen.

Ten minutes later, Ryan and Billy were both scanning the incoming lists of parking employees from Belfast International and George Best Airports. They also had a breakdown of airport and airline personnel. They saw no names that jumped out. Another email popped into Ryan's inbox. It read 'Part-time and Consultant.' Then another. 'Recently terminated.'

Billy got it too and yelled, "Hang on, hang on. Look at that, Ryan, in the consultant list, third name."

Ryan whistled. "Dermot Feeny. Parking Consultant."

"I'll be honest," Billy said, reading on down the page, "I thought he was dead."

"And we know Feeny is a documented friend of Brendan Doyle."

"What the hell is a parking consultant anyway?" Billy shook his head. "I'll tell you this for nothing Ryan, Feeny won't talk. He'll never admit to passing information to Doyle."

"No, I grant you it's unlikely, not with everything I know about Brendan Doyle. But at least we have a possible tie-in. Maybe Doyle found out when Kevin was due back through Feeny. But what's the damn motive? Brendan's mum likes Kathleen and is upset when she's killed? Upset enough to have her son murder Kevin? I don't know. She'd only known her for what? Seven, eight, months? Although by all accounts, they were close. Could there be another reason to take the risk? There's so much at stake for Brendan Doyle now. Everything he has. His family, his reputation, everything. Would his mother want him to risk all that for a young woman they barely knew?"

"What is it, DS McBride?" Brendan Doyle sounded agitated on the phone. "My mother had a stroke and was taken into the Royal Victoria Hospital in Belfast on Friday."

"I'm sorry to hear that, Mr. Doyle. But you and I will need to talk. And soon." Ryan saw the bustling, fiery little woman in his mind's eye—the fruit and nut chocolate bar. It was too bad.

"About what?" Doyle said.

"About Kevin Coulter. You know he turned up dead, same place as Kathleen McGuire?"

"Ah, yes. The man who was kidnapped, it was on the news. Kathleen's friend, as it turns out, right? A little bird told me he's dead, but I'm not privy to all the details."

Ryan could hear traffic noise in the background. "Are you in Belfast?"

"I'm in my car heading home to sleep for a few hours. I've been up at Mammy's bedside. My wife Kelly is with her, and our boys will pop in later."

"I still need to talk to you," Ryan insisted. "I'd like you to come into the station for an interview. Otherwise…." Ryan left the threat hanging.

"I have to get some sleep. I'd be no use to you at the moment. I will come in tomorrow. Give me the morning with Mammy then I'll come up. You're at Antrim Road now, right?"

He has a lot of information about me at his fingertips, Ryan realised.

"Yes. Make it noon," Ryan said and ended the call.

Ryan signaled to Billy. "Maura's handling the Sam Burns stuff, for now, Brendan Doyle's coming in for a chat tomorrow, and I'm heading home."

He was bone-tired. He signed off, grabbed his jacket, and headed for the car. He decided to call Bridget. Since that evening at his farm, they'd spoken a few times, and she'd been rushed and dismissive. He couldn't understand it. They had come to an understanding that night, or at least he thought they had. What else did she want him to do? He'd asked her to move in with him, she had refused for the time being. She was the one who was keeping the pregnancy quiet.

Don't tell anyone.

He could call her. She'd be on shift. He knew that, knew she wouldn't like it. She would be brisk. No. He needed to see her, talk to her face to face. Now that it was happening, he realised he wanted to tell Billy about the baby, see his face. God, that would be something. He smiled briefly at the idea. And Erin, she was his sounding board, and she would be thrilled. He wanted to share it with her now, and was surprised at himself, he was. But Bridget was behaving strangely. Not answering messages. What was going on? Tired or not, he'd had enough. He jumped into the car and headed for the Mater Hospital. He would confront her.

And her brothers, he wasn't afraid of them, if that's what this was about. He had never been intimidated by Malachy and Marcus, dark, glowering, bitter youths. He didn't like them—and knew they hated him. This whole situation had left him feeling lost and abandoned.

At least Bridget's parents would be home in a few days. She could tell her mum—and her dad could talk the brothers down, if that was the problem.

CHAPTER THIRTY-TWO

He parked on the street outside Emergency.

"Hello, is Bridget Doherty on the floor?" he asked a passing nurse. She frowned, thinking. "Yes, maybe on break. Let me page her for you."

A few minutes later, Bridget came through the double doors and saw him. "What is it? Is everything all right?"

"Let's get a coffee." He steered her away.

Starbucks was open, and they grabbed a table in a quiet corner.

"Bridget, what the hell is going on?"

Surprised, she pulled back a little. "Ryan, it's crazy here at the moment, some new flu strain going around. I've been called in for extra shifts. Sorry I haven't been returning calls."

"That's not what I mean. I thought we were settled, had talked it out at the farm."

She hesitated. "It's with everything. I need some space. It's overwhelming."

"It's overwhelming? Is that what you're saying to me now? It's overwhelming? You need space? What the hell are you talking about? It doesn't have to be. I'm here now. Talk to me and let me help. We're in this together, right? Move into the farm. It's going to happen eventually."

Again, that pause. "Ryan, Mum and Dad will be—"

He pushed his chair back, looked away over her shoulder into the corridor with the nurses and doctors—the worried visitors, low level tension hanging in the air. Christ, he hated hospitals. And he was tired of this, bloody tired of being confused and unsure. Hadn't he given up Rose? Hadn't he told Bridget he would be there for her? What else could he do? "I know all about that. Your mum and dad and your brothers. It's you and me I'm interested in. I'm talking about us." He hesitated. "And the baby."

He heard a tinny announcement in the background. Could hear the chatter of customers and other nurses getting a caffeine fix.

"Listen, Ryan, I'm sorry, I have to go. You're right. We need to sort things out. I'll come over tomorrow night, and we'll make solid arrangements."

She looked tired, Ryan thought, strained. He felt sorry that he needed to push her.

"We'll sort it tomorrow. I'm on until two in the morning, and I already have a splitting headache. I'll call you." She grabbed her coffee and pressed the lid on. "We have a lot to talk about."

Chapter Thirty-Three

Tuesday, November 8

R yan contemplated his buttered toast and took a bite. His mobile rang and he swallowed quickly, almost choking. Brendan Doyle. "Mammy's slipped into a coma. I'm on my way there now. I need to cancel our meeting."

Through his kitchen window, the garden dripped green and grey like a watercolour painting left in the rain. He needed to resolve this case and felt strongly that Brendan Doyle held one of the keys.

"I am sorry about your mother, but we still need to meet. Tell you what, I'll head up there to the Royal myself and find you."

"You have my number." Doyle rang off.

Great, another hospital...Ryan walked to reception, the tang of antiseptic and hospital food hanging in the air around him. He asked a bright-faced intern for directions to heart and stroke and called Doyle before he got there. They decided to meet in the restaurant.

Spoons was busy, a shiny, well-intentioned attempt to distract visitors and patients alike from the reason they were there. He walked in and saw the big man at a table by the window. Doyle had a coffee cup in front of him. He waved Ryan over. *He knows who I am.*

"Are you eating? The food's not too bad, considering." Doyle gestured to the seat across from him and sat down.

"A coffee will do," Ryan said.

The waitress bustled over, and Ryan ordered. "So?" he asked Doyle, "How is your mother?"

"She'll likely not pull through."

"That's bad news."

"Aye, well."

Doyle looked away for a moment, over the flat roof and the car park beyond. Underneath the man's ruddy complexion, Ryan could see a sallowness. Grief, perhaps, the creeping realisation of impending loss.

Ryan's coffee arrived, and he stirred it, thinking of what to say and deciding just to ask. Doyle struck him as a man who did not need to be finessed.

"Tell me about the connection between Kathleen McGuire and your family. And Kevin Coulter."

Doyle said nothing but reached into his inside pocket and removed his wallet. He took a photograph from it and laid it on the table between them. Then he slid it towards Ryan.

Ryan picked it up and saw a youthful Mary Doyle at the seaside. She seemed happy, and she had two children with her. Brendan Doyle, skinny, but recognizable with his wild brown hair and strong features, had his arm around a little girl of about five. The child had long black hair and light eyes.

"Mammy went through hell with our da. A right bastard. He beat the shite out of all of us." He took a moment. "People think I'm a hard man, and maybe I am, but he was harder. It was him gave me this…." He smiled and touched his nose, "And a few more knocks besides. But he never touched Ailish. I think he knew that if he did, Mammy would have reared up and killed him. You see, Mammy was surrounded by boys, and she loved us mind, but she lived for her wee baby girl."

Ryan's perception of Doyle subtly shifted. A man struggling with memories and love. A criminal and a murderer, probably. But he cared deeply for his family. Ryan flashed to his own mother. He loved her, and his father—probably, despite their differences. And Erin, of course. And soon, someone else to love. Christ, McBride, cue the frigging violins.

234

"What happened?"

"Da gave Mammy a bad hammering one night, and they took her into the hospital. They would never have thought to charge him in those days. Even the local police were wary of him. And she never made a fuss, said she fell, you know, that old carry-on. While Mammy recovered, Ailish contracted pneumonia, and Da couldn't be bothered to take her to the hospital. He said she had a bad cold. He was drunk most of the time then. A terrible, mean drunk.

By the time he could be arsed to call a doctor, it was too late. I should have done something, but I was too young to realise she could die from it. They pointed a finger at the bloody pigeons, how they carried it, but Da killed her right enough. Mammy never totally recovered."

"What age were you?" Ryan could imagine this big man as a splintery youth, long hair and burning anger.

"Fifteen."

"And what age would Ailish be now?"

"She's every age to Mammy. At first, she only had to see a wee girl in the town, and she would start to cry." Doyle leaned back in his chair. "I've a story to tell you. Now mind, we never touched a hair on Kathleen's head. She gave our Mammy a second lease on life. Mammy protected her. I think she saw something of Ailish in the lass. She's been looking her whole life, you know? For something."

"The days before she died, Kathleen stayed with you, didn't she?" Ryan understood then. "She had nowhere else to go. She was running from Coulter. We saw the bruises on her body. He'd threatened her, and you protected her. That's where she went."

"Yes. She stayed with us, then drove off to meet her sister. We never heard from her again. We saw on the news she'd been murdered. Mammy was shattered. Seemed like she'd lost Ailish all over again. That's why she didn't—couldn't—go home to Belfast right away." He paused for a moment. "She put on a good show, my mam, she'd done that all her life you know, had to put a brave face on everything, but Kathleen's death broke her for the second time."

"And you believe Kevin Coulter killed Kathleen?"

Doyle hesitated, then seemed to make up his mind. "We knew about Coulter. He abused Kathleen and bullied her like Da did to Mammy. When Kathleen ended the bloody thing, Coulter came to our Belfast house and tried to beat her up. And he hit our mammy." Doyle regarded Ryan with dead eyes. "I took both women out of harm's way. Mr. Coulter thought he was dealing with a defenseless young woman and an old lady." Doyle looked away for a moment, and Ryan heard a bitter laugh. "But no. Detective. He was fucking with me."

There it is, Ryan thought, the old Brendan Doyle. Oh yes.

The waitress appeared with a fresh coffee, and Brendan thanked her, then something caught his attention over at the door. Ryan turned to see. A couple of men crowded the entrance, hard men, older. One of them, bald and stooped, nodded respectfully to Brendan.

I know you, Ryan thought. Not dead. Brendan Doyle had acknowledged the courtesy by tipping his head.

"Dermot Feeny. Popped in to see your mammy, I daresay?" Ryan said.

He recognized the other man too. A face from the past. "I imagine, Mr. Doyle, if we positioned Serious Crime Officers outside your mother's room, they'd be busy for a while."

Ignoring the comment, Doyle sipped again from his cup. "Kathleen had decided to go to the police with allegations of abuse. Also, she was convinced Kevin Coulter had killed her old boyfriend, Liam McKenna. Not to mention an ex-girlfriend, a woman who was suing him. Or maybe getting someone to do it for him. A nasty piece of work, Kevin Coulter, a dangerous man."

"It doesn't mean he killed Kathleen."

"Ah, you see, that's just it, Detective McBride. He didn't."

Ryan paused. "But—"

Doyle shook his head, and Ryan saw the ghost of a smile touch his lips. "And I didn't kill him."

Chapter Thirty-Four

Sunday, October 23

BEFORE

Early Sunday morning, Kathleen sat in the big farmhouse kitchen drinking a mug of strong tea while Mary cooked breakfast, ordering her son and daughter-in-law around like a sergeant major.

"What are you smiling about?" Mary asked her, sliding another egg onto her plate.

Kathleen held up her hand. "That's enough food, for goodness sake. I'm just one person."

"You could do with a bit more beef on you," Brendan added, turning to his mother. "She's desperate skinny."

Mary Doyle nodded her head in agreement. "You look nice this morning, dear. I like your shoes. All dressed up for your sister, then? Can we not persuade you to come to mass with us instead? You could see your sister after."

"I haven't seen her for months, Mary. I want to tell her what's happened. I haven't been returning emails. You know what it's been like with Kevin. I want to explain. I called her..."

"You used the phone I gave you, right?" Brendan asked.

"Yes, yes I did. We're meeting later in Portstewart. She tried to put me off until next week, and I didn't want to go into the whole thing with her on the phone, I insisted we meet..." Her voice trailed off. "She was angry with me."

Kelly, who had been loading the dishwasher, turned around. "Didn't you say she got in yesterday? She'll still be tired, pet, that's all."

"Yes, probably, but I need to see her. I thought I might take a country drive on the way. Avoid the motorways as much as I can. It's going to be a nice day."

Brendan put his plate on the counter. "Be careful, Kathleen, that's all I'm saying. We haven't seen yer man yet. We've been watching his place, and there's no sign of him or his car. Hard to get inside that parking garage, but I think we've found a way."

"They have a corporate rate at the Europa," Kathleen said. "We've stayed there together. They know him. If he was out in Belfast drinking Saturday night, he might be there. But it's also possible he's with his dad. They have a flat in London. He hops back and forth all the time. He usually leaves his Mercedes at the long-stay parking at George Best Airport and flies from there."

"George Best, eh? Kelly, love, which one's the rubbish drawer again?"

"There, under the window. Why, what are you looking for?"

He rifled in the drawer, and with a grunt, he pulled out a notebook.

"This. My old address book. I know a fella at the parking. Remember Dermot Feeny?"

"My God." Kelly barked out a laugh. "Don't tell me that auld eejit's still breathing."

"Still breathing, still drinking, and has a finger in every car park in Belfast." Brendan held the book open. "I'll give him a wee ring later on, ask him to keep an eye out. You wouldn't have the registration plate number, would you, Kathleen?"

She wasn't much into cars, but Kevin's plate was personalized, she rattled it off, and he jotted it down.

"You be careful till we talk to him, eh? We'll straighten him out, but before that...go meet your sister and come right back, do you hear me?"

Brendan turned to go, and his mother called to him from the cooker, "Is that what you're wearing to chapel, son?"

Kathleen saw him glance over at Kelly, who rolled her eyes.

"No, Mammy, sure, I'm just away up to change."

She called Rose's mobile again and left a message saying she was on her way. It was less than a two-hour drive, give or take, depending on weather and traffic. She wanted to take the country roads where she could and enjoy the scenery, take her time. It had been a while since she had relaxed and had an outing. She checked her mirrors every little while, in case, but how could Kevin find her? She had even noticed Donny doing a desultory check of her car, for heaven's sake. It was like some tawdry film. Her life in the pictures. A life in scenes....

She would take the motorway if necessary but avoid it if she could. It felt good to be free of Kevin, like something heavy had been lifted, and with Mary's family behind her....

Once she made it to Belfast, she took the ring road and headed west towards Maghera. She stopped in Antrim for a break to stretch her legs and have a coffee. She locked up and wandered along High Street. Sophie lived around here and always said how lovely it was. As she returned to her car, she made a promise. She would travel around more, maybe go on some trips with Rose, stay at B&Bs, have a laugh. Drink more wine, eat more pasta, have more sex—oh, bad girl.

Back on the road, at the top end of Lough Neagh, she saw a signpost for Portglenone Forest. Ah, Portglenone, the small town her family had visited when she was little. Rose and her, running and playing by the River Bann, splashing and chasing each other. She had a flash of her father, hitching up his dark, baggy trousers and paddling in the water, laughing and shouting, 'Happy days are here again.' She had a sudden urge to see it and decided to go in that direction. It was still early. As she turned onto the small road that ran parallel to the river Bann, the sun disappeared, and the landscape, previously bright and vivid, darkened to a somber, shadowed green. It was beautiful here, sun or shade, and a little detour would do no harm now, would it? She had time, a whole lifetime ahead of her. She would lose that worthlessness she felt sometimes, find a proper boyfriend and be a better sister. She wondered briefly about that detective. I wonder if he's sorted that ex-girlfriend out yet. She'd liked him. God, he was attractive. And when they were making love…she smiled, remembering. She still had his card somewhere….

The narrow road wound gently at this point, and she slowed down, enjoying the drive. Only one car passed her, coming the other direction, a white Range Rover. The driver slowed and lifted a hand in greeting.

It started as a tiny wobble, hardly noticeable, but as she steered around a tight bend, the car started to bump, and she felt it then, a flat tyre's slap-slap. Oh, no. Up ahead, she saw a break in the hedgerow, a lay-by.

She pulled over and stopped, checking her watch. Already eight o'clock.

As she sat there thinking, tyres crunched, and she looked up, surprised, sun in her side mirror bright now, blinding her. Another car had pulled in behind. She opened the door and grabbed her handbag and mobile. Change a tyre? Her? Get a grip, she thought. Maybe this person could help. Would help.

But no. It was Kevin, the sight of him almost a physical blow. She stumbled back.

"You've been following me?"

"Yes, and aren't you the busy bee? Worth keeping an eye on."

"Where I go has nothing to do with you, not anymore." She could hear the quiver in her voice, and it embarrassed her, showing the bastard fear.

"How can you say that after all, we've been to each other? After all I've done for you?" he said, moving a little closer.

How had she not seen that before, his smugness?

"I see you still wear the watch."

She glanced at the Rolex, loose on her wrist. She unclasped it and threw it at him. She couldn't stand his sarcasm, his smirking face. She was done with that, although that first jolt of fear stayed with her, coiled in her stomach, slowly twisting.

He made no attempt to catch the watch, and it fell at his feet. He crushed it beneath his shoe and kicked it away.

CHAPTER THIRTY-FOUR

"Kevin, we are done. You need to leave me alone."

"What, so you can run back to Liam? I wouldn't bother trying."

He moved closer still, and she held her ground for a moment, transfixed by his expression, his fury. He was hardly recognizable as the man she knew. Backing away, she rummaged through her handbag, through tissues, her mobile, and makeup, until she felt the gun's grip. Could she do this? Brendan had told her—no, hammered into her—that having a gun would somehow make things better. She had been unsure. In all the interactions with Kevin, even with the home invasion and the attack on Mary, she never thought she was in mortal danger. Now she did.

"Looking for your phone? Who are you going to call? A friend? I told you, Liam's not available."

He started towards her again, and she moved away, her hand still in her bag. Why did it have to be so quiet here? Why did she turn up this road? Her hand was on the grip, yet still, she hesitated. "I have a gun." Those words. They had power. She felt it. Some strange electricity surging up her arm and into her being.

He stopped short. Then he smiled.

"And where would you get a gun? Marks and Spencer?"

She withdrew it from her bag, lifted it up, and deliberately released the safety with her thumb.

He remained motionless, staring at it. Like he couldn't believe what he was seeing. He knew what a gun could do, especially in her inexperienced hands. Thank God, thank God, Brendan had given it to her.

"Leave me alone." She started to lower it, and he moved toward her again. She jerked her hand back up. That dark anger, her fury, roared back.

The gun went off.

She absorbed the recoil as she was shown, and the noise surprised her as it had in practice with Brendan. Everything stopped. The wind in the trees, birdsong, the long grasses sighing in the field. All she could hear was the gunshot echoing on and on.

He wasn't hit. But the look on his face—surprise? Fear? She couldn't tell.

He got the message and sprinted back to his car, jumped in, slammed the door, and roared off in a shower of gravel and clumps of grass. For at least a minute, she remained immobile, terrified. Of Kevin, yes, but also by what she had done. What if she'd killed him, what then? And she had come so close, just her bad aim.

She walked to her car and stopped. The bullet had gone into her front tyre.

And at the back, the other tyre had a gash in it; someone had stuck a knife in it, huh. Kevin must have been following her this whole time and done it while she stopped in Antrim.

She got into the car and tried to think. What if he came back? He could easily get a gun; she was sure of that. He might even have one in his car, in the boot? Once he settled himself he would be back. It wasn't in his nature to be humiliated by a woman, and he had been. Again.

Who could she call? Not the Doyles, not for a while. They had their phones off for chapel, and according to Kelly, Mary dragged the whole family to the hall for tea and a meet and greet afterwards.

It would be hours before they were back.

Angus was in Dublin.

There was Rose. She groaned at the thought. Could she stand it, all the recriminations? It would take Rose ages to get to her, and Kevin may have come back by then. She guessed she had maybe half an hour to an hour at most. She didn't want to drag her sister into this, perhaps place her in danger too...

The police were not an option. Okay, they were—but not right now. How could she explain Brendan's gun and the bullet in the tyre? A garage? What if they decided to report the bullet hole? She could try to flag down a passing car, but this damn road was deserted, and she didn't fancy standing out there in case Kevin came back.

There was always Sophie, but she was good friends with Kevin and his father. Although she didn't have to tell her everything, did she? At the end of the day, she only had a couple of flat tyres. She needed to get away from here.

She felt it again, that roaring in her head. Outside the car, sporadic sunlight caught edges of the outer branches of bushes, while beneath, she could see deeper shadowed greenery and dark leaves. If Kevin came back, she didn't care what she had to do. He wasn't going to take her.

Chapter Thirty-Five

Tuesday, November 8

"When I heard someone lifted Kevin Coulter, I asked around." Doyle sipped his coffee.

"You did, did you?" Ryan settled back in his chair, ready to listen. This should be good.

"Some people roughed him up a little. By the end of it, they were convinced he had told them the truth. Liam McKenna aside, under pressure, he swore he did not kill Kathleen McGuire."

Doyle leaned back, thought for a moment, then continued.

"Coulter did admit to placing a tracker and to following her from time to time. I failed her there. I should have checked her car myself. I'm getting soft in my old age. Kathleen told us earlier that he had likely killed Liam, her ex-boyfriend. He kept telling her he had. And there was another incident in his past, another girlfriend, but he denied involvement in that. Kathleen wanted to go to the police, have him investigated. He did follow her on the morning she died. They argued at the lay-by, and she pulled a gun on him. He bolted."

"He said all this?"

"Yes, he said all this. They released him."

"You let him go?"

"They let him go, near St. Anne's Cathedral, late Friday night, early Saturday morning. You might get lucky and have some traffic cameras

there, or CCTV? He was alive early Sunday morning, Detective McBride."
Doyle paused, smiled that half smile again. "According to my sources."

"Did your sources tell you the exact time of release?"

"Around three in the morning, I believe."

"We'll check that out."

"Do. I don't like being accused of a murder I didn't commit."

Something in his tone rang true. It would be easy to assume Doyle did it,
especially now they had a motive of sorts. But still, Ryan believed him.

"I wonder where she got a gun, don't you? Nice girl like that."

"Someone who wanted to keep her safe, I expect," Doyle replied.

He knew he couldn't prove the gun was Doyle's. Better chance of linking
it to the Pope. "Whoever took him is guilty of attempted murder. During
the abduction, someone opened fire on me several times."

"Several times? Lucky you, then, your abductors must have been bad shots
indeed."

Ryan's mobile rang before he could reply. It was Billy. Doyle started to
leave.

"I'll need to speak with you again, Mr. Doyle."

"Sure," Doyle said, half-smiled again, and walked away.

Ryan watched him. Hadn't made up his mind about him. "Billy. What's
up?"

"Ryan, the Mini's tyres match the ruts at the lay-by. They also found hair
and prints. I would say it points to Sophie there in the Mini with Kathleen."
Billy took a breath.

"Yes, and I have motive," Ryan interrupted. "Kathleen believed Kevin
murdered Liam McKenna and also possibly the ex-girlfriend who tried to
sue him. She planned to expose him. Listen, I'm coming in. We have a lot
to talk about. I had an interesting heart-to-heart with Brendan Doyle."

Half an hour later at the station, Ryan got Billy, Derek, and Maura together.
The day had not brightened up. The atmosphere in the squad room settled
around them, grey, damp, and noisy.

"Bottom line is, Brendan Doyle said he interrogated Kevin Coulter, decided he was telling the truth about Kathleen, and let him go."

"Doyle admitted to that?" Derek was gripped.

"No, no, the usual bullshit, a friend of a friend, but it was him. We need to go through the CCTV of that area in the timeframe he supplied. Can you do that, Derek?"

"What's he like? Brendan Doyle, eh? I read about him in school. He's a legend." Derek remained enthusiastically impressed.

"I've no doubt he's used to beating the truth out of people. If he says Kevin didn't do it, I'm inclined to believe him. Although if Kevin was desperate enough, he might have lied. Let's face it, he had to know he was a dead man if he confessed. Doyle doesn't care about Liam McKenna. That murder isn't important to him. He believes his mother is dying because of Kathleen and wants to find her killer as much as we do. We need to get Kathleen's prints and hair from the Mini. Then we have enough for a warrant to search Sophie's property. Now back to the other burning question. Who killed Kevin if not Doyle?"

"Sophie?" Maura ventured.

"No, I can't believe she would ever have killed him. She's devastated by his death. I heard her crying." Ryan paused, remembering. "A terrible sound."

"Perhaps she finally told him she was his mother, and he rejected her or something? You can't discount her altogether." Maura had that little frown thing going on.

They sat there thinking for a moment, and finally, Derek jumped up. "All right, I'll start checking the cameras, see if I can find Kevin. Next thing we know, Brendan Doyle will end up dead, then somebody else, and it will keep going and going." He glanced around, twitched.

Ryan took Billy's last crisp, crumpled the packet, and threw it towards the bin. "You know what, Derek? You might be right."

When Ryan called forensics for an update, Eddie laughed him off the phone.

"Prints and DNA from the Mini? Get a grip. Tomorrow for the prints, if you're lucky, and that's because Girvan asked. DNA a wee bit longer. Sorry mate."

On the bright side, with the location and time supplied, it didn't take Derek long to pull up Donegall Street CCTV just before three a.m. on Saturday, November fifth. He sent it over, and they all gathered around.

"See, there it is, there's the van." Derek pointed at a dark vehicle slowly cruising along in front of the Cathedral. They watched as it moved past St. Anne's shadowy mass and came to a halt.

"That's at Talbot Street and Commercial Court, right?" Billy added.

They stared at a black, shadowed road, deserted and slick with heavy rain. Faint intermittent triangles of reflected light shone down from lamp standards high above. A miserable night, with no lurking pedestrians. The van took off at speed. It skidded around the corner at Waring Street and disappeared.

"What happened?" Ryan said.

"Wait, wait." Derek had already viewed part of the video.

Something moved on the far pavement, a big black bundle.

"What's that?" Maura crowded the others for a better look.

The shadow coalesced into a man, hunched over and staggering. Once on his feet, he almost fell over, but managed to prop himself against a wall. He remained there in the pouring rain.

"Jesus," Ryan said. "Doyle's telling the truth. It's Kevin Coulter."

"How can you tell, though?" Maura's nose almost touched the screen.

"Let's assume it's him for now. We can try for other cameras on the street later."

They watched as the figure finally pushed away from the wall, shambled across the street, and vanished.

"What? Where the hell's he gone?" Derek rewound furiously. He hadn't seen this part.

Ryan pushed his chair back from the group. He felt a surge of energy. He knew where Kevin was headed.

"Commercial Court. Right, Billy?"

Billy laughed and slapped his knee.

"The gallery! He went to Sophie Walton's gallery."

"Come on, let's get down there, see if there are other cameras in the vicinity. I want to get a clear image."

"Right," Billy said, standing up. "It's almost five o'clock. I'm taking my own car there and heading home after."

Ryan hurried down the stairs to his car while Billy, still wrestling with his coat, stumbled behind him.

They arrived after five, parked their cars, and met in Commercial Court. They wandered into The Duke of York, along from the gallery, only to be told by the apologetic barman he had no working cameras facing Donegall Street. They walked a little further and decided to send a constable to double check other businesses in the morning. When they reached Sophie's Gallery, a notice on the door read, 'Closed until further notice.'

"You think he came here?"

"He didn't look to be in great shape, despite what Brendan Doyle said. He can't have gone far."

"But after three in the morning? The place would have been closed up. What would have been the point? To sit outside?"

Ryan looked through the front window. Beyond it the gallery stretched, pools of dim light illuminating the hallway. "Angus said there were three floors here, right? He said something about a studio above. Maybe Kevin had a key? He handled their security, after all. He would have known about the flat upstairs."

"Maybe. I wonder why he didn't call us? Or an ambulance."

Ryan thought about that, imagined Kevin, bruised, battered, and afraid.

"I imagine Doyle threatened him."

At the front door on the left side of the frame, on a panel half-hidden by an overhang, they found a keypad with a buzzer at the top. It was well hidden and protected from the elements.

"Hang on." Ryan fumbled for his little penlight and shone it at the panel. The button and the area around it were smeared with dried blood. "Kevin's prints and his blood, has to be. And he didn't even need keys. We have to protect this buzzer until the warrants come through tomorrow. Thank God we included the gallery in the request. Let's get a constable here overnight."

Ryan's phone rang. It was Erin. He turned to Billy. "Can you sort a constable?

One of us should wait, shouldn't be long, a few minutes. Hang on. I'll take this. It's Erin."

Billy moved away and called dispatch.

"Erin, what now? I'm still on the job."

"Ryan, I'm at the Mater. Bridget's in Emergency."

He met Erin outside the ward.

"How is she? What happened?"

"She's resting. She'd started her shift downstairs in Emergency when the pain started. You'd better go in and see her. She's asking for you." Erin touched his arm gently. "You should have told me."

The blinds were drawn in the private room, and he caught that sharp smell of antiseptic. He had never seen Bridget so pale. He took her hand. "Hey."

She stirred and opened her eyes.

"Oh, Ryan." She closed her eyes again and shook her head. A tear formed and ran down her cheek. She didn't wipe it away.

"I lost him. A little boy."

He sat on the bed and held her. She started to cry into his shoulder, her body heaving. She didn't smell like his Bridget. She smelled of dirty hair and sweat and pain.

"This is what I get," she said.

"No, no, don't say that." As he sat there, it hit him like a body blow. He had lost a son. He hid his face in her neck and cried with her, his tears mixing with hers, wet and salty.

In a little while, she settled, and he smoothed her hair and kissed her cheek.

"Can I get anything for you? Do you need water?"

"No, I'm fine, Ryan. I'm sorry, I...."

"What? Don't be sorry. This isn't your fault. If it's anyone's, it's mine. You needed to rest. These bloody cases. I didn't realise." He should have insisted she move to the farm and to hell with her family. "Jesus, Bridget, I'm the one who should be sorry." He hadn't wanted her at the farm, though, had he? God, God, what a bastard he was…didn't know what to think.

Erin popped her head in. "Okay, you two?"

"Yes, Erin, thanks," Bridget said. "I need to talk to Ryan for a minute. Can you make sure my brothers don't show up? One of the nurses may have called them before I warned everyone."

"Oh, sure, no problem. I'll be in reception. Nobody gets by me." Erin disappeared.

Ryan pulled his chair over to the bed. "What do you need?"

"I've something to tell you. I was going to tell you tonight before this…" Her voice trailed away. "I swear, but…" She turned her head away.

"The baby wasn't yours."

In the lift, a few nurses got on with him. He moved to the back as they chatted and laughed. On the floor below, the lift stopped, and a couple entered. The young woman held an infant and stood quietly beside her partner. At each floor, new people, new smells, new chatter, and as they descended, in the midst of normalcy, Ryan felt his sadness intensify.

Outside, dusk had settled in, and the usual blustery wind lifted his hair. He turned up his collar. Sirens from Emergency cut the air, heavy with exhaust. Drivers at the car park entrance blasted their horns, eager to get in or get out.

The night sky held towering clouds. Rain began to fall, and he felt its wetness on his face. Rain, that's all it was. He wiped his cheeks and started to walk to his car, then stopped when he heard quick footsteps behind him.

"Hey, you." Erin grabbed his arm and walked with him, holding him close. When they got to his car, she pulled him to face her. "I'm so sorry, Ryan. Bridget told me."

"What's she going to tell her brothers? I thought she had kept it quiet."

"Everyone knows to say it was a gallstone thing. The family won't know."

"Oh." He didn't care now.

"Can you drop me home? I was downtown when Bridget called," Erin said.

"Sure, c'mon."

They were easing out of the car park when Erin spoke again. "How are you doing with this?"

"I'm fine. Wasn't my baby." Wasn't his baby. He gripped the steering wheel tighter.

"Ryan, I know that, but you're not fine."

"I..." He stopped. No point in lying to Erin.

"She was planning to tell you the truth. This happened before she could gather her nerve. Ryan, I believe her. She was going to tell you."

"Why didn't she? She had plenty of time before."

"No, no, don't be like that. You know she could have left it. Never told you."

He thought about going back to the farm alone, to Finn and whiskey. Or he could call Rose, but that seemed wrong somehow. Too soon, too calculating.

"Can you stay at the farm tonight, Erin? Keep me company?" He didn't want her to see how much he needed her to come.

"Of course, I will."

Chapter Thirty-Six

Wednesday, November 9

This was not the way he'd wanted things to happen. My God, he would be a monster if he had wanted this. But there it was, his life was his own again, yet nothing would be the same.

Distracted, he skimmed the last few night's incident reports and almost missed it. Hillary Kerr. It was the Law Office that caught his eye. 'The victim was a legal assistant at the respected Law Offices of Mitchell & Cobb.' Ryan hesitated and pulled up the report.

Christ Almighty. He picked up his mobile.

"Abbott, we need to talk."

"Ryan, I—"

"No. No. Don't say anything. I can't deal with this over the phone. I can't."

"Right then, I'm at the gym tonight. See you there." Abbott hung up.

At around eleven o'clock, Girvan called Ryan into his office and handed him warrants for Sophie Walton's properties. Ryan scanned the papers. What should have been a victory felt hollow. He gave Girvan a quick update.

"We have three stray hairs found belonging to Kathleen McGuire, and different hair from the driver's headrest. It likely belongs to Sophie Walton. We can do that comparison when we bring her in. Remains of a license with enough of Kathleen's name on it, in a small damp spot in the base of the drum behind the garage. Sophie's smart, though. She put sugar in the petrol tank and ran it till it stalled so everyone would think the Mini was undrivable. I don't think she suspected we would ever find it."

"Ahh," Girvan said, nodding.

"Then she wiped the interior," Ryan added.

Girvan grunted. "Too clever for her own good then. Right. A team is on its way downtown to that gallery too."

Back in the squad room, Ryan asked Derek to go to the gallery and keep an eye on things for him. Maura had already been called to Carrick with another DS on a new investigation, so Ryan asked PC Valerie Stewart to ride along. A rosy-faced junior with light brown hair pulled back in a bun and freckles across her nose, she sat in the back of the police car, beaming. She only spoke when spoken to, thrilled, he guessed, to be asked to accompany them. Ryan found this disconcerting—a bit like having a well-behaved five-year-old in the back.

Billy chatted away to her. Ryan listened to them drone on, but his thoughts kept returning to Bridget. And Hillary Kerr. This was crazy. He needed to focus. He needed to concentrate on the case and Sophie.

They'd scanned the CCTV for hours after Kevin's first appearance with no other sign of him. Girvan's pressure was fast-tracking the DNA from the blood on the keypad. Ryan was positive Kevin had gone there. He hadn't been seen until he ended up at the river. Did someone kill him at the gallery?

Could he be that wrong? Ryan couldn't see it. Sophie, murder her own son? No. He wanted to check the studio and the whole damn place, but he had to pick Sophie up at her home, and he couldn't be in two places at once. If her arrest went smoothly, though, he could head downtown for a while in the afternoon.

No need for lights, he'd told the others, and everyone arrived quietly enough at Sophie's, driving up the tree-lined lane together and onto the forecourt with a light crunch of tyres.

"Can't see her Jag, Ryan, or the Range Rover," Billy said after jogging back from the courtyard behind the house.

At the front door, Ryan rang the bell while PC Stewart waited behind him. The other officers got out of their cars and adjusted their hats. Billy directed a few constables to head around back. Withered leaves on the vine that hung on either side of the door rustled in the wind. A few crows cawed in the distance. The sun shone intermittently from behind fast-moving high clouds. Ryan shivered and rang the bell again.

After a few moments, a tall, heavyset woman in her sixties opened the door and looked over Ryan's shoulder at the policemen. She held a pair of rubber gloves in one hand and wore a flowery cotton apron and a faint air of disapproval. She directed her gaze back to Ryan.

"Yes?"

"Ma'am, we're here for Ms. Sophie Walton. Is she home?"

"No," the cleaner said. She glanced over Ryan's shoulder again at the cars and officers, and frowned. "She's gone."

Ryan felt his whole body slump. He was exhausted, the last few days had drained him both physically and emotionally, and now this...she's done a runner. Took so long for the bloody warrant. She'd have seen the activity at the garage and realised. She'll have taken the ferry from Larne, then on to Europe. She could be anywhere. Rome, South America....

The cleaning lady interrupted his waking nightmare.

"She went off to the Ballygalley Castle Hotel for lunch about half an hour ago, never stays in when I clean. Mr. Walton goes with her if he's here, but he's away so she's gone alone. What's all this carry-on?"

Ryan showed her the paperwork.

"We have a warrant to search the house and grounds, and an officer will want to talk to you. Would you mind waiting in the living room?"

"You're not coming in, are you? I've done them floors."

Ryan smiled. "I'm afraid the officers will have to enter the premises. But they will be respectful."

"Well, they better take their boots off, that's all I'm saying." She opened the door wide and headed back inside.

"Come on. We'll leave the team to it and get over to the Ballygalley. Where's PC Stewart? Oh, there you are." She'd been standing so quietly behind him, he almost tripped over her.

They piled into the car, and Ryan floored it to the main road. The white fluffy cumulus clouds that had held so much promise earlier had turned grey and threatening. A sprinkle of rain peppered the windscreen, much to Billy's distress.

"Suffering duck. Here we go again, more flipping rain."

Ryan did the trip with the lights flashing, and they pulled into the front of the hotel less than forty minutes later. All the way, Billy did his usual grabbing the dash while PC Stewart remained stoic and silent in the back. In the rear-view mirror, Ryan noticed her swaying gently from side to side on the tight curves, smiling like a Buddha. Billy could take a few pointers from that young woman.

"She's here all right—there's the Jaguar." Billy pointed to the car park across the street. The shiny red car was parked, somewhat haphazardly, at the end of a row.

Sophie had to know they were closing in. No way she had missed the activity at the garage down the field. They crossed the road and entered the lobby. And there she sat, at a small table by the window, with a bottle of wine and some sandwiches. She looked up as Ryan approached but didn't appear to be surprised.

"Detective McBride. I was lost, and now I'm found."

"Yes indeed."

She smiled up at him.

"Will you sit with me for a moment?"

Ryan sat down. Billy and PC Stewart moved away and sat on a sofa near the door.

Sophie had diminished since he'd last seen her. It was as if something invisible had attached to her and was sucking her dry. Her cheeks had hollowed out and her eyes were huge and dark in her face. Even that lustrous hair with its curls had dulled, hanging limp around her shoulders.

"You know why we're here?" Ryan asked her.

"When I saw you all down there on Monday, I realised I haven't been as careful as I should have been. But it doesn't matter. I've nothing left, you see." She lifted her glass and took a mouthful of wine.

Ryan studied her. She had so much going for her on the surface. An attractive woman with plenty of money, a profitable business. Yet here she sat, struggling. He had sensed it, hadn't he? That sadness.

"Why? Ms. Walton," he said gently. "You have your family. Your mother, a brother, and a loving husband. Why would you throw that away?"

"He was my son, my only child, and he would have loved me if he had known...." She looked at Ryan, narrowing her eyes. "Do you have children, Detective?"

Ryan hesitated. He'd never done that before. Never had to. It had always been, no, I don't have children, thank God. Simple as that. And what would he have done? Would he have killed for the son he'd thought was his? Maybe, in the right circumstances. Never know now, would he?

Sophie stared at him, trying to understand his reticence, probably.

Ryan continued. "You murdered Kathleen McGuire and maybe another woman in a hit-and-run because he was your son. What else have you done for him?"

She shook her head.

"Let me tell you something about family, Detective. My parents didn't give a damn about me. My brother always came first with them. It stays with you, not being loved. And don't get me wrong, I can't have been an easy child. I had issues, problems growing up, but still, with family, you're supposed to take the good with the bad, aren't you? My mother did with my father, I can tell you that." She gave a little laugh. "God knows I have with Kevin." She drank some more wine, spilling a little when she placed the glass roughly back on the table. "Pathetic. I'm pathetic." She hesitated again, a strange look clouding her face. "And there's Anthony, but...."

"What about him?"

Sophie lifted her wine glass and then set it down again. "That's all over."

"Anthony didn't know about Kevin. You told him."

Sophie turned to the window, stared at the sea and the heavy sky above it. "'I must go down to the seas again, to the lonely sea and the sky.' I love that poem, don't you? And here especially, this coastline, these surging waves. The wildness of it, the endless crashing water. Especially on a day like this. So much beauty in bleakness, don't you think? I've always preferred days like this. I've never been a bright spark." She smiled briefly, looked away again.

He followed her gaze. He could see gulls soaring, skimming the whitecaps against a backdrop of grey clouds, swollen with impending rain. Wind picking up.

"I can't find beauty now, only loneliness. Yes, I told Anthony I was Kevin's mother. When I found out on Friday that Kevin had been kidnapped, it devastated me. I realised the kidnappers assumed he had murdered Kathleen.

"Anthony knew something had happened. He kept on and on, and finally, after too much wine, I told him all about it, about my relationship with Adam Coulter and Kevin being my son. I needed to confide in someone. I've held it close to me all these years. I thought Anthony would support me, but he didn't. We couldn't have children. We tried, but... Anthony's gone too. I drove him away."

Again, the hesitation. "I've never been afraid of anything until Kevin. Then I was afraid for him all the time. He was everything to me, and I couldn't tell him. Olivia's way of punishing me. I couldn't bear the thought of him being unhappy, or cold, or..." She trailed off. "I tried to make Anthony grasp this, but it only made him angrier, do you see? He was jealous. I'd never seen him so distraught. He thought he was the only one in my life, then he realized he wasn't. He had issues himself, in the past. A fragile man. You wouldn't think it. He puts up a front. People don't like him. He only has me."

"You told him everything?"

Sophie smiled again and shook her head. She ignored the question and continued to stare at the sea outside the window and drink her wine. How was it that despite everything, he felt sorry for her?

"We had a huge fight that Friday evening. I believed the worst, you see, that Kevin was dead already. This overwhelmed Anthony; he assumed I'd never loved him. That all our years together were a lie. He went upstairs, packed a bag, and left. I haven't heard from him since. The stupid thing is I probably do love him. As much as I can love anyone else."

Ryan hesitated. "Where might he have gone after you fought?"

Sophie, surprised at the question, thought about it briefly. "A hotel probably, then he would have caught an early car ferry. He said he never wanted to see me again. What does it matter?"

"We need to go, Ms. Walton." He signaled to Billy.

Sophie touched his arm. "You know, in a way, you remind me of Kevin. I thought that the first time I saw you. So smart and handsome like him," Sophie said, lifting her handbag. "Look, I'm a mess. I'd like to use the toilet and freshen up."

"PC Stewart will go with you."

She tried to smile. It came across as a grimace.

"Is that really necessary?"

"Yes, I'm afraid it is."

He watched her walk away toward the toilets on the other side of the lobby, amused despite the situation as PC Stewart tried to keep up. Sophie still cut an elegant figure in her red suit and high heels. The diminutive policewoman in her uniform and flat shoes looked like a little mouse scurrying behind her.

"She's an odd one, eh?" Billy joined Ryan, and they watched her go.

"Yes, and she told me an interesting thing. I think there's a chance Anthony Walton may have been in the studio that night. And Billy, it looks like he had been handed a big fat motive."

"Anthony Walton?"

"Sophie told him about her affair with Adam Coulter and that Kevin was her son. She thinks Anthony hates her now, but Billy, I think he loves her so much he might have killed for her. He blamed her son for coming between them. He may have even thought that by killing Kevin and leaving him where we found Kathleen, the kidnappers would get the blame for both murders."

"There has to be some forensic evidence at the studio, with Anthony as a possible suspect," Billy said. "If you're right, it lets Brendan Doyle off the hook." Billy wandered over to the great stone fireplace, warmed his hands, and came back. "It's nice here, eh, Ryan? At the other end, there's an old stone spiral staircase, and at the top, there's a Ghost Room with a whole legend around it. It's interesting. And all the *Game of Thrones* stuff along the coast too. That's a quare good show. Do you watch it?"

Outside, the Irish Sea roiled and crashed on the rocks beyond the car park. It had started to rain again. "What the hell's keeping them? Does it take this long to pee and slap a bit of lipstick on, or whatever?" This was the part he hated, getting the suspect, taking them in. More of a letdown than anything else, and never knowing how people would react.

Billy was rambling on. "Drive you mad, some girls would, the time they take. And speaking of which, I might pop into the gents. Me and Margaret stayed here. Mind you, that was years ago, before the kids, when it wasn't renovated or anything. We couldn't afford it now, of course, too expensive. I'll be right back."

Billy trotted off, and Ryan called after him, "Where are you going?"

"I told you, to the toilet. Are you deaf or what?"

"But aren't the toilets at the other end of the lobby?"

"Yes, but these ones are closer behind reception here. Those other toilets are way up the staircase to the Ghost Room. They were all those years ago, if memory serves."

They both looked across in the direction Sophie had led PC Stewart.

"Augh, come on, Ryan, you don't think...."

"Oh shit," Ryan said and started running towards the staircase. "Shit!"

Chapter Thirty-Seven

Wednesday, November 9

"She's gone."

They reached the stone staircase only to be met by a frantic PC Stewart. She had lost her hat, her bun had come loose, and her long hair hung in wild strands around her face, shiny with exertion.

"I waited outside the toilet door, but the staircase is so narrow, and all I had to come down here. She must have known I would. People were going up and down to that room at the top all the time. I went up to check because it shouldn't have taken so long, and she'd gone. I ran back down one flight and noticed a door at the rear of the lower landing. It's a banquet room with an exit at the back." PC Stewart stopped for a quick breath, then continued. "And, sir, she has a gun. She was about to run outside when I saw her. She stopped and pointed it at me from the far door before she ran out. I don't think she was going to use it…."

PC Stewart's explanation had only taken a few seconds. Sophie couldn't have gone far. Got to get her…Ryan ignored the rear door and raced out through the main lobby onto the forecourt with Billy following and PC Stewart gamely sprinting after him.

"Which way?" Billy yelled. He ran tilted forward, arms flapping like a toddler, and crashed into Ryan's side. The hotel faced the Irish Sea. Rain lashed down, water snaking across the road into the car park and continuing on past the huge, piled rocks and into the crashing waves.

The whole place, drenched and deserted. A grey mist everywhere.

"Look!" Billy pointed over at the car park—a flash of lights.

"She's making a run for it," Ryan shouted and charged across the road. Sophie had managed to wrench the driver's door open against a brutal, soaking wind howling from the Irish Sea. She had tumbled inside when Ryan body-slammed the passenger door. He battered on the window as she fired the ignition, and the car roared to life. Nothing else for it. Before she could lock the door, he hauled it open and jumped in beside her.

"Get out! Get out!" She screamed it at him.

He made a lunge for the keys, but she had already jammed the car into reverse, and he was thrust forward, then she shifted, and the car shot out of the car park like a rocket. He crashed back into the seat. They hit the road, engine racing.

She accelerated around tight bends, with the rain intensifying and the road ahead twisting away, running with water.

Don't mess with this road, Ryan thought, not on a day like this. He considered himself a decent driver, but the Antrim Coast Road, a narrow scenic route high above the Irish Sea, wound around sheer rock faces and right through jagged arches cut into the cliffs. He usually loved the exhilarating drive, but now he was scared.

"You're going way too fast, Sophie." He could do nothing. One wrong move, one jerk of the wheel, and they were over the cliff face and onto the rocks below. He pulled on his seatbelt.

They skidded through one of the arches as Sophie hammered on in the afternoon gloom, her tyres splashing through torrents of water, flowing freely down the crags and across the road. Great wind gusts buffeted the car.

Ryan cursed himself. He had seen despair in her eyes. Jesus, he had seen it. And more. Much more.

He glanced in the side mirror. Billy and PC Stewart, skidding round the curves behind them. He'll have called for backup.

They drove on to a background noise of tyres hissing and spinning on the slick tarmac, wind punches buffeting the car, and the constant drumming of the rain on the roof and the bonnet. Sophie's face was a mask, grim, determined. But determined to do what? Ryan was thrown from side to side in corners and pushed into his seat on straight sections.

Suddenly Sophie cried out and pounded the steering wheel. "No, no, no." She hit the brakes hard, and the car skidded, fishtailing wildly, then straightened. She pumped the brakes again.

A police car, its lights strobing, had appeared on the road ahead. Keeping its distance. Another slid in behind it.

They sat there. All cars poised, for what? Ryan didn't know, but something had to happen now. Exhaust puffing, rain beating down, down. Blue lights flashing. The road ahead, a black satin ribbon. The thunk, thunk of the wipers back and forth, windows steaming up. Ryan reached forward slowly and wiped the condensation away with his sleeve. Could he risk lunging for the keys? No. Bad idea. Sophie was wired. One sudden move and they would be off again, with nowhere to go but down.

"What now, Sophie?"

"Kathleen wasn't going to tell me when she phoned that day. She lied at first, but I could tell something was up. 'I have a flat tyre,' she said. 'Can you come get me?' I could tell by her voice something was wrong, and I got it out of her. How Kevin had threatened her and killed her boyfriend, Liam. Can you imagine?"

"But he did kill Liam, he did," Ryan said. He thought he sounded shrill, although under the circumstances—the engine was still running, and they were too close to the edge—who wouldn't whine a little?

"And what if he did? Kathleen planned to go to the police. She believed Kevin killed his last girlfriend too, but he didn't. I did. I had to protect him. Don't you see that? It would have ruined his life." She began to sob and started rummaging in the handbag wedged between the seats. Instead of a tissue though, she brought out a gun and pointed it at Ryan.

Was it here, then, that he would die? In this damp and steamy car, shot by a frantic, obsessed woman?

"The cut above my eye. You noticed it at our first meeting. Clever of you. It happened that day—with Kathleen. I worked it all out in advance. I gave my mother a sedative and changed the time on the clock in the bedroom. And the flat tyre, I did that myself too, threw a few nails about. Then I picked Kathleen up and drove her to the river to calm her down. I tried to get her to understand, I did—and do you know what she said?" She gave Ryan a quick side glance, a rictus of a smile. "She said I was jealous of her. That I was in love with him, my own son! I laughed. I did. And you said the same thing to me in our second interview, do you remember?" She blew out a breath.

"Listen to me, Sophie, please." She was vibrating with tension. She might shoot him at any minute. He lifted his hands in surrender. "I know you don't want to do this. You're under severe pressure right now. Put the gun down, let me bring you in, and we'll talk properly. Don't make this worse than it is. Please, Sophie."

But Sophie continued as if she hadn't heard him. "And Adam. What a fool. He believed that Kevin had mild schizophrenia. If only that was all it was. No, our boy had inherited some issues from my dear father, as did I. Not his fault, do you see?" She shook her head to clear it, but the gun remained steady in her hand.

Outside, Ryan thought he heard the thud of car doors opening and closing.

For God's sake, don't rush the car—don't do it. If they did, he had no doubt Sophie would shoot him and take off. He could see that at this moment, she had no intention of giving up. She wasn't even here in the car with him. She was back there by the river with Kathleen, furious at her for threatening her son.

"I told Kathleen, over and over, don't do this. He's a good man. I begged her—but in the end, it was no good. I'd brought some hot sweet tea for her to drink, to calm her, I'd added a little sedation. I couldn't stick it, you know, hearing all that vitriol about my boy. Not another word. She hated him. Can you believe that?"

"So you planned it? As soon as she called you?"

"Believe me, I didn't want it to go that way. I didn't enjoy killing her, if that's what you mean. I wanted to talk. I'm not naturally a violent person. Okay, there was that other woman, before, but she was suing him."

"Sophie, you drugged Kathleen. Why did you do that if you only planned to talk?"

"I needed her to be compliant, to understand. I told you."

She came back to the present. He saw something change in her eyes.

"My God, you do remind me of Kevin."

He thought he saw her smile for an instant. She moved the gun up a fraction. Then made a small movement with it. She twitched the barrel. He braced himself.

"Get out, now, before I change my mind."

He hesitated.

"Get out." She jolted the car forward a little, still looking at him, her left hand on the steering wheel. "I'm warning you...." She gestured with the gun again.

Ryan undid his belt and opened the door. "Are you sure about this, Sophie?"

"Get out."

He pushed the door open against the wind and sprinted down to Billy and PC Stewart. He jumped inside and slammed the door shut as Sophie accelerated away.

Ryan saw the rear of the car dip and the bonnet lift. "What the hell is she doing? The police cars are ahead there on the road."

Billy took off in the car after her. "Maybe she intends to ram them and make a run for it?" Then he slammed on the brakes again. Everyone jolted forward.

"Oh, God." PC Stewart finally spoke. "Oh my God!"

Sophie had jerked the Jaguar's wheel sharply to the right. The car shot directly across the opposite lane and sailed over the edge. It seemed to hang there, suspended in midair, before disappearing from view, down to the rocks below. Billy turned on all the blue lights and pulled the car into the middle of the road.

Ryan turned to PC Stewart. "Call it in again, Constable, update them. Then get out, take the flares from the boot, and set them up behind us at the archway. Watch for traffic. Billy, will you go tell those guys up ahead to put flares out further along behind them if they haven't already? I'm going to check on the Jag."

He ran to the cliff's edge and looked over, down a sheer drop into the water and the rocks and the beach. The rain continued to pelt down, soaking him, plastering his hair, and dripping from his nose.

The Jaguar had landed on its roof. Even if she had managed to survive the crash, he couldn't save her. No way he could get down there. The tide slid in relentlessly.

He thought back to Sophie by the window, telling him how much she loved the sea. Telling him, she'd lost everything.

Less than fifteen minutes later, the first pump arrived from Larne. Police cars had already taken over the road. The big red and yellow vehicle parked, and the firefighters tumbled out. The crew commander approached Ryan.

The rain had eased into a light shower. Ryan shivered, soaked to the skin.

"How many in the car again?" the commander asked.

"One woman. I'm assuming she didn't survive the crash, but I don't know about these things. Could she be alive?"

"We'll have to go down and see." He turned to his crew. "Martin, get the rope ladders out and fix them. Carson, you get sorted to climb down."

"Right you are."

"Tide's coming in," Ryan said.

"Yup, fully in by about eight o'clock. We have about four to five hours before the car's submerged. Carson! Get a move on." He turned back to Ryan and looked up at the heavy sky. "At least the rain's buggered off."

Carson, the first fireman to climb down, had changed out of his heavy boots and suit and sported a waterproof anorak and climbing shoes. He wore a yellow hard hat with a light, and had ropes and various tools strapped around his waist.

The crew commander pulled Ryan aside.

"We expected we'd have to do this, so we're lucky Carson could come in. He's a rock climber. We wanted him here. The others will get down, but he's your man."

They both watched as the fireman descended quickly and carefully. When he hit the rocks, he gave a thumbs up, and Ryan heard a walkie-talkie crackle. The commander clicked on.

"Go ahead, Carson."

"Looks pretty bad from here, but no sign of fire. I'm going in."

They watched him make his way across the rocks and approach the car. More static, then, "The airbag's deployed, but it's a mess inside. God, there's a lot of blood. She's crushed, compressed onto the roof."

"Any sign of life?" The commander sounded edgy, and he paused as an RRV screeched round the far bend and stopped by the fire pumper. A paramedic jumped out of the green and yellow-checkered vehicle and ran over.

"What's the situation, sir? Ambulance is on its way."

The commander held up his hand, then continued.

"Carson, a paramedic with a Rapid Response Vehicle, has arrived up here, and an ambulance is coming. Can you reach her to get vitals?"

"I'll try, but it's badly mangled in there. Tell the paramedic to stand by, but I can't see how anyone could have survived that."

They all saw a high beam torch click on as Carson gingerly approached the driver's window.

A burst of static jolted Ryan.

"She moved! Sir, she moved her fingers—she's alive! I can't fucking believe it. Bloody Jags, they're built like tanks."

They could see the fireman leaning into the car, then more static. "Send the paramedic down. I told her to hold on, we'll get her out." He moved away from the car.

"Commander, we need the Jaws of Life from the pumper asap. She's pinned. I told her she'd be okay but it looks bad. It'll be a long job to cut her free. We'll have to take it slow. She can only move her upper body and her arms a little."

"The paramedic is on his way down. Steady it for him, will you? He's got a lot of gear with him, and I'll get someone down there with the Jaws right away."

CHAPTER THIRTY-SEVEN

"Right, sir."

Ryan saw Carson go to Sophie's window again, say a few words, and then run to the ladder. The paramedic had almost reached the rocks. Carson took some of the gear. In the fading light, both men gave a thumbs up signal for the watchers, and, hefting the equipment, they started toward the Jaguar.

A shot echoed across the beach.

The men were about six feet away from the car, staggering a little from the weight of the equipment. Both men dropped their gear and fell to the ground.

"What the holy hell!" The commander clicked the walkie-talkie. "You two okay there? Did she hit you? Why is she shooting? Does she not know you're trying to save her?"

"Don't know what happened, but we're both fine. I'm going to take a look."

"Easy there, Carson."

"I have to get down there." Ryan made for the ladder. The commander grabbed his arm.

"Oh no, no chance. You'll slip and kill yourself dressed like that. If you must, at least get some proper footwear and a hard hat from the pumper."

Static again, then Carson's voice sounded strained, even through the walkie-talkie.

"Commander, Jesus! She shot herself."

Chapter Thirty-Eight

Wednesday, November 9

Another long day, and getting longer. It was late when Ryan parked outside the gym. Abbott's car was still there. Inside he saw a light in the far office and saw Abbott working in the corner with one of the younger boxers. He turned when the door banged shut and slapped the youth on the arm. He nodded over at Ryan and headed for the office. Ryan followed.

Inside, Abbott sat down, pulled out a bottle of rye whisky from the desk drawer. He poured two glasses, slid one to Ryan. They sat there for a moment, drinking.

"This stays between us, Abbott. Because we're friends. But what the fuck?"

Abbott's head shot up. "What?"

"No matter what she did, you told me you would never raise your hand to a woman. Jesus. You put her in hospital, cracked ribs, punctured lung." Ryan stood up, agitated. "A concussion? I never expected... I thought I knew you, thought we were friends."

"For Christ's sake, Ryan, stop ranting, will you? I never touched her. Never went anywhere near her. I thought you did it."

Ryan, caught mid outburst, took a gulp of rye, which he hated, shook his head and placed the glass back on the table. He squinted at Abbott. "You thought I did that?"

"I thought it was you." Abbott looked back at Ryan, unsure. "It wasn't?"

"But who then?" Ryan asked.

The door banged open. "I did." Bernie leaned over and pushed Ryan's glass towards Abbott. "And will you keep your voices down? We've a couple of lads from the senior team still out there. Abbott, give us a top-up will you, pet?"

"You?" Ryan was flabbergasted.

"Shannon and Tara helped. Boxercise."

"Bernie. You beat the shit out of her."

"Nah, we only roughed her up a bit. We tried to talk sense into her, and she threatened to sue me. Sue me! I laughed so hard I nearly wet my knickers." Bernie gave Ryan and Abbott one of her looks and shook her head.

"Dorothy got me and the girls through our grief when we lost Andy, she's a good-hearted wee woman, and I won't see her threatened. I owe her. That big bitch came back three nights in a row. Mental case right enough. A real nasty piece of work, no talking to her. I explained to her in a way she could understand." She took a swig of the rye. "Jesus, Mary, and Joseph, that is foul." She slid it back towards Ryan. "We'll say no more about it. Lock up, will you, Abbott? I'm away on home."

Ryan reached for the rye and took another swig. The stuff was growing on him. My God, what a day.… "I should arrest her."

"Yeah, yeah." Abbott topped him up again. "Ryan, my friend, you'd best drink up, because I have a confession to make.…"

Chapter Thirty-Nine

Monday, November 14

Ryan, Billy, Maura, and Derek had been summoned to Girvan's office for a debrief. Late afternoon sunlight streamed in, and a sky-blue wash hung behind bare tree branches. The room had a cheery feel to it, and Ryan suspected it wasn't the light making the office atmosphere so jolly. Girvan beamed with satisfaction.

"So, she'd already decided to kill herself before she left her house that morning?"

"It looks that way, sir," Ryan said. "She didn't expect to come home. She died not knowing Anthony killed Kevin. She'd written a note, asking Anthony to forgive her."

"Walton's been arrested?"

Ryan nodded. "He gave himself up to the police in Rome as soon as he heard about Sophie's suicide. He admitted to the murder of Kevin Coulter. Claims he'd been drinking heavily, was devastated by Sophie's confession. When Kevin arrived at the studio flat early Saturday morning, they fought. He said Kevin came at him, and he defended himself."

Girvan snorted. "By the state Kevin Coulter was in when Doyle finished with him, I can't see him putting up much of a fight."

"That's Walton's story," Ryan said. "According to him, he killed Kevin in self-defense then passed out. Later, in the wee hours of Sunday morning, realising what he'd done, he drove to Kathleen's crime scene at Portglenone

Forest with Kevin's body, dumped it, and took the ferry. Trying to muddy the waters. Sophie had given him all the details of Kathleen's murder."

"Right," Girvan said. "And PC Burns?"

"Oh, we've a boatload of evidence against him, sir," Billy said. "He won't even get bail. He's named the others from Musgrave too. He said they shared those drugs between them. Pointed to Wylie as the ringleader. Wants to get a deal."

Girvan remained quiet, then said, "For this room only, that isn't a huge surprise. Inquiries were underway about that group. Every single one of them. I took them up here to get them out of Musgrave's way so the investigation could proceed quietly. This would probably have come out sooner or later. Although not in such a public way. The only saving grace on all this is that bloody Burns was only a probationary constable. The other three, Wylie and his two associates, they'll be up for dismissal. Stealing drugs from evidence lockup. That's a big one. I can't see the Chief Inspector jumping into the ring to defend his nephew. This will be the final straw."

"It's a tangled web we weave, sir," Derek said.

Girvan shook his head, glanced at Ryan, puzzled.

"Yes, McGrath, be that as it may, I have some news too. At year's end, I will be leaving this lovely station for Knock."

"Headquarters. Congratulations, sir." Ryan was pleased for the big man, but yet....

"Thank you, DS McBride. The Chief Inspector's decided to take early retirement, what with the fuss regarding his nephew and all that, and the successful resolution of so many cases at once didn't hurt either. Good work, everyone."

So, thought Ryan, now he understood why Burns's arrest hadn't upset Girvan so much. He had another question to ask, one he dreaded. He knew the answer before he asked because that was the way things were going with him lately.

"Sir, do you know who might be coming in here to replace you?"

"There's some talk Inspector Carol Whelan may be transferred. We'll see."

"Right, sir, thank you." Ryan's good mood vanished. Perfect. Could things be worse? Carol Whelan…his potential new boss and the woman who was furious with him because he had taken first place in their graduating class. The single most competitive person he had ever met. She had dogged his every exam, field training exercise, and weapons test.

Girvan thanked the group again, and they all filed out. He gestured to Ryan. "Hold on for a moment, will you, McBride? What about Brendan Doyle?"

"We don't have solid evidence against him. And something he said made me think again about the night they took Kevin. It was him, no question, but he fired to miss, I'm sure of it. He could have hit me easily. But he didn't; the ricochet got me."

"And the attack on your car?"

"They aimed at the tyres. If they had fired through the window, with those bullets, I wouldn't have survived."

Girvan reached for his gold pen and started to tap it restlessly on the desk. Some of his previous good humour had disappeared, Ryan noted. Had he hoped to add the arrest and prosecution of the infamous Brendan Doyle to his resume?

"Sounds to me like you're making excuses for him."

"He's not stupid. He knows what killing a police officer would mean to him and his family. I don't want to waste everyone's time on a case I don't believe we can win."

"Damn, I would have liked to nab that bastard. But God knows we've enough to sort out on this investigation."

"And, sir, here's an odd thing. I spoke to Doyle a few days ago, clearing up some loose ends, and he told me his mother had passed away. She never regained consciousness. After Sophie died, while Mary Doyle lay there in a coma, he told her Kathleen's killer was dead. Mrs. Doyle died a few minutes later."

"How strange." Girvan frowned.

"Yes, very strange." Ryan had reports to file and a special dinner date later. "Is that it, sir?"

"I certainly hope so, McBride."

"Excuse me?" Janice popped her head in. "Got a young lady on the line for DS McBride. She says it's urgent."

Chapter Forty

Monday, November 14

T he night Bridget lost the baby, she had refused to tell Ryan who the father was. Just one of the many guys who hung around her. Ryan had left, angry and upset.

Now, she needed to see him. She had been desperate on the phone. "I've something to tell you. We have to meet."

Christ, he'd had enough confessions lately for a lifetime.

The Duke of York this time. Evening setting in, moon bright outside, warm and cosy in the bar. Was there a better smell than an Irish pub? Fried food, beer, and, if you were lucky, a peat fire burning at the back. Bridget was there when he arrived, a drink in front of her.

"What is it? I don't have much time. Rose is coming to the farm." He sat down and ordered a whiskey from a passing waiter. He was angry, couldn't help it.

Bridget ignored his tone. "I told you I had too much to drink one night, had sex with a guy, and got pregnant. All my fault."

What did she want him to say? He'd allowed himself to become accustomed to the idea of a family. It hadn't been easy. So gradual, in fact, that the thought of being a father had slid into his unconscious mind and started to take root like the baby in Bridget. Yes, maybe she had changed her mind, was going to tell him, but she hadn't, had she?

She started to speak again, and he interrupted her. "Bridget, you lied to me. You were carrying someone else's baby, but you chose me to be the father? What gave you the right?"

"Okay, I was wrong, of course, I was—but this isn't all my fault."

How was any of it his fault? How in God's name was this his fault?

"I know I was wrong to lie, I know. It was eating me up inside. I did plan to tell you the truth, but that doesn't excuse it. I am sorry." She took a sip of wine. "It wasn't until Sam Burns' case broke in the news last week that I realised what had happened to me...."

Ryan interrupted her again, "Christ no, Bridget. Don't tell me that." He could see the guy, the boyish grin, the eagerness. The short hair, better to fit wigs on, and that smooth face, ready for false beards. He remembered the frantic chase and what it felt like to punch him.

The waiter arrived with his drink, and he took the whiskey into his mouth and held it there. He let it burn. He didn't want to hear this.

Bridget frowned, then continued.

"The press conference when Girvan released the names. Those officers, they all shared the drugs, the Rohypnol, right? That's when I started to put it together. Took me a few days, but it made sense." She reached for his hand. He pulled it away.

"It wasn't Burns. It was Ed Wylie who turned up at the Chimney Corner, my favourite pub." Bridget took a gulp of wine. "He seemed surprised to see me, like we accidentally bumped into each other. He bought me a drink, and we chatted for a while. I knew you two didn't get on. I suppose I thought he would be sure to let you know, that it would make you jealous. That night at the Christmas party, that fight you had with him was the first time I had ever seen you so angry. You were jealous." "I thought, why not get a little dig in? I'd been thinking about you—would it have killed you to call me once in a while?"

"You can't be serious. You broke up with me, time and time again. What did you want me to do? Keep phoning, keep trying to get you back?"

"I only intended to have a drink with him, Ryan. It didn't seem like such a bad thing. I relaxed and had another—and next thing I know, I'm in his car, and we're making out. I'm sure that he slipped me something, targeted and raped me. Maybe he followed me there, had it all planned. At the time, I never suspected. And it wasn't much, because I remember bits and pieces." She sat staring into her glass. "I swear to you, Ryan, after those drinks, it was a blur. I can see it now. I just never thought…."

"You should have told me, Bridget. The whole thing."

"What? That the baby was Wylie's? You would have told me to get rid of it. I didn't want to, I couldn't. I shouldn't have lied, but it wasn't the baby's fault, and you two look enough alike, I thought it might work. The timing was off for it to be you, but it was close enough that I figured I could deal with that later."

Back at his farm, Ryan lit the fire, and the living room had that lovely smoky smell. Finn lay on the rug at his feet, and Rose came in from the kitchen with another bottle of wine. She sat down beside Ryan and tickled Finn with her toe. The dog rolled over on his back, luxuriating.

"Bridget never suspected," Ryan said. "She remembered some of it, just didn't have any reason to be suspicious, not then. This whole time, I felt something from him. He was dying to tell me, bursting to tell me he'd had sex with Bridget, but he couldn't risk it. He must have suspected they were being investigated, and if I put two and two together…."

"And Bridget was trying to make you jealous? Hoped it would get back to you?"

"Maybe, but she only meant to have a quick drink with him. She swears to it, Rose, and I believe her. He used her. I think he stalked her because he hated me."

He thought about that future he had imagined with Bridget and a baby that wasn't his. How would that have gone? If Bridget hadn't told him, would he have ever guessed? Would he have loved the boy and never suspected? His mind reeled away into a future that would never be there, to consequences that would never be faced.

"Are you okay?" Rose asked.

"Yes. It's just that right at the beginning, when she told me about the baby—that I was the father—I was angry. But after a while…."

"You got used to the idea. You started to look forward to it." Rose reached over and touched his hand. "There's nothing wrong with that. It's natural."

"Not for me. Or at least I didn't think it was."

"There you go, you're a changed man."

He took a moment to answer. "I suppose so." Hard to admit, even to himself.

"Why does Wylie hate you so much? That's what I don't understand," Rose said.

"I don't know. Not the whole thing. He was an arse in basic training, and his uncle made it worse, getting him special privileges. Nobody liked him. At the beginning, we were partnered, but I couldn't stick with him and asked to be assigned a new partner. That pissed him off." Ryan took a drink. "I suspect he thought we were going to be best buddies."

A slap of wind hit the window.

"Let's go into the garden." He took her hand, and they stepped outside. It was a supermoon night. The trees at the back of his property swayed, dark branches against luminous clouds.

"Look at the moon. It's huge," she said.

He had to tell her about Kathleen. Confess. Bridget had told him he kept too much inside. But how? How to begin. And when? Certainly not on this bright evening.

But he would.

Soon.

High above, crows started to caw, the sound eerie and desolate above them.

"That's odd, isn't it? Crows cawing at night like that?" Rose said.

Ryan thought back to that first morning in the car park. The beginning. The high trees, the birds. "I think it's the moon. And us, we've disturbed them."

She smiled at him, a silver sweep of moonlight on her cheek. As he leaned in for a kiss, his mobile rang. It was Erin.

"I can't talk for long. I'm with Rose." He listened. "Yes, I will. Yes, yes."

He looked over. "Erin says hello. And we're invited to dinner with her and Abbott on Friday night."

"Oh, that sounds lovely. Who's Abbott?"

Ryan shook his head. Smiled.

"Don't ask."

A Note from the Author

Look for book two in The Belfast Murder Series, *Blood Relations*, due for release summer 2023.

Acknowledgements

I have many people and organizations to thank. To Sisters in Crime and the Guppies, all of you, to a person. And also, Crime Writers of Canada, International Thriller Writers, and the Suncoast Writers Guild.

The wonderful dames of Level Best Books. Harriette Sackler, Verena Rose, and Shawn Reilly Simmons.

My early developmental editors, Gretchen Stelter, and Chris Stewart. And in the UK, Oliver James.

Renee Chastleton and Raimey Gallant, thank you for your careful, in-depth critiques of my original manuscript.

First readers, Marilyn, Marla, and Jacquie.

To writers Donnell Bell, Kate Charles, and Katherine Ramsland, thank you for reading the manuscript, encouraging, and helping me.

My Beta Readers, Marilyn Kay, and Lis Angus. Both wonderful writers. Your comments made all the difference.

To my current critique partners, who are also amazing writers in their own right, Elaine Wolff, and Ruth Setton. I can't thank you enough for your help and guidance.

Robert Rotenberg and Cathy Astolfo mentored and helped me. Thank you.

To Hallie Ephron and Hank Phillippi Ryan who, through their on-line classes and talks, and willingness to engage, always take extra time to critique and work with their students.

Marcia Talley. What can I say? Thank you so much for your friendship and guidance. You know how much it means to me.

A shout out to my good friends in Canada, the US., and UK. Gil and Mark, thanks for the support and the champagne!

I had a lot of help with police procedure. Sergeant Joseph Cardi here in Canada, for his patient, detailed answers to my varied questions on police matters and investigations. And in the UK., former Detective Chief Inspector Matt Markham. Matt, thank you for reading the book and making suggestions and corrections. Thank you for in depth and insightful answers to general policing questions specifically in the UK and your expertise in Northern Ireland. You are amazing.

And to Mrs. Carole Lyle Skyrme, and Stanley Adair. You are both in part, responsible for all this. And Dawn, my sister, and my wonderful photographer.

To my daughter Victoria, her husband Kean, baby Kai, and my husband Nicholas, I love you.

About the Author

J. Woollcott is a Canadian writer born in Belfast, Northern Ireland. Her first book, *A Nice Place to Die*, introduces Police Service of Northern Ireland detectives DS Ryan Mcbride and his partner DS Billy Lamont.

In 2019, *A Nice Place to Die* won the RWA Daphne Du Maurier Award for Mainstream Mystery and Suspense, and in 2021 was shortlisted in the CWC Awards of Excellence.

She is a graduate of the Humber School for Writers and BCAD, University of Ulster.

SOCIAL MEDIA HANDLE: @JoyceWoollcott

AUTHOR WEBSITE: jwoollcott.com

CPSIA information can be obtained
at www.ICGtesting.com
Printed in the USA
LVHW011934160922
728563LV00003B/198